Joseph Gordon

The Life and Writings of Rev. Joseph Gordon

Joseph Gordon

The Life and Writings of Rev. Joseph Gordon

ISBN/EAN: 9783337733964

Printed in Europe, USA, Canada, Australia, Japan

Cover: Foto ©Raphael Reischuk / pixelio.de

More available books at **www.hansebooks.com**

THE

LIFE AND WRITINGS

OF

REV. JOSEPH GORDON.

WRITTEN AND COMPILED BY A COMMITTEE OF
THE FREE PRESBYTERIAN SYNOD.

CINCINNATI:
PUBLISHED FOR THE FREE PRESBYTERIAN SYNOD.
1860.

PREFACE.

Rev. Joseph Gordon was one of a few ministers, who united and formed the Free Presbyterian Church, in 1847. In the midst of prevailing declension and Hunkerism, they came out from their ecclesiastical connections, with a manifesto of principles adverse to the popular religion of the day; and on these they based the new organization. During seven years he was the editor of the *Free Presbyterian*—the organ of the new formed church. After his death, the Free Synod at its next meeting held in Ripley, O., in October 1858, appointed a committee of two persons to write a biography of the deceased and compile a selection from his writings, and have them published. Of this committee, Rev. T. M. Finney, of Martinsburg, was one. The other member expected him to write the biography, and aid in selecting from the writings of the deceased. After a lingering sickness of some four months, Mr. Finney died on the 20th of July, 1859, without having begun the work. Amid a pressure of other duties the surviving member of the committee was compelled to dispatch the matter in a short time, and without the advantage that even his limited share of ability might have given it, with more leisure and attention. This statement extends to the biography, the selections and the arrangement, but of course not to the writings of the deceased. If, however, the humble effort helps to preserve the memory of one exceedingly dear to him, and in any good degree promotes the cause of truth, and righteousness, and church reform, he will be thankful and satisfied.

CONTENTS:

SCIENTIFIC AND MORAL ARTICLES.

CONTROVERSIAL ARTICLES.

MISCELLANEOUS ARTICLES.

INTRODUCTION.

THE thunderstorm and the tornado produce great ethereal commotion. There is a terrific war of elements—the heavens are covered with blackness—bolts of livid lightning stream and flash across the horizon—the hoarse thunders bellow—the storm rages—and the passive earth is swept with desolation. With the fertilizing rain it is different. It descends from the calm and quiet clouds with gentle distillation, and a luxuriant vegetation rejoices after it. Yet we gaze with emotions of grandeur and sublimity on the one; and are but little impressed with the dull quiet of the other. So it is with the men who have lived, and acted, and gone to their last resting-place. One class filled the earth with excitement and terror. Their course could have been traced by the stormy commotions around them, and could be readily followed by the cheerless and melancholy desolations after them.

To the eye of the common observer there are the scenes of exciting violence, and the success of brilliant achievements; but on closer investigation, there lie behind these conquests, the destruction of unnumbered ties of kindred and affection, and the desolation of hopes and prospects never estimated. Those of the other class are too quiet to excite much attention, yet their influence is on the side of peace, virtue and happiness. Like the course of the fertilizing shower, their way is strewed with benefactions to the race. The Alexanders, Cæsars and Napoleons employ many pens—fill many volumes, and these give deep interest to millions; while the Luthers, Melancthons, Howards, Judsons and Spensers, the real benefactors of the world, furnish but tame materials for the biographer and the historian.

To this there is an occasional exception. When a moral hero, in fighting the battles of the Lord for truth and righteousness, meets bloody opposition; when persecution lights her fires and brings forth her racks and tortures; and when, in the strength of faith, he triumphs or dies in the contest, then his life assumes poetic interest.

It is also true that men of violence and blood, are rapidly loosing their hold on human admiration. A Havelock must be robed in the white folds of Christianity, as viewed from one standpoint, to get general admiration for his character; while his very profession was that of one well qualified to inflict evil, spread desolation and destroy human life. The very incongruity, like that of another distinguished commander, who required a city under martial law, to observe the forenoon of the Lord's day, shows progress. Most of the world's heroes were prodigies of brutality and crime. Others possessed native and inherent nobleness, which would have made them blessings to their age and ornaments to the human race, had their energies by a proper education been turned in the right direction. Great minds must have some object on which to concentrate their energies, and if one worthy of their powers be not presented or sought, one of evil will necessarily be found and embraced. Had Alexander or Bonaparte lived in different ages, or been educated so as to see and appreciate real greatness, they had stood as high among the world's benefactors as they do amid its scourges; while Paul without his piety might have run the career of Alexander, and wept for another world to conquer.

But the world is changing, all boys are not now encouraged and educated to first glow over the siege of Troy—the conquests of Alexander, or the campaigns of Napoleon. Some get their first and generally lasting views of the true ends of life from the benevolence of a Howard, the piety of a Payson, the self-sacrifice of a Henry Martyn or the consecration of a Judson, a Moffat, a Livingston or a George Thompson. To multiply such characters, we need the numerous biographies of those who acted on their principles, and walked in their footsteps.

The best subjects for such books (other things being equal) are those who lately left the world. With the good of ancient ages we hold but imperfect communion. They seem to us more like angels than tempted, tried, feeling, suffering human beings, living and acting like ourselves. Few biographies are much read in after ages. A few like Paul, Luther or Howard become immortal. The majority fade way in a few ages and their memory is lost. Often important principles are esteemed and cherished, long after the persons who contended for their value and secured their adoption, are covered with oblivious veil. But the published lives of such are not wasted labor. They become an appendix to their existence, and carry on and finish their work. Should this humble volume share the common fate, the writer and compiler will still feel that his labor has not been in vain. Yet as the work will consist chiefly of the writings of the deceased; as these subjects are various, some of them lasting in their nature, and the writer's clear views on others were greatly in advance of the age, it is hoped they may present a legacy of thought to the coming generation.

Mr. Gordon was a varied and copious writer. His constant changes of employment of course rendered his articles miscellaneous. His ministerial life was only about twelve years in length. His editorial career ran over seven years, but the time of actual employment was only six. The last year his health failed so much, that his mind was somewhat enfeebled with his body. Of this he was himself fully sensible, and mentioned it in a letter to a friend. When we add to this his labors as a minister, his work in the printing-office, with the cares and anxieties incident to an establishment meagerly supported by a small subscription list, and yet which required to be so managed as not to sink him into debts beyond his means; it seems wonderful that he could write weekly editorials of any merit or power. Had his leisure permitted it, and his powers been concentrated on one or a few leading topics, no one can doubt that his success would have been brilliant in proportion.

It was remarked by a very sensible and intelligent reader of the *Free Presbyterian*, after his death, that when he made an argument on any of the great questions of the day, or on the principles advocated, other opposing editors never copied it, or replied to it. This statement was generally true. Hunker editors snarled at his side, and barked on his track, but never faced him. This probably arose quite as much from their convictions of the strength and correctness of the principles he advocated, and the weakness of their own, as from fear of him personally as an opponent. To keep their people from reading or hearing any thing on the other side of the controversy, has been the common policy of ministers and editors who continue the ecclesiastical fellowship of the slaveholder. Even so respectable and generally candid a paper as the *Presbyterian of the West*, with its talented and titled editor, manifested the conviction that discretion was the better part of valor, as the following editorial will show:

"No Response.—Our readers will remember that some weeks since we proposed to discuss with the editor of the *Presbyterian of the West*, the charge of schism which he made against the Free Presbyterian Church, and to publish two columns of what he might write on the subject for every one he should publish from us. To this proposal, as we expected, no response has been made. Why is this? It will not do for the editor to throw himself back on his dignity, and profess to regard us as beneath his notice. He has already made us the subject of a column of editorial. We have our own opinion of the reasons why the discussion is declined. If the reader is anxious to know on what that opinion is based, he will find some light on the subject, by referring to the Gospel of John 3d chapter, 20th and 21st verses."

In the selections made, the personal taste of the writer and compiler has alone been consulted; for since the death of Mr.

Finney, many controversial articles were necessarily omitted on account of their ephemeral nature. At the time of their appearance they were in many cases specially interesting, but the circumstances which drew them out have faded from the public memory, and their republication is therefore not desirable. Others were written in answer to articles from correspondents, and can not appear well alone. In his editorial career, the well written and sensible articles of persons differing in sentiment, were very freely published. The censorship of his columns was exercised with the largest liberality.

Were it possible for Mr. Gordon himself to be consulted in the selection of his own best articles, it were " a consummation devoutly to be wished." But that can not be. He has gone beyond the reach of praise or blame. From the " irrepressible conflict " between truth and error, he has passed away. His trenchant pen is no longer wielded, and his earnest voice no longer raised in vindication of the supremacy of God's higher law, and the rights of his down-trodden poor. The surging world sweeps on in its course over his lowly grave, unconscious of the good he labored in life and death to bequeath it. As he remained faithful unto death, and fell in his armor; may his mantle fall on us who survive him, and may we transmit the victory, rather than the conflict, to those who come after us.

MEMOIR.

Joseph Gordon was born near Washington, Penn., on the 28th of September, 1819. His parents occupied the middle walks of life, and his childhood and youth were spent amid the labors of a farm. He was one of the younger children of a moderately large family. Nothing very peculiar marked his early years. His habits were quiet, retiring and unobtrusive. From childhood he manifested a kind of careless independence—generally formed his own opinions, and seemed neither to seek those of others, nor to be over-anxious for the adoption of his own.

His intellectual powers were bright and vigorous—a good deal above mediocrity. The first rudiments of his education were obtained in the common schools of the neighborhood. In 1836 he became a student of Washington College, remained four years in its classic halls, and graduated in 1840. While pursuing his course as a student, he exhibited the same quiet, unobtrusive disposition which characterized his whole life. He was punctual in his recitations—had the general approbation of his teachers—never complained of the burden of his professor's demands—met their requirements alike without a complaint of their severity, or a boast of the amount of his achievements. At this point we insert an article published after his death, in the *Christian Leader*, from the pen of his special friend and classmate, Rev. T. M. Finney, who has since joined him in the spirit world. The attachment and confidence of the two friends was strong and mutual, and such as is seldom experienced in this selfish and wicked world. After their acquaintance they ran a parallel course. They graduated in the same class—both became Presbyterian ministers—both left the church in which they were born, educated and licensed, on account of its complicity with American slavery—both united with the Free Church— and both were cut down in the prime and vigor of manhood, and in the midst of extensive usefulness. Like Saul and Jonathan, "they were lovely in their lives, and in their deaths they were not long divided." Mr. Finney survived his friend but a little over one year. The article is copied from the *Leader*, April 2d, 1858:

The death of this faithful servant of God has been already noticed in the *Leader*, very appropriately, both by the editor and a correspondent. This might seem sufficient; but friendship claims the mournful privilege of placing another humble tribute to his memory, upon his new made grave. Twenty-two years ago, the writer became acquainted with Brother Gordon, at Washington, Penn., where we entered and passed through college together. During this time a friendship was formed, which has never been interrupted. There are very many personal reminiscences, which it would be pleasant to record; but for the present I must pass them by, to present a few of the leading incidents in the brief life that has closed.

During his college course Bro. G. was studious, but not what is usually termed "a hard student." He needed and took a great deal of exercise. But he never came to his class unprepared. He acquired knowledge easily, and mastered in an hour, what many others would labor upon for half a day. He graduated in 1840, and in most respects was the best scholar in the class. He took a part of the first honor. It was perhaps about two years before he ended his college course that he made a profession of religion, and united with the Presbyterian church of Washington, Penn. Before this he had thoughts of turning his attention to the Bar. In this profession he would at once have taken a prominent position. But God had other work for him to do. In the fall of 1841, he went to the Theological Seminary at Allegheny city, where he continued until he was prepared to be licensed as a minister of the gospel. After his licensure he supplied for a time the Presbyterian church of Ashland, Ohio. During ths time and while he was a student at Allegheny, he and the writer corresponded with regard to the sin of slavery in the church and our duty in reference to it, and at one time concluded to start a religious newspaper, vindicating the doctrine held by the Free Church on that subject. Not meeting with sufficient encouragement, and not having sufficient funds to commence the enterprise, it was abandoned.

In Nov. 1844, Bro. G. removed to New Philadelphia, Ohio, where the writer had settled as pastor of the Presbyterian church, and we commenced teaching an academy together, which we continued one year, and then gave it into other hands. During this year Bro. G. supplied the church of

Urichsville. During this year also, he was married to Miss Sarah A. Robertson of New York. During the summer of the next year he was elected professor of mathematics in Franklin College, and in the autumn removed to New Athens. Here he continued about five years, discharging with great fidelity, and ability, the duties of his office. He also preached to the church of New Athens. Meanwhile the General Assembly had met at Cincinnati and passed the pro-slavery action of 1845. That action which has caused so many to mourn over the degeneracy of the church and assisted to such a fearful extent in strengthening the hands of the slaveholders, and paralyzing the efforts of anti-slavery ministers, and members of the church. Bro. G. bore a faithful testimony against this action, and the position of the church upon the subject of slavery. He was not yet ordained, and the vigilant eyes of the defenders and apologists of slavery were upon him.

The church of New Athens gave him a call to become its pastor, and the Presbytery of St. Clairsville set a time for his ordination. He passed with approval through all his parts of trial, and just at the moment when the ordination services were about to commence, a member rose and objected to further proceedings in the case on account of Bro. G's sentiments in reference to the action of the General Assembly on the subject of slavery. The whole thing as it afterward appeared, had been preconcerted. This was the signal for unchaining the whole pro-slavery pack. It is said by those who heard it, that Bro. G's defense was manly, eloquent, and unanswerable. There was no crouching fear, no retraction of truth, no apology for having uttered the honest sentiments of his heart, in reference to the iniquitous position that "domestic slavery under the circumstances in which it is found in the southern portion of our country is no bar to Christian communion." Of course the Presbytery attempted to silence him. The church however stood by him, and he was shortly afterward ordained by the Presbytery of Ripley, which had left the New School body on account of its position on slavery.

Bro. G. joined with Bros. Bradford and McClain (who as pioneers in the Free Church movement in Western Pennsylvania had declined the jurisdiction of their Presbytery, on the same ground), formed the Free Presbytery of Mahoning, and this Presbytery uniting with that of Ripley formed the Synod of the Free Church. This was in Nov. 1847. Bro. G. continued at New Athens, and preaching in the church till (I think) near the close of 1848, when his health failing he was obliged to resign. The fatal disease which finally brought him to the grave, was already at work.

Meeting him soon after in Washington, Penn., the writer proposed to him the idea of starting a weekly religious newspaper, in connection with the Free Church movement, and of his becoming its editor. After serious and prayerful deliberation, he consented that the subject might be proposed to the Mahoning Presbytery, then to meet in a few days at Mt Jackson in Mercer Co, Penn. This was done, and all the members seemed to recognize in this arrangement the hand of God. It was resolved, that with the concurrence of the brethren in Southern Ohio, we would start a weekly journal at Mercer, Penn., to be published by W. F. Clark and edited by Bro. G. This arrangement was made. Bro. G. went to Mercer, and commenced the publication of the *Free Presbyterian*, in the summer of 1850. The paper, on account of the position it occupied, had necessarily a limited circulation; but one sufficient for its maintenance. Its list was slowly, but steadily increasing, when after two years it was thought best to unite it with the *Christian Press*, an anti-slavery religious paper, published at Cincinnati. According to this plan Bro. G. went to Cleveland, where it was proposed to have one branch of the publishing office. Owing to causes which I need not mention, but over which he had no control, the experiment was a failure, and it was resolved to resume the publication of the *Free Presbyterian*. Inducements were held out to the Synod, to publish at New Albany, Athens Co., and the press was removed thither, and was conducted by Bros. Gordon and Kephart as editors.

Before this Bro. G. had been a number of times very near the grave by a severe hemorrhage of the lungs. Still he labored patiently and perseveringly on, always seeming conscious that his time to work would soon be ended. This location was unsuitable, especially on account of its want of proper mailing facilities, and the press was removed to Yellow Springs, Green Co., where Bro. G. again became sole editor, it not being found practicable for Bro. Kephart to leave his other engagements, and go with him. Here he continued till last autumn.

During his stay at Yellow Springs, his labors were very severe. Often, with his poor health, he labored far into the night; till at last the feeble frame would bear no more pressure and sunk beneath it. Many of those who read weekly with delight, the soul-stirring words he wrote, did not know that the hand that penned them was becoming more and more feeble—

did not see the pale brow that was bending over the midnight lamp—did not realize that the glorious intellect that shone so bright and clear, was so fast ripening for heaven! But those of us who knew him best, knew that he was dying. Alas! that the good and gifted, so soon should leave us.

In October, he removed with his family to his native home, near Washington, Penn. He went back only to die; and on Sabbath morning the 28th Feb. he calmly fell asleep in Jesus. The closing scene has been feelingly described by another, and we shall not dwell upon it. He sleeps under one of the old, familiar trees, that he loved so well in childhood. There let him rest in peace till the resurrection of the just.

As a *Christian* Bro. G. was consistent, faithful and humble. His religion was that of principle. He knew no compromise with sin, and never sought popularity by betraying truth. As an *editor*, he was able and independent. His mind was of the first order. He thought deeply and expressed himself clearly. In argument he had but few equals. He wrote with great facility, and the subject that was clear to his own mind, he could always make clear to others. There was a clearness and directness about his style, which was admirable. He had no honied words for *sin*, but always called it by its right name. He plead for pure religion, and longed to see Christians coming out from their connection with the sins of the world. He plead the cause of the poor, and enslaved, and on his dying bed claimed the sweet promise of God in the 41st Psalm. Oppressors, time-servers and trimmers, hated him of course. And although they said "all manner of evil against him," his death-bed confirmed his upright course, and in near view of eternity he declared that he felt the position he had taken in the church to be right and good. He made a most interesting paper, for all who love to think and act aright. Eternity alone will develop the greatness of the work he has performed.

As a *speaker*, he was calm, collected, clear and often impassioned and eloquent. His language was always concise and pure, and he carried conviction to the hearts of his hearers by an irresistible aplication of *truth*.

As a *friend*, he was generous, frank and cheerful. His conduct was never fickle or wayward. The warm grasp and kindling eye, always told the pleasure he felt in meeting with acquaintances and friends. And now as I write, memory is busy with the past. He *my* friend. Through long years of trial he had always been the same. I have loved him as a brother, and now feel a *loneliness* even in the midst of busy life.

Yet I can rejoice that he is *happy*.   I know that he is with the blood-washed company.   The feeble body shall know no more trial and weariness—the overwrought mind no more anxiety and care. " Blessed are the dead who die in the Lord —they *rest* from their labors." He has gone "to be with Christ, which is far better." He has met again his little ones— the stricken lambs of his flock, the "Good Shepherd," has taken to the fold above.   May they who yet remain, his companion and his son, be prepared to meet them, and be an unbroken family in heaven.

Friends of my youth farewell!
  Life's changing day of sin and toil is past,
And from the gathering swell
  Of earth's rude tempests thou art safe at last.

Past are these scenes of care,
  The appointed nights of weariness are o'er,
No pain can reach thee there,
  In the bright mansions of that summer shore.

Brother I miss thee here,
  A shadow falls upon life's gloomy way,
But in thy brighter sphere
  The eye of faith beholds unclouded day.

Rest for the *weary*, rest!—
  Take back O native earth thy toilworn son,
And on thy peaceful breast
  Pillow the aching head whose task is done.

T. M. F.

•   LINES ON THE DEATH OF REV. J. GORDON.

Dead! in the manhood's golden prime,
  Ere life reached its zenith hour,
Ere long dark years of time had dimmed
        Thy spirit's power.

Yet in that life so quickly o'er,
  Rich triumphs have been won;
The work thy father bad'st thee do
        Was nobly done.

Hushed now the prayer that thou might'st live
  To battle 'gainst the tide of wrong
That now seems darkening o'er our land,
        Swift rushing on.

We only ask, the seed thou'st sown
  Of earnest thought, and purpose high,
Of kindly word, and noble deed,
        May never die.

We look abroad, for one like thee,
  Mighty in word, in spirit brave,
But seek in vain; sadly our hearts
      Turn to thy grave.

Mourn Afric's sons! from slavery's curse
  Fair Freedom's soil he strove to save;
To right thy burning wrongs, his life
      An offering gave.

Thy Leader's fallen; Zion mourn!
  'Twas *purity* he sought for thee,
A fitting Bride for "Christ thy head,"
      That thou might'st be.

Rest, weary one, we would not break
  Thy quiet slumber, calm and deep,
That sleep "God giveth His beloved,"
      Calm, peaceful sleep.

The rest for which thy spirit longed,
  Where all the strife of earth is o'er,
Where blight of sorrow and stain of sin
      Comes never more.

Great was thy work! great thy reward!
  A radiant crown thou now dost wear:
"An eternal weight of glory *now*
      Thou'st *strength* to bear."

Dost see thy Father face to face,
  And in his unveiled presence stand,
While thy song of rapture swells among
      The angel band.

We'd hush our murmuring hearts and say
  'Tis well, "Thy will, O God, be done."
We thank thee that our strength comes not
      From man alone.

ALBANY, Ohio.   M.

In addition to the above, a few things demand a fuller
notice. He was licensed by the Presbytery of Washington
in 1843. While he was a student of the theological seminary, some of his utterances on the subject of slavery, and
especially on one occasion, a truthful, but severe animadversion, on the criminal silence of the ministers and D. D's of
the church, gave special offense. An unsuccessful effort first
to flatter, and then to gag him into silence, was made by an
aged professor of theology (P.). He was licensed by the
Presbytery of Washington in the spring of 1843. After his
licensure, he labored a short time in Ashland, Ohio—a few

months in Claysville, Pennsylvania, and about a year in
Urichsville, Ohio, while he was teaching in New Philadelphia.
In May, 1845, the General Assembly of the O. S. Presbyterian church, passed the Rubicon in her downward march
from the hights of ecclesiastical liberty, into the territories
of despotism. Once, in common with other branches of the
Presbyterian family, she bore a strong and truthful testimony against slaveholding. The Assembly of 1794 declared
the slaveholder identical with the man-thief—the worst criminal designated in the Mosaic law. That of 1818 pronounced
it utterly inconsistent with the law of God, and totally irreconcilable with the gospel of Christ. But during all this
time the man-thief was permitted to preach the gospel and
commune in the church, under the delusive hope that a paper
testimony from the highest church courts would work a silent
destruction of the sin. Instead, however, of dying out, it
steadily grew, struck its roots deeply around the pulpit, the
altar, and the communion table ; and this year it felt strong
enough to throw off the mask, and claim that the Assembly
was originally organized, on the conceded principle that its
existence should be " no bar to Christian communion."

In common with many others, Mr. G. was greatly exercised,
and deeply grieved with this apostate action. In July following, he was invited to attend a convention of ministers
and elders at Mt. Pleasant, whose object was to try to induce
the Assembly of 1846 to rescind the action of that of 1845,
and re-affirm that of 1818, which had been the standing testimony of the church during twenty-seven years. The invitation found him prostrated on a bed of sickness; yet he
responded by letter. He always wrote with a trenchant pen,
and now disease probably added to its point. As this letter was
made the subject of flagrantly unconstitutional action, and
the occasion of bitter and relentless persecution afterward,
we here insert it entire :

NEW PHILADELPHIA, July 23, 1845.

Dear Brethren: A severe and dangerous attack of sickness, under which I was suffering at the time your letter was
received, prevented an immediate reply ; and now the feeble-
ness incident to but a partial recovery, will preclude a labored
answer.

Most gladly would I mingle with you in your proposed
convention, but the state of my health, and nature of my
engagements, forbid the expectation.

With the prominent object of the meeting you invite me to attend, I deeply sympathize—"to induce the General Assembly to rescind their late action on the subject of slavery." The emotions excited in my mind by perusing that action, have alternated between bitter grief and burning indignation. The *moral character of slavery*, I have ceased to regard as an *open* question. I no longer admit it as a *debatable point*, whether slavery be a sin. The *united voice of the civilized world*—the innate consciousness of every human heart—and the *plain teachings of the word of God*—have all combined to settle the question. Common sense alone is sufficient in its plain teachings.

With these views, I looked with anxious solicitude to our highest court, hoping to see them arrange themselves on the side of truth and Jehovah—hoping to hear the strong voice of affectionate, but stern rebuke to those who "deal in slaves and souls of men."

To blast these fond anticipations, came the *blasphemous* (the word is not too strong) report of the reverend committee, to which was committed the anti-slavery memorials of large and respectable numbers in the church; a report in which Christ and his Apostles are ruthlessly pressed into the service of "the vilest system of oppression that ever saw the sun," which is made up of a tissue of contradictions—in one breath pronouncing slavery the favorite institution of Jesus and his Apostles, and in the next, promulgating in the ear of the master as his rule of conduct, the broad principle of doing to others as they would have others do to them—which is destined to sweep the system of abominations from the earth; a report, which, in connection with the subsequent action of the Assembly, trampled on the right of free discussion, and manifested a reckless determination on the part of the majority, to earn the title of "brotherhood of thieves," and "wear it as a feather in their cap."

Is this language too strong? Look for a moment at the nature of the case. Slavery is either *right or wrong*—either a holy institution approved of God and pleasing in his sight, or a system of crime and blood, over which the Almighty frowns, and over which the Saviour weeps. A system so decided in its character and effects, precludes the idea of *neutrality* in its moral nature. If then it be a holy institution, as the drift of the report would make it, why in the name of all that is manly, this driveling policy of seeking to justify it, and yet not wishing to be understood as denying that there is *evil* connected with it? If it be a holy institution, let them proclaim it boldly, and call upon its opposers to cease their wicked efforts ; and should they refuse to do so, proceed to discipline and expel them from the church for seeking to contravene a Heaven-ordained institution, appointed by God himself, and baptized in the name of Father, Son, and Spirit, by Christ and his disciples.

But if on the other hand slavery be, as it surely is, the "sum of all villainies "—"a gross violation of the most precious and sacred rights of human nature, *utterly inconsistent with the law of God*, which requires us to love our neighbors as we love ourselves—and totally irreconcilable with the spirit and principles of the gospel of Christ ; " if such be the character of slavery, then no language is too strong in speaking of those who, while claiming loudly to be the ministers of the merciful Jesus, lend all their energies to uphold the vile abomination. Is slavery then the monster which the good and great of all ages and our own Assembly in years past declare it to be? As I have said, I shall not reason *that* question. Bring but one of its many constituent parts to bear on these reverend divines, and you shall hear a different response from their recorded action in the Assembly of 1845. Place one of them in the hands of a master possessing but one of the slaveholders' prerogatives—the power to separate him from wife and children—to compel him to toil without reward in the burning southern sun—the right to sell him to the most cruel tyrant—or the power to forbid him reading the word of God—and you would hear from that holy man no declaration that to " pronounce slavery a sin, would be to contradict some of the plainest declarations of the word of God." And yet not one, but *all* of these elements, and MORE, enter into the composition of slavery. And yet these *holy men* can say that Christ and his inspired followers did not condemn the system !!

> " How long, oh Lord ! how long
> Shall such a priesthood barter truth away !
> And in thy name, for *robbery* and *wrong*,
> At thine own altars pray ! "

The *time and circumstances* in which the General Assembly of our church have taken this impious stand, gives to their position a painful singularity. While the civilized, and even many parts of the savage world, are combining in one grand effort to crush the blood-stained monster; while almost all other branches of the Christian Church are uttering their

testimony against it; while just across the river, where the
Assembly sat, the voice of a former slaveholder—reared under
the influence of the system—a politician making no claim to
the Christian character, is pouring his denunciation in words
of burning eloquence, and calling, in language to which the
heart leaps as to the blast of the trumpet, upon all to marshal
to the death struggle with the demon of oppression, men
claiming to be chosen ministers of Him who came "to proclaim liberty to the captive," are seen rushing to plant their
shoulders in support of the tottering Bastile, as it reels beneath the sturdy blows that fall thick and fast upon it. Over
such a scene, surely Jesus and angels must weep; and that
such a state of things may soon cease to disgrace our beloved
church, will surely call forth the prayers of all that love the
truth. In all consistent and energetic action to secure the
great object of the coming convention, you have my most
hearty sympathy; and to the extent of my feeble powers, my
earnest co-operation. May God speed the day of the slave's
deliverance; and permit *us* to live to join our voices in the
jubilee shout, when "Liberty shall be proclaimed throughout
all the land, unto all the inhabitants thereof."

Yours, for Truth and Freedom,
JOS. GORDON.

Mr. McCullough, and others.

This letter, in connection with those of several others, was
published in the *Liberty Advocate* of Cadiz, Ohio. In the
following October he was invited to the church of New
Athens, and elected Professor of Mathematics in Franklin
College. Previous to this he had taken a letter of dismission
from the Presbytery of Washington, and put himself under
the care of that of Coshocton, Ohio. To that Presbytery he
was alone accountable for all the acts which were done while
he was under its care. It was rather an anti-slavery body,
and took no official notice of the published letter. After his
removal to Athens, he took a letter of dismissal from the
Presbytery of Coshocton, and put himself under the care of
that of St. Clairsville. That body, without any open objection, took him under its care, and appointed him to supply
the church of Athens a whole year, without a hint that his
conduct in writing the above letter, and permitting its publication, had been offensive. In 1846, one year afterward,
the church made out a call—the Presbytery without objection
put it into his hands—he signified his acceptance—and they

appointed a meeting for his ordination. The day came, and the body met. Their plans of operation were concealed. They proceeded with his examination, and heard his trials, as if nothing stood in the way of his ordination, till they were almost ready to lay on hands. Then a member arose and gave the information (which every member of the body knew a year and a half before) that the candidate had written an offensive letter in July, 1845, in reference to the action of the General Assembly. Pretending to receive this as a piece of new intelligence, the Presbytery appointed a committee to confer with the candidate, and endeavor to induce him to retract the sentiments of the letter. To the committee he made what he called "an explanation." He said the letter was written while he was on a sick bed—the language might not have been well chosen—and that it was not his right to judge the private motives of the members of the Assembly; but that in reference to the action itself, he had expressed his firm and matured convictions, and that he could not, and would not, retract them until they convinced him they were wrong. The explanation was pronounced unsatisfactory; the committee so reported to the Presbytery, and the whole body spent a considerable time in trying to wring from him something more. They put on the gag—prohibited him from making a public defense—confined him down to simply answer their questions—charged him with being "a young man "—"a mere tyro"—with many other phrases equally dignified, and rendered deeply impressive by the bitterness and anger with which they were uttered. All this heat, and zeal, and rhetoric he met with the calm serenity and self-possession of one who stood on the principles of conscious rectitude. No one attempted to convince him that his expressed sentiments were wrong, or to grapple with him in discussion of their truth or falsehood.

The Presbytery evidently designed to spring the matter on him suddenly—frighten him into some sudden concessions, and thus tie his hands, and gag his lips for the future. This was now a failure. What could be done? Should they give him a regular trial, as he demanded? This would entitle him to the right of being heard in defense. This they could not meet. They therefore suddenly arrested the proceedings and adjourned. This was supposed to be done to enable them to form some new plan for the future. They had persistently refused him a hearing. As soon as the body adjourned, he requested the crowded congregation to remain; and made to them an eloquent, manly and resistless defense of his course and conduct. A few days afterward his church met, and passed resolutions approving his course, and condemning that of the Presbytery. The Presbytery, through their stated clerk, published a one-sided statement of their action. The *Presbyterian Advocate*—a paper that seldom, if ever, manifested either candor, fairness, or love of truth, if their opposites seemed to better serve its purpose—refused to publish either his reply, or the resolutions of the congregation. The congregation, however, had them published in an extra sheet at the office of the *Liberty Advocate*, in Cadiz. These papers we republish. Some of the members of that Presbytery have gone the way of all flesh, and have passed themselves the ordeal of a higher tribunal. Most of them yet live, and their unrepented acts make a part of their reputation, and the one under consideration ought not to be forgotten.

[From the Presbyterian Advocate.]

PRESBYTERY OF ST. CLAIRSVILLE — CASE OF THE REV. JOSEPH GORDON.

The committee appointed by Presbytery to prepare a record of the proceedings of Presbytery in reference to Mr. Joseph .Gordon, for publication, submit the following :

Mr. Joseph Gordon, a licentiate under the care of the Presbytery of Coshocton, was, by virtue of a dismission from said Presbytery, received as a licentiate under the care of this Presbytery, at its meeting in June, 1846 ; and at-the meeting of the Presbytery, Oct., 1846, there was a call laid on the table of Presbytery, for Mr. Gordon, by the church of New Athens, to become their pastor. The call was put into the hands of Mr. Gordon ; and he having signified his acceptance thereof, Presbytery adjourned to meet at New Athens, on the 1st Tuesday of November next, with a view to ordain and install him as pastor of said church, provided the way was open. Presbytery having met at this time, pursuant to adjournment, heard the trial sermon of Mr. Gordon, from the text previously assigned him ; and also examined him on the Latin, Greek, and Hebrew languages, the Natural and Moral Sciences, the Sacraments and Church Government ; all of which examinations were sustained, as satisfactory parts of trial for ordination.

At this stage of the proceedings, and when Presbytery were about to have a recess, it was intimated to Presbytery that there had been some letters written by Mr. Gordon, and published in the *Liberty Advocate*, in reference to the General Assembly of 1845; in which there were improper and unbecoming expressions made use of by him in reference to that body. Whereupon it was

Resolved, That inasmuch as it had been represented to Presbytery that Mr. Gordon, the candidate for ordination, has written letters, published in the *Liberty Advocate*, in which there are expressions and sentiments which are slanderous to the Presbyterian church; therefore

Resolved, That a committee of three be appointed to examine such letters, and converse with Mr. Gordon on the subject, ascertain whether a retraction of such expressions be necessary, and how far Mr. Gordon is willing to retract; and report to Presbytery as soon as possible. The Rev. Dr. Rea, Rev. James Kerr, and Mr. Thos. J. Holliday were appointed that committee.

Presbytery having again met. it was moved that the report of the committee of the preceding evening be adopted. The report is as follows:

The committee appointed to examine certain letters written by Mr. Gordon, and to converse with him on the subject, report, That having examined one of the letters, acknowledged by Mr. Gordon to have been written by him, they found that the following language, in reference to the General Assembly of the Presbyterian church, that met at Cincinnati in 1845, occurs, viz.: "To blast these fond anticipations, came the *blasphemous* (the word is not too strong) report of the reverend Committee." Again: "A report which, in connection with the subsequent action of the Assembly, trampled on the right of free discussion, and manifested a reckless determination, on the part of the majority, to earn the title of 'brotherhood of thieves,' and 'wear it as a feather in their cap.'" Again: "And yet these holy men say that Christ and his inspired followers did not condemn the system."

> "'Great God of truth! how long
> Shall such a priesthood barter truth away!
> And in thy name, for robbery and wrong,
> At thine own altar pray?"'

Again: "The time and circumstances in which the General Assembly of our church have taken this *impious stand.*" The above are the principal expressions to which the Committee directed the attention of Mr. Gordon; and after much conversation with him on the subject, presented to him the following plain and simple questions; to which he himself appended the negative answers, viz.:

1. Are you willing to acknowledge that the language used in your letter to the Mt. Pleasant Convention is too strong?

Answer.—" I am willing to say that I impugned no man's motives; but that the language is not too strong, if applied to me, should I with *my* views, do the same thing."

2d. Are you willing to acknowledge that the language was inappropriate, as used, to that reverend body?

Answer.—" I would say as above, that I apply the language to the *act*, not the *men*."

3d. Are you willing to pledge yourself that you will refrain in future from using such language to your brethren?

Answer.—" I would again distinguish between the *men* and the *act*. Toward the action I hold the same language. Against my brethren I will in future use no abusive or slanderous language whatever."

After some discussion on the adoption of the foregoing report, the following question was presented to Mr. Gordon, and answered by him in open Presbytery, viz.:

" Is Mr. Gordon willing to say that he regrets having written the letter in question?"

Answer.—" I do not regret writing the letter, but I regret the construction that is put upon it."

Whereupon. the foregoing report was adopted by yeas and nays—yeas, 10; nays, 4; excused, 1. And hence all further proceedings in reference to his ordination were suspended.

BENJAMIN MITCHELL, Stated Clerk.

CADIZ, OHIO, April 22, 1849.

MR. GORDON—*Dear Sir:* I am sorry to have to perform, as Clerk of the Presbytery, the duty which you will perceive is enjoined in the following extracts from the minutes:

Extract from the Minutes of the Presbytery of St. Clairsville, met at Morristown, April 21, 1847.

" A communication was received from the congregation of New Athens, requesting that the action of the previous meeting of Presbytery in reference to Mr. Joseph Gordon be reconsidered, and that he be ordained as their pastor; and also a letter from Mr. Gordon himself on the subject.

"A motion was made and recorded that the request of the congregation be granted, which motion was lost by a unanimous vote.

"A motion was then made and recorded that Mr. Gordon be deprived of his license. After some discussion, it was moved that the subject be postponed till next meeting of Presbytery. This motion was lost. At this stage of the business the subject was committed to Messrs. Rae and Kerr to bring in a minute for the adoption of Presbytery.

"Presbytery had a recess till 7½ o'clock.

"After recess, the committee appointed to bring in a minute for the adoption of Presbytery, in the case of Mr. Gordon, presented the following, viz.:

"The committee appointed to bring in a minute for the adoption of Presbytery, in the case of Mr. Gordon, present the following, viz.:

"Whereas, The congregation of New Athens have presented a request that Presbytery should reconsider their action at last meeting in reference to the ordination of Mr. Gordon, and that he be ordained and installed as their pastor, accompanied with a letter from Mr. Gordon himself on the subject; and, whereas, Presbytery has now refused to grant the request of the congregation of New Athens; and, whereas, the letter of Mr. Gordon contains no manifestation of a disposition to retract any of his offensive expressions used in reference to the General Assembly, but rather a reiteration and defense of said expressions. Whereas, he has published in the *Liberty Advocate*, since the last meeting of Presbytery, a lengthened defense of said expressions, and thus continued to reiterate instead of retracting the accusations against the highest judicatory of our church, for which Presbytery arrested his ordination at its last meeting; and, whereas, a licentiate is a probationer for the work of the ministry, and Presbytery have now twice decided that they can not introduce him into the full work of the gospel ministry, Mr. Gordon's term of probation ought now to cease. Therefore,

"*Resolved*, That Mr. Joseph Gordon be and he hereby is deprived of his license to preach the gospel, and that his name be stricken from our roll of licentiates.

"*Resolved, further*, That the letter of Mr. Gordon, published in the *Liberty Advocate*, of Dec. 23, 1846, and his letter at the same time to the Presbytery, be kept on file.

"The report was accepted, and then the following resolution was presented and unanimously adopted. viz.:

"*Resolved*, That the previous report be postponed for the present, and that when Presbytery adjourns it adjourns to meet at Wheeling Valley on the second Tuesday of May at

11 o'clock, and that a copy of the records of this meeting in his case be sent to Mr. Gordon, and that he be cited to attend that meeting, and informed that in case he does not then answer satisfactorily the questions previously put to him, that then the preceding report will be adopted.

"By order of Presbytery.

"JAMES KERR, *Clerk*."

[For the Liberty Advocate.]

MR. HANNA: The following communication was prepared for the *Presbyterian Advocate;* but, (after publishing the report to which it refers) the editor refused to insert this; I, therefore, ask the use of your columns to lay it before the public. J. G.

[For the Presbyterian Advocate.]

MR. EDITOR: As the Presbytery of St. Clairsville have given publicity, through your columns, to their proceeding in reference to myself, at their late meeting in New Athens, I hope you will permit me to present to the public, through the same medium, my reasons for dissenting from that decision. *Public acts* of *public men* are *public property.* The humblest individual has a perfect right to call in question the justness of any decision of men in the highest stations; and when statements are published touching the standing of an individual as a Christian minister, he ought in fairness to have the opportunity of vindicating himself.

The history of my connection with St. Clairsville Presbytery is briefly this: Last June they received me as a licentiate from another Presbytery, and appointed me to preach to the congregation of New Athens till their fall meeting, which was all the time the congregation then asked for—intending to present a call for my pastoral labors at that time. A call was presented and put in my hands at the October meeting of the Presbytery, and after my acceptance of it, they proceeded to assign me a subject for an ordination sermon, and "adjourned to meet in New Athens on the first Tuesday of November, to ordain and install me pastor of this church, 'if the way was clear.'" At the time appointed, the Presbytery met, proceeded to hear the sermon, and attended to nearly all the examinations, which were all unanimously sustained as parts of trial. But at this point the proceedings were arrested, by a motion "to appoint a committee to examine certain letters written by me, and if possible, to induce me to retract certain expressions," which the Presbytery chose to consider offensive. The result of this conference, and the subsequent proceedings of the Presbytery, have been given to the public in their published report. The "letters" were written with reference to the action of the General Assembly of 1845, on the subject of slavery. My answers to the questions of the committee were, that so far as the language of my letter was an expression of opinion on the *action* of the Assembly, I hold the same language now; and hence, on that point had no retractions to make; but that I did not when I wrote the letter, and did not then intend to impugn or judge any man's *motives*. With this explanation the Presbytery was not satisfied, and hence adopted their report, which re-commended that all further proceedings be suspended, till I should make the required acknowledgments. On this decision I wish to offer the following considerations: First. *It is inconsistent with, and contradictory to, the previous action of the Presbytery in regard to myself.* The "*letter*" complained of was written in the summer of 1845—before I came into the bounds of the Presbytery of St. Clairsville at all—nearly a whole year before they received me as a licentiate, and sent me to preach to one of the churches, and more than one year before their last meeting, at which they refused to ordain me. The language, then, of my letter, which they call "slander-ous of the Presbyterian church," had been before them long before the time in which they took any action in my case. And yet, without the least objection, they took all these several steps preparatory to my ordination ; nor was any diffi-culty even hinted at, until they were almost ready to " lay hands upon me!" Now what is the inevitable inference from all this? Plainly this, that the Presbytery of St. Clairsville considered that there *was* no objection to my reception as a licentiate—that they considered me fit to preach by their authority, to one of their own churches—fit to receive a call through their hands—fit to be examined, and to have those examinations sustained—and yet (for an act done before I ever came into their bounds) *not fit to receive ordination at their hands!!* By their previous action in my case, the Presbytery virtually indorsed every *known* act of my life, of which they had no evidence that I had repented. They said explicitly, by their act, that they knew of no reason why I was not a proper person to preach by their authority. Now, is not the preaching of the gospel the most important and solemn part of a minister's work? and if I am in their judgment qualified for this, by what process of law do they come to the conclusion that I am unfit for the minor parts of the work? One of two conclusions seems therefore to *force* itself upon us—either that the Presbytery of St. Clairsville did not and do not consider the sentiments of the offending "letter" as a disqualification in one of their preachers, and therefore that they are insincere in their refusal to ordain me—or, on the other hand, that they are totally unfit for the oversight of the churches committed to their care, since they sent a man whom they profess to regard as a "public slanderer" to preach by their authority to one of those churches, and that too without one word of warning to that church to beware of the errors of this public slanderer. The Presbytery can exercise its discretion, in choosing between the horns of this dilemma.

In the second place, I object to the decision of the Presbytery, because I regard the language of my letter (in the sense in which I used it, and which I explained to the Presbytery) *as true, and capable of ample vindication from the word of God and the teachings of the Presbyterian church.* One of the expressions that gave most offense, was the term "*blasphemous*," applied to the report of the Assembly of 1845, on the subject of Slavery. Now, if I prove the term applicable and true, whatever consequences it may involve, I am not responsible. What is, then, the teaching of that report? The amount of it is this—"that slaveholding as it exists *in the Southern* part of our country, should be no bar to Christian communion." Now, the conclusion is irresistible from this, that by the decision of the Assembly it is no sin at all. What is the teaching and practice of the church on this point? That "EVERY SIN deserves God's wrath and curse, both in this life and the life to come." If it deserves God's wrath and curse, does it not deserve the church's censure? The *practice* of the church has been to exclude from her communion every man guilty of the open and constant practice of even the most *venial* sin, if he refuse, after proper admonition, to forsake it. Now, slaveholding is an open, constant practice, and slaveholders not only refuse to abandon, but openly avow their intention to continue it. Then when the General Assembly say that "to pronounce it a sin deserving the discipline of the church, would be to contradict the plainest teachings of the word of God," they say by the plainest inference, that it is *not a sin at all.* If, then, to pronounce slavery a sin would be to contradict the plain teachings of the

Bible, to pronounce it holy must be to accord with these "plain teachings." Slavery, then, they teach, harmonizes with the teachings of the Bible: it must of consequence harmonize with the character of the Author of the Bible: God's word is but a transcript or copy of his character. Then I understand the report to teach that American slavery accords with the character of God. Now what is blasphemy? Noah Webster says, "it is an indignity or dishonor cast upon God by writing or speech." If, then, it be not an "indignity and dishonor" of the grossest kind, and therefore *blasphemy* the most daring, to say even by remote implication, that American slavery harmonizes with the character of Deity, I am at a loss to know how God could be dishonored or blasphemed.

But to the same point we come by a shorter process. The report says explicitly, that slaveholders were taken into the church by Christ and his apostles. Their open practices were taken along. Into his Church nothing ever came with the approval of Christ, but what was holy and like himself. Slavery, says the report, came by his approval, *therefore is slavery holy and like to Jesus.* But what is slavery? The same authority that says this, defines it to be a gross violation of the most sacred rights of human nature—*utterly inconsistent with the law of God, and totally irreconcilable with the gospel of Christ.*" And yet there is no blasphemy in saying that *this thing* came into the Church with the approbation of God, and therefore bears his image!! I quote just one extract to show that I am not singular in the use of this language. The Presbytery of Chillicothe (and some of its members are *old men*) declares that "they can not hold fellowship with any Presbytery, Synod, or other ecclesiastical body, that tolerates the justification of slaveholding by appeal to the Scriptures, which in their judgment is *blasphemy of Almighty God,* and a shocking prostitution of his word."

There is one other expression in my letter that gave special offense—that "the majority of the Assembly of 1845 manifested a determination to earn the title, "brotherhood of thieves." This may seem harsh language from "a mere tyro," but the Presbyterian church ("our mother," as a venerable Doctor delighted to call her) has *taught me to use it;* therefore let me not bear the *guilt* of its use alone. If slaveholding be *theft,* then not only those engaged in it, but those fraternizing with them and sanctioning them in the practice, deserve the appellation, "brotherhood of thieves." That slaveholding is man-stealing, is the express teaching of the

Presbyterian church in former days. "Stealers of men are *all* those who are engaged in bringing men into slavery, or *in detaining them in it*," said the Church in 1794. Who are slaveholders, if not those engaged in "*detaining*" men in slavery? and, therefore, who are men-stealers, if slaveholders be not? Hear the Church again: "Men-stealers are *all* those who *keep*, sell, or buy slaves." Who, we ask again, are slaveholders, if not those who "KEEP slaves?" Yet these the venerable fathers call men-stealers. Now when the Presbytery of St. Clairsville has made out a clear distinction between a *man-stealer* and a *thief*, then, and not till then, will they have a right to proscribe me for the use of the phrase, "brotherhood of thieves." It is the language of *genuine* "*Old Schoolism*"—not of the patent, spurious, pro-slavery Old Schoolism so rife at the present time. Why then must I be condemned for using the language taught me by Dr. Ashbel Green, and other men, whose memories the Church delights to honor? Why this "building the tombs of prophets, and garnishing the sepulchers of the righteous," and yet persecuting the men that preach their principles?

But there is higher authority than even the Church for using the language. "Our mother" only borrowed it from the pages of inspiration. "The law, says Paul, "is made for murderers of fathers and murderers of mothers, for whoremongers, for men-stealers." The law here referred to may be found, Exodus xxi : 15, 16, etc. "He that smiteth his father or his mother shall surely be put to death, and he that stealeth a man and selleth him, or if *he be found in his hand*, shall surely be put to death. Now, in whose *hands* are the stolen sons of Africa found, if not in the hands of slaveholders? and who, I once more inquire, are slaveholders, if not those in "*whose hands the slave is found?*" Slavery came originally by theft and piracy : the stolen men, or their offspring (which is just the same) are now found in the hands of the very men who, the General Assembly say, should not be excluded from Christian communion.

Now, I call upon the Presbytery of St. Clairsville to meet these proofs and authorities fairly. I claim the authority of the Church, of the fathers and the word of God, for using the language I did use; and until this evidence is fairly set aside, I hurl back the charge of indiscretion and presumption so liberally heaped upon me, because, forsooth, I was not born quite so soon as some other men—because I am "*a young man*," or, as a venerable Doctor expressed it, "a mere tyro."

4

I close this communication with two remarks : First, Fairness would require of the Presbytery the publication of the whole letter, and not of detached sentences taken out of their connection. The language was based on two suppositions—that slavery is a system of theft and blood, and that the Assembly of 1845 gave it their approval. If these assumptions are correct (and it was never once attempted to prove the contrary), then the language of my letter was neither " too strong nor inappropriate." Was any of the Presbytery in place of the slave, he would not think the language " too strong." Yet God commands us to " feel for those in bonds *as bound with them.*" The second remark is, that I wish the majority of the Presbytery of St. Clairsville (and I have spoken only of the majority : to the minority I tender my thanks); to know that to retract *to authority is a proceeding I do not understand.* It is manly and Christian to recant error and abandon a false position, when the judgment is convinced; and thus I hope God will make me willing always to do. But it is base and pusilanimous in the extreme, to " take even a letter back " simply because other men choose to think it out of place, and offer no reason save that they *will* to have it so. Retraction on such grounds, I utterly and forever disclaim.   JOSEPH GORDON.

New Athens, Nov. 23, 1846.

☞ Wishing to occupy as little space as possible in the papers to which the above article was sent for publication, I said nothing of the unconstitutionality of the proceeding of Presbytery. It constitutes a further objection that it was a palpable violation of the Constitution. If the language of my letter was " slanderous," and constituted an offense deserving judicial investigation and censure—then the Presbytery of Coshocton was the only court competent to try the case. The Constitution expressly teaches, *that every offense shall be tried by the court under whose jurisdiction the individual is when he commits it.* (See *Discipline*, chap. 10, sec. 1 and 2.) If, on the contrary, it was for for my " views and *sentiments*," of the action of the Assembly, that they refused to ordain me, then their act was not only unconstitutional but tyrannical. On this subject opinions are left free. The Constitution prescribes the trials for ordination, and *leaves nothing to the discretion of the Presbytery save the branches of learning on which the shall be examined, and the number of his trial sermons.* On all subjects not authoritatively settled by the Constitution, a man has the right to hold and utter whatever sentiments he pleases; nor has any church court a right to call him to account for the proper expression of those views. If a Presbytery may exclude a man from the right of ordination for his sentiments on subjects in regard to which the Constitution has left opinions free, then that Constitution is a rope of sand; and the terms of admission to the ministry, are left to the whim of every Presbytery.

[For the Liberty Advocate.]

NEW ATHENS, Dec. 6, 1846.

The congregation of the Presbyterian church of New Athens, having met agreeably to adjournment, Judge Hanna was called to the chair. The meeting having taken into consideration the proceedings of the Presbytery of St. Clairsville, lately held in this place, to ordain and install Rev. Joseph Gordon pastor of said church, after due deliberation, unanimously passed the following preamble and resolutions:

Whereas, The Presbytery of St. Clairsville received the Rev. Joseph Gordon as a licentiate, *appointed him to preach to us as a supply;* put a call into his hands; adjourned to meet here to ordain him; and after hearing nearly all his examinations and his sermon, unanimously sustained them as parts of trial; and then, for sentiments published nearly a year before they received him, refused to ordain him, Therefore,

Resolved, That we regard the action of the Presbytery as a breach of implied faith—plainly given in their previous acts.

Resolved, That we feel *aggrieved* by said action of Presbytery.

Resolved, That as a congregation, we *cordially* sustain Mr. Gordon in the position he has taken before Presbytery.

Resolved, That we believe the language of Mr. Gordon's letter to the Mt. Pleasant convention of July 23d, 1845, is not "stronger" than *any man* would use if subjected to the condition of the slave, and, that we are required to "feel for those in bonds *as bound with them.*"

Resolved, That these proceedings be signed by the Chairman, and published in the *Presbyterian Advocate* and *Presbyterian of the West.*

JOHN HANNA, *Chairman.*

After the adjournment of Presbytery he continued the discharge of his duties in the college, and ministered to the church during the succeeding winter. In the following spring the congregation sent up two commissioners to the next stated meeting, requesting them to reconsider their action, and come back and ordain their minister. The request was refused, and a new plan was struck out. They took advantage of Section 11th, Chapter 14th of the book of discipline, which declares that "when a licentiate has been preaching a considerable time, and his services do not appear to be edifying to the churches, the Presbytery may, if they think proper, recall his license." This article did not in letter or spirit meet the case. The candidate could preach; the congregation thought him edifying and were urgent for his ordination. Still it was the best they could do. Sheltered behind it, they could keep their victim gagged, and pass him through their ecclesiastical guillotine in silence. To give him an opportunity of defense they dreaded. They consequently appointed a meeting at Wheeling Valley, some miles from Athens. By this time the people of Athens generally had very little respect for them, and its atmosphere did not suit them. They again demanded a retraction on mere authority, which was respectfully declined as before. They then by a large majority voted to strip him of his license and struck his name from the roll of candidates. The moderator contrary to the Constitution voted to swell the majority. Thus the Presbytery of St. Clairsville made a false and perverted use of an article in the book of discipline, never intended for such a case; and neither for alleged crime nor heresy, virtually deposed a young minister, and tried to degrade him from his office, and in the true spirit of inquisitors, refused him a hearing in his own defense. A license was taken away which was conferred three years before by another Presbytery immensely their superior in every desirable qualification. Mr. Gordon bore their persecution with that quiet, yet fixed determination for which he was remarkaable in all his movements. His friends wished him to carry the case up by "appeal or complaint" to the Synod of Wheeling next fall. This he declined. He expected but little sympathy from a body whose highest court had declared "domestic slavery under the circumstances in which it is found in the southern portion of the country, no bar to Christian communion."

It seemed to him better at once to seek an ecclesiastical connection where he could enjoy Christian liberty of thought and utterance. In the doctrines and order of the Presbyterian church he had been educated and to them he was strongly attached. He had often made the mortifying, but truthful confession, that the two branches of the Presbyterian church —the Old and New School in the United States, were the only members of the great Presbyterian family, that were false to the principles of civil and religious liberty. He resolved to seek ordination from the Presbytery of Ripley, a body which on account of their complicity with slaveholding had declined the connection of both Assemblies; accordingly he was ordained by that Presbytery in September, 1847.

In the meantime his church and congregation met and resolved to withdraw from the jurisdiction of a Presbytery for which they had lost respect. They believed the body had violated ecclesiastical law and order, and requested their minister to treat their action as a nullity, that is, continue to preach to them by virtue of his original license by the Presbytery of Washington, which they wished him to regard as still valid. To this he consented, and preached some three months in this way before he was ordained.

After his ordination the Presbytery of Ripley was divided into two, and Mr. Gordon was dismissed with a view of uniting with Messrs. Bradford and McLean, who had seceded from the Presbytery of Beaver; in forming the "Free Presbytery of Mahoning." This was soon afterward done. A short time afterward the three Presbyteries united and formed the Synod of the "Free Presbyterian Church of the United States."

The question has been asked, would the Synod of Wheeling have sustained this action, so manifestly unconstitutional and high-handed on the part of the Presbytery, in case an "appeal" or "complaint" had been regularly carried up? Of course the question can not be answered with certainty. The writer thinks it due to that body to say he believes they would not. The course afterward taken by the Presbytery, clearly indicated their own fears on the subject. The only way the Synod could reach it was by "review and control" when their minutes would come up for examination. Their stated clerk, Rev. B. Mitchell, brought them to the Synod, and after the committee to examine them was appointed he sent them home. The excuse given was that their temporary clerk had been sick, and consequently they were not completed. Why they were brought to Synod at all under these circumstances, and immediately sent away after the committee to examine them was named, they did not state. The only explanation that suggests itself was either that the plan of keeping them back a year, that the matter might to some extent fade away, was an after thought; or else that the committee of examination was one that did not suit them.

Several members of Synod manifested dissatisfaction. A Dr. of Divinity of high respectability and influence, said it was particularly unfortunate for that Presbytery to keep back their minutes, after the strange proceedings that were reported of them. One member of the Presbytery came to the aid of the stated clerk, seemed to wax warm and bold and said "they had done nothing they were ashamed of." That was a lower degree, and greater obtuseness of attainment, than their conduct seemed to indicate!

The circumstances under which men evince fidelity to God, to truth and to principle are immensely varied, but the spirit of such actions is in all cases much the same. The elements of real greatness may often be exhibited in an humble way. The mean and diabolical spirit of persecution with which such men are tried, is much nearer alike also, than is generally suppposed. The implements to be wielded by the enemies of Luther, were the stake with its faggots and fire, or the inquisition with its racks and tortures. We seem to see a sublimity in the courage that could calmly face these terrors, and adhere to principle while they flashed and threatened. Hence we gaze with emotions of grandeur and sublimity on Luther as he stood before the Diet of Worms, and plead the cause of God and truth; and when a retraction was vociferously demanded by the minions of the Papacy he calmly laid his hand on his breast and said "I can retract nothing, God help me." Still the lofty moral courage shown by the great reformer was the same in nature, and differed only in degree and circumstance from that of the man who can stand erect against the vociferous demands of a modern ecclesiastical court, armed with the power of public opinion and popular odium. Neither is there the difference between the spirit of the Ghostly Inquisitors who surrounded the monk of Wittemburg, and the ecclesiastics who apologize for slaveholding in our day, and persecute those who expose its fathomless abominations;— that at first view we would generally think. When human actions pass in review before the "judge of quick and dead," they will be much nearer alike than is generally supposed. John C. Calhoun said the war of the abolitionists against the South was more to be dreaded than one of devastation and blood; as it was a war waged against their characters. The great mistake of the statesman was that the war of which he complained, is not levied against the Southern people, but against this "peculiar institution." He was right in regarding a war against character as the worst. In Luther's case life was threatened. In our day the plan is to fulminate ecclesiastical censures and suspensions—destroy reputation—prevent congregations from giving employment—take away the means of living from a man, and thus afflict him with the wants of a dependent family; and by these and similar annoyances (as a popular divine expressed it), "keep order in Warsaw." Times and circumstances change but human nature remains the same. "If they have persecuted me, they will persecute you." "They that will live godly in Christ Jesus, shall suffer persecution."

After the church of Athens left the Presbytery, and their minister was ordained, and the Free Church was organized, nothing very special occurred with Mr. Gordon, during the next two years. The severe ordeal through which he had passed unscathed, resulted in his good. It enlisted the sympathies of good men generally in his behalf and brought him into notice. His quiet, unobtrusive disposition required something of the kind to rouse him, and draw him out. Small Free churches were organized at different points within his reach. With these he labored in season, and out of season. His friend—Rev. Thomas Merrill—who with a few intelligent and noble-souled elders had stood by him all through his persecutions in the Presbytery, seceded soon after he left, and became co-laborers in the cause of church reform. Their numbers were small, but what they lacked in this respect, was made up in union and zeal.

In the spring of 1849 he had a hemorrhage from the lungs, which eight years afterward resulted in his death. It came on as he was returning on horseback from his last appointment on the evening of the Lord's day. It seemed by no means improbable to himself that he might die on the road. His preaching was suspended, but his college duties were kept up during the year. In the spring of 1850, the Free Church determined to start a weekly paper, and with entire unanimity he was selected as its editor. He consequently removed to Mercer, Pa., and continued to edit the *Free Presbyterian*, till the summer of 1852. In the mean time his health improved, and he gradually resumed his pulpit labors. The Free church of Mercer, now under the pastoral care of Rev. J. W. Torrence, and the nucleus of the flourishing pastoral charge of Rev. A. B. Bradford, in New Castle, each enjoyed a share of his labors.

In the summer of 1852, the *Free Missionary* published at Cincinnati, and the *Free Presbyterian* were merged in the *Christian Press.* Mr. Gordon was appointed one of its editors, and also one of the Secretaries of the "American Missionary Association;" in consequence of which he removed to Cleveland, and entered on the duties of his office. He had but commenced in his new field, when his health suddenly again gave way, and he left Cleveland and retired among his friends, not expecting to live but a few weeks. After a time his constitution again unexpectedly rallied, and by the summer of 1853 he was able to resume his editorial chair. In connection with his colleague, Rev. Wm. G. Kephart, the *Free Presbyterian* was revived, and published at Albany, Athens county, Ohio. At the same time he was elected principal of the "Albany Manual Labor Academy." For some cause, or causes, not fully known to the writer, the situation did not suit him. After a year's hard labor, on the part of himself and colleague, they dissolved with mutual kindness and confidence, and he removed the paper to Yellow Springs, in April, 1854. Here he edited and published it till September, 1857. Though not a practical printer, necessity compelled him to learn the art, which he did in a very short time; and for three years and a half he acted as foreman in his office; did a journeyman's labor in setting type; besides editing the paper, and supplying the church of Clifton, and occasionally some other points with the ministrations of the gospel. But the labor was too great. The last year his health gradually declined, and in the fall of 1857 he relinquished the editorial chair, and removed to the home of his childhood. He hoped to recruit his constitution by light labor on a farm, but it was too late. It had twice rallied before, but now its vitality was too far spent. His voice so left him, that he could usually speak but in whispers; his strength also declined, and the grave was manifestly soon to inherit all that was mortal in his nature. He met the stern approach of the "last enemy," with the same cheerful and calm serenity, which always characterized him in the day of trial. He breathed his last on the morning of the Sabbath, 28th of February.

Death is always a solemn and melancholy scene. To the subject it is momentous — to the watchers impressive. It is the abandonment of the long-loved and cherished realities of

life, for the land of silence and of gloom. The passage from
the visible to the invisible; an abandonment of the warm and
tender affections, so long familiar, to a new and incompre-
hensible mode of existence. The whole passage and change
is such an act of unnatural violence, that we instinctively
shrink back from it, and cling with tenacity to the familiar
realities of time. Probably, no other beings in the universe
have such a passage to make, or such a change to undergo.
Angels are not required, like men, to pass at any time a dark
barrier, impenetrable to their vision, and full of vague and
unnatural uncertainties beyond.

On man's future, nature gives no light. She may stand
by the dying scene, see the form grow cold and ghastly, the
eye glazed and dim; but when the soul seems to float away
with the closing breath, she can not tell whether the living,
feeling, thinking soul passes into another mode of development, or sinks into the dark night of unconsciousness. Such
is death without revelation.

Faith alone reveals the future, and gives it substance and
reality. Its achievements are all wonderful. How often the
dying alone are cheerful, calm, and happy. They shed no
tears, feel no gloom, experience no fears, but look on the
separation from their friends as short, and catch a glimpse as
they pass the shadowy vale, of brighter and better scenes
beyond.

These consolations were sweetly experienced by the subject
of this memoir. We subjoin a short extract from a letter
written by his bereaved and widowed wife, a short time after
his death. The letter was written without any idea of its
publication, and the extract inserted without the knowledge
or consent of the writer.

"On New-Year's day he appeared very sad; he told me he
might never see another return of the day; that he had been
reviewing his life, had tried and wished to do right, but had
been a great sinner; that he thought the Lord had forgiven
him, and if he lived he hoped to live better, and do some
good in a quiet way. * * * At times he seemed very
happy, and would say that he could almost see the smile of
his heavenly Father. The peculiar and constant state of his
mind, seemed that of perfect repose, and confidence in the
goodness and wisdom of his heavenly Father, entire trust in
his Saviour, and complete submission to his will. He always
thought too much stress was laid upon the words of the dying,

and that a much better test of character was the tenor of their life.

"He said, not long before he left us, that he supposed some would think he delighted in saying hard things, and opposing others; but that *no one could ever know* how hard it had been for him to take the course he did: that he liked the good will and approbation of men, as much as any one, but that he thought duty called him to take the stand he had.

"How few live such a life! So self-sacrificing, so burdened with the woes and sins of humanity; so firm and unyielding in vindicating the honor of God. His last words were, 'I will go to sleep.' He then fell into a gentle slumber, and passed to the sleep of death."

To the above we add an obituary, from the pen of the Rev. Robert Burgess, a Free Presbyterian minister, and published in the *Christian Leader*, together with the preliminary remarks of the editor, Rev. William Perkins.

Rev. Joseph Gordon has Died.

Our whole church is bereaved. For years our deceased brother was its weekly teacher and faithful pastor. By his voice and pen, he spread abroad the whole truth, whether men would hear or forbear. He warmly and courageously espoused the cause of the poor, down-trodden stranger. Could these millions in their prison-house of despair now hear of the faithful friend they have lost, their weeping were like the widows of Joppa, over the body of Dorcas! Poor sufferers! we fondly hope that in the great mercy of Christ, not a few may greet their noble friend, where "the wicked cease from troubling" and "the weary" forever "rest."

Our cause has lost one of its most efficient advocates. The "*Leader*," in a double sense must credit Bro. G. with much of its humble influence. It succeeds the weekly he so ably conducted for years, while its unworthy editor was reasoned into his Free Church position, chiefly by his lucid arguments. So has it been with many others. He wore out his voice and his body in this blessed service. Did our success alone depend upon efficient laborers, our loss were irreparable. But we must remember that the race is not to the swift, nor the battle to the strong. Could we plant as did Paul, and water as did Apollos, all were vain till God chooses to give the increase. Never is he more ready to give it than when we feel our humble dependence upon Him. "When I am *weak*, then I am strong."

We sorrow then, not as others without hope. God having raised our Saviour, in whom our brother has fallen asleep, will, in due time, reanimate his slumbering body. So will he raise up other faithful servants to carry forward his precious cause. The war is not ended, though a good and great soldier be discharged. As the conflict waxes, needful means will be furnished, and the powers of darkness tremble. Left as we are on the field with the bright example of our fallen brother to animate us, let us put on the whole armor of God, and lead on his host to that victory which is made sure by the promise of Him who has loved us, and given himself for us.

Obituary.

Died, at his residence near Washington, Pa., on Sabbath morning, February 28, at 3 o'clock, the Rev. JOSEPH GORDON, aged 38 years, 5 months and 9 days.

O death! how rich are thy spoils! Another great man has fallen—another heart and home are made desolate—another household-light has been extinguished! Nay, more, a beacon-light to guide a ship-wrecked world; a watch-fire on the mountain-hight of eternal truth, to cheer the hosts engaged in the struggle which is to decide the world's destiny, in the war for the "rights of God and man"—the last great "war of principles." How rapidly pass away the flower of earth's nobility! He was the first and foremost in the conflict for the right, the first to fall upon his laurels won!

Truly a "Prince and a great man *has* fallen in Israel." "Our fathers, where are they? and the prophets, do they live forever." But if they have ascended in triumph, borne from our sight by the "Horses and chariots of fire," leaving behind their "mantle," by which we may smite the waters of opposition and death, is it not a great gain? Is not *their* triumph our own?

How fitting too, was the death of our brother! How suitable to his life of toil and sacrifice, and weariness, that he *should* sink to rest in the calm and quiet of a sweet Sabbath morn! Literally *worn out* in the sacred cause of God and humanity, it was REST that he needed. and it came in love, the symbol and the reality together. One of his last expressed wishes was, "That he might fall asleep, and awake in Heaven." It was granted. Near his last moments he called for drink;

he drank largely and remarked, "I will now go to sleep." His sad wife replied, "Yes, dear! you will soon be drinking the pure 'water of life.'" Accordingly he sank to rest, and while he seemed to be sleeping sweetly, he gently breathed away his life.

His wife alone was with him in the closing scene, having dismissed all the family to much needed repose. He had bid "good night" to his young son, with a conscious last kiss, following him with a yearning eye as he retired, aware that he should see him on earth no more. His dear wife had been for some time at his side, wiping away the death-sweat as it arose on his pale brow. Not thinking this was to be his long, last sleep, she turned a moment to stir the fire. Returning, he breathed twice, and was no more.

A few days before, he said, "That he preferred rather to die than to live; but that, for his wife and child, he was willing to live." At a former visit by the writer and Bro. Dyer Burgess, the latter had remarked, on parting, "That he thought he might live to do a great deal of sinning yet," a remark to which he often afterward referred, as a strange and sad saying, and as a reason why he did not "Wish to live, and return again to the world, and to sin." He had little pain to endure, and said, "That he had nothing to complain of; much to call for gratitude."

During all his sickness he uttered not a solitary complaint; and throughout gave *three* distinct proofs of preparation for death: a calmness and patience seldom equaled; a sensible increase, nay, an overflowing of "brotherly kindness," and a great delight in prayer. On his bed he said with emphasis, in reference to the opening of the 41st Psalm, "There is a promise I can plead! I have spent all my talents and strength in the service of the poorest of God's poor: I claim that promise." It was fulfilled. "Blessed is he that considereth the poor; the Lord will deliver him in time of trouble. The Lord will preserve him and keep him alive; he shall be blessed on the earth; and thou wilt not deliver him to the will of his enemies. The Lord will strengthen him upon the bed of languishing; thou wilt make all his bed in his sickness." His labors of love for poor down-trodden humanity, flowed from his fountain of unfeigned love to Christ. Christ forever made sacred our humanity, and all the "rights of man," by his union to our nature, "eternal in the heavens." So Bro. G. thought. Hence, when his wife inquired of him, "What do you now, in the full light of eternity, think of your course in the Church?" he replied, "That he had never written a sentence, which he did not then and now believe; that the position of his church was God's truth; only admitting, that he might have erred in the proper spirit."

A few days previous to his death, he was visited by Rev. Dr. Thomas Hanna, of the Associate Church, at which time the grounds of his hope were fully discussed. The Doctor remarked, that there was a true and a false hope; and defined the former. The sufferer added, "Such is *my* hope,—a hope founded on the blood of the Lamb, on the intercession of Jesus 'within the vail.'" He then quoted the promises, such as "In six troubles, I will be with thee; and in seven, I will not forsake thee. The mountains may depart, and the hills be removed; yet shall not my kindness depart from thee, nor the *covenant* of my *peace* be removed, saith the Lord that hath mercy on thee."

As to his character as a man, a minister, or an editor, I leave the task of drawing the sketch to his more intimate friends, and to abler pens. I write this hasty notice with a deep sense of my imperfection, and only because no other is on the ground possessing proper information. If we write to "comfort those that mourn," we must not delay till they too are in the grave.

At his funeral services, six ministers were present, including two of his own church, Bro. Dyer Burgess and the writer. The order of the exercises was as follows: Mr. Hanna opened by singing a Psalm and reading a chapter. This was followed by some very appropriate remarks by Dyer Burgess. Concluded by some additional remarks and prayer by the writer. The benediction was pronounced by the Rev. James I. Brownson, of the O. S. Church. A large and solemn procession, inclement as was the day, followed his remains to the grave.

He was much emaciated; and yet as he lay in his coffin, in his full suit of black, he looked so natural that we all felt as though he were just ready to rise, and "preach to us as of old." We laid him beyond the bustle of the busy town, in the still and beautiful new cemetery, beneath the shade of a native oak grove. The sunshine, as was most fit, broke through the wintry clouds, and fell upon his fresh grave, while we sadly turned away to come again with the spring, to plant evergreens and eglantine on his green grave.

Peace to his weary head! There let him sweetly "sleep in Jesus" till the glorious resurrection morn. He himself said, not long before, that "though a man of war, he was a man of peace." He had fought for a solid, reliable peace, under the banner inscribed, "First pure, *then* peaceable." He well knew that no other peace *could last*. He wanted a peace approved of God,—he hath it now. *Requiescat in pace.* Often will we and others return to visit that grave, to reassure our feeble virtue, to see the windows of heaven open above it, to kneel as in a temple, to plant not the cypress and yew, but roses and amaranths.

A short portrait of the character of the deceased will close our part of the volume. Like all the descendants of Adam, he had his faults, and imperfections. But like those of Goldsmith's village-pastor, even these "leaned to virtue's side."

Unobtrusive, quiet, and retiring modesty was natural to him, and was carried to an undesirable degree. Many men, with the same amount of intellect, scholarship, and gifts, would have more decidedly drawn the gaze of admirers, and been more prominent—sometimes more useful. Until their exercise was demanded, he seemed unconscious of his own powers; and no man of our acquaintance had less to say about himself. The reader may think this is labeled as a fault, though really an amiable virtue. Yet it is meant as expressed. A larger share of self-esteem would have pushed him forward more prominently, drawn out to better advantage his social nature, given him a wider range of private power, and secured the warm attachment of the many, instead of the intimate few, and enlarged his field of influence. Those social gifts, by which many good men talk others into their views, sympathies, and wishes, he possessed in but a limited degree. The tripod of the editor, and the stand of the orator were his places of power. The social gifts of the pastor, and imposing loquacity of the agent, he possessed only in a very moderate degree.

A more prominent, and perhaps the worst fault that belonged to him, was rather extreme severity in dealing with wrongs and wrong-doers. It is common to great minds to possess strong passions; and disease in his case probably sharpened them. His own "eye was single," and his purposes transparent, and he gave no quarter to opposite qualities in others. When, however, instead of consistent honesty he met selfishness, cunning, duplicity, jesuitism, and injustice, he was apt to become indignant, and express himself with a severity, of which few men are capable. Especially was this

the case in dealing with sinners in high places, and of large
pretensions. With corrupt politicians, making boastful pretensions to patriotism and democracy, when selfishness and
despotism marked their conduct; and with ministers of the
gospel, who ignored their profession by lower-law principles,
or pro-slavery proclivities, or any hypocritical drivelings, he
was severe and unsparing in exposure, and used scathing
denunciations. These were the only recollections of his
moral warfare, that gave him pain on a bed of death. He
said he had always vindicated what he believed to be right;
and opposed, without respect of persons, what he knew to be
wrong; but not always with a meek and quiet spirit. This is
a fault which probably no prominent reformer (except the
Lord Jesus Christ), ever entirely escaped. It belonged to
Luther, Calvin, and Knox; to Whitefield, Baxter and the
Wesleys.

In presenting a few salient points of his intellectual character, *his remarkable clearness of thought, and accuracy of
scholarship may be mentioned.* To investigate thoroughly, and
become master of the subject, was his motto when a student;
and on the well-formed habit, much of his success, no doubt,
depended. He grasped a subject in all its prominent bearings, was free from confusion or mixture, and presented it
with such clearness and simplicity, as often to make the
hearer think he understood it as well as the speaker, and
wonder that he never saw it so before. When he discussed a
subject, the intelligent hearer felt that it was finished, and
that nothing more was needed to fill it out. Some speakers
are brilliant and clear on detached parts, but leave the discussion incomplete; and when they close the hearer thinks of
" Ephraim " as " a cake unturned." This was not the case
with him.

2. *He was in the most desirable sense an original man.* His
was not the originality of mere novelty, but that of a clear,
accurate and independent thinker. Some persons surprise
and startle us by the newness and strangeness of their conceptions and expressions, and the novelty of their departures
from the old and familiar track; but too often they are
empty and fallacious. It is originality at the expense of
truth. It was not so in his case. His positions and thoughts
met us with something of the familiarity of an old acquaintance; but in a dress so new and improved, as to make us
wonder at the felicitous advancement. Every thing he said
bore the impress of having been elaborated in his own men-

tal alembic. The thinking power of the hearer was not exercised to know whether the idea presented was true; but was delighted to gaze on it for a stand-point from which he now viewed it for the first time. Some writers and speakers don't plagiarize, and yet their conceptions and views are so formed by those of others, as to impress the reader or hearer with a mere mechanical rehearsal of which he heard twenty times before. Their productions have no impress of their own minds. Such persons have no originality. Others will rehearse a common-place thought, or a familiar principle, with a freshness which makes us half fancy we have now heard them for the first time. This is the most desirable sense, in which, in this age of intelligence it is possible to be original.

3. As a debater he had the rare ability to look over the entire subject, and perceive at a glance the strong and the weak points in the arguments of an opponent. This gave him entire self-possession. He was never startled, or embarrassed in reply. He could unravel a sophism, uncover a weak point, and develop a false position of an opponent, with ease and power; and then overwhelm him with the momentum of the opposing truth. His unmixed sincerity kept him from ever using the arts of the sophist himself. Hence he never descended to "sap and mine" and quibble in a discussion. He attacked the arguments of an opponent openly; and always attempted to carry his fortifications by storm. From this course he seldom or never departed.

4. As a speaker he was clear in thought and utterance, rather deliberate than rapid, and always self-possessed. His command of language was copious, and accurate, and extremely free from any semblance of confusion. His style was racy and sufficiently adorned; yet, rather strong than beautiful. He usually addressed the intellect, yet had power, both to rouse the passions and touch the heart. When aroused, especially in debate, he was eloquent in thought, argument and manner. When the soul seemed to radiate from the countenance—flash in the eye—burn on the lip—and tremble on the tongue, the spell-bound hearer was enchained, and for the time being held under the mesmeric influence of the speaker, and confessed the glowing control of the mind that entranced him.

Of his moral and religious character, but little remains to be written. Its lineaments are interwoven in the narrative already given. His confidence in and obedience to God have been noticed. Practically and theoretically he was a "higher law " man. The will of the Lord was ever with him the paramount consideration. His piety was the religion of principle ; and to the claims of duty his life was one of steady and daily obedience. Possessing talents and acquirements with which he could, and most men would, have cleared a handsome fortune, he died poor. The only legacy that he left his wife and son was his stainless character and good name. He considered the interests of the poor, and looked for the blessing promised to such as do.

In all his intercourse with men, and especially as his editorial life was one of sharp controversy; he cultivated and manifested a constant love of truth. His aims, motives and actions were alike transparent. He was always frank. Few men were ever more free from cunning, and mere management. Had he not possessed a pretty fair insight into human character, that trait would have made him often the dupe of the wiles of others. He was, however, reasonably quick in perceiving in others, what he never harbored in himself.

The last trait we shall mention was his deep and strong sympathies and affections. These were more powerful and tender than a partial acquaintance would lead any one to suppose. In the hour of trial and separation they came out in full manifestation. As a watcher at the bed of a dying mother, and a mourner for the loss of two infant children, who died each at the age of about one year—one in 1850, the other in 1852 ; his depth of tenderness was intensely called forth. With some hesitancy about the propriety of publishing a letter so entirely written for a single person, the writer has concluded to give a short extract from one dated April 2, 1850, after the death of his little daughter. It is one of those productions in which .the writer unbosoms himself, and we see into the fountains of the soul. The object of its publication is, to show how a man of strength, of intellect and lofty moral courage—who fearlessly met opposition and relentless persecution for the truth of God, and the cause of humanity, could at the same time, show a depth of parental tenderness, that few experience. After describing the sickness and death of his child he adds :

" Thus died our little Mary. To us she was very lovely. She was too gentle and timid to attract the notice of strangers, but alone with us she was sweet, and playful and good ; and we loved her all the more tenderly for the timidity that made her cling to us alone. How tenderly we loved her, they alone can know who have lost a little one so gentle and sweet as she was.   *   *   *   I do not murmur at the sad loss, but *feel* as well as know that all is right. 'He doeth all things well.' Our little babe that nestled a little more than one short year in our arms, is now gathered gently as a lamb in the bosom of Jesus. Her sufferings are all over. She can never more feel pain or sorrow, and oh! to know that she is now infinitely happy is enough. She was beautiful in death. As she lay in her little cradle, with a plain white dress, and her little hands and bosom filled with flowers—a sweet smile on her face—her body seemed a meet emblem of her pure and gentle spirit. Death was divested of all terror—all gloom. It was like a quiet sleep. It is ours to suffer and struggle on a little longer. She has reached home before us, and awaits in her robes of white to welcome us there. God grant that we may be ready to follow when our time comes; to die as peacefully and sweetly as did our little babe. Life never before seemed to me so uncertain. Death, heaven, and the resurrection, never before seemed so near and real as now. The grave seems divested of all gloom, and I now feel that when life's 'fitful dream is over,' I can lie down there as to a place of quiet rest."

In his oratory he generally addressed the intellect and conscience, yet he easily could and frequently did point for the heart, and stirred the deep fountains of feeling. This power is necessarily based on personal susceptibility. One incapable of the exercise of tender susceptibilities can not reach and stir the fountains in other breasts, and start the tear in other eyes.

We here close. We have given a very imperfect portrait, but truthful as far as it goes, of as good and true a man as Heaven usually lends to earth. Could the wishes of hundreds have prevailed, he would not have left us so early in the conflict. His eloquent voice would yet be heard cheering on the Free Church hosts of freedom. His powerful pen would yet be puissant in defending right and exposing wrong; and urging forward the reign of peace, purity and righteousness. But he is gone. In him the slave, the church, the world has lost a friend, and no man has lost an enemy.

The balance of this humble volume will be his own. "Though dead he yet speaketh;" but speaks as one from the spirit land.

WRITINGS OF
REV. JOSEPH GORDON.

RELIGION AND REFORM.

True religion includes all genuine reform. The *Christian* is, from the nature of the case, a radical reformer. There may be a measure of reform without religion, but there can be no true religion without thorough reformation. Thus the drunkard may become habitually sober, without becoming converted, but no one can become truly religious without abandoning all open vices. True religion is supreme love to God, and equal love to man. But it is impossible for any one to love God with his whole heart, and cherish sins which God hates ; or to love his neighbor as himself, and practice vices which are at war with his neighbor's well-being. Thus, supreme love to God will purify the heart of secret sins, and leads to the cultivation of inward holiness, while love to man will restrain from outward crime, and promote the practice of pure benevolence. Hence the true Christian is a genuine reformer. To reform is to re-construct, to re-model, to *reform* or make over that which has been marred or broken. Man's whole nature, physical, mental, social, and spiritual, is marred and broken. Man is a ruin, and the work of true reform is to re-construct his shattered powers, and form them into primitive order and beauty. Sin is the great disorganizer. It is sin that has broken down this temple of God, the human body and soul, and spread ruin and disorder over all its fair proportions. Hence true reform is to forsake sin, to break its power, to undo its work of destruction ; and in opposition to it, to cultivate and attain a power of goodness and virtue. True reformation in its full extent is to gain a complete victory over sin, and to attain to the love and practice of genuine love and holiness.

Hence the reason why every true *Christian* is a radical reformer. The Christian is one who is like Christ. His heart has been reclaimed from the love and power of sin, and been filled with the Holy Ghost. His life is therefore, henceforward a battle with sin. He sees in it a cause of infinite dishonor to God, and the source of infinite ruin to the universe. Hence he sympathizes with Christ in the great object of his mission to earth, which was to destroy sin. In this sympathy with Christ is found the root and strength of every genuine reformation.

But it is altogether possible for men to be too religious to be genuine reformers. As true religion embraces true reform as a part of itself, so false religion is the most deadly and fatal enemy of genuine reformation. Fill a man's soul with the religion of superstition, of forms and creeds, or of mere excitement, and there is no room left for any real love either to God or man. The superstitious man is one whose soul is under the power of a slavish and crushing dread of a Supreme Being, whom it regards clothed with judgment and wrath. But servile fear is incompatible with love.

The being that is feared, whether he be God, man, or devil, is sure to be hated. Hence the spring of all purity of life, and of all benevolent effort is wanting. The soul becomes narrowed and shriveled under the influence of this degrading fear.

The man whose religion consists in periodic fits of excitement lacks the firm and steady principle which is necessary to nerve and sustain the reformer in an earnest grappling with gigantic social, political, or moral evils. Hence he can only be relied on when the reformation goes by excitement. So long as it can be urged on with the agency of large crowds, exciting speeches, parades, etc., he will shout with the loudest, and labor with great zeal and energy. But the *hard* work of all reforms is to be done before it reaches that point. It is when over-spreading and popular crimes are first attacked; when their opposers are few, weak, and despised, and their friends are many and popular, that the real strength of Christian principle is tested. The man of excitement is never found then battling with the heroic few, amid persecution and opposition against popular and rampant systems of crime. He will very likely be found in the ranks of the enemy.

Again, the mere formalist in religion is generally too selfish to make any efforts or sacrifices for the good of his race. This class generally contains the stuff of which "old fogies" are made. They are the well-to-do men of society; the conservatives, who dread change and innovations as the Pandora's box, filled with every imaginable evil and calamity. Their special horror is any thing which interrupts the steady flow of golden streams into their coffers, and which interferes with their growing "fat and sleek." The chief end of their life is physical comfort, and social respectability. Hence they are always found arrayed in solid phalanx against every reforma- tion. It matters nothing to them that slavery, or drunken- ness, or licentiousness, or any stupendous social and moral evil may devour hecatombs of the young and fair and lovely at a meal, and like the apocalyptic dragon, "draw down the third part of the stars of heaven." If they can draw fat divi- dends, if their stock can be kept above par, and their purses grow longer and heavier each day, it is all they desire. Their religion is in harmony with their ruling selfishness; and the cause of reform finds in them its most steadfast and uniform opposers.

From these principles we may derive a test by which to try any system of religious agencies. Do they harmonize with, promote, all true reformation? If so, it may be safely con- cluded that they are in unity with the gospel and spirit of Christ. Do they, on the contrary, tend to array those under their influence against vital reforms, or to render them indif- ferent? Then are they essentially anti-Christian. It is by the application of this test, that we have lost faith in the genuineness of many modern revivals. We have often no- ticed that men pass through scenes of religious excitement, and come out almost totally indifferent, if not utterly opposed to the *real* work of the Christian—the renovation of his own heart and life and of the world. We do not, indeed, as a general thing, find them any more ready than before to labor earnestly for the salvation of the drundard, the deliverance of the slave, or the conversion of the heathen. The probability is that they will be so filled with sectarian zeal as to have no heart for works of *genuine* Christian love.

It is a standing remark of the world, and one of the truth of which there is no question, that the existence, and the neces- sity for temperance, anti-slavery, moral reform, and other benevolent societies are a standing reproach on the Church. They are organized to do the very work for which Christ insti- tuted his Church; and it is because the Church is faithless to her mission that these voluntary associations are necessary. It is no true answer to this assertion to say that members of the church are among the most active members of these socie- ties. The Church should do this in her *organized capacity*.

Every local church should be a temperance, an anti-slavery, a moral reform society, by virtue of her divine constitution. But so far are the great majority of modern churches from being so, that the most bitter opponents of *all* true reforms are found in their pale; and the aggregate influence of the churches is against reform. Hence the reformers within the Church must be made so, not by the Church, but in spite of its influence. Thus the divinely appointed instrumentality for reforming the world, is robbed of the honor which it should reap in the fulfillment of its great and glorious mission.

We should be Men and Women of Devoted Piety.

There are many reasons for this:

1. In the first place, true reform can only be effected by the power of God. The best system of human agencies ever devised, is utterly powerless without his blessing. His spirit and truth alone can regenerate the human soul, they alone can truly reform the character; and the reformation of the world can only be effected by the reformation of each individual man and woman in the world. This being true, human effort in this work can succeed only so far as it takes hold of divine strength. While the means are put into the hands of men, the efficient power is of God. But only the man of piety can lay hold of the arm of Omnipotence for this end. A truly pious man is one who has sought and obtained the pardon of sins through the atonement of Jesus Christ; who loves and obeys God; who tries to do all the good he can; and who is a man of faith and prayer. It is to this man that God promises to look; it is upon the labors of such that he pours out a blessing. Only he who trusts God can look to him for aid in doing good. For " to the wicked God says, what hast thou to do to declare my statutes, or that thou shouldst take my covenant into thy mouth? "

No true reformation can be greatly promoted without the agency of prayer. For the aid of his spirit in converting and reforming the world, God says he will be inquired of by the House of Israel. Only as God's servants feel their dependence on him, and look to him in believing prayer, can they hope to be successful in doing his work. That reformation which ignores this instrumentality, must fail. But it is only the truly pious man who can pray in faith. He alone who loves, trusts and obeys God, can offer acceptable and prevailing prayer.

2. Again reformers should be men of ardent piety because none others can work in harmony with God in saving the world. The secret of all success in doing good depends on this harmony. All the plans, truths, principles and institutions necessary for the reformation of the world, have been provided and revealed by Jehovah. He furnishes each one of his moral soldiers a complete suit of spiritual armor. He has drafted a perfect chart of the work to be done ; has given a full description of that temple of holiness and love which his children are to labor in building up. The only work man has to do in reforming the earth is to use the instrumentalities which God has provided for the redemption of the world of mankind, in humble reliance on divine aid. But it is evident that none but the pious man can thus work in harmony with God. This is so because he alone is himself in harmony with his Maker. He alone has had his will, and principles, and purposes brought into unison with the will of God. The unconverted are at enmity with him. Their characters are discordant with his. Their aims and purposes are in conflict with his designs, and hence they are of course unprepared to labor for him in harmony with his plans.

3. A third reason why reformers should be men of devoted piety, is that none others will endure the persecutions and trials which are the lot of true reformers. To reform is to remodel the human character, and all the laws, customs, and institutions of man which are sinful. This work of re-construction frequently requires the destruction of existing habits and institutions. Thus before the human soul can be imbued with the principle of holiness, its native depravity must be destroyed. Before righteous laws and governments, and pure churches can be established, those which are oppressive and corrupt must be overthrown. Before holy and benevolent customs and habits can be introduced among men, those which are vile and selfish must be rooted out. But this work of overturning existing principles, laws, customs, and institutions is one which excites the fiercest opposition of the wicked. Hence he who engages in it must often expect the severest persecution. His motives will be misrepresented ; his character will be slandered ; his plans will be ridiculed ; and sometimes his person and life exposed to danger and abuse. This

has been the lot of reformers in all past ages, and it is their lot still.

Now, to endure this opposition patiently, the reformer needs a large measure of God's grace in his heart. He needs a strong, unwavering, child-like faith in God, and a deep baptism into the firm, meek, loving, gentle spirit of Christ. But these are the characteristics of the truly pious man.

4. Once more, reformers should be persons of devoted piety, because their teachings will be powerful for good only so far as their example corresponds with them. It is a well understood principle of human nature that example impresses more deeply than precept. No matter how great and important may be the truths taught us by a fellow-man, if his life is a violation of the claims of those truths, we reject him and his teachings. He who *lives* a truth is its mightiest preacher. He whose example is a standing testimony against sin, is its most effective opposer. He whose life is the exemplification of pure benevolence, is the most radical reformer. But to live the truth, to forsake sin, and to practice pure benevolence, are the works of the sincerely pious.

We may draw many practical inferences from these principles: It follows from them, for example, that he who rebukes slavery should not be hard and oppressive to his hired laborers; should not be grasping and dishonest in his dealings; should not cheat his neighbor in a bargain. He who reproves the drunkard should not sell his corn to the distiller; should not rent his buildings to the grog-seller; should not himself be a wine-bibber. He who preaches against the unfruitful works of darkness done in heathen lands, should not be a member of secret conclaves, whose midnight revelings bear close resemblance to the *mysteries* of a heathen temple. He in brief, who labors for the reformation of the world, should reform his own heart and life. "Let your light so shine before men, that they may see your good works, and glorify your Father which is in Heaven."

MISSION OF THE FREE PRESBYTERIAN CHURCH.

The mission of every true church is two-fold. First, general; second, special or particular. The general mission of every true church is to "go into all the world, and preach the gospel to every creature." To be "the salt of the earth" and "the light of the world:" To lift up Christ in her teachings and in the holy lives of her members, that all men will be drawn unto him; attracted irresistibly by the moral power and surpassing beauty of his character, as they are exhibited and exemplified in his Church.

The *special* mission of any particular church grows out of the peculiar circumstances in which she is placed; and consists in the specific application of the gospel to the most prevalent sins and the most pressing wants of the age and nation in which she exists. The Church is God's witness for truth, and against wrong; and her particular duty in any age is to witness against the most common and popular iniquities, and in behalf of the truths that are the most despised and rejected in the age in which she lives. It is of the duty of our church in this last respect that we wish now to speak.

The *great want* of the present age must be obvious to the most casual observer. It is a living *practical* faith in the religion of Christ, as the power that is to reform the world and govern the entire life and actions of men. Christianity as professed and practiced by the mass of nominal Christendom, is an abstraction. It is something to be worn as a Sabbath garment, and thrown aside during the rest of the week.

The idea that it contains a system of laws for the government of the whole life, has become almost obsolete. The consequence is that the Church, failing to embody and exemplify the religion of Christ, in this direction, has lost, to a great extent, her power to restrain men from sin, and to impress upon their hearts the constraining and converting power of the gospel.

As the most prevalent sin of our age and nation we do not name slavery, or drunkenness, or licentiousness, or any one particular practice, but that which lies at the foundation of them all—practical *Atheism.* These various developments of depravity are only the working out of this radical sin of the human heart.

The man who makes merchandize of God's image, or debases his own soul and body by the indulgence of low and sinful propensities, has lost a sense of God's presence, and of his government of the world.

The Apostle names, as the cause of all the hideous crimes and abominations of the heathen of his day, the fact that "they did not like to retain God in their knowledge;" and the Prophet says of the most abandoned sinners of his age, that they said in their hearts: "The Lord will not do good, neither will he do evil."

The mission of ours, as of every true church, is, therefore, to bear a practical testimony against this prevalent Atheism, and against the wide-spread and abounding iniquities to which it gives rise. This can best be done by exhibiting in her teachings and in the lives of her members the doctrine of God's special government of the world; and by manifesting in all their actions a sense of the divine presence, and of the constraining power of a belief in the supremacy of his law and kingdom. Let the world see by the conduct of a church that she is governed by a principle which chains every action to the throne of God, her power for good will be mighty indeed.

God has wisely adapted the organization of the Church to the successful accomplishment of the great object for which he has formed her.

A bond of closest union, and, consequently, an element of strength, is found in that brotherly love which is one essential trait of Christian character. In the diversity of gifts bestowed by his Spirit, he has provided for the discharge of various and diverse duties. The teachings, sacraments, forms of worship and orders of officers, are all adapted to enforce and impress the truth, and to give it a living power in the hearts of God's people. As different forms of church order and government have been adopted, each denomination is bound to show some peculiar excellence in that which it has embraced. The propriety or impropriety of denominational divisions among the people of God is not the question. Perhaps in the present state of the world such divisions are inevitable.

But while such is the case every Christian is bound to profess Christ in that branch of the Church which he regards as the purest in its doctrines and practice, and which he believes to conform most fully to the Scripture model of government and order. By his connection with a particular church every man *does* really profess to regard it as nearest the right standard.

Now the world asks and expects a *practical* exhibition of these *peculiar* excellencies which every member professes to regard as embodied in his church.

These thoughts suggest an important part of the special mission of the Free Presbyterian Church. Its members have a warm and decided attachment to their own order and form of government. They believe it to come nearest to the Scripture standard. They think it best combines that compact union which is essential to strength, with that individual freedom which is necessary to the full and harmonious development of Christian character. They hold these views in entire charity for other denominations. The very fact that they prize and love their own order, makes them tolerant to the conscientious preferences of others. But the fact of this preference to the form and order of their own church, imposes upon them the duty of giving the world a practical exhibition of what they regard as their peculiar excellency. They ought to show to the world that Presbyterianism makes the highest style of man. They ought to show that instead of the mere badge of a party or sect, it is the fullest embodiment of the spirit and principles of the Christian religion; and that those who are imbued with its doctrines are thereby baptized into the spirit of universal love and benevolence, and peculiarly fitted for every good word and work.

Presbyterianism *has* won for itself, in past years, a place among the reforming powers of the earth. It has uniformly until now been found on the side of freedom and right—the fast friend of civil liberty and of the poor and oppressed. It has brought forth and matured many a heroic apostle of liberty, whose names the world will not willingly let die. In view of its glorious achievements in the past it is melancholy to find the Presbyterianism of this age, as embodied in the Old and New School General Assemblies, in close league with the worst tyrants with whom the world has ever been cursed. These bodies are among the firmest pillars of that stupendous system of despotism in this country, which is now running riot over the crushed liberties of the American people. They have disregarded the hallowed names and memories of the past, and done what they could to make that system, which has hitherto been identified with many a heroic struggle for civil and religious freedom, the synonym of oppression and infamy.

In view of these facts it is a part of the mission of the Free Presbyterian Church to rescue the name it bears from the foul disgrace of being reckoned the handmaid of oppression. Let her voice be heard in all her pulpits in stern reprobation of the recent outrage perpetrated by Congress, and of the other schemes of the propagandists of slavery. Let her testimony against this giant iniquity be rendered still more pointed and emphatic. Let her speak through pulpit, press and ballot box to our godless rulers in such tones of rebuke and warning as John Knox was wont to utter in the ears of kings. Above all, let the lives of all her ministers and members be living epistles in which the world shall read lessons of the living power of Christianity in controlling *all* the actions and relations of life.

In fulfilling this mission it is pleasant to expect the coöperation of the other branches of the Presbyterian family that occupy the same ground on the great moral questions of the age. Let our church consecrate herself to this great work. Let her, by faithful believing prayer, secure the influences of the Holy Spirit; and she will accomplish a work that will glorify God and bless the world.

What Can I do to Bring the World to God.

You can do much. First and chiefly, you can give yourself to God if you have not done so already. The world of mankind is made up of individuals. You are one of the separate human beings who, taken in the aggregate, constitute the world of men and women. If each one will give himself to Christ the work will be done. The reign of peace and love will begin. The Saviour will see of the travail of his soul and be satisfied. The hosanna of the world redeemed will roll round the earth. And this is the work which every one must do for himself. You alone, his grace enabling you, can consecrate your own soul to Christ. You must repent, believe, love and obey for yourself. No one else can do this for you; no man can by any means redeem his brother, or give to God a ransom for him.

But if you have already given yourself to God, you can, as the first step toward bringing others to him, renew the consecration. You can make it more complete and unreserved. In looking over your course since you first tasted that the Lord is gracious, you can see, doubtless, that in many things you have come short. The world has sometimes divided your heart with God. Satan and the flesh have sometimes got the better of you. Often, perhaps, you feel that you have been very far from doing what you ought and might have done to bring sinners to the Saviour. Repent, therefore, and do your first works. Come again to the fountain, wash and be clean. Seek a fresh baptism into the very spirit and temper of Jesus.

Do this, and you will be ready in the second place to set such an example before sinners as will bring them to Christ. A pure example is the mightiest agency in drawing men to Jesus. This, by God's grace, you can set before the world. You can show by a life of unsullied integrity, of earnest practical benevolence, and of holy christian love, how pure and blessed is that gospel that brings forth such fruits. You can be a living epistle wherein all who see you may read how rightous, holy, loving and pure is the faith of Christ. Doubt not that if your own life is true to the Saviour, you will be the means of drawing others to him.

In the third place you can speak a word of warning and invitation to this and to that impenitent sinner whom you meet in your daily walks. You will meet some who expect this of you. Their consciences have been pierced with the arrows of truth. They are weary and heavy laden with sin. They long to come to Jesus for rest. But they tremble and shrink, and fear to come. A word of kindly encouragement is just what they need to bring them to the foot of the cross. That word you can speak. If you have no words of your own you can repeat the ineffably tender and beautiful words of Jesus: "Come unto me all ye that labor and are heavy laden, and I will give you rest."

But some sinners you fear will scorn your words of warning and entreaty. Then for them, and for all, you can wrestle with God in prayer. His grace which was sufficient to humble a Saul of Tarsus and save a dying thief, can subdue the hardest heart. That grace is bestowed in answer to prayer, and the fervent, effectual prayer of the righteous man availeth much.

Dear reader, will you begin to work for God? The sands of life are running out. The shadows lengthen upon the plain, and ere long your sun of existence will set. If you would have its setting cloudless and serene, then be diligent for God. Work while the day lasts, for the night cometh in which no man can work.

WHAT IS NECESSARY TO THE EFFICIENCY OF THE CHURCH, IN DOING GOOD?

This is an important question. The Church is God's instrumentality for the salvation of the world. It is the salt of the earth, and the light of the world. It is therefore of the highest importance to know what is essential to the efficiency of the Church in the great work to which she is appointed, and how her moral power may be increased to the utmost.

It is a common answer to this question to say that the efficiency of the Church depends on the presence and power of the Holy Spirit. This reply is true, but it is not sufficient. God pours out his Spirit in accordance with fixed and certain laws; and the Church must be in the right position to receive the divine influence. God is always ready to pour down his Holy Spirit. Men are not straitened in him, but in themselves. But only when his Church comes up to her duty, and is prepared to receive the divine influence, can he consistently bestow it.

The practical view of the question then, is in the light of human agency. If the Church does her part, she need never doubt that God will do his. So far, then, as human instrumentality is concerned, the two essentials of an efficient church are a faithful ministry and a devoted membership.

By a faithful ministry, we mean a ministry that will preach the whole truth of God, and that will exemplify it in their lives. Every word of God is pure. All Scripture is given by inspiration of God, and is profitable for doctrine, for reproof, for instruction in righteousness. To preach God's word is the business of the ministry. To this they are set apart as their peculiar calling. And they are bound to declare the whole counsel of God; to preach *all* the truth. God knows what truth the world needs, and the fact that he has revealed a truth, is an all-sufficient reason why his messengers should proclaim it to the world. To suppress any part of divine revelation, is to set up our judgment in opposition to Jehovah's. To hold back any portion of revealed truth, for fear of offending the prejudices of men, is to prove faithless to our trust. The fact that truth is unpalatable, is the strongest reason why it should be faithfully proclaimed, because it is proof positive that men are living in violation of its claims. But for God's ambassadors to withhold the truth for that reason, is necessarily offensive to God, and is an abundant reason why they should not expect his blessing on their labors.

The whole truth of God is needed to make a symmetrical and healthy Christian, just as a whole diet is needed to make a vigorous body. Unless all the elements of nutrition which enter into the composition of the human body, are supplied in the diet of the child, its growth will be distorted, and its body will be imperfect. So unless the whole truth of God, which is necessary to form a whole Christian, is supplied as the spiritual diet of the convert, he can not grow up to the stature of a perfect man in Christ.

But it is not enough for the ministry merely to *preach* the whole truth. They must feel its quickening power in their own souls, and exemplify it in their lives. They must themselves practice the duties they enjoin on others. They must shun the sins they condemn ; and walk in the path they point out to others. When they inculcate the duty of benevolence, they must themselves set the example of giving as God has prospered them ; and when they teach self-denial, they must take up the cross. It will avail but little to preach the whole truth of God, if the life of the preacher does not exhibit its constraining and sanctifying power.

A devoted membership is not less essential to the efficiency of the Church, than a faithful ministry. It will be in vain that ministers will preach and pray, if the members are cold and lifeless. The Church stands between the ministry and the unconverted. They will either receive, intensity and re-flect upon the world the rays of light and heat which emanate from the pulpit, or they will absorb and quench them. The Church will be either a wall of fire to throw the intense brightness of God's truth over the world, or it will be a mountain of ice to absorb its heat, and yet will itself derive no warmth therefrom.

Every Christian should be a missionary ; should feel that he has a *mission* to fulfill in the service of the Saviour. It may be a mission to a foreign land, but it is, in a majority of cases, to the neglected and impenitent around his own door. That mission, no matter who are its objects, is to make known in word and action the truths of Christianity. It is by this influence as much as any other, that the gospel advances in the world. It is compared to leaven, which works quietly and unseen, but actively and mightily, till the whole mass is per-vaded by its influence. This figure represents the silent but mighty power of Christian principle, as put forth in the faith-ful labors and holy lives of Christians. The kingdom of God cometh not with observation or outward show. It is not in noisy, ostentatious, spasmodic efforts, that God requires his people to expend their strength, but in the calm, constant, un-tiring exhibition of a godly example, and in the putting forth of *daily* exertions to do good, though they may be but humble.

From all this it follows that the efficiency of the Church depends greatly on each member *individually* devoting himself soul and body to the work of the Lord. If members of the Church feel that all *direct* efforts for the conversion of the world should be confined to the ministers, and officers of the Church, that they are hired by the congregation to do this work, and that private members do their whole duty when they employ a minister for this purpose, the cause of God can not prosper. Men can not serve God in this respect by proxy. They can not hire others to speak to the impenitent the words which they ought to speak themselves, and to set the holy example before them which they themselves are bound to exhibit. The gift of God can not be purchased with money. As each one must give account of himself to God, so each one will be held responsible for all the good that God has put it into his power to do, individually.

When the Church of God is composed of such members; when each one sets himself to cultivate his own part of the vineyard, and then all come together with one heart for the common and united efforts which the whole Church puts forth, the world will witness such triumphs of the gospel as have been but rarely exhibited in the past.

HAVE FAITH IN GOD.

There are moments when the spirit of the Christian grows weary of the burdens of life. Many causes there may be for this. Sometimes, perhaps, he may find an old sinful appetite, with which he had long struggled, and which he had thought was finally subdued, start suddenly into life under the power of strong temptation. He feels, consequently, discouraged. The battle with his besetting sin is to be fought over again. The ground which he thought firm beneath him, suddenly trembles and grows unsteady. The weary work is all to do over. Harder than he had thought, is the duty of self-conquest and self-control. His spirit sinks within him at the thought of past failure and of future conflict; and not strange is it if, in his despondency, he is led to doubt the reality of his conversion. Can it be, he asks himself, that a really renewed heart can contain so much latent corruption? Can the Holy Spirit have ever made that heart his temple, where so much depravity still lurks? Has he not deceived himself? Is not his hope vain? And will it not prove, in the end, as "the spider's web, or the giving up of the ghost?"

Something like this is, doubtless, at some period of their course, the experience of many Christians. At such times how appropriate to their case the exhortation of Christ to his disciples: "Have faith in God." Has God ever revealed himself to the Christian's soul as the God of mercy and salvation? Then will he not leave his work undone. He has promised that he will never leave nor forsake them; that he will perfect that which concerns them; and that he will finally bring them off more than conquerors through him that hath loved them. When by the power of a living faith these promises are fully received and rested on by the believer, the burden of despondency rolls off, and he feels his heart grow strong for fresh and more determined battle with his remaining corruption. "This the victory that overcometh the world, even our faith."

Another source of despondency to the Christian may be in the slow progress made in the conversion and reformation of the world, and in the apparent hoplessness of the work of finally bringing the whole race under the controlling power of the gospel of love and peace. In the fervor of first love, the Christian consecrates himself to this work. He feels the glow of gratitude to his Saviour in his heart. The Lord Jesus Christ has been revealed to him as "the chief among ten thousand, and altogether lovely." His heart burns within him to tell to others of the love of his Saviour, and urge them to come to him for life. He imagines that that which is so sweet and lovely to himself needs only to be presented to others to be joyfully embraced. Then the vision of a kingdom of justice, and purity, and love, and peace, and universal brotherhood, as revealed in prophesy, is so wondrously and surpassingly beautiful to his soul, that he thinks it need only be preached to the world, and men will crowd into it at the first invitation. With these thoughts and hopes glowing in his heart, he goes to his work. But he soon meets with bitter disappointment. He finds, as did the meek compeer of LUTHER, that the "old Adam is too strong for the young Melancthon;" that men have hearts that are by nature enmity to God; hearts deceitful above all things, and desperately wicked. The truth he proclaims, instead of being joyfully accepted, is scornfully rejected. The pride of the human

heart spurns the humbling terms of the gospel. From hatred of the truth the transition is easy to hatred of him who
urges it on their acceptance, and he finds himself the object
of the fierce opposition of men whom he seeks to bless, and
whom he expected to hail him as a messenger of good tidings
of great joy. Disappointed, surprised, and grieved, how natural
is it for the heart of the Christian to despond and grow weary
in these circumstances! When he first fully realizes the
depth and strength of man's enmity to God; and then looks
out on the world and sees how crime and woe and sorrow
walk the earth on their mission of death, his heart sinks
within him. He is ready to ask in the spirit of incipient unbelief, "Can these dry bones live? *Can* this world be redeemed? Is the gospel of Christ adequate to the mighty
work? Why does not Christ come and bring light out of this
darkness, and order out of this confusion? And where is
the promise of his coming?"

Here, again, is the time for the work of faith. Only by its
living power can the soul thus cast down continue to hope in
God. But it is adequate to its work. The weary soul of the
Christian turns to his Father's Word, and reads promises like
this: "They shall not hurt nor destroy in all my holy
mountain; for the earth shall be full of the knowledge of the
Lord as the waters cover the sea." He knows that the waters
cover *all* the sea; and faith in prophesy assures him that thus
shall the knowledge and peace of God cover all the earth.
He reads again that Christ shall have dominion from sea to
sea, and from the river to the ends of the earth; that the
heathen shall be given to him for an inheritance, and the uttermost parts of the earth for a possession. And all over the
Holy Book he finds promises like these glowing and flashing
on every page. "By faith he realizes that all the promises of
God are yea and amen in Christ; the burden is lifted from
his heart; the weary spirit grows strong in faith, and nerves
itself for new efforts in the glorious work of persuading men
to be reconciled to God."

Thus in all scenes of weariness and discouragement, faith
is the anchor of the soul. It brings near the promises of God.
It lifts the soul out of the darkness of the present, and permits it to look onward and upward to the time when the
clouds that now lower over the earth, black with crime and
sorrow, shall be dispelled, and the earth shall bask in the sunlight of God's peace and love. Ever appropriate to the
Christian worker is the exhortation: "Have faith in God."

"Stingy Christians."

There are none such. It is as great a contradiction of terms as to talk of an honest thief. But there are stingy professors of religion in most churches. One mark of these men is their ingenuity in contriving excuses for not giving to the cause of Christ. Ask them for a missionary contribution, and if they have heard of the slightest error in the management of the particular society to which they are asked to give, they triumphantly parade that as an all-sufficient excuse, forgetting that all human instrumentalities are imperfect. If they have not that excuse they will talk perhaps of their great sacrifices to support the gospel at home.—Ask them for a contribution to the cause of Christian education, and they will tell you of a donation they made years ago to some institution of learning, which was not managed exactly to suit their notions. They will not be cheated again. Ask them for money to send the Bible to the poor, or to print religious books or tracts, and they will tell you that the affairs of the publishing society are not managed economically. This or that officer gets too much salary, and they will not give their precious dimes to be squandered in that style. Ask them to take a religious newspaper, and they have more papers now than they can read. Their stock of newspaper reading probably consists of one or two dollar weeklies, filled with moral poison, for the ruin of their children.

The simple truth in regard to these professors of religion is that they love their money more than they love their Saviour. Their excuses are mere pretense. They may cheat their own consciences with them, but they deceive nobody else. The true Christian *loves* to give to the cause of Christ. He feels it to be a *privilege* to give. He regards himself merely as a steward of the property God has given him; and his experience is that it is more blessed to give than to receive.

Power of Prayer.

The Bible tells us that "the effectual, fervent prayer of a righteous man availeth much." A simple history of what it has accomplished will be the best commentary on this text, as the narrative of the apostle, in the 11th Chapter of Hebrews, is the best possible illustration of the nature and power of faith.   The history of the achievements of prayer is a record of wonders.

Abraham prayed, and in answer the destruction of Sodom was suspended on the contingency of finding ten righteous men among all its inhabitants.   The servant of Abraham prayed, and the appointed wife of his master's son comes forth in accordance with his request.   Jacob wrestled with the Angel of the Covenant in prayer, and the fierce heart of his brother melts.   The hoarded enmity of years, with all its dark purposes of revenge, is subdued; and he who had come forth with his men of war to imbrue his hands in his brother's blood, falls on his neck and weeps the gentle tears of forgiveness and love.

Moses cried to God, and the east wind drove back the waves of the Red Sea, and piled them up as a wall to guide the chosen people over.   In the wilderness he prayed, and the waters of Marah were healed and became sweet to the taste.   When, on another occasion, his hands were raised in supplication, the hosts of Amalek were scattered in battle; but when they sank the armies of Israel were spoiled.   The parents of Sampson prayed, and the Angel of the Covenant came back to their sight, and kindled the miraculous fire that consumed their accepted sacrifice.   The mother of Samuel prayed, and the prophet child is given, a precious boon from heaven.   "Elias was a man subject to like passions as we are, and he prayed earnestly that it might not rain; and it rained not on the earth by the space of three years and six months. And he prayed again, and the heavens gave rain and the earth brought forth her fruit."   The same prophet prayed, and the dead child of the widow of Zaraphath was restored to life.

Again he prayed on Mt. Carmel, and the fire fell from the sky and consumed the sacrifice, to the confusion of the worshipers of Baal.   When the king of Israel sent forth a company to seize the prophet Elisha, and the heart of his servant was affrighted, the prophet prayed and the eyes of the young man were opened, and he saw the mountain covered with chariots of fire.   Again he prayed, and the Syrians were smitten with blindness, and led helpless captives into Samaria. He prayed again, and the son of the Shunamite was restored to life, and delivered into the arms of his mother.

Hezekiah prayed, and the Angel of the Lord went forth and smote in the camp of the Assyrians " a hundred fourscore and five thousand, and when they arose in the morning they were all dead corpses." Again he prayed, and the Lord added fifteen years to his life, and as a sign of his recovery caused the shadow to go back ten degrees in the dial of Ahaz. Solomon prayed at the dedication of the temple, and fire came down from heaven and consumed the sacrifices, and the visible glory of the Lord filled the house. Nehemiah prayed, and the heart of King Ahasuerus was moved to send him back to repair the city of his fathers; and to give him letters of recommendation to the governors beyond the rivers to aid him in the work. Again he prayed, and the counsels of the enemies of Israel were brought to confusion, the walls of Jerusalem were rebuilt, and much of the ancient glory of the city restored.

Passing from the Old to the New Testament, and the narrative of wonders is continued.

In answer to prayer addressed to the Saviour, when personally on earth, the lame walked, the deaf heard, and the blind received their sight, the lepers were cleansed, devils were cast out, and the dead were restored to life. The disciples "continued with one accord in prayer and supplication," after the ascension of Christ, and in answer the Spirit came down as a mighty rushing wind, on the day of Pentecost, "cloven tongues as of fire" were given to the apostles, and three thousand souls were converted to God. Saul of Tarsus prayed in his blindness, and the messenger is sent to him at whose coming the scales fell from his eyes, and he received the Holy Ghost. Cornelius, the centurion, prayed, and the angel of God appeared to show him the means of procuring instruction in the gospel of salvation. Peter prayed, and the heavens were opened, and the vision which showed that to the Gentile as well as to the Jew the gospel was to be preached, was presented to his view. When the same apostle was cast into prison by Herod, prayer was made for him without ceasing by the Church, and the angel of the Lord opens the door of his prison, strikes off his chains and sets him at liberty. Paul and Silas prayed in the dungeon of Phillippi, and the heaving of the earthquake opened the doors of the prison, the keeper was converted and set them free. Paul prayed, and the ship in which he sailed to Rome was saved from the violence of the tempest. Again he prayed, and the father of Publius and many others were healed of their diseases, and the word of God was greatly spread abroad. "And what shall we say more? for the time would fail to tell of Gideon, and of Barak, and of Sampson, and of Jephtha, and of David also, and of Samuel and the prophets. Who through *prayer* (as well as faith) subdued kingdoms, wrought righteousness, obtained promises, stopped the mouths of lions, quenched the violence of fire, escaped the edge of the sword, out of weakness were made strong, waxed valiant in fight, turned to flight the armies of the aliens."

Here, then, is the Christian's strength and hope. When darkness gathers over his own soul and shuts out the light of the Divine love; or when moral gloom overspreads the earth, the ways of Zion languish, oppression and war and violence and every wrong riot in scenes of guilt and suffering, let him kneel at the mercy-seat and pray; and he whose arm controls the winds and waves, and moves the stars in their courses, has promised to hear and answer. "Prayer moves the arm that moves the world." And the record of God's faithfulness in answering it in all past time, should encourage his children "to draw near to him that they may find grace and mercy to help in every time of need."

Peace with God.

Peace is thirsted after by the human heart. Amid all scenes of strife and turmoil, a dream of rest and quiet, when those scenes shall have passed away is most fondly cherished. The man of business, in the feverish toil of the counting-room and the mad chase for wealth, consoles himself with thoughts of the quiet country residence. The statesman, riding on the angry waves of political strife, looks forward with keen delight to the time, when having gained the elevation he seeks, he shall be permitted to wear his laurels in *peace*. The sailor on the stormy ocean, the soldier in the din of battle, cherish fond visions of a return to the quiet cottage by the hill-side; and of exchanging the roar of the strife that rages round them, for the murmur of the rivulet, whose gentle music soothed the slumbers of their childhood.

But the peace which the soul needs to meet and satisfy this ardent longing, is one which the earth can not impart. A voice to still the *inner* strife which sin rouses in the heart, and to point the way of peaceful reconciliation with an offended God is what the soul demands; and that voice speaks in accents of melting tenderness in the gospel of Jesus. *"Come unto me all ye that labor and are heavy laden, and I will give you rest." " Peace I leave with you, my peace I give unto you; not as the world giveth give I unto you: let not your heart be troubled, neither let it be afraid." " Therefore, being justified by faith, we have peace with God."*

In language such as this is this blessing described. The invitation to seek this peace implies that man is *now* at enmity with God. This is the necessary result of sin. Sin is a violation of the divine law, and the man who does this proclaims himself God's enemy. The man who violates the laws of the State in which he lives, by that act, both makes and declares himself the enemy of the State. His crime is a declaration of war against the government. It is setting its authority at defiance, and declaring its laws unworthy of respect and obedience. Just so sin, which is breaking God's law is a declaration of war against the Almighty. It is an open repudiation of his dominion and government, and, therefore, the highest treason in the universe.

It is no arbitrary proceeding on the part of Deity that makes him the enemy of the sinner. It is the transgressor's own act. The law he breaks is based on infinite justice and goodness. His own happiness can be secured only by observing it. The breach of it is an open declaration on his part of his hostility to God, not of God's to him. It is a necessity, therefore, of his own choosing, that God shall be his enemy.

The gospel reveals a plan for the pardon of the past offenses of the sinner, and provides the means of changing his disposition, so that he shall no longer take pleasure in sin. The result of an interest in this plan is peace with God. The transgressor becomes a dutiful, obedient child of God. The smile of his heavenly Father rests upon him, and he finds an unspeakable peace in keeping his commandments. "Great peace have they that keep thy law, and nothing shall offend them."

The results of this reconciliation are, first, peace among all the powers of the soul. Man, as a sinner, is not only at war with his Maker, but at war with himself. The passions war with the judgment; the appetites with the conscience; the claims of truth and duty and God with the selfish and sensual desires of the soul. Love and hatred, hope and fear, forgiveness and revenge, all struggle for the mastery. But, by the voice of the Holy Spirit in the work of regeneration, all this wild tumult is stilled. The angry waves are hushed to peace. The mental and moral powers assume their rightful supremacy over the merely animal part of man's nature. The soul becomes as a well regulated machine, all parts of which work in beautiful harmony—as a happy family, every movement of which is in unison and love.

2. A second result of this reconciliation is a peaceful submission to all the afflictive dispensations of providence. The soul, at peace with God, looks up, by the eye of faith, and sees his heavenly Father seated on the throne of the universe. All the events of life are referred at once to his disposing hand. Afflictions are felt to come in the order, and as part of his wise designs. They are even hailed with joy as tokens of a father's love; for the child of God reads in the book of inspiration, "Whom the Lord loveth He *chasteneth*, and scourgeth every son whom he receiveth." He sees in these trials a necessary part of his discipline. He "glories in tribulation, also; knowing that tribulation worketh patience, and patience experience, and experience hope, and hope maketh not ashamed, because the love of God is shed abroad in the heart."

3. A third effect of peace with God, through the gospel of his Son, is a greatly enhanced pleasure in prosperity. The soul at one with God is at peace with all around it except sin. It looks abroad on nature, and sees the perfect smile of God in the sunlight, on hill-top and valley. The sparrow preaches to it of his tender care; the flower of his love for the beautiful. The rock-piled mountain and the roaring cataract are tokens of that almighty power which is pledged for his own salvation. The streams of domestic love are sweetened. Parental, conjugal and filial affection flow on in deeper and holier channels. The full cup of blessings causes the fuller heart to go up in ascriptions of boundless gratitude. The heart whispers to itself in accents soft as the quiet murmurs of the gentle stream, "The Lord is my shepherd, I shall not want. He maketh me to lie down in green pastures, he leadeth me beside the still waters." "Goodness and mercy shall follow me all the days of my life, and I will dwell in the house of the Lord forever."

4. A fourth result of the peace the gospel imparts, is a calm and heavenly triumph in death. The soul hears the voice of its beloved, saying to the waves of death's dark river, "Peace, be still." When the eye grows dim, and the curdling life-blood trembles faintly along the quivering channels, a tide of immortal vigor is poured through all the powers of the soul. It bursts like the chrysalis from its

shell, and floats away through the new element of its existence, lit up with glory from the opening heaven. In the parting hour the voice of promise sounds in his ear with words of blessing: "Blessed are the dead that die in the Lord, yea, from henceforth, saith the Spirit; that they may rest from their labors, and their works do follow them." "And the ransomed of the Lord shall return and come to Zion, with songs and everlasting joy upon their heads."

CHRISTIAN INTEGRITY.

The design of the Christian religion is two-fold. First, to save the souls of men; second, to reform the world. It is intended and adapted not only to save believers from hell, but also to make them pure, and honest, and benevolent in life. The last mentioned of its effects is the first which it produces. It makes men upright, just and good, and afterward takes them to heaven. The one result is both the evidence and surety of the other. It is by transforming human character that Christianity evidences, in a great degree, its power to save from future punishment. It follows that none but those who are *transformed* will be *saved* by the gospel. An impure, selfish or dishonest Christian is as great a contradiction in terms as an honest thief, or a reverent blasphemer. Purity, benevolence and honesty are essential elements of Christian character. If any one of these elements of character is manifestly wanting, it is an evidence of the want of all; for "he that offends in one point is guilty of all."

Overwhelming evidence of the spurious character of "the current religion of the country" is found in the want of strict integrity among professing Christians. Many of the prevailing maxims of trade are palpable violations of that honesty enjoined by the Christian religion. Let us look at some of these.

1. It is considered a fair rule in business to "buy cheap and sell dear." In both particulars this rule is grossly dishonest. To buy cheap is to buy for less than the real value of the article; to sell dear is to sell for more than its true value; because if articles are bought and sold for their real worth, they are neither cheap nor dear. Now, no *Christian* will habitually trade on any other principle. His simple rule will be, both in buying and selling, to give and receive the

7

real value of the articles bought and sold. He may honestly, if he chooses to be generous, pay more for articles bought than their real worth, but never will he knowingly take them from others for less. Yet to such an extent is this rule of simple justice violated, that a professor of religion who should rigidly adhere to it, would be a marked exception. He would be set down at once as fanatical, impracticable, "righteous over much," etc.

Excuses for this want of strict integrity, as for any other vice, are never wanting. Sometimes the plea is urged that the seller parts with his wares *voluntarily*, and hence no injustice is done to him. If this were true, which in the vast majority of cases is not, it is no excuse to the buyer. That state of mind which induces a man to *offer* less than what he knows to be the full value of an article, is itself dishonest. It shows a covetous desire for what belongs to his neighbor, for the value of the article over the offered price is honestly his neighbor's. But the excuse in most cases rests on falsehood. There are often circumstances surrounding the seller which amount to a virtual *compulsion*. Ignorance of the market price (known to the buyer) often induces him to take less than value. Combinations among merchants often enable them to carry into effect the motto, "Buy cheap and sell dear." Necessity again often forces the poor to part with the products of their hard labor without an equivalent. There are many other ways (known to the *initiated*) of taking the advantage in a bargain.

In business transactions, conducted on such principles, the *truth* of all parties suffers quite as much as their honesty. This introduces a second practice as dishonest as the first.

2. It is very common among professing Christians, as well as others, to violate the truth both in praising their own wares and depreciating those they wish to buy. Graphically does the prophet describe this: "It is nought, it is nought, saith the buyer, and straightway he goeth his way and boasteth." The simple rule for the Christian is to tell "the whole truth and nothing but the truth" in his business transactions. He should tell the imperfections as well as the virtues of his wares. He will "nought exaggerate," either in setting forth the superiority of what he wishes to sell, or depreciating what he designs to purchase. He will in this, as in other things, act in the spirit of the golden rule: what he wishes others to do to him in business transactions he will try to do to them. Every one feels, when he is himself the

sufferer, the injustice, not only of false representations, but of withholding part of the truth, and of thus deceiving by silence as well as by words.

3. A third and perhaps the worst indication of the want of strict integrity among professors of religion, is found in the habitual disregard of their promises. The promise of a professor of religion is considered generally as worth no more than the promise of any moral man. Men will no more trust a man because a professor of religion, without bond and security, than they will many others. Now, this fact is a standing reproach to religion. The word of every truly consistent Christian is as good as his bond. So the world regards it. There have been men, and some are now living, whose simple promise the men of the world consider the most ample security. Thousands of dollars will be entrusted to them with nothing but their simple promise as pledge of its return; and those who know them well feel that it is as safe (if they are not utterly deprived of ability to refund) as if a whole community were legally responsible for the amount.

But that such is not the confidence reposed in the vast majority of professing Christians is a most notorious and most humiliating fact. What is still more disgraceful is, that when implicit confidence is reposed in any of this class, it is not, in any degree, because *they are professors of religion.* This fact, in itself, is not regarded as any security whatever. Men feel generally that they must guard as carefully against being cheated by members of the church as by any other class. They feel it as necessary to have them bound in bond and security, and as little count on their strict punctuality in fulfilling their promises, as on that of any other portion of community.

The influence of these things on the honor and power of religion is most disastrous. These facts are a standing discredit thrown on the Church and a profession of religion. If men understand the Christian religion, they know that it inculcates the strictest justice and honesty in business, and the most scrupulous regard for truth. When they see its professors habitually violating these principles, they set them down as hypocrites, and make their delinquencies an excuse for their own neglect of the claims of Christianity. If men do not understand the Christian religion, they naturally load it with the evil doings of its professors—imagine that their religion has made them dishonest and false. In either case the effect is ruinous and melancholy. Thousands stumble into ruin over the example of these faithless professors of religion. They daily "crucify afresh" the Saviour they pretend to love, and "put him to an open shame."

The Religion of Principle.

The form and shape of the religious principle in man is very much diversified—as diversified as the influences by which it is developed. It sometimes takes the type of mere formality—observes days and times, and forms and ceremonies, with scrupulous exactness. In this it consists, and hence exerts no controlling power over the life and conduct. It is, therefore, no uncommon thing to find the most scrupulous formalist, the most dishonest man. It is not at all unusual to find men who would be shocked at the thought of breaking the Sabbath, who can cheat a fellow-man without any compunction. The religion of *mere* formality is, therefore, worthless.

Another form of religious development is that of mere feeling. This type of religion is spasmodic. The person under its influence, makes religion consist in excited feeling—in ecstacies and excitements of the emotions. It is, therefore, periodical in its exercises. It manifests itself at irregular intervals, and usually leaves its possessor under the controlling power of worldly motives and feelings during these periods. Hence it is not generally the case that those whose piety *all* consists in mere feeling, exhibit a high regard for justice and strict integrity in the conduct of life.

The religion the Bible inculcates, is the religion of principle. It does not exclude forms or feelings, but controls them, and makes them subservient to the claims of duty, which with it are paramount. Its essence is doing right—doing the will of God from the heart. This is declared to be the condition of admission to God's kingdom. "For not every one that saith unto me, Lord, Lord, shall enter into the kingdom of heaven, but he that doeth the will of my Father which is in heaven." The soul under the power of this living principle regards the revealed will of God as the expression of eternal righteousness. To conform its own desires and feelings and actions to that revelation is, therefore, its highest aim. Religion is with the man of principle a practical reality, controlling his daily actions and all his intercourse with his fellow-men. His piety may not, and usually does not, rise into ecstacy or sink to corresponding depression; but with calm, steady current, moves on in the regular channels of usefulness and duty.

There is always deep feeling in the religion of principle. It is not, however, the fitful outburst of transient excitement, but a calm, deep under-current of love to God and man. This, indeed, supplies the motive and energy to the true religious principle, for while that is a principle of faith, yet "faith works by love." The affections and feelings are chastened and made subservient, and not superior to the obligations of conscience and duty. The habitual conviction of the man of religious principle is, that duty must be done. If his feelings and desires stand in the way of duty, they must be crucified; but his constant desire is so to discipline these, that they may work in harmony with the claims of right and duty.

<hr>

"AMBASSADORS FOR CHRIST."

Ministers of the gospel are ambassadors for Christ. They are sent to propose to men God's terms of reconciliation, and to urge their acceptance. "Now then," says Paul, "we are ambassadors for Christ, as though God did beseech you by us; we pray you in Christ's stead be ye reconciled to God." Several important truths are brought to light in this figure:

1. In the first place, ministers are not to preach their own words, or to propose their own terms of pardon to sinners. An ambassador sent to negotiate a peace between parties at war receives fixed and definite instructions. His fidelity consists in adhering strictly to these instructions. He may neither change nor abate one jot or tittle of them all. His mission is confined to the simple duty of stating the terms of peace, proposed by the party from which he receives his commission, and of urging their acceptance. Especially is this the case when the guilt and wrong of the quarrel are all on one side. It is then the exclusive prerogative of the other party to dictate the conditions of peace. Still more is this the case when subjects are in unnatural and guilty rebellion against their lawful ruler; when creatures are in revolt against their Maker; when children are in wicked mutiny against a kind and good Father. Proposals and terms of reconciliation can then come only from the latter; and His ambassadors are

doubly bound to adhere with strictest fidelity to the very letter of their instructions. If they depart from them, they themselves assume the attitude of rebels.

Ministers of the gospel are ambassadors to make known the condition on which God, the creator and ruler of all things, proposes to be reconciled to the race of men, who are in guilty rebellion against him. It is Jehovah's exclusive prerogative to propose terms of peace, and it is the business of his ambassador to expound these to their fellow-transgressors, and to pursuade them to accept. If they fail to declare his whole counsel they are false to their trust, and will be held guilty of the blood of those who may perish through their unfaithfulness.

2. Another truth brought to view by this figure is, that the people are most deeply interested in having their ministers preach the whole truth. It is their interest surely to know precisely the terms on which their offended Creator and Judge will pardon their guilt, and restore them to his favor. If they are deceived on this point they must be infinite and eternal losers. And it is quite possible to be deceived. There is a false peace which may be mistaken for that which is real. The evidence that God has become reconciled to the sinner, is peace of conscience, a sanctified heart and a holy life. But a scared and stupid conscience may be mistaken for a good conscience, and mere selfish morality may pass current for genuine obedience. God may be really angry with a soul that fancies itself in loving fellowship with him. The only way to guard against this fatal mistake is to examine critically the terms of pardon and salvation proposed in the gospel, and to examine strictly the heart and life, to see if they have been really accepted. To aid men in doing this, God has appointed a ministry as his ambassadors to declare and enforce these terms. If they are false to their mission, the people are the more likely to be deceived. From this we see the superlative folly of men becoming angry with God's ambassadors for the faithful and pungent preaching of the truth. Their own eternal interests may depend on the word being thus preached.

3. Again: In the light of this subject we see that it is the duty of the people to examine for themselves the terms of reconciliation proposed by their ministers. The instructions of God's ambassadors are not sealed. The word of God is not bound; and God commands all men to search the Scriptures. The Jews of Berea were commended for searching to see if

the word preached by the apostles was in accordance with the inspired oracles of God. Christians are commanded to *prove* all things, and hold fast that which is good. They are enjoined not to believe every spirit, but to try the spirits whether they be of God. All these and many other injunctions in the Bible are totally inconsistent with a blind and unquestioning reception of the teachings of the ministers of the gospel. Men are bound to receive those teachings with all submission so far as they are true. But they are also bound to bring them to the test of the inspired word of God, and to see if they *are* true before they receive them. And this, all true ambassadors of God desire. The true minister of the gospel desires to preach nothing but the truth. He feels the solemn responsibility that rests upon him as a watchman, at whose hands the blood of the wicked will be required, if he fails to warn them of their danger. Hence he desires that those to whom he preaches should use the faculties of their minds in investigating the word of God, that by their labors in this behalf, thus united with his own, they may all come to a more perfect understanding of the lively oracles. He desires this also because those who thus examine for themselves are thus prepared to receive his message with a more ready mind. And from the nature of the case, this is the duty of all who have access to the word of God. While the unfaithful ambassadors will have a fearful account to render for themselves, they can not answer at the judgment for those whom they have led astray. The soul that perishes through their unfaithfulness will bear its own iniquity. For this reason should men examine for themselves, with most scrupulous care into the terms of their acceptance with God.

Duty of the Christian Minister.

The chief duty of christian ministers is not to battle the dead heresies of the past age, or the obsolete sins of a bygone generation. Neither are they to spend their strength in proving points, on which their hearers are already convinced, or in dealing out abstractions having no special bearing on their immediate duties. The preacher of the gospel sees before him a congregation of dying men and women, each having a mighty work to do, to secure his or her *personal* salvation; and another work equally momentous in bringing

the world under the power of the truth of God.   Hence his
great concern is to show them, first what they must do to be
saved; second, how they can best labor for God.   And as sin
is that which destroys the present and eternal welfare of men,
and robs God of his honor, the work of the faithful preacher
of the gospel brings him in direct conflict with all the sins
of all his hearers.   It is his duty to hold up the law of God
in all the extent of its claims, and show his audience how
they personally, politically, or socially violate it.   As every
sin is destructive of the peace of men, so every sin is the object of his reproof.   But his special efforts ought to be against
the prevalent, besetting sins of his hearers, as these are always
the most dangerous.   Every one has a favorite sin which he
loves above all others, and this is the one he needs to be
most warned against.   This is the one most likely to ruin his
soul.   Now for a preacher to rebuke every crime except just
those his hearers are most addicted to, is worse than for a
physician to prescribe remedies for all diseases save just the
one his patient is suffering with.   Suppose him called to a
man having one fatal disease preying upon his body, and several of less dangerous tendency.—If the physician has a remedy for the worst disease, and for fear of causing present pain
neglects to apply it, and contents himself with prescribing for
the others alone, he is simply a murderer.   Just so the minister of the gospel who for fear of offending his hearers, neglects to expose and rebuke their favorite sins is guilty of the
worst kind of murder—the murder of the soul.

17 Son of man, I have made thee a watchman unto the house of
Israel; therefore hear the word at my mouth, and give them warning
from me.

18 When I say unto the wicked thou shalt surely die; and thou
givst him not warning, nor speakest to warn the wicked from his wicked
way, to save his life; the same wicked *man* shall die in his iniquity; but
his blood will I require at thine hand.—Ezekiel 3: 17, 18.

It follows from the principles laid down that the preacher
of the gospel in selecting truth to be presented to his congregation, ought to choose that bearing most directly on their
condition.   It is cruel mockery of a soul which asks in the
eager agony of conviction for sin, "What must I do to be
saved?" to hear a labored argument to prove the doctrine of
predestination or the perseverance of saints.   For a preacher
to spend his time in curious speculations about the origin
of evil, and the way in which it was transmitted from Adam
to his posterity, while he never once exposes and warns
against the sins that are sending the souls of his hearers to

perdition, is "daubing with untempered mortar." To preach to the drunkard against the sin of lying, or to the liar against the sin of drunkenness, is folly. To preach to a congregation of slaveholders, or those cherishing a pro-slavery spirit, of the horrors of heathenism in a foreign land, is worse than folly. To entertain these or any other class of sinners with long discussions about abstract theology, or points of doubtful disputation is to be a traitor to God.

Practical conclusions of great importance may be derived from these principles. If a man is called to a congregation imbued with a pro-slavery spirit, and giving ecclesiastical or political support to the system, he ought at once to exhibit in all its enormity the sin of slavery, show his people how they are involved in it and urge them to repent and reform. If his hearers are living in the breach of any one commandment in particular, its solemn obligations ought to be most prominently held up to their view.—Such a course on the part of the ministry of this land, would redeem it from disgrace; would stop the mouth of Infidelity, and make the church "mighty to the pulling down of strong holds."

"THE HARVEST IS PAST, THE SUMMER IS ENDED, AND WE ARE NOT SAVED."—Jer. viii: 20.

The revolution of seasons has brought us again to that period of the year, when the imagery of this passage of holy Scripture, is most vividly appreciated. The natural harvest is past, the summer is nearly ended. The earth has yielded her increase to the hand of the reaper, and now while the incense of praise and the voice of thanksgiving should go up from grateful hearts, the mind may turn to study with profit the moral lessons which the occasion is designed to teach.

God speaks to man in the dispensations of his providence, and the works of his hands. Each one of the seasons teaches its own lessons. When spring comes forth with its reviving breath and clothes the earth in beauty, the whole scene speaks of the goodness of God, which adorns even a sin-cursed earth with so much that tells of heaven. Winter teaches the lesson of decay and death. Summer and autumn are witnesses of the boundless love of God, in causing the earth to bring forth its fruits in rich luxuriance, that they may give "seed to the sower, and bread to the eater:" and at their close they admonish us of the importance of improving all periods of time; they call us to consider that the seed-time and harvest of life are passing, and that if we fail to improve the precious hours, we will at last be compelled to take up the mournful wail, that "the harvest is past, the summer is ended, and we are not saved."

The simple idea of this passage is that life is a probation, that it is rapidly passing away, and that if neglected or mis-improved, the soul will not be saved. As the husbandman who should fail to sow in spring or reap in harvest would starve in winter, so if the soul fail to sow the seed and gather the fruits of holiness, it will wail its loss when forever too late to repair it.

A probation is a time for favorably affecting the future. From the present we may send an influence forward which will meet us there, and be of more value to us, than all the pains and labor it will cost us now. The actions of men are not confined in their results to the time when they are put forth. They run on into the future with an influence for good or evil, and often the most trivial actions apparently, are fraught with the most far-reaching and momentous results. It is indeed a solemn truth that the whole future of man's existence may be, and often is, fixed by a single act. There is a crisis in our history when the whole future is suspended on a single point.

Many illustrations of this might be given. The moment when the youth who has been reared in habits of sobriety, is invited to drink the first glass of intoxicating liquors very often decides his fate. If he yield now other and more pressing temptations will follow, while his power of resistance will be weakened, and his doom will in all probability be sealed. But if the first temptation be resisted and overcome, a second will come with weakened force, while the power of resistance will be proportionately increased. The first act is important as it settles a principle, and gives direction to the future life.

The hour when the youth is first tempted to pilfer a few dimes from his employer, under the delusive expectation of being able soon to return them, is another turning point, when the destiny for time and eternity is decided. His path in life is chosen, and his downward course, if he yield, is henceforth, without almost a miracle of grace, swift and steady.

So we doubt not there is a crisis in the history of the soul when its destiny for eternity hangs suspended in the balance, and the slightest force may turn the beam toward heaven or toward hell. There are moments when the spirit of God presses the decision of the great question of accepting Christ on the terms of the gospel on the soul, until it is almost persuaded to yield. The motives are about equally balanced. The person comes to the very door of the ark of safety, and the next decision will either land him safely within, or behold him turning his back on God and salvation. As "there is a tide in the affairs of men, which taken at the flood leads on to fortune," so there is doubtless a tide in the spiritual affairs of men, when their fortunes for the eternal world are suspended on a single act, or it may be a single thought of the heart. These are the summer and harvest moments of life. Once wasted they can never be recalled, but through eternity the lost soul must pour the bitter but unavailing lamentation, "the harvest is past, the summer is ended, and I am not saved."

How is it with you, dear reader? Are you sowing the seeds of holiness and love? Are you wisely improving the summer and harvest seasons of life? The time is favorable for serious reflection. Another harvest is over; another summer is almost gone. Nature will soon wear the somber dress of autumn; tree and flower will be stript of their beauty by winter's chilly winds. The notes of song will die away from woodland and meadow, and the joyous melodies of nature will be hushed and still. So man passes away—"He cometh forth as a flower and is cut down, he fleeth also as a shadow and continueth not." "We spend our years as a tale that is told." Soon those forms which glow with beauty and rejoice in their strength will be cold and still in the grave. The flowers of spring will wave above our quiet resting-places. Our probation will be closed, our destiny sealed. Shall we be then rejoicing in the presence of God with joy unspeakable and full of glory; or, shall we be wailing with the lost that "the harvest is past, the summer is ended, and we are not saved?"

"O Lord Revive Thy Work."

Christian reader are you praying for a revival of religion? Do you earnestly desire that God's work should be revived in your own heart, and in the Church? Unless you really desire this you can not, of course, pray for it in earnest. True prayer for a revival of religion always contemplates it as God's work. The prophet's prayer is, "O Lord revive *thy* work." There are so-called revivals which are the work of men. Revivals of religion are not uncommon in the Roman Catholic Church, yet few will believe that the spirit of God has any agency in their production. No part of this country is more frequently visited with revivals than the slaveholding States, and men go from the altar of the church, where they have just professed to "get religion," to tear the mother from her babe and sell her where she shall never see it again. Revivals followed by such fruits are the works of Satan or of men.

The genuine converts of a true revival immediately set about doing the work of God. It is the Lord's work to call them into his kingdom, enlighten and regenerate their souls. The inevitable result of this is that they begin at once a life of obedience to God. And what doth the Lord require of all his own children in this world? "He hath showed thee, O man! what is good, and what doth the Lord require of thee but to do justly, to love mercy, and to walk humbly with thy God?" Piety toward God, and justice and benevolence toward men, are the great duties here required. No revival is genuine which is not productive of these results. A pretended conversion which leaves the convert as selfish, worldly, and regardless of justice and benevolence as he was before, is utterly spurious.

Now acceptable prayer to God for a revival of religion will have reference to these truths. All true prayer is based on an intelligent understanding of what is prayed for, and of God's promises in respect to it. Acceptable prayer is only for such blessings as God has commanded us to seek for, and has promised to grant. Hence our prayers for a revival of religion, to be heard and answered, must be for holiness of heart and life in ourselves and others. Unless we really desire God to rule in, and reign over us, we can not pray in earnest the prayer, "O Lord revive thy work."

But will we not all strive for grace to offer that prayer in sincerity and truth? Surely, Christian brother and sister, a revival of God's work in our own souls, in the Church and the world is greatly needed. Souls are going unprepared in multitudes to the judgment-seat of Christ.—May it not be that our coldness and worldliness are in the way of the salvation of some of them? If needed so much, surely then a genuine revival of religion is infinitely desirable. The world is full of the works of men and of the Devil, but oh how little of the work of God is seen in the lives even of his professed followers.　The subjects of Satan's kingdom in this world are multiplying faster than the subjects of Christ.　Most of the professed *churches*, even, of this land are supporting a system which makes heathen faster than all the churches of the country are converting them.　Where all this must end, without a revival of God's work, it is not difficult to see.

A revival of true religion is also practicable.　God only awaits the prayer of faith from his people.　For the outpouring of his spirit he will "be inquired of by the house of Israel."　But he is more willing to give his Holy Spirit to them that ask, than earthly parents to give good gifts unto their children.　If we ask, therefore, we shall receive, if we seek we shall find.

CHRIST'S DIVINITY AND ATONEMENT.

Were a man to sit down for the express purpose of teaching the proper deity and vicarious atonement of the Lord Jesus Christ, he could not employ language more explicit and precise than that of the Bible.　All the names, attributes, works, and worship of God are given to Christ.　He is called "the true God."　He is called the "Everlasting Father," the "mighty God."　The glory of "Jehovah of hosts" seen by Isaiah, as' recorded in his sixth chapter, was the glory of Christ, as is declared in John 12, 41.　Christ claimed for himself divinity with all its attributes, and was therefore properly God, or else an impostor.　He repeatedly declared that he and the Father are one.　He made himself equal with God by declaring that he was his son.　Thus the Jews understood him, and when they charged him with blasphemy for claiming equality with God, instead of correcting their error, as he must in honesty have done if he were not God, he goes on to defend his claim to divinity.—Again: Christ and He alone is the son of God by generation.　He is the "*only*-begotten son."　All other creatures are God's sons by creation.　Now however impossible it is for us to conceive of the process of generation in the divine nature, the term yet irresistibly conveys the idea of the perfect sameness of the Son *in nature*, with the Father.　A son by creation is inferior to the father, but a son by generation is of necessity equal to him.　The son of a human father is perfect man, because begotten, so Christ, the "*only* begotten of the Father" must be perfect God.—If this is not so the use of this term is calculated to wholly mislead the human mind, and the Scriptures can not be received as a safe and sure revelation of truth.

Based on the divinity of Christ is the doctrine of his vicarious atonement.—This doctrine is simply that Christ obeyed the law in our place, and "died for our sins according to the Scriptures." He died that he might satisfy the truth and justice of God, and magnify his law, and thus provide pardon and life for the guilty race of man. The work of atonement consists of obedience and sacrifice. But unless Christ is God, as well as man, his obedience, and suffering unto death, could have no merit that could be imputed to others, or avail for their salvation. If he were a mere creature (though the first born of every other) he would owe perfect obedience for himself, and therefore his obedience could not be acceptable as satisfying the claims of the law upon the guilty. As a mere creature he would hold his life from God, and would have no right to lay it down for sinners. It is not true of any creature that he has "power to lay down his life and power to take it again." But Christ declared that he had this power, thereby claiming that he is Lord of life, which is not true if he be not God. The divine nature of Jesus united to the human gave infinite value to his obedience and sufferings, and also gives assurance to the convicted and anxious soul that "he is *able* to save to the uttermost all who come unto God by him."

With this view of the teachings of the Scriptures on these points accords the experience of every truly earnest and anxious soul. They alone give peace to the deeply convicted sinner. The soul that has been brought by the Spirit of God to feel the infinite guilt of sin, feels at the same time that the blood of a mere creature can never wash that sin away. He whose spiritual eye has been opened to see the number and power of the obstacles and enemies that are opposed to his salvation, feels that none but a *divine* Saviour can bring him off victorious over them all. He feels that he needs a Redeemer who is " mighty to save." From the darkness and terror of deep and pungent conviction of sin, the soul can emerge into light and peace only through faith in a divine Saviour and an infinite atonement.

We have been led to these remarks by reading some extracts from a volume of sermons by Professor Huntington of Cambridge, Mass. The Professor has been a Unitarian, and is yet, we believe, nominally in connection with that people. He

is a man of powerful intellect and of fine scholarship. He
is also a man of deep spiritual experience, and as such, he
finds peace only in Christ as properly and really a divine being, and as making in his death a vicarious sacrifice for sin.
On these points he makes the following explicit avowal of his
faith.   He is speaking of the Apostle Paul, and says:

"Like all men since, of very deep and intense moral experience, and such always find themselves interpreted and
satisfied only by Paul, he came out at last upon the ground of
acceptance on account of faith in Christ, and entire giving up
of the soul to the free mercy of God; the only permanent
ground for Christian theology to rest upon."

Equally clear and scriptural are his views of the nature and
office of Christ, as the following extract will show :

"There are two prevalent apprehensions of the character
and office of Jesus the saviour of the world. One contemplates
him as specially appointed to represent the perfection of humanity, meaning by humanity what we have hitherto known
or conceived of the spiritual powers and possibilities in a
human being. This view holds Jesus to have been a perfect
man ; the completest moral example and religious genius
of our race in exhibiting in his life and death the utmost that
human excellence can do or be ; as showing the ultimate
achievement, thus far at least, of a man's virtue, love and
faith ; and as having withdrawn his personal presence and
power from the world at his ascension, so that the communion
of his followers is not literally a communion *with him*,
but is only a commemorative observance for a Teacher
living on earth in the past, but retired now into the heavens.

"The other view regards Christ as showing forth not only a
perfect humanity, but also and primarily God himself; representing God to man, as well as man to himself; being God in the
act and character of revealing or manifesting himself ; creating
and saving the world ; separate at no point from God's sover-
eignty, nor knowing in his divinity, any limitation or abridgment from the fullness of God ; exhibiting, as in God's behalf,
through a union of nature with the Father, not explicable to
to us, the divine attributes ; and reconciling alienated souls
by manifesting God in his flesh. According to this doctrine,
he survives in his Church to this day, and will survive, not
only by influence and memory, but by the presence of his
person ; a distinct and everlasting person in himself, without
beginning of days or end of years, the same yesterday, to-
day and forever.

"The latter of the two views appears to me not only incomparably the most benignant and precious, but to stand toward the other in the relation of truth to error ; to be charged with inestimable benefit to our religious progress ; to be liable to fewer theological perversions, and less dangerous abuses ; and to need also that it be more distinctly asserted and impressed. on our present habits of thinking, especially among the inquiring and the young."

The promulgation of such views in such a quarter will probably mark an era in the history of New England Unitarianism. The Professor will gather around him all that is vital and evangelical in that denomination. A separation of the elements will probably ensue. The one party will come out on the ground of distinct evangelism and orthodoxy. The other party, cut loose from this vitalizing element, will probably gravitate to the congenial infidelity of Strauss and Parker.

Samuel Lewis

Died on Friday last at half past 12 o'clock, P. M., in the fifty-sixth year of his age. Although this event has been expected for a considerable time, yet the announcement falls sadly on the ear of all who knew, and consequently loved the deceased. Indeed every friend of the slave, whether personally acquainted with him or not, will mourn the loss of one of the truest, ablest, and noblest advocates of the cause of the poor. Every one who has ever listened to the eloquent voice of the departed, will feel a sad regret that its tones of warning, entreaty, and touching pathos will be heard no more. One of the purest and bravest soldiers of the army of freedom has fallen at a time when his services were eminently needed. But he died in the harness; and has bequeathed to his comrades in arms a name of which they may be proud, and an example which if they will faithfully emulate, will, to some extent, compensate the loss. We have not the materials nor the space for a biography of Mr. Lewis. A few points of his character, hastily sketched, are all that our limits admit of.

1. He was an eminently earnest and honest man. This high praise even those who most strongly oppose his views, freely accorded to him. No one ever listened to his voice, we presume, without being fully convinced of the deep earnest-

ness of feeling, and honesty of purpose which pervaded all his words and thoughts. The sacrifices he made for the cause nearest his heart, are abundant evidence that he was actuated by an earnest and honest conviction of duty. No man stood higher in the confidence and affection of the people of the State, at the time he threw himself, soul and body, into the then unpopular anti-slavery cause. Through his valuable and persevering labors in the cause of education, he had become known and loved by the great mass of the people. Had he chosen the field of political preferment, there is no honor in the gift of the people which he might not have attained. But the mute appeal of the dumb and suffering slave touched his heart. His soul was fired with indignation at his wrongs, and with deep sympathy for his woes. And without "consulting with flesh and blood," he threw himself a living sacrifice upon the altar of humanity. He made no reserve in the consecration, but gave mind, soul, body, influence and property freely to the holy cause. And from that time onward never wavered from his high purpose, amid all the obloquy, reproach and violence that were poured upon the hated advocates of the down-trodden and the poor.

2. In the second place, Mr. Lewis was a man of great *energy*. He was, in the true sense of the word, a self-made man. His early opportunities of education were very limited. A pioneer in Ohio, he came before the school-house opened its doors for the admission of youth. His training was his own work. Yet no one ever listened to the compact logic of his speeches, and marked his great command of the English language without feeling that he was, in the truest sense of the word, a well educated man. It was his great energy that triumphed over the difficulties and privations of his early life, and which bore him on in all his subsequent career. What his hand found to do, he did with all his might. And he lived to accomplish a great work. The common-school system of the great State of Ohio is one of his monuments; and when the fetters shall at last be stricken from the limbs of the toiling slave, few names will be more gratefully remembered than that of SAMUEL LEWIS.

3. He was an humble, devoted Christian. This is his chiefest praise. This at once stamps him as the noblest and highest style of man. It may be doubted whether his natural earnestness, sincerity and energy of character, would have sustained him in all the trials and persecutions to which he was exposed had the power of high Christian principle been

wanting. But when to these natural traits was added the
constraining power of the love of Christ, a life of noble purpose and of great usefulness was the certain result. There
is nothing comparable to the influence of Christian principle
in nerving a human soul for the endurance of trial, or the
accomplishments of great ends. Amid the many allurements
of the world, adapted to turn men away from the path of
duty, it is the only safe and certain guide. It was to this
principle, no doubt, that the subject of this notice owed most
of his success.

The dispensation of God's providence, which has removed
him from the field, has its lessons for the living. They are
called by it to watchfulness and prayer, and to renewed consecration to the Christian work. They are taught that their
entire dependence is in God, and not in an arm of flesh.
And they are called to emulate the virtues of the deceased,
and follow his example in so far as he followed Christ.

" ULTRAISM."

There is no term more flippantly applied than this by men
of small minds to unpopular reforms. The changes are rung
upon it through all the notes of the gamut. Owl-faced conservatism, with its canting affectation of wisdom, mutters it
in solemn tones, when any curtailment of hoary abuses or
canonized wrongs is proposed. Pigmy politicians, whose
glory is to follow their leaders and do the bidding of their
party, prattle glibly of the ultraism of those who propose any
higher aim in politics than power and spoils. Lilliputian
divines, who live in the smiles of the titled dignitaries of the
Church, use this term as their mightiest argument against
those who " walk not with them " in sustaining the infallibility of their ecclesiastical organization. Ultraists are given
over, in their charitable judgment, to the " uncovenanted
mercies of God."

This term has been applied, in times and ways innumerable, to the opposers of slavery, drunkenness, Free Masonry,
war and other evils in this country. Being misunderstood,
it has become a term of reproach, and has, probably, served
to deter timid souls from the investigation and adoption of
right principles on these subjects. It is really a term of
honor. No man ever benefited his race by any great discov-

ery in science or art, or by the exhibition and defense of
great truths in morals and religion, without being counted an
ultraist by the men of his own generation. Ultraism. in any
one's estimation, is simply getting beyond himself. The term
is, therefore, entirely relative. The position which exposes
any man to this charge depends entirely on the ground occupied by those who make it. Sad, therefore, would it be for
men—sunk, as the mass of them have ever been, in ignorance
and error—if no one ever got beyond them in the investigation and discovery of truth. It is by raising up men to
explore the paths of truth and wisdom, and announce their
discoveries to the world, that God promotes the real progress
of the race. But those men are, from the nature and necessity of their vocation, ultraists to the men of their own times,
who fail to make the same advancements. And though the
progress of these discoveries may be but small, yet it is still
ultraism to those who make no progress at all, but who plod
on, from generation to generation, in the beaten path their
fathers trod before them.

The history of the world furnishes an illustrious catalogue
of ultraists. On it are enrolled the names of all the great
and good of past ages. When Moses and Aaron " agitated "
for the abolition of slavery in Egypt, their notions were
thought exceedingly ultra by Pharaoh and the Egyptians.
" Who is the Lord that I should obey him ? " was his indignant question. What new-fangled fanaticism have we
here? Has not *four hundred* years of legislation " *sanctioned
and sanctified* " the bondage of these Hebrews? Away with
such *ultraism*, I will not let the people go.

When the decree went forth from the King of Babylon that
no petition should be asked for thirty days of any god, save
of King Darius, the conduct of Daniel was exceedingly ultra.
Why could not he have drawn the curtains of his window
and prayed to his God in secret? Why could he not have
refrained from assuming the attitude of devotion? He
could still have prayed to his God in silent ejaculations.
What fanatical ultraism to expose himself to the fury of the
lions that were fasting to whet their appetites for blood.

When the image was set up in the plain of Dura, and the
people commanded to fall down and worship, it was ultraism
that kept the three young Hebrews erect. What need for
them to brave the wrath of the king about so trifling a
matter as falling down on their knees with the rest of the
crowd? Could they not embrace that as a time for prayer to

the God of heaven? Would not the intention sanctify the deed? Then what fanatical ultraism not to have the fear of the glowing furnace before their eyes.

Isaiah was deemed so ultra for commanding the Jews, in the name of the Lord, to "break every yoke and let the oppressed go free," that he was sawn asunder as the only cure for fanaticism. Jeremiah was repeatedly imprisoned, and punished in other ways, for his ultraism, in denouncing woe unto him that used his neighbor's service without wages, and gave him not for his work.

The Lord Jesus Christ was the very Prince of ultraists. When he denounced the Scribes and Pharisees as serpents and vipers, exposed to the damnation of hell—when he drove out the sacrilegious trafficers from the temple—when he called the Jews, who boasted of their freedom and of their descent from Abraham, the servants of sin, and the children of the Devil, his words and conduct were deemed intolerably ultra and fanatical. Not less so were some of his sayings deemed by his own disciples. When he pronounced blessings on the poor in spirit, when he exhorted to seek first the kingdom of God and his righteousness, and to have no thought for the morrow in regard to the things of this life; and when he assured his followers that it was easier for a camel to go through the eye of a needle than for a rich man to enter into the kingdom of heaven; so ultra were these things regarded, that even his disciples exclaimed in utter astonishment, "Who, then, can be saved!"

Examples of the same character multiply upon us when we come to the history of the apostles and martyrs. What ultraism to refuse to throw a handful of incense on the altar in the idol's temple, and to eat of the meat offered there in sacrifice? When commanded to speak no more in the name of Jesus, their declaration that they "ought to obey God rather than men," was thought then, and is now, the most ultra fanaticism. The rulers thought the "*peace and harmony*" of the nation endangered by such radical doctrines. The supremacy of the laws could not be maintained if such notions should prevail; nay, the very union of the (Jewish) States would be dissolved "if men should thus set up conscience above the Constitution and laws."

As with the apostles and the Saviour, so with the doctrines they taught. There are very plain and explicit precepts given in the sacred writings, which if *now* reduced to practice by members of any of the leading denominations of Christians,

will expose them to the imputation of the very folly of ultraism. For instance, the following: "Be not conformed to
this world, but be ye transformed by the renewing of your
minds, that ye may prove what is that good, and acceptable,
and perfect will of God." The world has its maxims and
fashions, and the man or woman who conforms not to these,
is at once set down as ultra and fanatical. Instances will
suggest themselves to every mind, and need not, therefore,
be specified. Another explicit command is, " I say unto you
that ye shall resist not evil, but whosoever shall smite thee on
thy right cheek turn to him the other also." Let this teaching be proclaimed now, and urged as a practical duty, and
lived out by its advocates, and at once they are denounced as
impracticable ultras; as promulging principles that will overturn all order, and all government.

Again: an express command of holy writ is, "Remember
those in bonds as bound with them." Let any one manifest
but a tithe of the zeal for the oppressed, that he would
feel if himself enslaved, and the English vocabulary is exhausted to stigmatize the ultraism of his conduct. The Bible
is full of passages which we could quote to the same effect,
but our limits do not admit it.

We hold it just as impossible for men to be too earnest in
the advocacy of truth, justice and right, as it is for men to be
too holy in their character and conduct. That truth may be
defended through wrong motives, and under the influence of
bad passions, is of course true. That men may be ultra in
wickedness is equally true. All sin—the least, (if there be
any least)—is ultra rebellion against God. We have used
the term only as it is commonly applied, in reference to the
advocacy and practice of truth. That men can ever say too
much, or do too much, for truth, and justice, and right, is
simply impossible.—Equally impossible is it to carry out
truth and righteousness too far in the practical duties of life.

Death of Henry Clay.

This long looked for event has at length transpired. Minute guns and tolling bells have proclaimed to the nation the
statesman's departure. Were the nation but wise it would
learn a solemn and impressive lesson in the event. That lesson however will not be learned in the fulsome adulation of
political admirers, or in the wholesale panegyrics of the pul-

pit and the so-called religious press. Nothing more dangerous to the morals of the young can issue from these sources
than the indiscriminate eulogy which is habitually meted out
to the worldly great, on their departure from this life. The
true moral of the life and death of a man like HENRY CLAY
is not learned in those high wrought funeral sermons and
orations which hold him up as a model of every political,
moral and social virtue. But in a calm contemplation of
the great object of such a life, in the contrast between what
it did accomplish and what it might have accomplished, and
in the view of its last reckoning at the bar of eternal justice,
there is a volume of rich and impressive instruction.

It teaches the vanity of mere worldly ambition. What
now are the honors of successful statesmanship, or the triumphs of his glorious powers of oratory to Henry Clay? If
rescued from oblivion his name will go to posterity as one of
the chief pillars of the worst system of wrong and oppression
that ever cursed the earth. Often in the day of their extrem-
ity has his clarion voice rallied the fainting cohorts of slavery
to a renewed and successful charge upon the hosts of freedom.
Now as the result of his efforts the dark pall of slavery is
settling down over millions of acres of territory until lately
free from its polluting touch. In the light of eternity as
these "works of his life do follow him," how must they appear
to the vision of the departed statesman?

In contrast with what he might have accomplished for God
and humanity, the actual results of a life like that of Clay
presents a saddening object of contemplation. Seldom have
his powers of oratory been equaled. But rarely has man
possessed the power to draw around him, and fascinate by the
spell of his social accomplishments such crowds of admiring
and devoted friends. With these qualities were combined an
iron energy and will and an unyielding firmness in defense of
his position. Had these glorious gifts been sanctified by the
Holy Spirit and consecrated to the service of God, what
unspeakably blessed and happy results would have followed!
Had the fires of genius been purified and fanned to a higher
glow by the coal that touched Isaiah's hallowed lips, what
clouds of moral darkness would have been dispelled by their
light. Had the battle-axe of truth ever been wielded by the
strong arm of the departed statesman, how many a frown-
ing Bastile of error would have been leveled in the dust.

For what have these glorious objects been sacrificed? For
the idle flattery of political admirers, and for the unrealized

hope of reaching the highest office in the gift of the people. Alas that so glorious a birthright should have been bartered for so mean a price.

During his long public career, though we admit that he has "done the State some service," truth compels us to say that he has also done it much injury. Of his connection with the pecuniary policy of the country, we need only remark, that he had the peculiar misfortune of living to see the death of almost every question of public policy of this nature which he took under his special protection. But it is the influence he exerted when the great question of freedom came up for action before the councils of the nation, with which the present and the future will have most to do in writing his history.

No period in the annals of the legislation of this country has possessed deeper interest than when Missouri applied for admission as one of the States of the Union. The pregnant question was then presented—shall this Government, formed to establish justice and secure the blessings of liberty, falter in its holy mission? The issue was watched with intense interest, and the hopes of the friends of humanity beat high, as indications were given that the right would triumph. But in an evil hour Henry Clay, summoning all the intellectual powers he possessed, threw his influence into the opposite scale, and gave the victory to the side of robbery and wrong. The result was that Missouri was admitted with a Constitution making human slavery perpetual; and we may add that this triumph of the slave power did more, probably, to paralyze the efforts of the friends of freedom in this country than any other single act since the foundation of the Union.

The next issue presented was the terms of the admission of Arkansas. When that State presented her Constitution for acceptance on the part of Congress, an amendment was offered providing for the emancipation of all the slaves within her bounds at a given time. This amendment was defeated by the casting vote of Mr. Clay, and slavery was thus left to curse the soil of Arkansas.

We need hardly say that to Mr. Clay, more than to any other individual, is the country indebted for the series of acts known as the Compromise Measures of 1850. It has been stated by his physician that the labor he bestowed and the anxiety he felt, when these measures were before Congress, did much to shorten his life. We need not here analyze those measures—they have been fully discussed, and are now fresh in the public mind.

These, then, are some of the most important measures in which Mr. Clay acted a conspicuous part, and they will tell more upon the character of the country than any others. Those who approve of them, will of course feel prepared to laud his memory for the part he acted in them. Not being of that class, we dissent in this particular. He has gone, however, from the scene of his earthly labors, to appear before the Judge of all; and it is said by those who were with him as his confidential friends during his last illness, that he looked forward with calmness to the hour of his departure, expressing the hope that he was prepared to meet the great change.

We would speak no evil of the dead. Let the veil of oblivion be drawn over his vices, and let his soul be left in the hands of a just and merciful God. But let not the fulsome eulogies of a venal press and a hireling pulpit drown the voice of solemn warning and instruction that speaks in his life and death.

Jesus Christ Driven from the United States.

The Bible represents believers as "one with Christ." They draw their spiritual life from him, and live in him as *part of himself*. "I am the vine, ye are the branches." Christ is the head, believers are the members; for says the apostle, "We are members of his body, of his flesh, and of his bones." Hence the Lord Jesus Christ regards things done to his children as done to himself. This is repeatedly and explicitly taught in the Scriptures. At the final judgment the righteous are rewarded because they ministered to Jesus when sick and in prison, when a stranger and when suffering hunger and thirst. When they inquire when they saw him in want and relieved him, he says, "Inasmuch as ye did it to one of the least of these my brethren ye did it unto me." The wicked are condemned for withholding this assistance; and in answer to their inquiry it is said, "inasmuch as ye did it not to the least of these my brethren ye did it not to me." When Saul of Tarsus was on his way to Damascus, the question that arrested him was "Saul, Saul, why persecutest thou me." In reply to his question "Who art thou Lord," it was said, "I am Jesus whom thou persecutest." But it was not Jesus in person that Saul persecuted, for he was then in heaven, but it was Jesus in the person of his disciples. This is a plain and unquestionable principle. Let us look at some recent facts in the light of it.

By the passage of the Fugitive Slave Bill large numbers of professing Christians have been driven from the United States. One hundred and thirty members from the Baptist (colored) church of Buffalo, left for Canada. A large number went from the Methodist (colored) church of the same place. One hundred and twelve members of the Baptist (colored) church of Rochester, including their pastor, a native Kentuckian and a fugitive, were driven off. From the colored church of the same denomination in Detroit eighty-four members fled. Many others have gone from other places. All these were forced to flee, contrary to their wishes and interests, by an enactment of the American Congress. Among these professors of religion are no doubt many real Christians. They belong to that class to which in especial manner "pertain the promises," for " hath not God chosen the *poor of this world*, rich in faith, and heirs of the kingdom which he hath promised to them that love him." Every true Christian among them is really and spiritually "one with Christ" —in fact a part of the Saviour. In the person of every one of these, therefore, has the Lord Jesus Christ been driven, by violence, from the United States.

The question here arises who is guilty of this fearful crime? —a crime no whit less than that of nailing Jesus to the cross, and mocking his dying agonies. To this question there can be but one answer. The authors and supporters of the fugitive slave bill are the men. And these include not merely the evil Congress that enacted it, and the parties by which they were elected, *but the mass of the large denominations of professing Christians in the country*, with one or two exceptions. Look at facts. The vast majority of professors of religion belong to the Whig and Democratic parties, by which the fugitive slave bill was enacted. They, therefore, voted for the men by whom it was passed. Being done by their agents, therefore, it was done by themselves. Again : the leading doctors and ministers of these churches have come out in justification, or extenuation of the bill, and in opposition to its repeal. Large ecclesiastical courts of these bodies, after discussing the matter for days, refused to express the slightest opposition to it, and recommended obedience to its provisions. These facts are notorious and unquestionable.

Again : the man who advocates a principle or supports a

measure, is individually guilty of all the evils flowing naturally from that principle or measure. If I deny the existence of God, and the truth of the Scriptures, I am guilty of all the evils flowing from the atheism and infidelity I advocate. If others proclaim the same doctrine, their guilt is just the same as mine. Crime does not divide into fractional portions, so that each of twenty millions, that commit a single murder, is one twenty-millionth of a murderer. There are in such a case twenty millions of full-sized murderers. In the light of this principle, then, we see that every church which by silent acquiescence or avowed defense, upholds the fugitive bill, is guilty of all the wrongs and crimes flowing from it. Among these crimes is the forcible expulsion of the Lord Jesus Christ from the territories of the United States. We defy the world to successfully controvert this conclusion. The *Lord Jesus Christ, in the person of his poor disciples, has been driven from the United States by his own professed churches.*

The conclusion just stated would seem to throw considerable light on the mooted question, whether these churches are really churches of Christ. Are churches which drive the Saviour from the country, through the fugitive slave bill which they uphold, the churches of Christ? With just as much propriety might we ask, were the Scribes and Pharisees who crucified the Saviour his disciples?

It seems to us high time that the advocates of secession from slaveholding and slave-catching churches, should cease admitting that these are churches of Christ. This *may* be the fact, but it is not a fact to be assumed on one side and conceded on the other. The evidence at this day is *prima facie* against it. Facts like those adverted to above, and many others, are fearfully against the claim of the leading sects of this country to be the churches of Christ. It can, therefore, only be admitted on evidence of the most direct and unquestionable character.

But it may be said that a part of these churches protest against and oppose the fugitive bill, and similar abominations. This is true, but these protesters are not the churches to which they belong, but on the contrary a despised and insignificant minority. Their number is becoming every year less, and their voice of remonstrance more feeble. Their principles and measures are utterly repudiated by the vast majority in the churches to which they belong. The claim, therefore, that these churches are not apostate, because a few oppose the reigning policy and practice of the church, would apply with equal force to the apostate Church of Rome. God has doubtless "a people" in her communion, but that fact makes her none the less "the Mother of Harlots." Yet what has Rome ever sanctioned worse than the fugitive slave bill? What has she ever *done* that was worse than expelling the Lord Jesus Christ from the country?

Is it Consistent for Free Presbyterians to Commune with Churches which Fellowship Slavery?

This question has been submitted to us by a brother. We answer it by asking another: Is it consistent for a man, after signing a total abstinence pledge, to tipple occasionally? Or for a "penitent thief," after professing reformation, to pilfer on occasions? The very ground on which Free Presbyterians left the communion of the Old and New School Presbyterian Churches, was that membership in those churches involved them in the guilt of religious fellowship with slaveholders. The Presbyterian theory of the Church is that it is a unit, that each particular congregation is a part of one body which is made up of all the several congregations comprised in its communion. It follows that a communion table spread in an Old or New School Church in Ohio, has an end stretching into Georgia and South Carolina, and that he who takes his seat at the Ohio end, acknowledges as a Christian brother him who sits at the Georgia end.

This theoretical unity is made visible to the world in the Synods and General Assemblies of these churches. In these ecclesiastical gatherings the representatives of the churches from all parts of the Union meet together. The slaveholder from Alabama, who openly and defiantly affirms that he " buys, sells and holds his fellow-beings for gain," takes his seat at the council board and around the communion table with the Abolitionist from Wisconsin, who holds with the General Assembly of 1798, that "slaveholding is the highest kind of theft, and the slaveholder a sinner of the first rank." As these churches jog now, these antipodes meet, shake hands, sit down in council together, take their place side by side at the Lord's Supper, while the infidel world looks on and beholding this attempted fellowship of Christ with Belial, sneeringly exclaims, " Behold how good and how pleasant it is for brethren to dwell together in unity ! "

Now this communion, thus rendered visible, extends to all the members of the Presbyterian Church. These Synods and General Assemblies are representative bodies, and their constituents are all the members of the church,—men, women and children. Every member of the church, therefore, is in the closest possible religious fellowship with every other. Hence we repeat, the act of communing with a local Old or New School Presbyterian church in a free State, is an act of fellowship with the whole church, including their thousands of slaveholders. For a Free Presbyterian to do this is to commit the very sin of holding religious fellowship with slaveholders, to get free from which was the very object of seceding from those churches and organizing a separate ecclesiastical body. Such Free Presbyterians had a great deal better stayed in their former connection.

We have known a very few nominal Free Presbyterians—men molded after the fashion of Ephraim of old—who from the very hour of their deliverance from their spiritual Egypt, were seized with a strange hankering after its leeks and onions, and flesh pots. They would go still to the communion of the church they had left, thus stultifying themselves, causing the enemy to rejoice, and weakening the testimony of their brethren. We had the conduct of one of these half-baked professors once brought up in argument by a venerable doctor of divinity now dead, to prove that Free Presbyterians acted inconsistently with their profession. We could only reply that the man was an exception to the generality of the members of our church, and *was* acting most inconsistently. From *such* members may the good Lord in mercy deliver all our churches.

These men of course have the privilege of remaining in the fellowship of the slaveholding churches. But they have no moral right to leave the communion of these churches, unite with those who are free from fellowship with that unfruitful work of darkness, slavery, and then go back to their former connection. By such a course they convict themselves of folly and inconsistency, and bring weakness and reproach on those who are testifying against the sin of holding religious fellowship with slavery.

RADICAL AND CONSERVATIVE.

It has become the fashion of the hunker presses and preachers in this country to represent the principles expressed by these terms as the opposites of each other, and to apply the first term to reformers as a term of reproach, and the second to themselves as a term of praise. But there is no opposition between true radicalism and true conservatism, while there is a very wide difference between the latter and hunkerism. Genuine radicalism is laying the ax at the root of evils, while true conservatism is holding fast that which is good. The one therefore is the complement of the other. The most ultra radical may be the truest conservative. The best, and indeed the *only* way of preserving what is good, is to root out the opposing evil.

This is true of individuals, and true of society. The love of falsehood must be eradicated from the mind before the truth can be implanted and cherished. The ax must be laid at the root of selfishness, lust, pride and hatred, before the graces of benevolence, purity, humility and love can grow in the soul. He who would preserve his soul from sin and ruin must abhor and root out that which is evil, and cleave to that which is good.

So, also, in society. Evil and good, light and darkness, justice and injustice, peace and discord, can not co-exist. Neither can opposing laws, customs and institutions exist and operate in harmony. The good and the bad are destructive of each other, and one must finally prevail to the extinction of the other. Hence the truest conservatism of good is in seeking the most speedy and thorough eradication of the bad. It follows that genuine radicalism and conservatism instead of opposing, co-operate harmoniously together.

On the contrary there is not only a wide difference, but oftentimes a total antagonism between true conservatism and hunkerism. While the former will preserve only what is good, the latter will maintain the existing order of things, whether good or bad, simply because it *is* the existing order of things. Its motto is the atheistic sentiment, " Whatever is, is right." Whatever is received and established as law and custom, it will preserve whether right or wrong. Hence it often comes to pass that the hunker will at one time defend with the utmost obstinacy, laws and customs which at other times he has most bitterly opposed. True to his one idea of resisting all change and all reform, he is a bundle of contradictions. Consistency with his ruling principle leads him into endless inconsistency. With him the destructive radicalism of to-day, is the object of his intensest conservatism to-morrow.

True conservatism has nothing in common with such a

spirit as this. It is not in haste to adopt proposed changes, for in its vocabulary change and reform are not synonymous terms. Neither is it doggedly bent on maintaining established laws and institutions, simply because they *are* established. But examining carefully into first principles, it accepts what is good and rejects what is evil. It "proves all things, and holds fast that which is good."

It is evident from these principles, that those in this country who are laboring to abolish slavery, both in Church and State, are the true conservatives; while the politicians and Drs. of Divinity who seek to maintain that system are radicals of the worst and most dangerous character. Both slavery and freedom have been "proved" by their fruits—the one to be the prolific parent of every conceivable crime and abomination, the other to be the source of numberless blessings. The abolitionists see that the only way to hold fast the latter is to abolish the former. Both can not exist. They are in utter and deadly antagonism. If slavery lives freedom must die. Hence it follows that he who is truly conservative of liberty is radically destructive of slavery. The radicalism that lays the ax to the root of this upas of oppression, is near akin to the conservatism that would water and cherish the tree of liberty.

SCHISM.

SCHISM, in the Church, stands opposed to Unity, and signifies division. On no subject do more confused and mistaken notions prevail. Very many members of the church, and preachers too, who pass for intelligent men, think that schism is nothing else than leaving a visible church organization. If this were correct then all Protestants are schismatics; for all the various sects among them are secessions, more or less remote, from the visible organizations of the Catholic Church. Nay, Christianity itself is schism, for the Lord Jesus Christ and his apostles left the Jewish Church organization, and formed the Christian Church. Christ having solemnly excommunicated the Jews when he said, "The kingdom of God shall be taken from you, and given to a nation bringing forth the fruits of righteousness," afterward, on the night preceding his betrayal, organized his immediate followers in the Christian Church, and thus, without being excommunicated, seceded from that visible church organization. Thus, this notion of schism, if true, would unchurch the very men themselves who hold it.

Another class hold those schismatics who proclaim the whole counsel of God, when a portion of a professed church reject portions of it : and urge discipline for sins which have become popular and prevalent. That this course will often divide, and even break up professed churches, is certain. It is not therefore schism, however. The church that is divided by preaching the whole truth of God, is necessarily, in part or in whole, apostate. The church that can not bear the whole truth on every subject, is living in practical rebellion. It is therefore nonsense to say, that dividing such a church is causing division in the body of Christ, for it forms no part of his mystical body.

Schism may exist in a church, which yet retains an external appearance of unity. Outward union and inward discord are found often together. Paul says to the Corinthian church, " I hear that there be divisions among you, and I partly believe it." The word translated divisions is, *scismata*, the Greek for schism. That this would be a correct translation all scholars admit. Here while no secessions were taking place, there was divisions or schisms among the members of the church of-Corinth. Indeed, schisms of the very worst description have been most common in the Church, when outward union of organization was most compact. The Jews were schismatic every time they turned aside to the worship of idols. When most devoted to religious forms and ceremonies they were guilty of causing wicked divisions. They even made those religious exercises the occasion of such divisions. " Behold," says God, " ye fast for *strife* and *debate*, and to smite with the fist of wickedness." When they rejected the messengers of God, " killed the prophets and stoned those that were sent unto them," they were yet visibly organized into one church. The word of God through the prophets, by stirring up their rebellious passions, occasioned strife and divisions. On the principle of many modern interpreters these prophets were schismatics. They " caused divisions," by denouncing popular sins, such as oppression and cruelty. Yet the Jews who practiced these wrongs, were the true schismatics ; while the prophets who faithfully proclaim God's will were doing what could alone produce true unity.

This point may be illustrated in a simple way. Suppose a father to lay down right and proper rules for the government of his family. He leaves his house for awhile, and on leaving commands his children to obey during his absence, the laws of the household. The children, however, all find a strong propensity to do something the father has forbidden. In his absence they fall into these practices, and all agree that they will disobey the father. Now there may be perfect unity, of a certain kind, in that family. The children all agree that it is necessary to their peace and quiet that some of the father's just commands should be violated. Is this a righteous unity? Is it honorable to the father? Suppose further, that one or more of the children become convinced of the wickedness of their conduct and resolve to reform. They begin to remonstrate with the other members of the family, on account of their disobedience. At once the cry of *schism* is raised by the offenders. They gravely assert that the peace and prosperity of the family imperatively demand, that all such " distracting subjects" as that of filial obedience, ought not to be agitated. It is easy to see in this case who are in the wrong and who in the right. It is also obvious, that it is the duty of the repentant children to rebuke the others, and urge them to change their course, even if the entire disruption of the family should be the result.

This case illustrates several points. The Church of God is his spiritual family. Now a peace in that Church, which is founded on open or tacit agreement to disregard some of his commands, is a false peace. It is most dishonorable to God, and must prove ruinous to man. It is also evident that it is the duty of all God's obedient children to urge his claims to the obedience of all ; and especially to denounce and warn against those particular acts of disobedience that are most prevalent.

Now, whenever it is necessary to the peace of a church that anti-slavery truth, or truth bearing on the subject of temperance, must not be preached, then that peace is spurious and false. Those who talk of it " cry peace, peace, when there is no peace." God's express command is, to "open the mouth of the dumb, and plead the cause of the poor and needy." Every professed Christian, minister or layman, who neglects this command, who does not plead the cause of the slave, the poorest of all God's poor, is guilty of disobeying his Heavenly Father. Hence, as in the case of the family, it is better that such a church should be broken up entirely than continue a union founded on open breach of God's command.

Again : it is evident in such a case that the real schismatics are not those who obey God's command to plead for the poor, but those who reject the truth, and refuse to do likewise. It is not in such a case a question of numbers. If there were ten disobedient and one obedient child in a family, that one child would be the only one entitled to a place in the father's household. The others by their disobedience cut themselves off from the name and privileges of children. So in the Church—God's spiritual family. If but ten obey God's command to plead for the poor, as well as all other commands, and ten thousand disobey it, those ten are God's true family, his true Church. If cast out for their faithfulness, or withdrawing to avoid participation in the disobedience of the majority, God still owns them as his true spiritual household.

There are then but two ways of committing the sin of schism ; one is by disobeying the laws of God in the Church : the other by withdrawing from any branch of the visible church without a sufficient reason. An example of the first is found in every member of the church that does not labor and pray, and do all in his power for the deliverance of the slave. God's express command to all his professed children is, " Remember those in bonds, *as bound with them.*" That is feel and act and pray for the oppressed the same as you would if you were yourself in bondage ; or do for them as you would wish others to do for you in that condition. Now, true unity among God's followers, consists very much in a cheerful, affectionate obedience to his will, therefore to habitually break this command by doing and feeling nothing for those in bonds, is directly destroying the unity of the Church ; and is schism of the very worst description.

In regard to withdrawal from any professed church, if the toleration and practice of the " sum of all villainies " in such church is not just cause of secession, then there never can be such cause. If the churches of this land, should search for a system of crime for the express purpose of apostatizing. through its reception to their communion they could find none so bad as slavery which they *have* thus received. Their cordial welcome of those practicing this " most atrocious of all institutions " to their communion tables, is schismatical to the last degree. It follows that the course of those churches, which have excluded these criminals from their communion, is to the same extent promotive of the real unity of the Church.

10

CHRISTIAN UNION.

This subject is just now occupying a large share of the attention of various churches. This fact is our apology, if any apology is needed, for the space we devote to it. On our first page will be found a discussion on this question in the General Synod of the Reformed Presbyterian, or New Side Covenanter Church.—The same subject occupied the largest portion of the time of the Associate, or Seceder Synod, which met a week or two since, in Xenia. The conclusions at which they arrived, will be found in another place, and indicate a decided advance in the right direction. The Union of the Associate Reformed, Seceder and N. S. Covenanter Churches, appears to us far more likely to be accomplished now, than it has ever seemed before. The bigots in these bodies may succeed in delaying the consummation, but it is sure to come ere long.

A proposal for the union of the Reformed Presbyterians and the Free Presbyterian Church of Canada, is now under discussion in that province, and some late indications are promising. Of the proposed union between the United Brethren in Christ, Wesleyan Methodists, and Evangelical Association, our readers are already informed.

These various movements toward the same point, are full of significance. In the first place, they are without concert. Each is impelled forward in this movement by a power within itself. It is not the result of a concerted and previously arranged plan. Hence, it is manifest that the hand of God is in it. There can be no doubt in the mind of the Christian that these various churches are moved upon by the Spirit of God; and that the desire for union is his suggestion. How else can we account for the fact that churches having no outward fellowship with each other, and which are supposed to be widely apart in doctrine and order, should simultaneously and without consultation, start forward with zeal and energy in the holy work of gathering into one the scattered fragments of the Saviour's family?

Another significant fact is that this movement is confined to the anti-slavery churches of this country. Among the pro-slavery churches the tendency is toward wider division. The New School Presbyterians and Congregationalists are getting further apart every day. Each of these denominations has been seized of late with an intense sectarian spirit, which is the very essence of the spirit of disunion. The Old and

New School Presbyterians are more completely at arm's length to-day than they have been since the excision of 1837. The Methodist Church has divided once, and there are symptoms of a second rupture in the Northern branch, growing out of the efforts of the living piety within it, to throw off the dead carcass of slavery. But among the churches which exclude slaveholding and its kindred evils, this simultaneous. movement for closer union has commenced, and the spirit of unity and brotherly love is becoming more and more prevalent. Now this fact certainly means something, and we think it is not difficult to read its significance. An anti-slavery religion can alone save the world, for no other religion is Christianity. A pro-slavery religion is the religion of hell, and to call it Christianity is to blaspheme the Son of God. The Church is the agency appointed by Christ for preaching and extending his gospel over the earth. To do this successfully, she must be a united church. This is clearly implied in the prayer of the Saviour, John xvii : 20, 21. Again, the time for the universal establishment of the kingdom of Christ on earth is near at hand. All interpreters of prophesy agree in this. The time of the birth of the Saviour was not more clearly foretold, than the time of the destruction of the Man of Sin, and all antichristian powers, and the establishment of the Redeemer's reign; and upon this time we are just verging. But the only church that he can use as an instrument for this work, is a church which embraces his religion, which is a religion at war with slavery in all its forms, at war with drunkenness, secresy, popery, and every system of darkness and oppression. Is it then presumptuous to conclude that God is bringing the churches which embody this religion, into one, in order to use them as his instrument for the triumphant establishment of his kingdom of righteousness on earth?

We may be sneeringly asked at this point, if we mean to teach that to the comparatively small band of anti-slavery Christians alone will be committed the mighty work of propagating the gospel over the earth; and if no use will be made of the Christians in the large and popular church organizations of this country?—We mean nothing of the kind. We have never doubted that the Lord has thousands of his own blood-bought people in the slaveholding churches of this land, and we have no doubt that he will use them as honored instruments for the establishment of his kingdom. But we have just as little doubt that he will bring them out of their pro-slavery church organizations, before they will be made largely useful in this work. These organizations are anti-christian. An organization, whether ecclesiastical or political, which supports slavery, is of *necessity* antichristian, for slavery in its every element is anti-Christ. Hence, before the Saviour's reign on earth can become universal, these organizations must be destroyed, just as the Roman Catholic hierarchy must be destroyed. But the Lord's people in these corrupt bodies will be brought out, and united with those already out in one mighty phalanx, for the last and triumphant onset upon the kingdom of the Devil.

This thought suggests another mighty reason for the union of the anti-slavery reforming churches of the land. United, their power to break up the antichristian, pro-slavery church organizations of the country, would be ten-fold what it is now; and, united, their moral power would irresistibly draw the pure members of these corrupt churches to themselves. There will be a moral power and grandeur in the spectacle of all the reformed and reforming churches of this land, laying aside the shibboleths that have heretofore divided them, and coming together on the foundation of Christian purity, and in the spirit of Christian love, which would be irresistible. Before the combined influence of this host made mighty through the living God, the huge ecclesiastical structures which constitute the bulwark of American slavery would be broken in pieces, and all the living, spiritual stones in them would be gathered together and builded into this new and holy temple of the Lord.

The effect of all this on the conversion of the world, opens a theme so vast and grand that we can hardly trust our pen to touch upon it. Emancipated from their bonds, as the slaves would then soon be, educated and Christianized, they would become missionaries to the land of their fathers; and through their instrumentality, "Ethiopia would soon stretch forth her hands unto God." The religion of this country, cut free from the incubus that has hitherto weighed it to the dust, and with the warm, fresh blood of freedom in its veins, would start forward anew in the missionary work, with an energy and success that would find their only parallel in the Apostolic times.

If we have read aright the indications of God's providence in the union movements of our day, it follows irresistibly that those who oppose these movements are planting themselves directly athwart the path of the Divine purposes and operations. A fearful responsibility is theirs!

UNITY OF THE CHURCH.

The unity of the Church is its *oneness*. The Lord Jesus Christ distinctly intimated that his Church should be one :

"That they all may be one ; as thou, Father, *art* in me, and I in thee, that they also may be one in us ; that the world may believe that thou has sent me.

" And the glory which thou gavest me I have given them ; that they may be one, even as we are one.

" I in them, and thou in me, that they may be made perfect in one ; and that the world may know that thou hast sent me, and hast loved them as thou hast loved me."—John 17 : 20—23.

The Church of Christ is his appointed instrumentality for the salvation of the world. Its power as such depends on its unity. Its union is its strength. It is, therefore, very important to know wherein this unity consists; how it is destroyed and how it may be promoted.

The oneness of the Church does not imply that all its members are exactly equal in bodily and mental power; that they shall be equally learned and wise; follow the same calling in life, and believe exactly alike on all scientific, political or historical questions. These are simple impossibilities in this world. Again : it is not essential to the true unity of the Church that all its members should believe exactly alike on all religious subjects; that they have the same spiritual gifts, and possess in equal measure the power of the Holy Ghost. Diversities of mental structure are the work of God, and so long as these exist, men will differ in their modes of thought and expression, in the views they take of various questions, and also in their religious experience and exercises. A vast variety in all these is consistent with the highest degree of Scriptural unity. "For there are diversities of gifts, but the same spirit. And there are differences of administrations, but the same Lord. And there are diversities of operations; but it is the same God that worketh all in all."

Wherein, then, *does* the unity of the Church, or the oneness of believers consist?

1. In the harmonious blending of these various "diversities" in one body. Instead of causing divisions, these differences of character, gifts, etc., are designed to produce the directly contrary effect. They are all essential to a perfect church, just as all the members are necessary to a perfect body. This is the figure of the apostle: "For as we have many members in one body, and all members have not the same office, so we being many are one body in Christ." These varied gifts and characteristics fit the members of the Church of Christ for the different posts of labor in the Church. Through them believers are fitted to encourage, strengthen, aid and comfort each other. The lofty courage of one blends with the timid gentleness of another, and by the mutual union both are benefited. The ardent hopes of one preserves others from despair, while the humble fears of the latter saves the former from presumption. Thus are the members of the Church fitted "to bear each others burdens, and so fulfil the law of Christ." - So, also, are the followers of Christ fitted for the various duties connected with the propagation of the gospel. As in its first proclamation, the daring courage of Peter, the loving gentleness of John, and the iron energy of Paul were all required, and all answered their end ; so now the various gifts of Christians are all to be brought and consecrated on the altar of the Saviour. And when each one comes forward to do the work for which God has fitted him, and as one united host the Church moves on in the strength of this union, the triumph of the cause of Christ will not be distant. Unity amid diversity is universal among the works of God, and of this, such a church will be a beautiful example.

2. A second thing essential to the unity of the Church, is the belief of all its members in the fundamental truths of the Bible. While opinions may differ as to what are and are not essential truths, every one will admit that the belief of *some* truths is necessary to make men Christians. For instance, they must believe that such a person as Jesus Christ lived, taught, wrought miracles, was crucified, rose from the grave and ascended to heaven. Christianity is revealed in the Old and New Testaments. To deny these as authentic and true histories of real events, renders it impossible for him who denies to be a Christian ; just as the man who should deny the history of Mohammed and the truth of the Koran could not be a Mohammedan. The belief of all the essential truths and doctrines of the Bible is, therefore, necessary

among other things to constitute men Christians. In this oneness of belief is found another element of the true unity of the Church. The power of a belief in the same truths to unite men together is every where seen, especially when those truths are of great practical interest and importance, which is eminently the case with the truths of the Christian religion. This is one important link in the chain that binds together the various religious sects in the world. Hindoos, Mohammedans, Catholics and the various sects of Protestants, unite together in consequence of holding the same belief on the essential points of their religion. The same is true in political and other voluntary associations. The bond of union is a common belief in certain truths. Hence a lively faith in the essential truths of the Christian religion will draw believers into intimate union and fellowship, and make them one in Christ.

3. A third essential element in the unity of the Church is a oneness of aim among all its members. The great object of life is with all true Christians essentially one—the promotion of God's glory—through and by the advancement of their own and neighbor's highest temporal and spiritual welfare. Though the temporal callings in life of Christians are as various as among the men of the world, yet with true believers those callings are only means to a common end. In the pursuit of this one great object there is no jealous rivalry, and no disappointment. The success of one is the success of all, as all harmoniously co-operate together. Now this unity of purpose and aim begets a oneness of feeling and desire. By a law of our mental constitution, it binds together in closest bonds all that truly love the Saviour, and thus " they being many are one body in Christ."

4. Again, the Church of God is one, as subject to the same king and head, and governed by the same code of laws. Christ is " head over all things to the Church." He has given her a perfect code of laws in the Bible, and by those laws each and all of the true members of the Church are governed. They are thus one community, one nation, one kingdom, one family. In the kingdom of God, there is no forced submission to the government of a king, and code of laws which the subjects hate. It is a joyful and ennobling obedience to a government which they love. Thus the king and laws of the Church are a bond of union among its members of the strongest kind.

5. Once more: the true members of Christ's Church are

essentially one in character. The elements of Christian character are in all the same. It is character by which the followers of Christ are distinguished from the rest of men. They have been "transformed by the renewing of their minds;" "changed into the image and likeness of God." Through the principle that "like seeks its like," the true disciples of Christ unite together in closest unity.

Thus is the true Church of the Lord Jesus one body, one in faith, one in aim and purpose, subject to one king and law; one in character, spirit, feeling, desire; having the same hopes and fears, joys and sorrows, and the same eternal home in prospect.

From these principles important conclusions follow. Outward, visible unity to be lasting and profitable, must be founded on this inward unity of faith and character. Hence the way to promote it is not through Evangelical Alliances, to patch up an outward union of incongruous elements: but by proclaiming in all its fullness the word and law of God; submitting ourselves to its power; and laboring to bring all others to the love and obedience of Christ.

Another conclusion is that the unity of the Church is violated, not by proclaiming the whole counsel of God, and exercising discipline on *all* offenders, but by the contrary. By suppressing the truth, admitting known transgressors to the Church, under the plea of reforming them there, refusing to exercise discipline on open, acknowledged sinners, and thus throwing the doors of the church open to those influences which will not only mar its unity but destroy its very existence. Christ, as King in Zion, merits and claims implicit obedience to the laws of his Church. The known and willful transgressor of those laws, therefore, unfits himself for membership in that Church. To retain him in her communion is, therefore, in direct contravention of the law and will of Christ; and, therefore, destructive of all true unity.

When the Church of Christ shall (as she will) become really one; when one in faith and purpose, in obedience and character; she devotes herself in her combined energy to the glorious and benevolent work entrusted to her by her head, the triumph of his truth on earth—the downfall of all oppression and crime, and violence and every form of evil, will speedily follow. Her true union, will give her a strength which earth and hell will in vain oppose.

SOUTHERN REVIVALS.

The following item is circulating in the papers:

The Editor of the *Western Christian Advocate* says—"We have the following on authority that admits of no questioning: Recently in a town of a certain slave State, a revival took place in the church under the charge of the Rev. Mr. ————. During the meeting a slave-trader *professed* conversion, and joined the church, and a local preacher became much encouraged thereat. Soon after the close of the meeting, the slave-trader made a purchase from the local preacher of a slave woman, who had a child at her breast. The trader not wishing the child, and the mother refusing to go without it, strong cords were obtained. A dray was sent for, she was tied hands and feet, and was carried by main force, and strapped down to the dray, and was thus driven off."

Our exchanges, from time to time, contain accounts of "revivals of religion" in Southern slaveholding churches. These revivals are held up as evidence that God has not forsaken those churches, and that therefore Christians in the North should not forsake them. We never publish these accounts, because we have no faith in the genuineness of these revivals. We find no evidence at all that those who are the subjects of them are in the least degree changed in their character and conduct. They continue to rob and oppress the poor, just as before. As the foregoing item shows, they are just as cruel as ever. They can tear the tender infant from the mother, just as ruthlessly as they were wont to do before they professed conversion. Indeed, the evidence we have in the case, goes to show that the subjects of these revivals are generally made worse instead of better, and it is in accordance with the philosophy of human nature, and with the teachings of the Bible, that this should be the case.

All men have some ground on which they base a hope of happiness in a future existence. Very often the "men of the world," as they are called, place their hope in their natural humanity and justice. Hence it is their religion to "do justly and love mercy," so far as they conveniently can. But as the gospel of Jesus Christ is preached in many places, in these modern days, it is made the minister of sin. A free pardon, through the blood of Christ is proclaimed, and men are taught that if they rely on Christ alone for justification, then salvation is secure. The teaching of the Bible that sanctification is the necessary accompaniment of justification, is not so presented as to awaken and alarm the conscience. Without any real, radical change of heart, the convert settles down into a false and carnal security, and with a conscience at rest for the future, feels at liberty to indulge his wicked propensities to the full, for the present. In the practice of that guilty abuse of the doctrine of justification by faith, which the Apostle Paul so pointedly condemns, he "continues in sin that grace may abound." The parallel to these conversions is found in a passage from the sayings of Jesus Christ: "Woe unto you Scribes and Pharisees, hypocrites! for ye compass sea and land to make one proselyte, and when he is made, ye make him *two-fold more the child of hell than yourselves.*"

We believe in genuine revivals of religion—revivals which stir the conscience of the sinner to its profoundest depths; which bring him an humbled, heart-broken penitent to the foot of the cross, and then send him out to the world a pardoned and sanctified soul, to lead a life of holiness and true benevolence. But those "revivals" in which loud shouting is received as the evidence of conversion, and from which the "convert" goes out to "tear the mother from her babe, and chain her to a dray," are the Devil's own peculiar work.

Revival Excitements.

The long article on this subject which will be found in to-day's paper, we publish by request. We suppose it is intended as a reply to our article headed "The Religion that Saves," published two weeks ago. But as a reply to that article, it strikes wide of the mark, for we have never opposed genuine revivals of religion, but on the contrary have ever taught that they were the great need of the world. We think that the "Old Carmelite" was a very stupid old fogy. But we think also that the scenes sometimes witnessed in what are called modern revivals, bear a much closer resemblance to the frantic ravings of the priests of Baal on Mt. Carmel, than they do to the calm but intensely earnest prayer of Elijah. From the immense force of lungs that is often expended in the prayers heard at these revivals, we have sometimes thought that the suppliants must believe that the God to whom they were addressed, was "either talking, or pursuing, or on a journey, or peradventure asleep and must be awaked." There is very often a fallacy in illustrations of spiritual things drawn from material objects. Thus, in the article in question, the comparison of the influences of revivals to rain, would prove that all revivals are genuine, because rain is always rain, whether it flows in gentle showers or in overflowing torrents. But the most enthusiastic advocate of religious excitements will hardly contend that *every* such excitement is a genuine revival. All sorts of religion may be revived, and every kind of church has its revivals. Again, the smoke and fire anecdote, at the beginning of the article, is utterly absurd and fallacious. If a man must take part in every scene that he witnesses in order to judge correctly of its effects, we should find ourselves in a bad condition truly. A company of revelers, for instance, are indulging in scenes of drunken mirth. A looker-on reproves them for their sin and folly. Oh, you have got smoke in your eyes, say they, and can't see clearly; come down and partake with us of *spiritual* refreshment, and you will be able to see clearly. Must men become slaveholders, or gamblers, or Mormon polygamists, or pagan idolators, or Roman Catholics, before they can judge correctly of these various practices and systems? We do not wish to compare modern revival excitements to any of these things, but the anecdote proves as much in the one case as in the other; and proves just nothing in either. Then we would hope that modern revival prayers are not always mere "*smoke*," for every one knows that the greater the smoke the less the fire.

But passing by these things, we come to other matters. We have already remarked that any kind of religion may be revived, and that all sorts of churches have revivals. The Roman Catholic Church often has extensive revivals. We were in Wisconsin a few years ago, when a legate of the Pope, just from Rome, was visiting the churches. Revivals every where attended his labors. In a single town, after a protracted and excited meeting of three weeks, he received about eight hundred persons into his church. Mormonism often enjoys seasons of revival, during which large numbers are taken into that fold of adulterous "saints." No part of our country "enjoys" so many revival seasons as the South, and yet the "converts" do not keep "the fast which God has chosen." It is only a few weeks since we published an account from the leading Methodist paper of the North, of a Southern revival, in which a slaveholder and slave-trader were both "converted," and during which the former sold to the latter a mother, reserving to himself her infant child. The mother resisting their efforts to part her from her babe, a dray was procured, to which she was chained by the "converted" trader, after being forcibly torn from her infant, and driven away, uttering the most heart-rending cries of anguish. Now in all these cases, and many others which we might name, no one believes that these so-called revivals are the work of God's spirit. Hence, the mere fact of a church having a religious excitement, and bringing many to profess "conversion," and "indulge" a hope, proves nothing one way or the other. It only proves that the religion professed and practiced in that particular church has been revived. That religion may be Mormonism, Roman Catholicism, the religion of form and cant, or it may be genuine Christianity. The character of the religion and of the revival must be determined by another standard altogether.

We are then brought to another inquiry. *Is* the religion professed and practiced by the majority of the large popular Protestant churches in this country, the religion of Jesus Christ? Let us look into this question a little. The religion of these churches fellowships, and thereby sanctions American slavery. This assertion is so notoriously true, that we shall not stop to prove it. But American slavery is a system at deadly war in all points with Christianity. Never has there been a definition of the system so comprehensive and so literally true as that of the great founder of Methodism, JOHN WESLEY, "American slavery, the *sum* of *all* villainies." The mission of Jesus Christ was to *destroy* " all villainy." For this was he manifested that he might destroy the works of the Devil." Is that his religion which fellowships and sanctions the "sum of all villainies?"

Again, the popular religion of this country sanctions offensive war. A few years ago our government made a wanton and unprovoked attack upon a feeble neighboring nation. This government was the aggressor from beginning to end. The assertion of the President of the United States, on which the declaration of war was based, that " war existed by the act of Mexico; American blood having been shed upon American soil," was a deliberate and willful falsehood. But upon that falsehood war was declared and carried on, till the feeble Mexican Republic lay helpless at our feet, and a vast portion of her territory was wrested from her possession. There was guilt enough contracted by this country in that crusade to damn ten thousand worlds. But no sooner was it over, than the American people picked up from the blood and dust of its battle-fields one of its successful captains, and amid wild huzzas elevated him to the highest office in their gift. His *only* qualification for the office was his success in that murderous and infamous war. It was by that alone that he became known to the nation, and on the strength of the fame won in the work of human butchery was he elected to the highest office in the government. And the popular church of the land sanctioned the deed. Nineteen-twentieths of her members, we presume, voted for the successful commander, and joined with others in the wild acclamations amid which he was borne to the presidential chair. Four years later and both the leading candidates for this office were selected from those whose hands were dripping with the blood of this murderous crusade, and again voted for by the mass of those professing to be the followers of the Prince of Peace. Is that Christianity which thus does homage to the spirit of aggressive war, by honoring its successful captains?

Once more: Some thirty years ago freedom and slavery had a pitched battle in our national Congress. It was a time of intense excitement. Momentous consequences hung upon the issue. But the forces of freedom were worsted in the conflict. They made a "compromise" which was a hard bargain for freedom. But it secured the prohibition of slavery North of 36 deg. 30 min. A third of a century passed away. Slavery had possessed the lion's share which she gained by the compromise, without molestation. At the end of that period, with malice prepense, the bargain was deliberately and foully broken. With a degree of fraud, villainy and impudence that would disgrace a gang of pirates, a majority of the U. S. Congress tore down the barriers, that the overflowing scourge of slavery might sweep over vast portions of virgin and free soil, in the very heart of the continent. By this act the heathenism, licentiousness, cruelty, and all the matchless atrocities of slavery, are likely to be spread over vast regions that, under the magic touch of free labor, would bloom as the garden of God. We can not help believing that this was the Devil's work, and that those who did it, and those who *justified it when done,* were the Devil's servants. But the churches of our country claim a large number of these covenant-breakers as members "in good and regular standing." Some of them even desecrate the sacred desk as professed ministers of Christ. Is that Christ's religion which such men teach and practice? Are those *genuine revivals* which such men assist in getting up and carrying on? Yet we have heard of such "revivals" not a thousand miles from the spot where we write.

We have no space to multiply the proofs of the essentially antichristian character of the popular religion of this country. They *could* be multiplied a thousand fold. The religion of Christ says, "Love your enemies, do good to them that hate you and despitefully use you." The prevalent religion of the American people says, kill your enemies, and do honor to those who can destroy them most successfully. Christ denounced in terms of awful severity the rich, and powerful, and haughty sinners of his day; but spake in words of winning love and gentleness to the poor and lowly. The popular churches of this land reverse the order. They fawn upon and court the great and the guilty, but trample and scowl upon the poor. Christ declared that unless a man denied himself, and took up his cross and followed him, he could not be his disciple. But it is no cross to profess religion in any of the large denominations of this country, but on the contrary it is often a stepping-stone to wealth and respectability. But it is a pretty severe cross, as we have been learning for the last ten years, to expose the iniquities which find a safe nestling-place in their bosom. The true Church of Christ is the salt of the earth. But while the popular churches of this nation control, or might control public sentiment, the most abounding and alarming evils are sweeping almost unchecked over our land, notwithstanding these churches enjoy their yearly "revivals," and are constantly adding to their numbers and wealth and power. "By their fruits ye shall know them;" and until we see different fruits, we must be pardoned our want of faith in the vast majority of the so-called "revivals of religion" which annually visit the churches.

Yet we repeat what we said two weeks ago. We speak of things only in general. We rejoice to believe that God has a people in all the ecclesiastical organizations of our land, the Roman Catholic not excepted. We war upon no man for his creed, or his opinions, in regard to things not essential to salvation. If his *life* only gives evidence of the practical power of the love of Christ in his soul, we hail him as a brother. We moreover earnestly pray, and are trying in our poor way to labor for, the upbuilding of pure and undefiled religion all over the world. But until the professed churches of Christ are prepared to bear a decided and consistent testimony against *all* sin, and until they become pure enough to exclude known criminals like slaveholders and their abettors, we have little hope of any great good to come from their revivals.

In conclusion, we have only space to say, that those

churches or individuals who feel that they are free from participation in the popular iniquities we have named, will not be offended at our remarks. But we do expect that those who feel that they are *not* free from a guilty participation in these crimes, *will* be offended.

REVIVALS OF RELIGION.

The fact that revivals of religion take place in slaveholding churches of this country, is held by many to be conclusive of God's favor. It is plead that those churches must be owned as his on which he pours out his Spirit, and in which he revives his work. If such revivals of religion were genuine, and were really followed by the fruits of righteousness, there would be force in this plea. But such is not generally the fact. A few months after these excitements, called revivals, the subjects of them are usually as frivolous and as worldly as ever. It is an exception if in any case a marked change in the *life* of the convert is the result. Even during their progress the grossest crimes are sometimes perpetrated by those professing to be the subjects of converting grace. A true revival is a revival of *God's work*. The result is that those whom he converts live henceforth to do the work of God.

But we did not commence this article to pen an argument, but to relate a few facts. If revivals of religion prove the church in which they occur to be genuine churches of Christ, then the Roman Catholic Church is such. In no church do more extensive revivals of religion occur than in this: — and these revivals are followed generally by the most punctilious observance of the outward ritual of the worship of the church. During our recent visit to Wisconsin, extensive and powerful revivals of religion were in progress in the Catholic church in parts of that State. A Legate had just come on from Rome, clothed with apostolic powers. He exercised the function of forgiving sins; and we were told he had pardoned the sins of some persons for the next three years. This man held daily and nightly meetings in the larger towns, and in the cities of Wisconsin, and his labors were usually followed by extensive revivals of the *Catholic* religion. In the town of Green Bay, a place of fifteen hundred or sixteen hundred inhabitants, I was informed that he received eight hundred

people into the church. He preached there night and day
for weeks, and the whole community was moved by his preaching. Protestant schools, in which Catholic children were
receiving education, were broken up. Backsliders were reclaimed, the faithful were strengthened, and converts were
gathered into the fold.

Now this was really a revival of religion ; but it was a revival of the current religion of the Roman Catholic Church.
The converts would not, of course, embrace higher principles
than those preached to them by the Pope's Legate ; and his
principles permitted him to engage in the infamous traffic of
indulgences, in denunciation of which, when practiced by
Tetzel, the voice of Luther sounded the first notes of the
Reformation. But if the argument from revivals be valid,
then the Catholic Church can plead it, and it will prove her
a true church of Christ. But the plea is fallacious. The
fact usually is that the current religion of the church in
which these revivals occur, is that to which their subjects are
converted. In the Catholic Church they are converted to the
Catholic religion. In slaveholding churches the converts
embrace the prevalent type of religion which permits them
to trade in slaves and souls of men, and covers the atrocities
of slavery with its mantle of protection. In churches which
permit their members to sell and drink intoxicating poisons
revivals are frequent, but their *spirituality* is not of the Holy
Ghost's imparting. Thus it will be found that revivals of
religion take their character from that of the church in which
and the teachings under which they occur. To plead, therefore, that such revivals prove these churches to be truly of
Christ is simply absurd.

But the question may here be asked, whence comes the interest in religion which attends and marks these revivals, if
not from the spirit of God? With the same propriety we
may ask whence the interest which attends Roman Catholic
revivals? If the one is of God, *simply because excitement exists*, so is the other. But do men need to be taught that
religious excitement is no evidence of genuine piety? True
religion leads men to do justly, love mercy, and walk humbly
with God. It is not every one that says Lord, Lord, that
shall enter into the kingdom of Heaven, but he that *doeth*
the will of the Father which is in heaven. Excitements,
hopes, fears, joys and sorrows, mental exercises and im-
aginary experiences are no evidence of true piety. John
Newton had "sweet experiences" while pursuing the slave-

trade on the coast of Africa. If alive now, and similarly engaged, these sweet experiences would not save his neck from the halter. Excitements on religion may be from beneath as well as from above; hopes may be false, joys may be unfounded, fears may be slavish, sorrows may be of the world and work death, exercises and experiences of mind may be very fallacious. By their fruits ye shall know them. If, therefore, the fruits of revivals, in the lives of their converts, are not justice, mercy, faith, truth, honesty, love, peace, and all the graces and fruits of God's Holy Spirit, the revival is not of God, and does not prove the church in which it occurs to be his.

Decay of Public Virtue—Its Cause and Cure.

That public morality is declining, year by year, in this country, is a fact of which even politicians are becoming sensible. High-toned honor and strict personal integrity are hardly looked for now among public men. Charges of wholesale bribery against Congressmen and Judges excite no surprise. Peculation of the public treasury has almost ceased to be disgraceful. There is no conceivable villainy that is not freely practiced and fully justified, if the success of a political party is supposed to require it. Attempted assassination, of the most beastly and cowardly sort, in the halls of Congress, only prepares the assassin for a splendid ovation of public honor at his death. Profanity is looked for in office-seekers, and, in fact, a man can hardly succeed in the rough-and-tumble of politics without it. Some of the law-makers of the country are noted for the ingenuity and intensity of their blasphemy. To be able to coin a new word of insult of Almighty God is a passport to the society of a class of public men. That chivalrous sense of personal honor which would scorn to strike a man from behind, or to take any unfair advantage even of an enemy, is altogether out of fashion. That nice and scrupulous integrity of character which shrinks from the offer of a bribe, as from the touch of a leper, is obsolete. That reverential fear of God, which characterized those who planted the seeds of our free institutions in New England, and elsewhere, is a forgotten legend.

From those high in place the corruption spreads down through all ranks of society, as is to be expected. Profanity, licentiousness, fraud, swindling, embezzlement are lamentably common. Human life has become wondrously cheap. The cowardly practice of carrying concealed weapons is becoming general. Assassinations and murders now excite less commotion in a neighborhood than an assault and battery did a few years ago.

It is a hopeful sign that thoughtful and upright men are beginning to inquire for the cause and the cure of this alarming condition of things. The main cause, however, appears to have escaped the notice of those whose opinions on the point we have seen. That cause is undoubtedly the low state of religion in the churches. The connection between piety in the Church and morality in the world is as intimate as between the heart and the pulse. This connection may be stated and solved with mathematical accuracy. The problem would stand thus: Given the state of piety in the church of a country to find the state of public morals therein. This intimate relation is alluded to in the words of Jesus to his disciples, "Ye are the salt of the earth." "Ye are the light of the world." The Christian influence emanating from the Church is the salt that preserves society from corruption. But that influence is preservative only so far as it is Christian. "If the salt have lost its savor, it is thenceforth good for nothing but to be cast out and trodden under foot of men." If the influences that emanate from a church are unchristian, instead of staying, they hasten the process of decay. To the extent to which the influence of the Church is mighty for good, when she is true to her mission, to the same extent is it powerful for evil when she proves false to her trust. "If the light that is in her be darkness, how great is that darkness?"

However the wicked may affect to despise, and may really hate a holy church, they are yet powerfully restrained by its influence. There is a power in goodness before which vice shrinks abashed and confounded. The pure and burning light of the holy religion of Jesus, reveals and shames the dark schemes of the ungodly. A single man, "strong in the Lord and in the power of his might," is often more dreaded by the ungodly than an army with banners. John Knox was more feared by the Queen of Scots than all the military force the Protestants of Scotland could muster. Calvin did more to restrain and confound the schemes of Popery in France than all the Huguenot armies of Conde and Coligny. Before the meek eye of Jesus the most hardened sinner quailed in conscience-stricken terror. Hence it is that a church, in any community, which is deeply influenced with the Spirit of Christ, and exemplifies his doctrines in all its conduct, is the most truly restraining and conservative power that can exist in its midst.

In the light of these truths the cause of the present deplorable state of public morals in our land is manifest. The Church has ceased to be the light of the world and the salt of the earth. Instead of being the terror of evil-doers, she has become their safest hiding-place. The robber and oppressor are among her most honored members and ministers. The wine-bibber and the distiller are welcomed to her fellowship. The most flagrant political crimes may be perpetrated by her members without rebuke or question, for the current doctrine is that the Church has nothing to do with politics. The wealthy church-member may lease his buildings for rum holes or brothels, and the blood-money which he draws from these sources is freely received into what is called the treasury of the Lord, and his name stands high on the subscription list, and he is lauded for his *Christian* (!) benevolence. Ministers (?) of the gospel may sell virgins into forced prostitution without compromising their ministerial standing in the least. These statements are true of all the large and widely influential denominations of this country.

With this state of things in the Church, the wonder is that it is no worse in the world. It *would* be worse if all the churches, without exception, were involved in this fellowship with crime. "But there is a remnant, according to the election of grace," who have not "bowed the knee to Baal." There are those also, in the large and corrupt ecclesiastical organizations, who sigh and cry for the abominations that are done within their pale. It is owing to the influence of these classes, who embody and exemplify all of practical Christianity that is left in the land, that any vestiges of public virtue are left, and that the nation is not left without righteous men enough to save it from a political, social, and commercial conflagration.

With this knowledge of the cause of the low state of public virtue, there can be no mistake as to the remedy. "Judgment must begin at the house of God." The sanctuary must be cleansed before the purifying streams can be poured through the Augean stables of social, political, and financial corruption. A general revival of religion can alone raise the standard of public morality. But it must be a revival of true

and not sham religion—of that religion which consists in
"doing justly, loving mercy, and walking humbly with God;"
which consists in "visiting the widow and fatherless in their
affliction, and keeping unspotted from the world."

CREEDS.

There is no subject, scarcely, upon which there has been
such an infinite amount of twaddle, as that which we have
placed as the caption of this article. One would be almost
tempted sometimes to think that all " the ills that flesh is heir
to " are the result of *creeds*, and that their universal abolition
would be the consummation of the millenium!

Now what is a creed? It is simply a system of religious
faith, it matters not whether written or unwritten. The man
who has no creed has no faith—no system of religious truth,
and is simply a pagan or an infidel. There is no intelligent
Christian who has not a *creed*.

But, says the objector, my objection lies only against *written* creeds. Do you, then, object to the *Bible?* for that is the
written creed of universal Christendom. Oh! no, says the
objector, I only war upon creeds of human composition, the
Bible is my creed. Nay, my brother, your creed *is your
understanding of the Bible.* Suppose, for example, that you
should *write out* your opinion (or belief, if you please,) of
what constitutes Bible regeneration, repentance, faith, justification, sanctification, etc.; or of what the Bible teaches concerning the character of God, his nature and attributes; or
of the resurrection of the dead, or the judgment, or future
rewards and punishments. You certainly have some fixed
opinions or belief concerning these and all other Bible teachings, and this *belief* written out would be your written creed.
But is it any the *less* a creed because not written? Are you
not just as tenacious of your *unwritten* creed as the veriest
creed-monger? and do you not as certainly recognize as *error-
ists* all who do not subscribe to your *unwritten creed*, which is
simply *your understanding* of what the Bible teaches?

Now, although Christianity is not *merely* a science, yet it is
as *certainly* a science as astronomy or political economy. If
a science, it has certain fixed and definite principles, and
these principles, so far as understood, constitute, whether
written or unwritten, the *creed* of him who embraces it.

You, my brother, who have an *unwritten creed*, pronounce those who have a *written* creed all wrong. But suppose you should write out your creed, would there not be quite a probability that the world would find as much wrong in yours as any other? And do you not subject yourself to the suspicion that it is to avoid this very judgment that you do not commit *your* creed to writing?

But creeds are an abridgment of Christian liberty. So far, then, they are wrong. Admitting, for the sake of argument, that this is true of all existing creeds, and still it is far from being proved that this is an inherent or essential defect in creeds. It would only prove that those who drew them up had inadequate conceptions of what constituted true Christian liberty.

Suppose you should *write out* your ideal of Christian liberty, is there not a strong probability that it would be found quite as objectionable as any other? Here again you escape the judgment of the world by retreating into the dark labyrinths of an *unwritten* creed. But certainly your brother, with his written and published creed, has this advantage, that by the very publication of his creed, he has given evidence that he is not ashamed of it, nor afraid to have it submitted to the test of strictest investigation.

We might pursue this course of argument much further, but we think it is a matter *comparatively* unimportant. We are no creed-worshiper, and no advocate for creed supremacy. In their proper place and their legitimate use, we believe they answer a good purpose. If any have been found to give them an improper place, or pervert them to the destruction of true Christian liberty, or have exalted their authority above the Word of God, it is no more the fault of the creed (though no creed, we presume, is faultless) than the monstrous assumptions and aggressions of the slave power are the fault of the Constitution or the Declaration of Independence. That much evil has resulted from creeds—that creeds monstrous in wickedness have been promulgated—and that others, as a whole correct in theory, have been monstrously perverted in their application, is all doubtless true, but it would be a strange freak of logic to infer, *therefore*, that all creeds are necessarily and essentially wrong. Up to the present day every civil government ever organized has been organized upon principles subversive of human right, ignoring the doctrine of God's universal fatherhood and man's universal brotherhood. Must we, therefore, necessarily infer that *all* civil government is of the Devil, or that man is incapable, with the light and teachings of God's Revelation to aid him, of drawing up a form of government which, properly administered, shall secure the great ends for which government was instituted?

But while we thus speak, we enter our unqualified protest against all creed-worship and creed-supremacy. They are matters of mere convenience. They have no authority in themselves, nor can they derive any merely from the will of the body enacting them. Their sole authority is derived from the Word of God. All creeds must, like the stars in the firmament, shine with a borrowed light. Let them, then, occupy their humble, subordinate, but not useless sphere, receiving and reflecting the light of God's holy truth, and the world may be blest by their beneficent influence. We believe the doctrine of our Confession of Faith is the true position upon this question:

"The *Supreme Judge*, by whom all controversies of religion are to be determined, and all decrees of councils, opinions of ancient writers, doctrines of men, and private spirits, are to be examined, and *in whose sentence we are to rest*, can be no other but the Holy Spirit speaking in the Scriptures."—*Con. F.*, chap. 1, sec. 10.

Again: "An offense is anything in the principles or practice of a church-member, *which is contrary to the Word of God*."

"Nothing, therefore, ought to be considered by any judicatory as an offense, or admitted as matter of accusation, *which can not be proved to be such from Scripture*, or from the regulations and practice of the Church, *founded* on Scripture," etc.—*Book of Discipline*, chap. 1, sec. 3, 4.

SCIENTIFIC AND MORAL ARTICLES.

CHRISTIANITY AND SCIENCE.

THE pertinacious efforts and oft-vaunted success of infidels in trying to extort from the revelation of nature a contradiction of the truths of the Bible, have caused many serious Christians to fear and distrust scientific investigations into the teachings of nature. They hence look coldly on all attempts to fathom her secrets, regard the man as little better than an infidel who avows his faith in any alleged new discovery, and regard as deceptive any new light that may be thrown on the laws and properties of matter or mind. This feeling may find some apology in the thousand pretended discoveries of superficial observers, which for a time have occupied the attention of men, and have then been exploded and succeeded by some new wonder equally foolish and false. But this attitude of hostility to the researches of science, and this tremulous apprehension lest some evidence should be extracted from the volume of nature to throw discredit on the records of revelation, is unworthy of intelligent Christians, and dishonorable to their holy religion.

All Christians believe that the Creator of the universe is the author of the Bible. They believe that the revelations of nature and of the Scriptures have both emanated from the same infinitely wise and perfect mind, a mind that is alike incapable of mistake or contradiction. It follows that these revelations must harmonise with and mutually confirm each other. The object of both revelations is the same, the exhibition of the glory of God through the holiness and happiness of men; the one is in part a history of the other. Both are intended for the instruction of the same intelligent beings, and relate in many things to the same subject. It follows as an inevitable conclusion from all this, that these revelations must mutually illustrate and establish each other, and that it must be the very madness of atheism that leads any person to try to extort from the perverted pages of the one, a contradiction of the other.

As was to be expected, therefore, we find all the past efforts of infidels in these attempts, have signally failed. Again and again, indeed, has the world rung with their boastings over some alleged discovery of science that had completely exploded the credibility of the Christian Scriptures. But no sooner have these pretended discoveries been investigated than it has been found that they have been false in themselves, or that their alleged opposition to the Bible has been founded on an entire misrepresentation of the teachings of the holy volume. The weapons with which the unbelievers have sought to destroy the citadel of revealed truth, and the foundation of the Christian's hope, have been turned with terrible effect on the cobweb theories of the infidel.

Of the truth of these remarks the present position of geological science furnishes a pertinent illustration. In nothing more than the alleged revelations of geology has infidelity sought for evidence to destroy the claims of the Bible to be the word of God. For a time the Christian world looked on with alarm, and investigation into the phenomena of the geological formations was discouraged and distrusted. This was just what the infidels wanted. Loudly did they scoff at the fears of Christians, and boastingly did they proclaim that they were afraid to examine into the structure of the earth, as the evidence furnished would inevitably overthrow their faith in the Bible. But the field was at last entered by the believers in revelation, and at every step of their investigations have they found the most abundant confirmation of the truth of the inspired records. The contradiction to its teachings which the infidels pretended to have discovered, were found to rest upon the most superficial observation of the phenomena of nature, and upon the most false and distorted views of the facts.

A single instance is all we now have room to furnish in illustration of these remarks. A work was published a few years since, called the "Vestiges of Creation." One object of the work was to establish what is called the "development" theory of animal existence. This theory is, that all animal life, from the lowest form up to that of man, is a result of the operation of the laws of nature—that currents of electricity passing through small masses of matter in a certain state generated monads, or the lowest forms of animal life; that from these the developments and improvements went on to reptiles, fishes, birds, four-footed animals, monkeys and men. The "great fact" that was adduced in support of this theory was, that the only fossil remains found in the first or lowest geological formations were those of the lowest order of animals, and that the development and perfection of these fossils kept pace with the geological formations, thus proving that they began and proceeded together. The object of this theory was to disprove the Mosaic account of the creation, and thus throw discredit on the Bible. This was considered for a time a triumphantly established theory. But, alas for infidel confidence! subsequent investigation has proved the pretended "fact" on which the theory was based, to be no fact. The researches of Miller and others have resulted in the discovery of some of the most perfect forms of vertebrated animals, in the lowest geological formations. Thus the flimsy foundation of the superstructure of air has been overturned, and the faith of the Christian in the truth and inspiration of his Bible vindicated.

Many similar illustrations of the truth of our remarks might be furnished. We waive them for the present to make room for the following observations by an able writer, which will be found interesting:

"While revelation thus lavishes its favors on science, science in its turn, illustrates and confirms revelation. Seeming facts have, indeed, at times, been promulgated, which appeared to contradict and bring discredit on its statements; but further research, on the part of scientific men, exposed their fallacy, and confirmed the Scriptures. For example, the accuracy of the Mosaic chronology has been more than once impugned. Toward the close of the last century, the astronomical tables of the Indians formed the topic of protracted discussion. These tables professed to record observations conducted during millions of years. Attempts were made to verify this remote chronology, and to show that there was internal proof that the observations must have been actually made at the time specified. This theory was adopted by several philosophers in this country and on the continent; it was advocated by some of the leading journals, and infidelity seemed to have gained a victory. Its triumph however was short. By Bentley, Delambre, La Place, and others, these tables, to which the Brahmins had assigned so high an antiquity, were subjected to a more rigid and scientific scrutiny. The result was an unanswerable proof that they had been fabricated only a few centuries before.

Again, when the celebrated zodiac of Dendara was brought from Egypt to Paris, Dupuis and his disciples expected to derive from it an argument in support of their skeptical reveries on the "origin of religions," and of pretended civilization, which they maintained had existed in Egypt long before the times of either Moses or the deluge. The calculations by which they attempted to prop their fallacious theories were investigated by men distinguished in the scientific world, and proved to be erroneous. Still the adversaries of revelation were unwilling to acknowledge defeat, and persisted in ascribing to their zodiac an antiquity of more than six thousand years. Quite recently, however, Champollion, in his researches among the mysterious paintings and hieroglyphics of the Egyptians, found, on the very temple from which it was taken, two inscriptions, one of them in Greek, containing the names of Ptolemy and Cleopatra and the Roman emperors, by whom it had been built about the commencement of the Christian Era._ Thus the truth of the Mosaic narrative, instead of being subverted, was confirmed, and its opponents covered with confusion.

The inquiries of the learned into Egyptian documents and monumental inscriptions, have thrown light on sacred history and furnished independent evidence of its accuracy. The sojourn of the Israelites, their state of slavery, the occupations at which they were compelled to labor, as well as the period of their abode, are all recorded in the documents to which I have referred.

Had Voltaire been now alive, he would not have ventured to put the sneering question, how, and on what materials the Hebrew lawgiver would write the Pentateuch; for it was proved that papyrus was in common use for writing in his time. Nor would he have tauntingly asked how, after an interval of a thousand years, Hilkiah, could find in the temple of Jerusalem, the autograph of the law; for writings and contracts on papyrus, as old as the times of the Pharaohs, still exist, and are still legible. Nor would he have incredulously inquired, how so many objects of art for the tabernacle, and the sacred vestments and vessels, could be wrought in the desert; for the arts then flourished in Egypt, and there Moses had acquired a knowledge of them. Nor would he have insinuated against Ezra the charge of having forged the sacred books which he had collected; for the written and monumental history of Egypt so coincides with these books, in dates and facts, as to demonstrate that they could not be the work of an impostor. The remark respecting this celebrated infidel, made by Benjamin Constant, an eminent philosopher who had abandoned infidel opinions in consequence of the numberless difficulties which the facts of science oppose to skepticism, is very pungent: "He who would be gay with Voltaire, at the expense of Ezekiel and Genesis, must unite two things, which will make his gaiety sufficiently melancholy—ignorance the most profound, and frivolity the most deplorable."—*Robson.*

Science and Christianity—Another Coincidence.

One man of real science, Agassiz, and several smatterers, Gliddon, Nott, etc., have lately been trying to prove that the human race have not all descended from one original pair. They pretend to find such differences of physical conformation among the different nations of men, as preclude the idea of their having the same ancestry. This idea is, of course, at variance with the teachings of the Bible. Its history is, that Adam and Eve were the progenitors of all the race. The apostle's declaration is, that "God has made of one blood all nations of men to dwell on all the face of the earth." If the theory that there was more than one original pair could be established, of course the testimony of the Scriptures on this point would be discredited.

But the recent discoveries of science come in at this point to confirm and establish the testimony of revelation. By the aid of the microscope it has been discovered that the blood of every animal is specifically different from that of every other, and that human blood is entirely distinct from that of all animals, while it is the same in all races of men. A writer in the *Presbyterian Banner and Advocate* thus states the proposition of the apostle in his speech at Athens:

"I. There is a common life-stream flowing through the veins of all men, of whatever tribe or nation, which, notwithstanding its accidental modifications caused by influence of climate, food, health, and habits, is yet everywhere characteristically the same, and can be recognized as such.

"II. This life-stream of the human race is characteristically different from all other life-streams, found in all other creatures: in other words, the blood of beasts, birds, or fishes, or any other creeping thing, and can be clearly distinguished therefrom."

These propositions he demonstrates thus:

"Science has actually established our interpretation of the

Pauline statement as the true one! The light breaks at last upon our path! The achievement of scientific naturalists furnish to our hand the materials for a true interpretation, and bring vividly to mind the pertinent and far-reaching remark of Bishop Butler, that 'Events as they come to pass will open the fuller sense of Scripture.' The microscope accomplishes to-day a splendid work in behalf of the living oracles of God. It interprets to-day a part of the oration of Paul. It has superseded the tedious and circuitous method of chemical analysis relied upon for the last twenty years, but with so much misgiving and dissatisfaction. The most that could be accomplished by this means, was simply the detection of coloring matter in the blood, without any evidence, whatever, whether the blood was that of a man, a beast, or a bird. But the microscope has done more. It has done for the blood just what the telescope has done for the nebulous stream in the heavens. It has resolved the mazy mass into separate *globes*, and determined the variety, character and size of each. First, came the discovery that the blood of every animal is composed of an infinite number of minute, red globules, floating in a colorless fluid. Next, that in the Mammal class, these globules were uniformly *circular* and somewhat *flat;* in thickness equal to one-fourth the diameter. Next, that in birds, fishes, reptiles, these globules are *oval* in form, and last of all, that 'every *kind* of animal has its blood globules differing in *size* from those of every *other kind.'*"

GEOLOGY.

So far as our Brother Bradford is concerned with the foregoing communication, "he is of age and can answer for himself." Having admitted the assumption of the geologists that the earth is more than six thousand years old, he is bound to reconcile the supposed fact with the Mosaic account, or reject the latter as false. *We* have made no such admission, though in our former article in reply to the question of a " Sincere Inquirer," we showed one way in which the assumptions of geologists in regard to the age of the earth and the history of creation as given by Moses, could be reconciled. Our want of success in " fully satisfying " our correspondent. does not encourage us to repeat the attempt in that direction. We shall content ourself, in the present article, with defining our position and giving a true statement of the point at issue between the infidel geologists and the Bible.

We neither admit or deny the assumption of the geologists that the " earth's monuments prove her to be tens of thousands of years old." It seems to us quite too soon to make such assertions with overweening confidence. Geology is too young, and, hitherto, too confined in her researches to speak as those who know whereof they affirm of the age of the world. Let her votaries content themselves with examining phenomena, collecting and classifying facts, and thus laying the foundations of a true science. When the entire field of investigation open to their research has been thoroughly explored, it will be time enough to call in question the hitherto received interpretation of the Mosaic cosmogony. That they have yet furnished any thing approximating a " *demonstration* " that the earth is more than six thousand years old we deny. The alleged demonstration is derived from the fossil remains found in the secondary formations, and the following extract from Professor Silliman is, perhaps, a fair specimen of the mode of reasoning from these discoveries :

" We will not inquire whether Almighty Power inserted plants and animals in mineral masses, and was thus exerted in working a long series of useless miracles without design or end, and, therefore, incredible. The man who can believe, for example, that the Iguanodon, with his gigantic form, seventy feet in length, ten in hight and fifteen in girth, was created in the midst of consolidated sandstone, and placed down one thousand or twelve hundred feet from the surface of the earth, in a rock composed of ruins and fragments, and containing vegetables, shells, fish, and rolled pebbles—such a man can believe any thing with or without evidence. If there be any such persons we must leave them to their own reflections, since they can not be influenced by reason and sound argument; with them we can sustain no discussion, for there is no common ground on which we can meet."

Now can the learned Professor, or any one else, affirm that the huge monsters of which he speaks, were not antediluvian animal productions, cotemporary and corresponding in magnitude with the " mighty men which were, of old, men of renown," and that they were not buried in the fearful convulsions attending that event, when the fountains of the great deep were broken up ? Or can the geologists tell what effect six thousand years, with its earthquakes, volcanoes, its one general deluge and thousands upon thousands of violent floods have produced upon the earth? Well may the language of Jehovah, to one of old, be addressed to these speculators: "Where wast *thou* when I laid the foundation of the world? Declare if thou hast understanding."

The state of the question then as between the infidel geologists and the Bible is this. The Bible does not rest on geology for evidence of its truth, but geologists appeal to their science for evidence to prove the Scriptures false. It is then evidently for the geologists to make out a case for their science, as against the Bible, so clear that the shadow of a reasonable doubt can not rest upon it. Until this is done it is both impudent and absurd to set up their speculations to prove the Scriptures false, and then clamor against the bigotry of those who refuse to cast aside the only book that holds out any hope for man in time or in eternity. The Bible presents better authenticated historical records than any other book. There is more and better historical evidence that Moses led the Israelites from Egypt to Canaan—gave them the law and established their system of religious worship, than there is that Cecrops founded Athens, and that Greece became the seat of learning and arts. There is more and better historical evidence that Jesus Christ lived, taught, wrought miracles, was crucified and rose from the dead on the third day, than there is that Julius Cæsar lived, subdued Gaul and Britain, led his armies back to Rome, crossed the Rubicon and became Emperor. The evidence from prophesy is so remarkable that some ancient enemies of the Bible were compelled to resort to the silly plea that they were written after the events they professed to foretell. The evidence from this source is cumulative, and is growing stronger by the lapse of time. Now, if the accounts of the miracles of Moses, the Prophets, and of Jesus, were published and believed at the time in which they are said to have been wrought—and to deny this is to falsify and discredit all historical evidence—they must have been true. If events were foretold hundreds of years before they transpired so clearly that they are a true history of the events, then the book which is attested by these miracles, and which contains these prophecies, must be divinely inspired.

But the Bible presents evidence of its own truth and inspiration, above the testimony of prophesy and miracles. In the correspondence of its parts, the agreement of its writers one with another—writing as they did during a period stretching over fifteen hundred years, in different parts of the earth—being men of different habits and education and mental endowments—in all this, and in the *practical effects* of the Bible, there is evidence that it is of God, that amounts to the very strongest moral demonstration. Whatever progress the world has made in knowledge, and virtue and happiness, it owes directly or indirectly to the Bible. The institutions under which the infidels of the present day have been educated into the outward decencies of civilization, and into the knowledge and practice of some moral virtues, owe their existence to the Bible. Serpent-like, these men would destroy the bosom on which they have been warmed into whatever of intellectual and moral life they enjoy.

The Bible goes to the rude hovel of the Hottentot, breathes over him its own divine spirit, awakes his debased and feeble intellect to newness of life, and transforms his fierce and more than brutal soul into the divine likeness of Jesus. The lion becomes the lamb. The revengeful, blood-thirsty savage, becomes the meek, non-resisting, peace-making Christian. The lustful become pure, the proud are made humble, and the selfish become benevolent. Following in the track of the Bible, the arts and sciences of civilized life take the place of the debasing institutions of heathenism. Thus, by its practical effects, the Bible vindicates its claim to be the book of God. The life of one Christian Africaner, before and after conversion, is an argument for its divine inspiration which infidelity in vain attempts to gainsay.

Again: the Bible goes to the bedside of the dying believer, and transforms that scene of mortal agony into the lofty triumph of the conqueror. Its voice of hope and promise rises high and clear above the roar of the billows of death. Its light of future glories throws a hallowed radiance over its dark and bitter waves. While the infidel tremblingly and in agony exclaims, "Remorse! remorse!" the Christian shouts, "O death, where is thy sting! O grave, where is thy victory! thanks be to God, who giveth *us* the victory through our Lord Jesus Christ." *Thus*, also, the Bible vindicates its claims to Divine inspiration.

We might pursue this train of argument to an indefinite length, but we stop here. So much evidence do the Scriptures afford that they are of God, that men like Locke and Newton—giants of intellect, before whose colossal proportions the sciolists of this age that call in question the inspiration of the

Bible, dwindle into microscopic dimensions—bowed in profoundest veneration to their infallible authority.

Now this is the book which geology—a science of yesterday,
having dug a few holes one eight-thousandth part of the
earth's diameter in depth, and extracted therefrom a few bones
of extinct species of animals—would set aside as a forgery and
a lie. The theories of geology, built upon this most superficial and narrow examination of the earth's monuments, have
been legion. It has been the fate of one theory after another
to explode, after new facts have been brought to light by further examination. Yet these structures of gossamer, rising,
sparkling, and bursting, like the soap-bubbles which the
child blows up for a moment's amusement, are to overturn the
adamantine pillars of revelation, built on the moveless foundation of the Rock of Ages. And when the infidelity of Low-
ell peddles out at second hand these flimsy speculations, to
discredit the truths of revelation, a " Sincere Inquirer," and
those he represents, are ready to " beg for quarter ! "

We have said nothing about the matter of the obligation of
the Sabbath, because that question depends on the truth or
falsehood of the Bible.

War.

One of the brightest revelations of Prophesy is the entire
cessation of war. It is thus announced by the Prophet
Isaiah :—

"And it shall come to pass in the last days, *that* the mountain of the
Lord's house shall be established in the top of the mountains, and shall
be exalted above the hills; and all nations shall flow unto it.

"And many people shall go and say, Come ye, and let us go up to
the mountain of the LORD, to the house of the God of Jacob; and he
will teach us of his ways, and we will walk in his paths: for out of
Zion shall go forth the law, and the word of the LORD from Jerusalem.

"And he shall judge among the nations, and shall rebuke many people: and they shall beat their swords into plough-shares, and their
spears into pruning-hooks: nation shall not lift up sword against
nation, neither shall they learn war any more."

The time thus foretold is called by Christians generally,
the Millenium. This is the time of the Lord's reign on earth,
either personally and visibly, as some believe, or spiritually
in the hearts of men, according to the faith of others. Before

this period arrives, war must universally cease, and the reign of peace extend over the earth. This consummation is to be brought about by the gospel of Christ. When the Christian religion shall become prevalent in the earth, and the hearts and lives of all are brought under its power, " wars will cease unto the ends of the earth."

War is, therefore, opposed to the spirit and principles of the gospel. It is a practice which is undesirable, the existence of which all the good deplore, which no one with any feelings of love to God or men, desires to see extended and perpetuated. This is enough for our purpose. It is abundant proof that it is every one's duty to labor for the abolition of war and the war-spirit. It is an all-sufficient reason why no Christian should seek a justification of war, even in extreme cases, from the gospel of Christ. War is one of the Devil's favorite agencies for the ruin and misery of men. Satan, no doubt, never feels better pleased than when he beholds two armies engaged in slaughtering each other. How far Christians may adopt and employ one of his favorite instrumentalities would not seem difficult to determine. That this has been done extensively, by *professing* Christians is as much out of character, and as much a matter of wonder, as the fact that they have engaged in the foreign and domestic slave-trade, and in holding men in slavery; or that they are found engaged in the making, vending, and drinking of intoxicating liquors. Their conduct in these and many other instances, is a libel on the religion they profess; a gross misrepresentation of the teachings and spirit of Christ. Even though a plausible argument for war in an extreme case might be made out, it proves nothing. *Extreme cases are not the rule of action, but the exception, and exceptions only establish the rule.* We therefore, oppose war to the same extent that we oppose slavery, drunkenness, caste, polygamy, or any other organic sin. Ranking it with these, we would be faithless to our convictions of duty if we did not raise our feeble voice against it.

There are different grounds of opposition to the practice. It appeals to different motives. We oppose it,

1st. On account of its fearful and wasteful expenditures. The wars of what are called *Christian* nations, have cost more than all other purposes of government besides. Confining our attention to our own land, and we find that the expense of preparation for war in time of peace, is *four times* greater than all other expenses of the Government. A few facts will abundantly establish this position; and we shall use only those which are familiar to all. The army and navy of the United States cost the nation *eighty per cent.* of all the public revenue. This percentage is higher than in any other nation on the globe. In Austria it is 33 per cent; in France 38; in Prussia 44; in Great Britain 74; and in the United States 80 per cent! That is eighty cents out of every dollar of the public revenue, paid by the laboring classes of the country, is swallowed up in making and sustaining preparations for the work of human butchery. The remaining twenty cents answers all the civil purposes of the nation. Pays the salary of all the public officers; the outfit and salaries of foreign ministers; the light-houses, from Maine to California; all public buildings of the nation; the complicated, extensive and most useful machinery of the post-office department, together with various other expenditures. A few items in this account may be looked at with profit. The military academy at West Point has cost the nation more than four millions of dollars. Each cadet receives, besides a gratuitous education, twenty-eight dollars a month for the privilege of being educated at the public expense. There are kept there 100 horses, with grooms, blacksmiths, &c., for the accommodation of the pupils. A single lesson at target-shooting costs the nation fifty dollars.

The salary of a colonel of dragoons is $2,000; of a brigadier general $2,958; a major general $4,500; a captain of a ship of the line receives on service $4,500, out of service $3,500. A larger salary for doing nothing than any minister of religion, or president of a college, receives in the United States. A single regiment of dragoons costs annually $700,000. There are now at least three of these in the nation, costing yearly $2,100,000. The cost of two ships of the line has been $2,000,000. Every gun carried across the ocean costs $15,000. The building and outfitting of the line ship, Ohio, cost $834,485. The expense of the same for one year is $220,000.

During the fifty years of peace from 1789 to 1843, there were devoted to the army and navy $538,964,000. A moderate estimate of the expenses of the militia for the same period gives the enormous sum of $1,335,000,000. Of these sums there were spent in time of peace more than *seventeen hundred millions* of dollars—a sum beyond the power of human conception. All this spent in peaceful preparations for war in times of profound peace!

These are a few of the facts and figures in the case. They are such as may well arrest the attention of every thoughtful mind. Had this immense expenditure been devoted to the education of the people, and the dissemination of Christianity over the world, a Christian civilization would ere this have been attained which would render future wars utterly impossible.

Since the foregoing calculations were made the Mexican crusade has been carried through, involving the nation in a direct expenditure of probably two hundred millions of dollars. The actual sum of money paid, however, in sustaining military operations is but a small part of the waste of property in actual war. The withdrawal of troops from industrial occupations, and the consequent loss of their productive labor, and the destruction of property attending the march of an army, would swell the estimate to an amount beyond the power of human conception.

Resting our estimates of the cost of war and military establishments here, many serious questions arise to the mind. Could not the objects for which all the wars of this nation have been waged, have been attained by peaceable arbitration ? Would not the nation and those with whom she has been at war, have all been immense gainers by such a mode of adjustment?—Can a nation professing to be more completely under the influence of Christian civilization than any other on the face of the earth, fail to have incurred fearful guilt, by this destruction of those things which a beneficent Providence has provided for the wants and happiness of man? These questions we can not now discuss. They are indeed their own answer. Another question, full of important suggestions, immediately presents itself. What has been gained by all this fearful waste of property? By the Mexican war a vast territory, which has become the cause of more wide-spread agitation and strife than any that ever distracted the country. A strife that threatens to tear down the very pillars of the Government. Territory has been acquired, immense portions of which will be given up to the withering curse of slavery, if the purposes of the authors and supporters of the war be attained. In addition to this the nation thinks it has gained a little glory. A little empty fame. A crop of Presidential aspirants, in the shape of military commanders. And this is candidly and really all. On the other hand, what has been lost? What is always lost by the prosecution of war? All the immense amount of property of which we have spoken ; thousands and thousands of precious lives ; the respect of all other nations among whom any sentiments of honor prevail,

—the force and efficacy of a high and beneficent example to the nations of the earth. Depravation of public morals, and the prevalence of a military spirit among the people, have resulted; the disposition to give military renown the precedence to statesmanship and virtue, as a qualification for civil office. These evils every candid man must see as following inevitably in the train of wars, waged under circumstances similar to those attending that with Mexico.

But we must leave these considerations to a future article. We were speaking in this merely of the expense of war. The war debt of Christendom at this day would plant and sustain a school, with a competent teacher, for every thirty children in the world. It would build a church and support a preacher of the gospel for every five hundred inhabitants on the earth; sustain a printing-press, and endow and support a college or university for every county; feed the poor of all nations; sustain the alms-houses, hospitals, and other public charities, of the world. In short, it would supply and sustain all the instrumentalities needed for the redemption of the whole world from ignorance, superstition, idolatry, caste, slavery, and all other evils that afflict the race; and then be scarce half exhausted.

And all this incalculable amount of property, that might have been devoted to these beneficent objects, has been worse than wasted in the prosecution of the work of human butchery. Brethren—children of one father—made of one blood—destined in a few brief years to a common resting-place—have wasted money enough to furnish the means for *flooding* the earth with the light of science and salvation, in the fiendish work of each other's destruction! Terrible will be the reckonings of the Judgment Day for this.

Remarks on other aspects of the subject must be deferred to future numbers.

WAR.

There is an allegory which tells of one of the "Elder Spirits of Heaven" being appointed to conduct a youthful angel down to earth, for the purpose of learning the character of this world and its inhabitants. The guardian spirit conducted his charge first to the scene of conflict between the fleets of two hostile nations. The battle was raging with fearful carnage. The roar of cannon was incessant; the wounded lay weltering in their blood, mingling their groans and cries of agony with the din of battle. The combatants, with faces begrimed with blood and smoke, stood by their dread engines of death, that at every discharge revealed their grim and ghastly countenances, glaring with all the fierce passions of incarnate fiends. For miles around the ocean was discolored with blood; while fragments of broken spars and masts, and mangled human bodies, were floating on the reddened waters. The youthful spirit turned to his conductor with an air of displeasure, and exclaimed, "What is this? You were appointed to guide me to earth, and you have brought me to *hell!*"

The moral of the legend is obvious. There is no doubt that every human being, imbued to any extent with the Christian spirit, would be similarly impressed by such a spectacle, if he had never read of war or battle. The idea that those whom God has made of one blood to dwell upon the face of the earth—brethren possessed of a common nature and common interests, partakers of the same joys and sorrows—should resort to the work of each other's wholesale destruction, for *any* purpose whatever, is one which were it not a stern reality, would be regarded as one of the wildest freaks of a distempered fancy. Were the proposal to resort to war for any of the purposes for which war is waged now, for the first time, made, it would strike the whole civilized world with horror. Yet the guilt of the first war would be no greater than if ten thousand had been waged before. The frequency of the recurrence of warlike collisions between hostile nations, while it blunts the impression of their guilt, at the same time really increases it. From such a point of view as we have supposed there would be but one opinion of the character of war. There would be but one verdict from the civilized world. In this may be found, therefore, with unerring certainty, the testimony of nature and of nature's God against the practice of war. In strict harmony with the revelation of nature on this subject is the fuller revelation of the Bible. We shall now enter into the discussion of that branch of the question; but basing our opposition to war on those broad grounds of inexpediency and immorality, on which all the virtuous and humane may stand together, we propose now to inquire what can be done for the entire suppression of the system, and for the substitution of other more rational methods of gaining the ostensible ends for which wars are usually waged.

1. The first thing essential to the establishment of universal peace on earth, is to dispossess the minds of men of the

idea that wars are necessary for self-defense among nations. A strictly defensive war is, in this age of the world, a simple impossibility. Let a nation observe strict justice in all its intercourse with other nations ; let it say to them, "We desire to live in peace with all the world ; any injury done by our agents or citizens, to the property or lives of any of your subjects, shall, when brought to our notice, be promptly redressed ; ' let there be no strife between us ; for we be brethren ; ' " let a nation proclaim such principles as these, and act in accordance with them, and that nation is safer from invasion than if its fleets darkened every sea, and its forts and arsenals frowned on every hill-top. There could then be neither motive nor pretext for attack ; and the nation that without these should invade its soil, would raise a storm of indignation against itself more terrible than fleets and armies. Bad as the world is, it is too far on in civilization to tolerate such open, wanton aggression. Besides, "There is a just God who presides over the destinies of nations," and who, "when a *nation's* ways please him, will cause even its enemies to be at peace with it."

But so long as a strictly defensive war is admitted as a probable, or even a *possible* event, so long will preparations for war be thought necessary ; and so long as men are trained for war—so long as navies and armies are kept up—so long will wars continue to devastate the earth. This assertion is susceptible of the clearest demonstration, both from the truths of history and from the necessary tendency of such preparations. Frederick the Great, of Prussia, gave once as a reason for invading a neighboring State, that "*he had an army of one hundred thousand men under his command.*" There is a volume of meaning in this honest confession of an atrocious motive. The only chance for distinction among military men is in the occurrence of actual war. The end of their entire education is to fit them for the work of death on the field of battle. It is only there that they can show off their accomplishments. Now, while a standing army and navy are kept up, with officers and men stationed all over the country, enjoying, through a false public sentiment, admission to the best society, and permitted to exert a controlling influence over the public mind, pretexts for war will be found just as often as these trained and respectable murderers may wish for an opportunity to distinguish themselves by military achievements.

But let it once become a settled conviction in the public mind, that preparations for military defense are unnecessary, and the army and navy will be disbanded. The vessels of war will be employed for the useful purposes of commerce; and the soldier compelled to resort to the peaceful pursuits of life.

2. A second thing which each one can do to hasten the time "when wars shall cease to the ends of the earth," is to resolve never, under any circumstances, to vote for the military man for any civil office of profit or trust. If the road to political promotion was once fast closed against the professional soldier, the days of the demon of war would be numbered. The very reverse of this is now true among all civilized and savage nations. The army offers the surest and shortest road to civil and political promotion. The qualifications of a man for office are generally counted by the number of his battles and victories, and by the number of victims he has slain. This has come to be more and more the case in this country, and in the last Presidential election a large majority of the voters of the country, by electing a man who had been forty years in the army, and had never performed an hour's civil service, thereby announced their belief that nothing but military prowess was necessary to fit a man for the highest office in their gift. If the "signs of the times" are not deceptive, the same thing is to be acted over again at the next electoral canvass. Those things augur badly for the Republic. Military rule, and the disposition to honor military achievements more than political wisdom and integrity, and moral worth, are the surest precursors of the ruin of public virtue, and the prevalence of anarchy and licentiousness.

Now, the half million of voters in this country, who are the professed followers of the Prince of Peace, have it in their power to arrest this dangerous tendency. Let them resolve, as one man, that no man who follows a profession opposed to the entire letter and spirit of the pure any peaceful religion they profess, can ever under any circumstances, secure their votes, and the politicians will look elsewhere than to the army for their Presidential and other candidates. Every professing Christian who refuses to do this, ought to feel the blood and guilt of every war which grows out of a reckless ambition, resting on his conscience.

Other means of hastening the overthrow of war and the war spirit, might be named. The dissemination of light and truth on the subject. Facts, arguments and appeals, showing the utter failure of the ordeal of battle to establish any right principle, or secure any valuable end, ought to be brought to bear on the public mind. Petitions should be circulated for the abolition of the army and navy, and the substitution of rational and Christian modes of adjusting national difficulties. And above all, the fervent prayers of God's people should be offered up without ceasing for this glorious consummation. When the public heart shall be awakened to this great subject, and become more deeply imbued with the spirit, of Him who " came not to destroy men's lives, but to save them," the days of legal and wholesale murder will be numbered. The orator and poet will then cease to enshrine the bloody achievements of the warrior, in eloquence and song. Their " gifts divine " will then be consecrated to the conquests of the moral hero. The triumph of intelligence over ignorance, of light over moral darkness, of love over hatred, will then claim the admiration of men. The vision of the Prophet will then be realized; the swords will be beaten into plow-shares and the spears into pruning-hooks ; and the nations learn war no more.

MARTIAL LAW DESTROYS PERSONAL ACCOUNTABILITY.

At a time when our public servants are voting increased and most extravagant appropriations to the army and navy, it is highly proper that the people should look closely at the organization of these institutions, which they are taxed so heavily to support. A well written article on the subject of martial law will be found in another part of this paper. From the incontrovertible facts and principles laid down in that article, the conclusion is inevitable that, so far as human instrumentality can do so, martial law destroys individual responsibility. Let us look at what is implied in personal accountability ; and then we shall see how military law interferes with it.

It is a doctrine both of natural and revealed religion that every one shall give account of himself to God. The very idea of a moral government over intelligent beings, involves the doctrine of their accountability to their ruler. Man's moral nature corresponds with this obligation. He is endowed with a judgment to discriminate between right and wrong, and with a conscience to approve the one and condemn the other. A law also has been given by the Creator, commanding all duty, and forbidding all crime ; and it is to this law that he is accountable, and by it that he will be judged. But to render this accountability just, it is necessary that man

should be perfectly free to exercise his judgment in considering questions of duty, and free to follow the convictions of
his conscience.

But this freedom of judgment and of conscience is just the
thing which martial law takes away from every soldier, from
the commander-in-chief, down to the private in the ranks.
Every man below the commander-in-chief is bound, under
terrible penalties, to yield the most implicit and unquestioning obedience to the orders of his superior officer, and the
commander-in-chief is bound to render the same obedience to
the commands of his government. Prompt and unhesitating
obedience to orders, coupled with skill and courage in their
execution, are the essential elements of good soldiership. The
soldier has no possible use for a conscience, or for any moral
faculty whatever. His whole conduct, as a soldier, is laid out
for him by others. A cultivated and enlightened conscience
would indeed be utterly incompatible with military regulations,
as it would cause its possessor to revolt from the execution of
many a command of his superior. All the soldier needs is
intelligence enough to understand his instructions and courage
and vigor in carrying them into execution. But the question
irresistibly arises here, if God had intended men for soldiers
would he have endowed them with faculties which unfit them
for that position? Would he have given them a judgment to
distinguish right from wrong, and a conscience to approve or
condemn, as their conduct accords or conflicts with their convictions of duty, when the only result of these faculties is to
unfit them for the work of the soldier? Such incongruity
between means and ends is found in none of the works of
God.

Let it be noted, moreover, that this absolute snbmission to
orders is essentially necessary to the organization of an army.
No army could hold together for a day, in which every man
had the right to think, decide, and act for himself. Discipline would be completely at an end. But it is a military
axiom, that discipline is the soul of an army, and every one
knows that when the soul is out the body is dead. It was not
an arbitrary love of power merely, which led to the enactment
of the Draconian code of martial law. It was the necessity of
the case. Entire unity of counsel and purpose is indispensably necessary to the efficiency and success of military operations, and that unity can only be secured by placing the whole
mass under the absolute control of a single mind. To divide
the supreme command even between but two persons, as has

sometimes been done, is found to lead almost invariably to divided counsels. weakness, and defeat. But it is not only necessary that the command be in one person, but also that his authority be absolute. Even a *murmur* against it is not to be tolerated for a moment. The organization and efficiency of the army can only be maintained by every subordinate officer and soldier becoming a mere animated machine, to execute, without question or scruple, the will of another.

Now we repeat, that if it is right to place men in this absolute subjection to the authority of another, it is wrong to hold them individually responsible for their actions. They have no choice but to obey. There is no room for the exercise of judgment and conscience. The soldier, for all moral purposes, is as much a tool as the sword, in the hands of his commander.

But God's laws may not be thus set aside by human arrangements. He still holds men to their accountability, and by no act of their own can they throw it off. It still remains true that we must all appear before the judgment-seat of Christ; and that every one must give account of himself unto God. The soldier's oath to obey his leader does not free him from his obligations to the higher law of God; nor will the plea that he only obeyed orders, excuse him at the bar of God, for the crimes he has committed. No man has any right to place himself in a situation in which he can not exercise his own free agency; and that must of necessity be an inherently vicious institution which can only be maintained by annihilating men's freedom of choice and action.

The fact that there is no despotism so absolute and relentless as that established by martial law, furnishes the reason why standing armies are ever the willing and ready tools of tyrants. Men educated in the school of despotism can not be expected to love liberty. They who are voluntary slaves themselves, can have no true regard for the freedom of others.

True and False Heroism.

At the present moment a hundred thousand of the chivalry of Western Europe, are gathered in deadly conflict with a greater number of Northern barbarians, around a Russian stronghold, on the shores of the Black Sea. War there rages in all its fury. Death riots on prey, and banquets daily on hecatombs of the slain. By battle, by disease, by hunger and exposure, by shot and shell, by bayonet and dagger, the work of slaughter goes on. The wild excitements and fierce passions of war are fanned to a fearful glow. The fields around Sebastopol are fattened with human blood, and whitened with human bones. All the enginery of destruction which modern skill, and science and energy have devised, is there employed. Stratagem and plot are brought into play. The fierce sortie, and the dogged and desperate resistance, are almost nightly repeated. The angel of death waves his dark wing over the embattled hosts, and his foul fiends hold daily and nightly revel in the crammed and reeking charnel-house which engulfs the slain.

And this fearful work of death has not even the extenuation of being, on either side, a contest for a great and holy principle. It is not a struggle of the oppressed against the oppressor. It is not a fight for liberty against despotism, nor a battle for the protection of the weak against the strong. It is only a conflict of despots over points of barren and tortuous diplomacy. The tyrant adventurer, who controls for the time the destinies of France, and the effete aristocrats, who rule the English cabinet, have just as little sympathy with freedom, as Nicholas or Alexander. The crushed masses of Europe have nothing to hope from either party, but everything to fear from both. As now waged, the war is a wanton, useless, reckless waste of human life.

Yet every man who is thus sacrificed, is the center of a circle of home affections. Each one is bound to father, mother, wife, children, brother, sister, or friend. None there so friendless as to fall utterly unregretted, while over the fall of the vast majority, loving eyes will long weep tears of bitter anguish. Many a lovely home will be desolated forever. The light on thousands of happy hearth-stones will go out, never to be rekindled. And the soldier who escapes the dangers of the campaign, will in many cases come back so depraved by the vicious influences of the camp, as to cause deeper sorrow by his life than would have been excited by his death.

And this fierce strife of man with man, the world calls heroism. The more successful the man in the work of death, the greater the honor accorded to him. When either party gains a partial advantage over the other, whole nations shout in triumph. Public thanks are returned to the same God, alike by Russian for the slaughter of Frank or Englishman, and by the latter for the destruction of the Russian. In temples professedly dedicated to the worship of God, *te deums* are chanted over the gory triumphs.

But it requires no high courage to be a soldier. A moderate share of the lowest animal courage, combined with a large infusion of the most brutal and ferocious of human passions, are the best material for the warrior. In entering the camp as a professional soldier, the man of necessity gives up his conscience to the control of his superiors. That high sense of right which shrinks from the very appearance of evil, and that lofty moral courage which adheres to the right, not only in the face of personal danger, but in the face of scorn and hatred, and bitter obloquy, are utterly incompatible with the profession of arms.

But turning from the picture of strife and carnage, a spectacle of another kind meets our view. The war that has been the *cause* of all this display of wrath and blood, has been the *occasion* of the exhibition of pure and true heroism. A young female, of ample fortune and high social position, beautiful in person, refined in manners, surrounded by all that could minister enjoyment to cultivated and elegant tastes, leaves all the endearments of home, and all the pleasures of refined social life, to minister to the sick and suffering victims of the war. She incurs not only the loss of all the comforts and enjoyments which her position commanded, but even the sneers and insinuations of some who were base enough to hint that her mission of mercy betrayed a want of modesty. And there, in that ghastly receptacle of the wounded and the dying, on the shores of the Bosphorus, this heroic woman may be seen, day after day and night after night, moving like an angel of mercy among the long lines of the suffering and the dying. Her gentle hand administers the healing balm to the wounded, and cools by its soft touch the brow of the fevered sufferer. The sight of ghastly wounds, of gory and mangled bodies, the cries of the agonized sufferers, and the groans of the expiring victims, so shocking and revolting to sensitive nerves, are all borne and braved with a lofty moral heroism, before which the brute courage of the soldier is totally eclipsed.

Look at the two pictures. On the one side "the smoking hell of battle," where all that is fierce, and foul, and fiendish in human passion, seethes and rages in its fiery flow. On the other, the gentle ministry of purest and holiest benevolence. From the battle-plain goes up the roar of cannon, and bombshell, the fierce shouts of the combatants, the shrieks of the wounded, the groans of the dying, the mingled cry of agony from horse and man. From the receptacle of the wounded sounds clear and soft the gentle tones of love; the voice of Christian sympathy and soothing consolation. Almost in hearing of the conflict breathes forth that still small voice, with its music of love.

> "Like lutes of angels, touched so near
> Hell's confines, that the damned can hear."

On the one side, the rage of man mutilates and destroys his brother; on the other, the loving ministry of woman binds up the wounds and soothes the pains of the victims. The one curses, the other blesses. The one destroys, the other saves. From the one goes up the hoarse imprecation, the foul blasphemy, the shriek of rage and hate; from the other the tones of kindness, the voice of hope, and the accents of prayer.

And yet, of these pictures so broadly contrasted, the first fills by far the largest portion of the world's history, even among nations calling themselves Christian. The heroes, falsely so called, of blood and carnage, are those whose names stand highest on the scroll of earthly fame, while the deeds of sacred charity and love, from earth's true heroes and heroines, are altogether unnoted, or passed by as things of little worth. But it will not be always thus. Even now the faint dawning of a better day may be detected by the spiritual eye. "The soldier's name will be a name abhorred," while earth's true heroes will be recognized in those whose lives are given to bless and save the race.

"Look on This Picture, and on This."

Congress has recently passed a bill creating the office of Lieutenant General, conferring the office upon General Scott, giving him $30,000 for past services, and adding $1,600 a year to his salary, which was $7,000 per annum before. The bill has received the signature of the President, and gone into effect. This act of Congress is in harmony with the received and prevailing sentiment of the country. To honor and pay her military commanders is part of the standing policy of our country. The general, the commander of a man-of-war, and even "the swearing frontier colonel," receive from three to six times the salary of our college presidents and professors, and our ministers of the gospel. Then the former are the stuff of which Presidents and Senators are made. The act of pensioning General Scott, therefore, is consistent with past policy and the prevailing public sentiment.

But, while we admit the consistency of the measure with the popular practice and opinion, we condemn the morality of both the act and the sentiment that sanctions it. Without asserting any extreme views of the wickedness of war in all cases, we yet maintain, with all confidence, that the *professional soldier* is neither more nor less than a *professional murderer*. His contract with his Government is to kill whomsoever it may order him to kill, without ever asking the question whether those he is commanded to destroy are innocent or guilty. The first and last duty of the soldier, from the commander-in-chief down to the private, is to *obey orders*. He has no right to exercise his own conscience and judgment in considering whether the order is right or wrong. The exercise of his moral sense in this way would destroy all discipline, and discipline is the life and soul of an army. If the soldier has the right to judge of the right or wrong of his orders, he must also have the right to *carry out* his convictions; and if he concludes, on a calm and conscientious review of the case, that his orders, in any instance, are to commit a great crime, he should have liberty to refuse to obey, otherwise his right of private judgment is a farce. But the attempt to do this will cost the soldier his head. It is neither more nor less than mutiny, and a court-martial would make short work with the mutineer. The general gives himself over, body and soul, to his Government, and binds himself to do just what that Government commands him, "asking no questions for conscience sake." The private soldier gives himself up to the same unconditional subjection to his superior officer. Without strict subjection there can be no discipline, and without discipline an army becomes a mob.

But aggressive war is wholesale murder, whatever defensive war may be. Every life lost in a war of aggression is a murder with malice aforethought, and if hanging were right, ought to cause the execution of the officers of Government that declare the war and the army that wages it. There is no escape from this conclusion, unless a multitude may nullify the law of God. If the private man who makes aggression upon his neighbor, and hires a professional assassin to kill him, is a murderer, so the government which makes aggression on its neighbor, and sends its hired butchers to kill its subjects, is guilty of wholesale murder. And as the hireling who kills in the service of one man is judged guilty of murder, so the hireling who kills in the service of twenty millions of men is also a murderer.

But this is just what General SCOTT and the whole of his subordinates have done. This is just what the Government ordered them to do, and for doing this he is now rewarded. The war in which his *freshest* laurels were won, was a war of wanton aggression, according to his own assertion, and the unanimous vote of the political party to which he belongs. It was his exploits in this war that brought him prominently before the American people. And for his great skill and success in blowing out the brains of innocent men, women and children, he is promoted and rewarded, and the President promptly sanctions the act of Congress conferring title and wealth upon the professional assassin in epaulettes.

This is one side of the picture. Let us turn the canvass, and look upon the other.

A few years ago a young female, moved by the compassionate spirit of Christian love, devoted her life to the cause of the suffering. Those unfortunate members of the human family who have lost the use of their reason, were the especial objects of her sympathy. Like an angel of mercy, she passed from asylum to asylum, and from prison to prison. Her pathway was as a line of light over a dark background of sin and sorrow. Wherever her deep, low tones of love fell on the ears of the raving maniac, his passions were stilled. In mute rapture he drank in the heavenly music, and the demon of his breast was for the time cast out. She penetrated like HOWARD and Mrs. FRY, the most dismal dens of suffering. Like them she carried hope and life to many of their inmates. Through her efforts the old and barbarous modes of treating the insane, were superseded by others more rational and more merciful. Love was substituted for fear, in their management. Physical comfort took the place of squalid misery. The means of intellectual and moral training were provided. The fruits of these efforts have been the restoration of the shattered powers of many an intellect to their wonted harmony. Many a raving maniac, touched by the magic power of her Christian love and sympathy, has been seen sitting at her feet, "clothed and in his right mind."

To aid in the enlarged and comprehensive schemes which

her expansive benevolence devised, Miss DIX sought an appro-
priation of a part of the public domain for the use of the
wretched objects of her sympathy. She sought no wealth for
herself, but only the accomplishment of her noble schemes of
philanthropy. And the present Congress, to their praise be
it spoken, after long and earnest solicitation, granted her
prayer. The bill appropriating a portion of the public lands
to this object was passed. But no sooner does it reach the
hands of the President, elected though he was by people
claiming to be Christians, than it is promptly vetoed. Just as
the long-cherished hopes of that loving and gentle heart were
about to be realized, the tyrannical one-man power interposes
to dash the sweet draught from her lips. The hopes of thousands of the unfortunate and suffering were crushed by the
same cowardly and perfidious blow; and the " outer darkness,"
over which bright gleams of hope were beginning to shine,
was rendered blacker than before. Heart-sick and sorrowful,
the angel missionary of the unfortunate left our shores to
pursue her work of mercy in a foreign land.

These pictures teach their own moral. FRANKLIN PIERCE
is an average representative of the statesmanship, morality
and religion of our country. He is neither far above nor far
below the standard of benevolence and religion by which the
mass of the people, in and out of the church, are governed.
The religion of the land has no quarrel with the leading acts
of his administration. The mass of the ministers and members of the churches voted either for him or General SCOTT at
the last Presidential election, and gave no evidence of peni-
tence for the deed. What is the obvious inference from all
this? Evidently that the people of this country esteem him
who destroys life worthy of more honor and reward than him
who tries to save it and alleviate its woes. Yet, Christ " came
not to destroy men's lives, but to save them." Is that his
religion which honors the professional destroyers of life, while
it denies the means of relieving human suffering to the
benevolent?

DRUNKARD MAKING.

This infamous business is frightfully on the increase in all
parts of the land. Never before were the manufacture, sale
and consumption of intoxicating poisons so great; and never

before were these poisons so deadly and fatal to human life. The pure liquors which our fathers drank were harmless compared with the drugged and adulterated compounds which the tipplers of this age imbibe. One of the most alarming features of this increase of drunkenness is that it embraces, more than ever before, the female sex. When the mothers of the people become intemperate, then, indeed, may we expect to become actually a nation of drunkards. The children will literally drink the poison with their mother's milk, and become possessed of the depraved taste of the inebriate by natural inheritance. That things are tending rapidly to this terrible state admits of no serious doubt.

The invariable results of this increase of drunkenness are witnessed every day. Crime keeps pace with its cause. Our nation, though young in years, is old in guilt. Murder, rape, arson, burglary, thuggery, are commonplace. The proverbial ingenuity of our people is exercised with dire success in the invention of new modes of transgression. The catalogue of crime is rapidly lengthening. "Hoarse, horrible and strong," rises to heaven the cry of guilt and the skies grow black with its portentous clouds.

This state of things presents to every serious mind a subject of the most anxious reflection. Where is all this to end? How shall it be remedied? Has the temperance reformation been, after all, only a signal and disastrous failure? To what causes is this immense increase of drunkenness to be attributed? and how shall those causes be removed? These are questions that call for the most serious and anxious thought. The subject must be probed to the bottom. It can never be successfully dealt with by superficial thinkers and flippant declaimers. School-boy rant about the evils of intemperance, or the inefficiency of prohibitory laws is vastly out of place. None but minds that can trace effects to causes with logical precision, and that are wise to apply the adequate remedy to the evil, are fit to grapple with this momentous subject.

That the temperance movement, which has occupied so large a share of the attention of the public for the past thirty years, has been at least a partial failure, admits of no denial. It has not freed the nation from drunkenness. It has saved thousands undoubtedly from the drunkard's grave, but for every one thus saved, probably hundreds have perished. And now the force of the movement seems nearly spent. The barriers which it erected to the progress of the black tide of intemperance are being swept away, and the weary work is all to do over again.

Now, if we can ascertain the cause of this failure of past efforts for the suppression of drunkenness, the knowledge of that cause will guard the friends of temperance against like failure in future. The prime cause of that failure is undoubtedly the fact that the cause failed fully to enlist the religion of the country. The religion of a nation, whether true or false is the controlling power of that nation. The reason is that the religious element of man's nature is the controlling power of the individual man. The Church and priesthood of a nation, as the embodiment and exponent of its religion, are consequently its controlling institution. By these the public opinion of the people is molded. By these the government is shaped, and the laws framed.

Now this which is true, more or less, of all nations, is preeminently true of this nation where the people are the government. Any cause, therefore, in this land, which does not array the religion of the people in its favor, must fail, and hence the partial failure of the temperance reformation. It has only had a partial support from religion, and has therefore been but partially successful. The Christianity of the country has all been in favor of temperance, as it is the foundation of all true reform, and as temperance is one of the Christian virtues. But the Church and clergy of the nation have, to a large extent, been arrayed against the cause. There is not a large and influential denomination of professing Christians in the country in which the makers and sellers of intoxicating drinks do not enjoy full fellowship. But a few of the smaller churches make these practices a bar to communion. The popular religion of the country has no quarrel with drunkard-making. The true Christians in all the sects are opposed to the iniquity, but these are probably largely in the minority. Ministers, elders, class-leaders and deacons may and do carry on grog-shops and run distilleries without losing their standing in the professed church. Thus the cloak of religion is thrown around these practices of atrocious criminality. They are made respectable by the Church, and find their safest resting-place beneath the altars of the professed churches of the Lord of hosts.

If we are correct in these positions, then the true course of the temperance reformers is evident. They must begin at the foundation. They must purify the fountain. They must array the religion of the country against the infamous and guilty business of drunkard-making. They should call upon the churches to array themselves on the side of temperance. They should abandon every church organization that refuses to do this. A church at this day, which fellowships the crime of drunkard-making, or even refuses to denounce and oppose it, is that far false to God, and, on that point, in league with the Devil. Their true character should be exhibited, and the cloak of affected piety torn off. A professed church which will not raise its voice and wield all its power in opposition to a business which sends annually thirty thousand souls to the drunkard's hell, is a curse to the world, and a libel on Christianity. Its influence, if it can not be brought into the right channel, should therefore be destroyed.

When the religion of the country is separated from its complicity with drunkenness, and arrayed on the side of temperance, the work will be done. Laws for its suppression can then be made and executed, as the public opinion in which laws have their origin and efficiency will be pure and right.

CONTROVERSIAL ARTICLES.

[From the Free Presbyterian.]

COMMUNICATION FROM THE HON. HORACE MANN.

MR. GORDON :—I thank you for your laudatory remarks upon the performances of the graduating class at our late Commencement. Coming from so good a judge as yourself, they confirm the opinion which I hear from so many other sources, that the members of that class acquitted themselves in a highly reputable manner.

The commendation you were pleased to give to the main points of my Baccalaureate Address, was most acceptable ; for it gives me assurance that you will labor with me for effecting the great reform there advocated.

It may seem ungracious in me, after accepting your general approval of my performance, to except to your single criticism or animadversion upon it. But such is the way with what we call "poor human nature." We think a man very wise while he agrees with us, but how suddenly is he bereft of wisdom when he comes to differ.

I fully acquit you of any intention to misrepresent me ; and yet, the omission of an idea which I several times repeated, gives, as it seems to me, all its plausibility to your criticism. My position was not, as you aver, that "supposing there were fifty different sects, forty-nine of them *must* be wrong, and the whole fifty *might* be." Each time I had occasion to refer to the differences between the sects, I said, "forty-nine out of the fifty must be wholly or partly wrong." By the alternative words "or partly," which you did not hear, or forgot, one of the points of your criticism becomes wholly inapplicable.

At the same time the starting-point of my argument is left untouched ; which was, that, so far as the sects differ from each other, all but one (possibly all) must be wrong. So far as the fifty sects inculcate their hostile views upon the minds of youth, they inculcate forty-nine errors at the least, to one truth. For, if we say that the fifty, in their distinctive points, are all true, we affirm truth and error to be identical.

This being mathematically certain, what is the best method of discovering that truth which lies wholly, or partly, *outside* of them all, or outside of all but one?

How is *Truth* to be discovered? Doubtless, according to the order of God's providence, by human instrumentalities; for we do not expect a new and special revelation from God on that subject. Now, what are the best and highest of possible instrumentalities for the discovering of truth by men— by the sects? I answer, diligence in searching for truth as the supreme good, and candor and impartiality of spirit in discerning between truth and error; in one word, a power of honest investigation and reception. And what does more than all other things to destroy this candor and impartiality of spirit—this power of honest investigation and reception? I answer, the notorious fact that each sect trains up its children and youth to believe that its own dogmas—those in which it differs from others not less than those in which it agrees, are true, and that all conflicting ones are false.

Now the authorities and arguments by which these conflicting points are to be vindicated or assailed, demand the most extensive research, the soundest and best trained judgment, and, above all, a mind so poised in impartiality, that the slightest preponderance of evidence will turn the beam. Yet nothing is more certain than that the teachings of these dogmas to children and youth, in catechisms, creeds, or by oral instruction, as ultimate truths, unfits the mind—the very instrument to be used for the discovery of truth—for making that noblest of all discoveries. This early inculcation does all it can to make present differences perpetual; so that if each sect could fulfill its own desires in regard to its own disciples or pupils, a thousand years hence would find the Christian world quarreling on the same points which would now embitter and disgrace it. Now, instead of kindling in the youthful mind the supreme love of truth, and training it to the honest use of all those methods of exegesis by which Scriptural truth can be discovered, almost all our private schools, our Sunday-schools and our colleges, are disabling the rising generation from discovering where truth lies; and are thus perpetuating these strifes and contentions of the sects by which the body of Christ is wounded and pierced with pains, I have no doubt, sharper than those of Calvary.

Now, what I would venture to suggest as a better course, is, that sound morality should be made a peremptory condition in all cases of college standing and graduation, and that all the knowledge and argument which can bear upon controverted points should be honestly and impartially communicated; and then, that the mind of our youth should be left free and unbiased to form its own conclusions. Who does not see that such a mind would have a far better chance of discovering truth than you or I ever had?

Nor does this suggestion of mine lead to any laxity of Christian doctrine. It tends rather to establish the true doctrines of the gospel on firmer ground than ever before.

It is as in science. When the great body of accredited scientific expounders agree, we teach youth accordingly. When there are two schools, we announce the prevalent doctrine, but always qualify it by a full and fair statement of the dissenting authorities. If I departed from this rule, and suppressed the views of acknowledged great men because I did not agree with them, I should consider myself a bigot in science and unworthy to teach it.

So when we encounter controverted points in religion, let us frankly state the great names and fairly present the arguments on all sides—acting magnanimously toward our antagonists—so that the new, unsophisticated, unpreoccupied mind may hold the balances more steadily than the teacher was able to do. It is in this way that science has made such immense advances, and that conflicting philosophies are so rapidly harmonizing and blending into one; while the *science* of theology remains nearly or quite stationary, and the Ishmaelitish sects, whose hands are against every man, are on the increase.

In closing this topic, you say you "can understand why an infidel should seek to magnify the alleged differences among Christian sects, but can not understand what interest a *Christian* has in so doing." As you must now perceive that so far from having any desire to "magnify differences among Christian sects," my sole aim is to obliterate those differences by eliminating the errors which make us differ, and evolving the truth on which we can agree, you must also see that the sting which you inserted in that paragraph is beautifully extracted.

Again you say: "If a particular denomination establishes a college, they must do one of three things in this matter: they must either teach what they themselves believe to be the true religion, or they must teach what somebody else believes, or teach no religion at all." And again: "So far as Presi dent Mann teaches his students religion, he teaches what he himself believes to be true, and not the notions of somebody else."

Now, my dear sir, in the first of the above quotations, which is matter of opinion, I think you are wholly wrong; in the second, which is a matter of fact, I know you are so. So far as I teach religion—and I have a very large Sunday-school class every Sabbath—in elucidating points upon which there is a substantial agreement between all Christian sects, I have no occasion to note any differences; but when I come to a contested point, I endeavor, with the utmost honesty of my heart, and the utmost ability of my head, to set forth the views of others as fully as my own. Indeed, on those points, I refrain from announcing that I have any views. I assume, as far as in me lies, a judicial character. I present the evidence fully and impartially to the jury, whose province it is to decide. I refrain from doing as many judges do, getting down into the jury seats, and usurping their functions. If, then, in any point, you and I differ, I mean they shall understand your views as completely, as profoundly as they do mine, so that, after full opportunities of investigation, if they discard your opinions, they shall see the reasons why; and if they should afterward encounter you, or one of your one-sided, half-taught disciples, they will know the holes in your armor through which they can perforate your vitals, and let the day-light of truth shine in where it had never shone before.

You must now see, that by the three methods enumerated in your paragraph, above quoted, you did not exhaust the subject as you supposed, but left out wholly what I conceive to be the best method of all, and the only true one, namely, that of a full and fair presentation to the minds of the young, of all the facts and arguments which have a bearing upon contested points, so that their minds may not be fettered by the prejudices which all who have been educated in the common way can not help bringing to the subject. When an exciting cause is to be tried in a civil court, does not every honest judge examine the jurors upon oath, to learn whether they have expressed or formed an opinion on the case; and does he not set aside, as unfit to be upon the panel, those who have formed such an opinion? Every man sees and feels the reasonableness of this course. Yet this is just the reverse of what is done in regard to controverted religious doctrines,

in most of our private schools, Sabbath-schools, colleges, and
theological seminaries.   Hence, Truth, claiming by divine
warrant to be heard, is silenced; error, worthy of annihila-
tion, is perpetuated, and hostile sects, the scandal of the
Christian religion, are increased.

I trust I need not assure you that it is not at all from any
personal feeling, excited by your animadversion (for I believe
you wholly incapable of desiring to do me injustice), but
only because I believe a truth, most sacred in itself, and
most indispensable to human progress, has been assailed, that
I trouble you with these remarks.

As I am expecting to leave town, I may not see your comments upon this communication (should you deem it worthy
of any), but, trusting to your candor and sense of justice, I
leave it in your hands without apprehension.

Yours, very truly,

HORACE MANN.

YELLOW SPRINGS, July 13th, 1857.

REPLY.

We publish very cheerfully the preceding article of President Mann.   We had not the remotest intention to misstate
his position.   We have long since learned that truth gains
nothing by misrepresentation.   For the President, personally,
we entertain none but feelings of the highest respect, and the
most unaffected kindness; and if there is the appearance of
"a sting" in a single sentence of our former article, we beg to
assure him that it was not so intended.

But after a re-examination of the subject, since the reception of Mr. Mann's communication, and with the light of his
explanations before us, we are fully satisfied of the substantial
justness of our "criticism."   Let it be distinctly noted that
the only thing to which we excepted, in the President's most
eloquent address, was the application of his strictures on sectarian education to Protestant evangelical sects.   That they
may be abundantly just, as applied to all other sects, it is not
for us to deny.   The terms Protestant and evangelical have
a well-defined and well-understood meaning, and it is only of
sects answering to these descriptive terms that we assume to
speak.

Two things must be true to form a valid basis for the President's argument. First: There must be, if not vital and fundamental, at least grave and important doctrinal differences between these sects. Second: The teaching of their distinctive principles must be extensively, if not generally practiced in the literary institutions under their control: For if the theoretical differences among Protestant denominations are comparatively trivial, and if they teach these differences in their schools and colleges only in a few obscure and exceptional cases, then it was hardly worth the President's while to spend his eloquent reprobation upon them; and certainly, in that case, he would not be justified in representing the differences as important, and their inculcation in denominational schools as general. Now we venture to question the truth of both these alleged facts. Certainly, in the great majority of cases the doctrinal differences among evangelical denominations are comparatively trifling, and even where they differ the most, theoretically, they agree practically. For instance, no parties among these sects differ more widely, perhaps, than Calvinists and Arminians. But while they differ in points of speculation, they harmonize in views of duty. For example, the Calvinist—to use the technical, theological language of these parties—believes in " the perseverance of the saints," while the Arminian believes in " falling from grace." But both believe that it is a man's duty to " take heed lest he fall "—that watchfulness is necessary in him who would live a true Christian life. The one believes in election, and the other don't. But each believes that he should " give all diligence to make his calling and election sure." Then in regard to fundamental morality and the great duties of life, which we agree with Mr. Mann in regarding as of the very first importance, there is absolute agreement. All Protestant sects profess to believe that man's great duty is to " do justly, to love mercy, and to walk humbly with his God "—that the sum of all duty is to love the Lord with all the heart, and our neighbor as ourselves. Hence our former remark remains substantially true, that " Supposing there are fifty different Protestant sects, instead of forty-nine of them being wrong, to any important extent, the whole fifty may be essentially right." Now we submit that to base an argument against the sects on alleged differences between them which do not exist in fact, is virtually to " magnify " those differences, though we doubt not such a purpose was entirely foreign to Mr. Mann's intentions. The *practice* of these sects on some of the great moral questions of the day we do not defend; and when Mr. Mann shall employ his almost unrivaled powers of wit, argument, and eloquence, in exposing and denouncing their *practical* inconsistencies, no one will shout a heartier amen than we. But the source of these practical wrongs is not in their creeds, for they are perpetrated in violation of their teachings.

But admitting, for the argument, that there are grave and important differences between the Protestant sects, the next question is, do they teach these discordant views generally, or even extensively, in their literary institutions? A man's opinions on such questions are governed by his knowledge of facts, and from our knowledge of facts, we should answer this question emphatically in the negative. We spent five years as pupil in an institution wholly under Presbyterian control, and we do not now remember to have heard the theoretical differences between Presbyterians and others once alluded to. We are very certain that no systematic effort was made to teach them. We spent nearly five years more as teacher in another institution under the same control, and of it the same statement is true. Nothing was taught on the subject of religion but its great principles, on which all Christians agree. So far as we have learned the practice of other literary institutions, under the care of different sects, the same thing is true of them. Mr. Mann's acquaintance with institutions of learning is, doubtless, far more extensive than ours, and we of course do not deny that he may know of different practice in some sectarian schools.

But admitting both these supposed facts—that there are great differences of doctrine among these sects, and that they teach their distinctive doctrines generally in their colleges,—and they may still be justified, provided they teach them fairly and impartially, and do full justice to the views of those who differ from them.

This brings us to the second point in dispute. An addition of two words to our statement, that a college controlled by a sect " must teach in religion what they themselves believe, what somebody else believes, or teach no religion at all," would more fully express our meaning. The sentence as amended would read, that a college under the control of a particular denomination "must teach *for truth* what they themselves believe, or what somebody else believes," etc., and with this qualification we think these "three methods" do "exhaust the subject." We would respectfully ask Mr. Mann whether, when he teaches his students a religious doctrine which he wishes them to receive as truth, he does not teach it solely because he himself believes it to be true, and not because some other great man so believes? and whether, if all the other great men in creation received a dogma as true which he believed to be false, he would teach it for truth to his students on the ground of their faith? If he answers the first of these questions in the affirmative and the second in the negative, then does he not teach for truth "what he himself believes, and not the notions of somebody else?"

We agree with the eloquent President as to the mode in which controverted points in religion should be taught. But his remarks on this subject only confirm our position, for this impartial method is the only one by which *any* views can be thoroughtly taught. A student is but half instructed in a disputed dogma when he has been taught only the arguments for its truth. He must likewise be taught the objections to its truth, and the mode of answering those objections. If we desired to impress what we knew to be an error on the minds of others, we would try to state, with at least the appearance of candor, the objections to it; much more if we wished to teach what we believed to be a truth. Candor and impartiality in a teacher are the surest means of gaining a lodgment for his own views in the minds of his pupils. But this impartiality may be carried too far. When it reaches the point of *neutrality* it becomes in the highest degree pernicious. If an important controverted point is so presented as to create the impression on the minds of a class that the subject is involved in great uncertainty, that much can be said plausibly on both sides, that definite and *truthful* views on the point are hardly attainable, and that it is not very important which side of the question they adopt, thus leaving them, with their comparatively undisciplined faculties, as likely to adopt wrong as right views, we can only ejaculate, in the language of the litany, "from such teaching, good Lord, deliver us."

Mr. Mann will probable agree with us, that a religious teacher ought to have fixed and well-defined views on all the important doctrines of religion, controverted or not controverted (we admit the existence of radical differences between many nominal Christian sects, although we deny their existence as between one class of the sects); that these views ought to be the result of the most thorough and impartial investigation, and that he ought to believe them with his whole strength of conviction. Now a religious teacher holding thus opinions which he is fully convinced are true, and knowing that truth is infinitely important to his pupils, *must* earnestly desire that they should adopt his views, not because they are *his*, but because in his judgment they are *true;* and thus desiring, we do not see how he can honestly do otherwise than seek to impress his own opinions on the minds of his scholars. But a teacher who thus acts teaches what " he himself believes to be true, and not the notions of somebody else." He will, of course, if honest and impartial, present fairly the objections to the truth of his own views, will admit that he may possibly be wrong, will gladly receive new light from all sources, and when convinced that his opinions are erroneous, will modify or change them. But so long as he believes them to be true, and consequently of infinite importance to all men, he *must*, as an honest man, seek to instill them into the minds of others. Mr. Mann will thus see that, as our method of teaching controverted points is the same as his, our " disciples " would be no more "half-taught and one-sided " than his own, nor would our "vitals," perchance, be in any more danger of perforation by the Ithuriel spear than his.

The analogy between the position of a judge and of a religious teacher fails in important particulars. An honest judge has no personal interest in the issue of the cases brought before him for trial, but the religious teacher has the same deep personal interest as his pupils in the right decision of the questions with which he has to do. He therefore combines the functions of judge and juror. Again, a jury are presumed to have minds sufficiently disciplined to form right decisions, if the law and the facts are fairly laid before them. But a class of youth are in process of discipline, and therefore need more careful and fuller instruction than a jury. But taking the illustration as employed by Mr. Mann, and it seems to us to confirm our view of the matter. The great aim of an honest judge will be to administer exact justice in all cases. That this may be done he knows that correct views of the law and the facts must be adopted by the jury. To arrive at such views himself he will investigate each case with all possible fairness and thoroughness. But, having thus investigated the case, and formed his opinion, and fully believing that opinion to be the true one, he *must* desire that the jury should adopt the same. Now we hold that it is neither possible nor desirable for a judge in such a case to so charge the jury as to lead them to believe that he " has no opinion in the case." The man who is so *very* impartial between truth and error, justice and injustice, as to argue with equal force and earnestness in behalf of each, is just the man whom we would not wish to sit in judgment on us in court, or instruct our child in religion. A profound conviction of the vast importance of truth to his pupils will lend a force, depth, earnestness and power to a teacher's reasonings in behalf of truth, which he can not, and ought not, to bring to the defense of error.

In view of what has been said we can not possibly see how instructing youth in religion, according to this impartial method, even when the teacher has deep personal convictions and labors to impress them on his students, can unfit their minds for the "discovery of truth," as Mr. Mann assumes it does. On the contrary, it seems to us that its effect would be to create such a conviction of the importance of truth as to form a good guaranty of the success of the young in its pursuit.

We join with our highly-esteemed friend in deploring the divisions of the Christian world; and agree with him that those divisions are the result of prejudice and pride of heart and opinion. When we can all lay these aside, and come to the study of truth with the docile spirit of little children, these divisions will soon cease. If Christians could enter into discussion with each other, feeling that if they are convinced of the falsity of their present views, they will come out of the friendly contest, not disgraced and humble captives to grace the chariot-wheels of an opponent's triumph, but glorious victors over their own past errors, the unity among his followers for which Jesus prayed would not be remote. We join with all who love the Saviour in devout prayer that we may all come soon to such a mind as this.

IMPRISONMENT OF W. L. CHAPLIN.

The *National Era* is out in condemnation of Mr. Chaplin formerly editor of the Albany *Patriot*, for assisting the escape of the slaves of Messrs. Toombs and Stephens from Washington City, for which he was arrested and imprisoned. We have no heart to join in this censure. The slaveholder is simply a pirate, holding by a thief's title, his fellow-man in bondage, who has precisely the same right to be free as himself. This being the case, it is not only the right, but the duty of the slave to get free whenever he can by lawful means. The *only* lawful means in his power is to run away. It is, therefore, his right and duty, whenever a chance of escape is presented, to embrace it. If it be right for him to make his escape, it is of necessity *right to assist him.* Therefore, the act of Mr. Chaplin, for which he has been arrested and committed to prison, was, we honestly believe, pleasing in the sight of God.

The *Era* quotes, in condemnation of this act, from an article written by the editor, in Cincinnati, commencing thus: " The human mind is so constituted, that it will attach something dishonorable to that which has to be done in the dark, or by stratagem."

On this principle the editor would condemn the primitive Christians, who assembled " in the dark," in the " caves and dens of the earth," to worship their Saviour. He would condemn the Waldenses and Albigenses of France, the Covenanters of Scotland, and the Puritans of England, whose only "freedom to worship God " was obtained by meeting " in the dark and by stratagem ? " Would it be " dishonorable " for a man taken captive by Algerine pirates to escape " in the dark or by stratagem ? " Then why is it wrong for the captives of Toombs and Stephens, and other *Congressional* pirates, to do the same thing ? Was it " dishonorable " for the persons taken prisoners by the Indians, during the first settlement of this country, to avail themselves of " stratagem and darkness" to escape? Yet slavery is more intolerable than Indian captivity ; for who does not know that one object of the Seminole and Florida Wars was to recover the slaves who had escaped from the " tender mercies " of Christian civilized slavery to the " horrors of life in the wigwam ? " We fancy that if Dr. Bailey's wife and children were reduced to slavery, and he had a chance to recover them " in the dark or by stratagem," his scruples would vanish marvelously soon. If Mr. Chaplin shall be doomed to follow the lamented Torrey, it will be for an act on which we have no doubt Jesus and angels smile with approbation.

Can Crime be Legalized?

The *National Era* takes the affirmative of this question. In some comments on the proceedings of the Illinois Convention, these sentences occur : " A legal relation is one which the law allows, creates or protects." Again : " The *legality* of a relation is one thing—its *morality* another. It is legal if it is established by the law-making power of the State, acting under the Constitution which prescribes its extent and limitation."

We demur to the above sentiment. The proper meaning of the term law, as applied to intelligent beings, *is a rule of duty.* That which is immoral is never duty, and, therefore, can never become *law* in the true sense of that term. It is not, of course, our intention to deny that men may pass enactments which "allow, create or protect" crime. But are those enactments, laws? Do they impose the duty of obedience? Does it require a person to obey such enactments, to earn the character of a law-abiding citizen? For illustration, suppose Congress should pass a bill offering one thousand dollars for the scalp of every Indian, belonging to any of the peaceable tribes in this country, and should "command all good citizens" to shoot down and scalp unoffending Indians, wherever they had the opportunity. Would such an enactment be legal? Certainly not. But it will be said such a bill would be a violation of the Constitution, and, *therefore,* illegal. Exactly so. But why does this make it illegal? Because the Constitution is *above the laws passed under it,* and whatever violates the Constitution is illegal. This is precisely our position, and because we recognize (as everybody else except an atheist does) a code of laws above all human Constitutions, we conclude that whatever violates that higher code is illegal. A Constitution which "allows, creates or protects" that which violates the higher law, is itself null and void. It has properly neither legal nor moral force.

The highest Constitution in the universe is that which obliges men to do right. The law of justice, of equity, of eternal righteousness, or in other words, the law of God is first and supreme. Next to that are the Constitutions which nations adopt for themselves; and next to these Constitutions are the laws passed by the proper authorities under them. There is in all a just and beautiful gradation. Now, as enactments, passed under human Constitutions, which violate these Constitutions, are null and void, and illegal because of this violation, so requirements framed into these same human Constitutions, which violate that which is above them, are void also, and for the same reason.

All ethical and legal writers of any authority, so far as we know, lay down certain qualities as essential to constitute an enactment a law. One of these is that they be passed by a competent law-making power; another is *that they do not violate the eternal principles of right and justice.* Now, if an enactment declaring one human being the *property* of another, is not a violation of the eternal principles of right and justice, no such violation is possible. Yet the *Era* holds that these enactments are laws, that the property relation is really a legal relation. The doctrine of this paper is, therefore, identical with the famous (or rather the *in*famous) dogma of Henry Clay, "That is property which the law makes property." Of course, then, if the law declares the wife and children of the editor of the *Era* property, they are legally such. We are greatly mistaken if there is a freeman on earth, who would not think such an enactment as destitute of all legal, to say nothing of moral force, as any of the worst regulations of a gang of Algerine pirates.

We hold that all enactments, passed by any of the States of this confederacy, which allow one man to hold another innocent man as property, are in violation, not only of the law of God, but of the Constitution of the United States. The great object of the Constitution, as set forth by that instrument itself, is to " establish justice and secure the blessings of liberty ; " and if enactments which establish *injustice* and *deprive* men of the blessings of freedom, are not violations of the Constitution, how are such violations possible ? If that which wars upon THE object which the Constitution was made to promote, does not war upon the Constitution itself, we confess our inability to see how *anything* can conflict with that instrument.

There are other sentiments in the *Era's* strictures on the Illinois Convention which we think erroneous. It is not our special vocation to defend the sayings and doings of that Convention. The men who composed it are abundantly competent to vindicate their own positions. But the sentiment to which we have especially referred in this article, is general in its bearings ; and we are sorry to see the *Era* using its great influence to give currency to doctrines which we think false in themselves, and of mischievous tendency.

CAN CRIME BE LEGALIZED?

The *National Era* responds to our notice of his position on this question as follows :

" The *Free Presbyterian* is rather anxious we fear, to disagree with the *Era* The difference between us is one of *definition*, not *principle*. We agree with the *Free Presbyterian*, that no human enactment can justify a relation, or impose an obligation upon an intelligent being to do an act, which the law of nature or revelation forbids. In common with the editors of that paper, and with every man who believes in the existence of a God, we acknowledge the absolute supremacy of the divine law. In *principle* we agree. Wherein, then, lies the difference between us? In *definition*—nothing more. The *Free Presbyterian* defines law to be, a *right* rule of conduct: one of the essential elements of law, in its judgment, is, *its harmony with justice*. It follows from this, that the phrases — 'bad laws,' 'wicked laws,' 'tyrannical laws,' 'cruel laws,' are all misnomers: there can be no such laws. A 'bad law' is no law at all. No enactment is law which commands, sanctions, or allows anything wrong.

"Need we say that this definition is not warranted by the etymology of the word 'law,' not supported by authority, not in conformity with popular ideas or modes of expression?

"The word is derived from a Saxon root, meaning 'laid, set, or fixed,' and means simply a rule of *conduct*—not of *duty*, as the *Free Presbyterian* has it. Human law is a rule of conduct prescribed by the supreme power of the State; Divine law, a rule of conduct prescribed by the Creator. The latter can never be otherwise than just and good, because its Author is always just and good. The former may be short-sighted, absurd, or unjust, bearing the stamp of its fallible or corrupt author.

"Human laws may be right or wrong, humane or barbarous—allowing in one country what they forbid in another, prohibiting to-day what yesterday they legalized."

Again, the *Era* says;

"The *Free Presbyterian* says that the doctrine of the *Era* is 'identical with the famous (or rather infamous) dogma,— "That is property which the law makes property." ' The dogma is true—and the offense of Mr. Clay was, not in giving utterance to it, but in *using it as a reason to justify slavery* —for, he added, 'two hundred years of legislation has sanctioned and sanctified negro slaves as property.' Two hundred thousand years of legislation can not sanction and sanctify a wrong. The law in the free States makes the soil and its products, capital, and the productions of capital and labor, property—and in the slave States it makes men, women, and children, property. This is a fact; and it is because it is true, that what the law makes property is property, that we so utterly detest the system of slavery. Our heaviest charge against that system is, that it takes man, who was created a little lower than the angels, and to whom was given dominion over the fish of the sea, and the fowl of the air, and the beasts of the field; drags him down to their level, and makes him property in the same sense that they are made property. This is the very element which makes slavery the monster crime against humanity—dishonoring human nature and insulting its Creator."

We are not "anxious to disagree with the *Era*," but happy to coincide in the main with that excellent paper. We rejoice in the *Era's* prosperity, and had we the power it would . afford us unmixed pleasure to multiply that prosperity a hundred fold. We have dissented publicly from the teachings of the *Era twice*, in about eight months—once in the case of Chaplin, and again in the present instance. This does not appear to us often enough to justify the "fear" of the editor that we "are *anxious*" for such disagreement. But to the point at issue.

The *Era* thinks the difference is merely one of definition. There is, of course, no difference of opinion as to the fact, that many wicked enactments exist in the world, which are regarded as laws. All the wrongs specified by the *Era*, and many more, have a legislative sanction in different States. But are the enactments which create, allow, or protect these wrongs, properly laws? We still think not. The *Era* says, a law is a rule of conduct, not of duty. But does not all legislation proceed on the assumption, that the conduct of the citizen shall be coincident with his duty? Does the law make any provision for the perpetration of acknowledged wrong? Is not obedience to the very worst enactments—the Fugitive Slave Bill, for instance—urged on the ground of duty? This shows the universal conviction, that law and justice ought to be one—that duty and conduct ought to coincide. If, then, a legislature enact, as a rule of conduct, what is not a rule of duty, its enactment lacks the essential attribute of law.

The main question is, Has *law*, or has it not, *moral* character? The *Era* makes it a moral nondescript, having all characters, and no character, and opposite elements of character, at once. If his idea of law is correct, then it seems to us quite as desirable to cultivate lawless as law-abiding sentiments among the people. If "a bad law" has all the legal force of a good law, then the people ought to be taught that it may be their duty to disobey, quite as often as to obey human laws. According to the *Era's* doctrine, ANY enactment which a competent law-making power may choose to pass, is in the proper sense of the term a law. Now there are surely some things which would not be law if enacted by all the law-making powers in the world. We adduced an example or two in our former article; they might be multiplied indefinitely. An enactment commanding murder, is the example given by Blackstone, and he declares such an enactment has no legal force.

But we are no lawyer, and perhaps have no right to express an opinion on this subject. We are, however, only reiterating principles taught by the masters of jurisprudence. Let us look then at some of the authorities.

" *Law is an intelligible principle of right*, necessarily resulting from the nature of man; and *not an arbitrary rule*, that can be established by mere will, numbers or power."—*Spooner.*

"Jurisprudence is the science of what is just and unjust." —*Justinian.*

"The precepts of the *law* are to live honestly; to hurt no one; to give to every one his due."—*Justinian and Blackstone.*

"All laws derive their force from the law of nature; and those which do not *are accounted no laws.*"—*Fortescue. Jacobs' Law Dictionary.*

"*Law.* The rule and bond of men's actions; or it is a rule for the *well* government of civil society, to give to every man that which doth belong to him."—*Jacobs' Law Dictionary.*

"Of law no less can be acknowledged, than that her seat is the bosom of God, her voice the harmony of the world. All things in heaven and earth do her homage; the least as feeling her care, and the greatest as not exempted from her power."—*Hooker.*

"Lawful: Agreeable to law; conformable to law; legal; *legitimate;* constituted by law; *rightful.*"— *Webster.*

"Jurisprudence: The science of law; the knowledge of the laws, customs, and *rights* of men in a State or community, necessary for *the due administration of justice.*"—*Ib.*

For most of these references we are indebted to Spooner on the Unconstitutionality of Slavery, where others are given of the same import. In view of them what becomes of the *Era's* declaration, that our definition is "not supported by authority"?

We are surprised that the *Era* should assert the truth of the dogma, " That *is* property which the law makes property." That is property which God made to be the proper subject of property, and that is *my* property of which I have obtained honest possession. If I steal a horse all the enactments of all the governments of the earth can not make him my property, because he belongs to another. The right of self-ownership is the inalienable right of every human being. Every man properly owns himself, and hence can never be made the property of another. The man who claims and uses him as such is a thief; the so-called laws which uphold him in the act, are the most *lawless* outrages possible. The regulations of a banditti, or a gang of pirates, by which their prey is divided are just laws as much as these.

The practical tendency of this popular notion of law is most pernicious. Reverence for law is deeply instilled into the minds of American citizens. They are taught to regard it as sacred; hence, when any enactment, no matter how atrocious, is passed, the people are taught that it is law, and the reverence they feel for law is at once appealed to, and enlisted in its support. The man is blind who does not see that it is through this principle that profligate politicians and apostate doctors of divinity are now leading the people to acquiesce in and obey the infamous Fugitive Slave Bill. The remedy is to teach the people the true nature of law—that justice is its essential element; and that lacking this it lacks that which is indispensably necessary to make it law.

PROSCRIPTION.

It is stated in the papers that the *National Era* has lost seven thousand subscribers through the influence of the Know-Nothings. The *Era* has never shown any friendship for the *Free Presbyterian*, and, so far as possible, has ignored our very existence. It will not exchange with us, and hence we know of its condition only from statements we see in other papers. But these facts shall not prevent us from bearing our testimony to the fidelity of the *Era* to the great cause of freedom, and against the proscription that is crippling its circulation and endangering its existence. The position of the *Era* at the seat of the National Government, the very center and focus of the slave power, gives it an incalculable importance. Hence the antislavery people of the country have always felt that one of their first duties was to give it an ample support. Then the ability and fidelity with which it has been conducted have been all, in the main, that its friends could desire. It has steadily and fearlessly exposed the schemes of the propagandists, and from time to time has lifted up the warning cry, as a faithful sentinel upon the watch-tower of freedom. And yet, because the *Era*, in common with the vast majority of the true and tried friends of freedom, suspects danger to the cause from the new secret order, and has faithfully exposed its pro-slavery tendencies, thousands of those who profess to regard slavery as the paramount issue before the country withdraw their support, and pursue a course to endanger the very existence of that paper.

This secret proscription is one of the most dangerous and detestable features of secret associations. Bound by solemn oath to the strictest secresy, their members can by common concert strike down whom they will, and yet never permit the victim to see the hand that gives the blow. Men who are too honest and upright to seek concealment find themselves crippled in their business, often without even suspecting the cause. They are placed under the ban of a secret, irresponsible order, each member of which does all in his power to ruin them in their calling in life, while these very members are probably themselves receiving, in some other branch of business, the support of the men they are trying to ruin. The member of a secret society has this double advantage. He is sure of the support of all the members of his order, and has an equal chance with others, to secure his share of the patronage of the rest of the public. Should these things continue and increase, it may yet drive the opponents of secret societies into an *open* combination for their own defense. Certainly the members of these secret conclaves would have no right to complain if the cup they fill for others should be commended to their own lips. An open league among the opposers of secret societies, to patronize none but those who agreed with them in sentiment on this subject, would be a very legitimate fruit of the secret obligation which the members of secret societies take, to patronize none but those of their own order.

We trust it may not, through necessity, come to this. Free and fair and honorable competition is the right law of trade. But " What a man sows, that shall he also reap."

These remarks have led us away from the subject with

which we started—the condition of the *National Era*. And yet the positions we have been stating are strikingly illustrated by the proscription of that paper by the Know-Nothings. Dr. Bailey stands where he has stood for years, on the broad platform of the equality of men in rights. The so-called antislavery Know-Nothings have left that platform and adopted another, which makes man's rights depend on the place of his birth—a matter over which he had no control. The order is also developing, in most of the States, the most thorough pro-slavery proclivities. It is becoming clear, almost beyond possibility of doubt, that Know-Nothingism is but the ghost of Hunker-Whiggery, trying to sneak back to life. Yet there are thousands of antislavery men in the order who have been blinded to its real purposes. And these men, regarding the slavery question as the one great over-shadowing question of the country, and as controlling all other questions, can yet be so hoodwinked by their connection with a secret society as to proscribe and try to destroy one of the most important antislavery agencies in the country. Can stronger evidence be needed of the dangerous and pernicious influence of secret oath-bound associations?

The *Era* is not the only paper that has suffered from the same cause. The *Ohio Columbian*, the able and efficient anti-slavery organ at our State capital, has been the object of the same unrighteous proscription. That our own list has not suffered in the same way is owing, we presume, entirely to the fact that we have probably not a dozen Know-Nothing sub-scribers on our books.

That all the members of this secret order sympathize with its intolerant spirit we do not suppose. Once in a while a man can be found in their ranks with magnanimity enough to tolerate a difference of opinion on a few points while there is full agreement on many points. But such magnanimity is, we fear, exceedingly rare ; and the direct tendency of the influences of the order is to destroy it.

IS THERE A LAW FOR THE RENDITION OF FUGITIVE SLAVES?

We take the negative of this question. We deny that there is either moral or civil law binding the people of the free States to aid in the recapture of fugitive slaves, or even to *permit* them to be pursued and captured on their soil.

This question may be regarded as stale and unprofitable by some, but the outrages upon the feelings of the North which slave-catchers are constantly perpetrating, force the question upon us as one of the highest *practical* import. It is, after all the discussion that has been had on the subject, an unsettled question, and until it is settled the country can enjoy no real quiet.

So far from God's law sanctioning the return of the escaping slave, it forbids it in express terms. "Thou shalt not return unto his master the servant that is escaped from his master unto thee," is the explicit mandate of Jehovah. The return of the fugitive is also forbidden by direct and necessary implication in all those passages which command to show mercy to the poor, to feed the hungry, to clothe the naked, to hide the outcast, etc. A more direct, flagrant, impious and diabolical violation of God's law than the infamous fugitive act of 1850, was never conceived or executed by man. Every person who gives the least aid in executing this act, does it at the peril of his soul's salvation. It is a sin that will inevitably secure his eternal damnation unless he repents; and those professed ministers of the gospel who defend this atrocious enactment will be doubly damned without the most deep and bitter repentance.

But not only is the return of the escaping bondman a violation of the revealed will of God, but also of the law of nature, written on every human heart. Heathen nations have always held the right of hospitality to be sacred. It is considered by them intensely base and wicked to betray the wanderer who takes shelter under their roof. Even his bitterest enemy is safe if he breaks bread in the tent of an Arab. This is not the only instance in which the virtues of heathenism shame the crimes of nominal Christendom.

But leaving this point, we inquire is there civil law for the rendition of fugitives? We deny that there is, for the three following reasons:

1. All civil enactments which violate God's law, are null and void.

2. The Constitution of the United States gives Congress no power to enact such a law, and Congress has no power of legislation except what is conferred by the Constitution.

3. If there had been a Constitutional compact for the return of fugitives, the repeated and habitual violation by the South of other provisions of the Constitution, have freed the North from all moral and civil obligation to keep such compact.

The first of these positions is distinctly taught by all writers on civil law of any standing. It is, moreover, a position which none but a downright atheist will deny. If there be a God, the creator and upholder of all things, it is not only his right but (speaking after the manner of men) his duty to govern the universe he has made. None but an almighty and infinite being is fit to rule over intelligent spirits. Hence he only can rightfully govern. But his law must be supreme and above all other laws, or his power is not absolute and his right to rule is a farce. It follows from this that those professed ministers of the gospel who teach that human enactments, like the fugitive bill, which contravene God's law, shall be obeyed, are the worst practical atheists.

Our second position is that the Constitution invests Congress with no power to pass a statute for the recovery of fugitive slaves. The article of the Constitution claimed as conferring such power, refers to persons owing service or labor in certain States by the laws of those States. But according to the so-called laws of the Southern States, the slave is a chattel, and not a person held to service by law. The slave is held to labor by brute force, not by law. Legal obligation to labor is always based on the assumption that an adequate compensation is paid to the laborer. But the very essence of slavery consists in making the slave property, and forcing him to labor without wages. Eminent Southern statesmen deny that there is any law in the Southern States establishing the relation of master and slave. The government of those States found the slave in the hands of his captor, and merely interposed to regulate the relation. The slaves are held to labor precisely as the captives on a pirate ship are held to labor; and it is an abuse of the holy term *law* to apply it to any enactments made either to establish or to regulate this piratical robbery.

Again, the so-called fugitive clause of the Constitution speaks of service and labor as *due* from one person to another. But is any thing *due* to the man-thief from his victim? Nothing, unless it be cold lead or a halter. The law of God pronounces the man-thief worthy of death, and it would be passing strange if an innocent man could owe life-long service to a culprit condemned to die. He who forfeits his right to life, forfeits his right to every thing else, and, of course, to all claim of service or labor from his fellow-man.

But, finally, admitting the existence of a Constitutional compact for the rendition of fugitives, and we claim that the

South, by its habitual violation of other parts of the compact, has released the North from all obligation of whatever character, to keep it. A compact or bargain always implies two parties and mutual obligation. It is an undisputed doctrine, both in law and morals, that when one party violates any part of the bargain, the other is legally and morally free. Now, the slaveholding States have habitually and persistently trampled down the plainest provisions of the national compact, and have violated every act of Congress passed under the Constitution when it suited their purposes to do so. The Constitution declares that the citizens of one State shall enjoy all the rights of a citizen of the United States in all the other States. But in the South the citizens of the free States are seized the moment they step on Southern soil, thrust into prison, and then, if no one appears to buy them out, are sold to pay their jail fees. The freedom of speech and of the press is guaranteed to all persons by the Constitution, but in the South it is certain death to attempt to exercise this right in speaking or writing against slavery. Compacts which stood a generation are coolly repudiated by the South. After securing their own part of the property in stipulation, they turn round, and, without a word of excuse, attempt to steal that part which had, by their own solemn compact, been secured to the North. By these and a thousand similar acts of villainy, the slaveholders have proved themselves incapable of keeping faith, and hence no faith should be kept with them. They should be commanded to give up their stolen goods, including three millions of men, women and children, and if they refuse, should be hunted from the earth as pirates are hunted from the seas.

In view of these indisputable facts and principles, we are amazed that the Republican party, and nearly all the papers in its interest, continue to concede to the slaveholder the right to pursue and capture his escaped victim on Northern soil. If justice and manhood prevailed, every free State would pass a law securing freedom to the fugitive slave the moment he set his foot upon their soil, whether he came with or without his so-called master's consent; and making it a penitentiary offense for the latter to pollute their territory by his presence in pursuit of his victim. If God's law were in force in Ohio, the poor fugitives now on trial for their liberty, in Cincinnati, would dwell safely "where it liked them best" in the State, and their pursuers would be doing the State service in a public institution at Columbus.

16

HIGHER AND LOWER LAW.

The reader will find a specimen of each in our paper to-day. On the first page is the eloquent, thrilling, *Christian* speech of Mr. Jolliffe ; on the fourth page is the weak, inhuman, atheistic decision of Judge Leavitt. How great the contrast! The antagonism between light and darkness, holiness and crime, Christianity and atheism, we have rarely seen more broadly marked. The decision of Judge Leavitt, as a mere specimen of legal ability, is weakness personified. The whole question of the relative rights of the marshal and the sheriff to hold the fugitives, is made to turn on the mere accident of the marshall having come *first* into possession of them. But in the nature of the case it could not possibly be otherwise. They were arrested by warrant, issued by the commissioner under the fugitive act, in the hands of the marshal. At the very moment of arrest, the killing of the child, which gave rise to the indictment for murder, took place. The arrest was the cause of the killing. The act was barely consummated when they were seized by the marshal, and hence it was an utter impossibility that an arrest for murder should take place before the arrest under the fugitive act. But on this mere casual incident, Judge Leavitt decides the broad and momentous question of the relative jurisdiction of the State of Ohio and of the United States. Could the fugitives have been first arrested on charge of murder, the right of the sheriff to hold them in spite of the commissioner's warrant, according to Judge Leavitt, would have been undoubted. Was ever such a grave legal question before decided on such trivial grounds ? Was there ever judicial trifling equal to this?

But the legal weakness of the decision is not its worst feature. It moral character is even worse. The Hon. Judge reiterates the lower law atheism, which has been the current teaching of venal pulpits and religious presses for the last five years. Speaking of that compound of meanness and villainy, the fugitive act, he says :

"And I may here remark, that, speaking judicially, this question is not affected by the fact that the law of the United States under which the process issues, and these persons are in custody, may be viewed, even by a majority of community, as inexpedient, unjust and oppressive. Until repealed, or adjudged void on the ground of unconstitutionality, by the proper judicial tribunal of the Union, it must be be respected and observed as law."

Then, of course, the midwives of Egypt were rebels against law and government, and deserving of severest censure. Then Daniel was guilty of rebellion, and his three brothers were wicked fanatics. No doubt if Judge Leavitt had lived at Babylon in their day, he would have thought them guilty of causing a very foolish and sinful waste of fire-wood in the heating of the furnace for their martyrdon. According to his doctrine, Paul and Peter, and the other apostles were traitors to the government, deserving of death. They should have "respected and observed as law" the decree that forbade them to teach and to preach in the name of Jesus, until it had been "repealed, or adjudged void by the proper tribunal." All who have ever stood out for right against power, and for justice against oppressive and infamous statutes, were traitors and fanatics. But when this doctrine is taught in the pulpit, it is not strange that it should be taught as good morality from the bench.

Injustice and oppression, if embodied in the form of law, according to Judge Leavitt, are worthy of respect and obedience. Then all that is necessary to make any injustice and oppression worthy of respect, is to enact them into statutory law. If the Legislature of Ohio should pass an act to sell Judge Leavitt and his wife and children on the auction block, he would be bound on his own principle to "respect and obey" it. This doctrine is subversive of all distinction between right and wrong. It overturns the very foundation of justice. It will produce the very worst anarchy and disorder. It is practical atheism of the most dangerous character.

OUTSIDE THE RANGE OF THE DIVINE OPERATIONS.

The forces of God's kingdom, both of nature and of grace, operate ordinarily within fixed boundaries and in certain directions ; and it is quite possible for men to place themselves outside the range of their operations. Thus the natural laws by the operation of which rain falls upon the earth, act only within certain limits. There are portions of the earth, as the Desert of Sahara, for instance, on which it never rains. Now, the man who desires the rain to fall upon his fields and render them fruitful, must not make his home and plant his seed in the barren desert. By so-doing he places himself outside of the forces of nature by which rain is produced.

It is a law of light that it will not penetrate opaque sub-
stances. Hence the man who would live in the sunlight must
not make his home in the deep mine. So doing he puts himself beyond the operation of the laws of light.

Those portions of the earth's surface which lie around the
poles, never come sufficiently under the rays of the sun to
become warm. Hence the man who desires the warmth of
the sun must not make his home amid the icebergs around
the poles. He is there outside the operation of the forces by
which the earth is warmed.

Now it is quite within man's power to betake himself to the
desert, the mine, or the polar iceberg. But so long as he
remains there he can not hope to enjoy the blessings of rain,
of light, or of heat.

In like manner, a man may put himself outside of the operation of the forces of God's kingdom of grace. The dew
and rain of the Divine Spirit fall not on the heart that has
made itself wholly desert and barren. Yet every man may
harden his heart until it is like nothing but the arid and
sandy desert. The heart is hardened through the deceitful-
ness of sin, and it is in every man's power to give himself up
without restraint to a course of sinful indulgence. But the
habitual indulgence of known sin will make the soul a waste
Sahara on which no dew of grace distills, and where not a single green blade appears to relieve the eye or give promise of
the least fruit. The man places himself beyond the range of
the operation of that Divine Power, by which the soul is
refreshed and quickened, and made fruitful in works of righteousness.

Again, the light of God's truth and Spirit can not fall on
the heart that is sunk in unbelief. Infidelity is a deep mine,
to whose dark recesses the rays of the Sun of Righteousness
never penetrate. And a man may make himself an infidel.
He has only to close his mind against the evidences by which
the inspired oracles are attested, and give himself up to the
lusts of an unbelieving heart, and the work is done. The
Bible forbids the lust of the flesh, the lust of the eye, and the
pride of life. But the natural heart loves these, and therefore hates the Bible; and man has only to give full scope to
this love of sin and this hatred of truth to become completely
blinded. His soul is then beyond the territories over which
the Sun of Righteousness shines.

Again, the natural selfishness of the heart, if freely
indulged, will soon render it a spiritual iceberg. Every

warm, generous, and benevolent emotion will be chilled and frozen. The soul may create around itself a moral atmosphere as cold as that which circulates around the eternal snow fields. So long as it resigns itself to the native selfishness of the carnal heart, it can feel no warmth from the sun of truth and love that shines in the moral heavens. The man has placed himself outside the operation of those Divine influences by which the heart is warmed. The genial heat of God's love can not reach his soul.

Now it is, of course, possible for God to exert his power outside of any fixed limits. He *could* cause the clouds to gather and empty themselves on the deserts of Africa. He *could* rive the earth asunder by an earthquake, and pour the sunlight into the deep mine ; and he *could* reverse the earth's axis, and bring the polar regions under a tropical sun. So he can, if he choose, pour the dew and light and heat of his Holy Spirit on the hardened, unbelieving and selfish heart. But such is not his way of action, and it is desperate presumption in the sinner to calculate on such miraculous interposition of God in his behalf. There is not a single promise in the book of God to the sinner who voluntarily places himself outside the limits within which the saving influences of the gospel usually operate.

SAVAGE.

The Memphis *Eagle and Enquirer*, alluding to the fall of Mr. Giddings from illness on the floor of the House of Representatives, says :

"We are pretty sure that some Southern members rather relished the peculiar manner in which the old Abolitionist occupied the floor then and there."

This is another illustration of the barbarism into which slavery is sinking the people of the South. None but a mind thoroughly brutalized could pen the above paragraph; and none but a half-civilized people would support or tolerate such journalism. Mr. Giddings has grown gray in a long life of faithful public service. His head is crowned with the honor which follows a life well spent. However men may differ with him in sentiment on particular questions, all must accord to him unshrinking devotion to his convictions of right, the manners and deportment of a gentleman, and a life of unspotted integrity, both public and private. To " relish " the sudden fall of such a man by the stroke of disease, betrays the heart of a brute or a fiend.

How different the spirit in which the Northern press chronicled the recent sudden death of a somewhat notorious Southerner. They point the moral which his departure teaches, and rebuke the unseemly eulogy which his comrades lavished upon him, but they express no exultation. Had his friends permitted they would have suffered him to be borne quietly to his grave, without allusion to the act that will make his name infamous in all coming time. Yet the memory of Brooks was crowned with lasting dishonor, while no stain of atrocious crime attaches to the name of Giddings.

Dr. McGill on the Free Presbyterian Church.

The Rev. A. T. McGill, D.D., professor in the Theological Seminary at Princeton, and permanent clerk of the O. S. General Assembly, was the delegate from that body to the Congregational Association of Massachusetts. His speech before that body, at its late meeting, was mainly a glorification of the position of his church on the subject of slavery. Speaking of the results of the " adjustment " of the question made at Cincinnati in 1845, he says :

" Some of our body were dissatisfied with the position in which this adjustment left us. I do not know personally all who left, to form what is called the Free Presbyterian Church. I know that some of them were estimable men ; but I know that the foremost and hottest man in repudiating the church of his fathers has, since that time, repudiated all religious organizations, has renounced the Saviour, has cursed the Bible, and has gone to the world a violent infidel—a miscreant reviler of all that is sacred and decent in the usages of Christian civilization. And I know that another of the most eloquent in leading off that exodus from us, on account of slavery, has since turned the sacred desk into a mere political stump, and takes every text to vilify all that is dominant in Church and State. Now, sir, if we had nothing else to justify this action in our eye, this ruin of those who have gone off would satisfy us that we are, in all probability in the right."

We have seldom read any misrepresentation of our church with as much regret as the above ; not so much on account of

the statements it contains (for they are too utterly unfounded
to do us any harm), as on account of the source from whence
they come. For the greater portion of two terms in a theological seminary, it was our privilege to enjoy the instruction
of Dr. McGill. The intercourse between us as teacher and
pupil was uniformly of the most kind and agreeable character.
We have ever regarded him as a man of the strictest truth
and integrity, and as a kind, amiable, courteous Christian
gentleman. We formed for him an attachment which the
lapse of years, and our separation from the Old School Presbyterian Church, have scarcely weakened. It is this which
causes our regret in reading statements so unfair and untrue
as are contained in the foregoing extract.

In the first place, it is not true that a single minister, who
left the Old School Presbyterian Church on account of the
"adjustment" of 1845, and aided in organizing the Free
Presbyterian Church, has become an infidel. The individual to whom, we suppose, Dr. McGill alludes, left the O. S.
Pres. Church two years before the year 1845, and never was
a member of the Free Presbyterian Church. He has denounced our church quite as freely as he has the O. S. Pres.
Church. His infidelity moreover is the work of the pro-
slavery teachings of Old School Drs. of Divinity, and others.
Whatever "ruin" there may be, in his case, is the result of
the persistent efforts of pro-slavery "divines" to prove that
the Bible sanctions slavery. Instead of indulging, therefore,
in self-righteous glorification over such cases, Dr. McGill and
his colaborers should take to themselves shame and confusion
of face over the "ruin" their own hands have wrought.

Again, the statement that "another of the most eloquent
in leading off the exodus from the Old School General Assembly, has turned the sacred desk into a mere political stump,
and takes every text to vilify all that is dominant in Church
or State," is not true. Free Presbyterian ministers believe
that civil government is God's ordinance, and that he has
defined the character of the civil ruler in his word. They
believe that men should vote as they pray; that they should
vote, as well as eat and drink, to the glory of God. They
have, therefore, preached these Bible truths to their people,
and have tried to show them *how*, in their judgment, they
could vote for the glory of God. To this extent and no more,
they have turned the "sacred desk into a political stump,"
and we defy Dr. McGill and every body else to show to the
contrary.

But the worst thing in the Dr.'s tissue of false statements is representing those who have gone off from the Old School as "ruined." Suppose the foregoing statements about two individuals were as true as they are false, and what a monstrous conclusion is it, that the whole Free Presbyterian Church has gone to "ruin" in consequence. The Free Presbyterian Church numbers about fifty ministers. Suppose two of them had gone to moral ruin, which is not the fact, what then? With far more propriety might an old Pharisee have represented the church and cause of Jesus Christ as gone to ruin, because out of a ministry of twelve one *did* prove a vile traitor, whereas, according to Dr. McGill's own showing, only two out of fifty, or one out of every twenty-five, of our ministers, has proved recreant to his high calling. This mode of judging and pronouncing sentence is monstrous. From time to time ministers of the O. S. Pres. Church are tried and excommunicated for heresy, for dishonesty, for adultery, fornication and other crimes. We could name more than a dozen such, within our own limited range of observation. Shall we, therefore, say that the whole body is ruined? Such cases occur in all churches, and it is the grossest injustice to charge their guilt upon the whole church, unless the church retains them in fellowship, after their guilt is brought to light.

There is another fact which renders the statements of Dr. McGill still more inexcusable. He represents Free Presbyterians as having gone to ruin, because they seceded from a church which proclaims that its own organization is based on the conceded principle, that slavery, as it exists at the South, is no bar to Christian communion, and because they have formed a church which denies Christian fellowship to slaveholders. This position he represents as the *cause* of their "ruin." Now what will the reader think, when he is told that Dr. McGill was baptized, reared, educated, studied theology, was licensed and ordained to preach, and actually did preach several years in a church which, as long ago as 1832, took the very same ground of non-fellowship with slavery, which our church occupies; and has maintained it ever since? Yet such is the fact. Dr. McGill had all his training, and spent the first years of his ministry, in the Associate Presbyterian (Seceder) Church; and he knows full well that the position of that church, of the Covenanters and Associate Reformed, all of which exclude slaveholders from fellowship, has not been their ruin. They have grown as rapidly in proportion to their numbers at first, as other churches; and they are distinguished above others for their steadfast adherence to the doctrines of the Bible, and to the Presbyterian form of church government. And, yet, with these facts before him, Dr. McGill can represent a church as going, or gone to ruin, because it refuses Christian fellowship to slaveholders. So saying, he reproaches and "repudiates the church of *his* fathers."

Dr. McGill is a man of powerful and brilliant intellect. The fact, therefore, that *he* can bring no better reasons than the foregoing misstatements, to prove that his church "is in the right," is the strongest possible presumptive proof, that on the question of slavery it is wholly in the wrong.

CANT.

In the course of a sermon, preached before the Old School General Assembly, at St. Louis, by Dr. Humphrey, of Louisville, on the subject of Domestic Missions, occurs this passage:

"In brief, ours is both historically and constitutionally, a free church in the bosom of a free people—a republic within a republic. It is identified at once, with all that is glorious in the history of the country, and with all that is far more exceedingly glorious in the hopes of another and better country, even an heavenly. For this reason it has a precise adaptation to the work of spreading the gospel throughout the land. *It is in sympathy with the common people, with all their patriotic sentiments, their passionate love of liberty, their most cherished institutions.* Our missionary on the most distant frontier, or in the remote wilderness, where a few hardy settlers are just letting in the sun upon the soil, may captivate at once their understanding and republican sympathies, by laying open the principles of our ecclesiastical policy; thus demonstrating that *Presbyterianism, though so long maligned, is but another name for truth and liberty.*"

These sentences are found in the midst of an eloquent disquisition on the sympathy of Presbyterianism, in past times, with civil and religious liberty. It is true of every form of Presbyterianism, except that represented by the two General Assemblies of this country, that it is the fast friend of the largest liberty. It is true that it was in the days of the

Westminster Assembly, and in the time of the American Revolution, "in sympathy with the people's passionate love of liberty." It is one of the glories of Presbyterianism, that it has in past times been the foe of tyranny, and the stern advocate of the rights of man. In the mouth of an old Covenanter, in the days of Cromwell, or in the mouth of any of their *legitimate* descendants, in this day, the language of Dr. Humphrey would be appropriate. But in the mouth of their author, and before the Assembly he was addressing, they are words of canting hypocrisy. Look at it.

The speaker himself, if we are not mistaken, is an Eastern man by birth and education, now a slaveholder in Louisville, Ky. The Assembly to which he was speaking, has adopted as her deliberate testimony, that she originally organized, and has since continued the bond of union on the conceded principle that domestic slavery, in the circumstances in which it exists in the southern portion of this country, is no bar to Christian communion. They affirm, moreover, that among the duties enjoined by Christ and his apostles upon slaveholders, that of emancipation is not enumerated; and that for them to pronounce the holding of slaves a heinous sin, demanding the discipline of the Church, would be virtually to dissolve their Assembly, and abandon the organization under which by the Divine blessing they have so long prospered. The practice of the church, taking the testimony of their own Synods, and Presbyteries and churches as evidence, is even worse than this declaration of sentiment. About eighty thousand immortal beings are held by her ministers and members in a state of bondage, the most absolute and unmitigated that exists on the face of the globe. They are without legal protection for a single right, and completely subject to the irresponsible will of their owners, however cruel and capricious that will may be. Their treatment in this condition by members and ministers of the Presbyterian Church is often infernally cruel. Take a few items of testimony. Says the O. S. Synod, of Kentucky: "*Cases occur in our own denomination in which professors of the religion of mercy sell the mother from her children, and send her into merciless and returnless exile, and yet discipline rarely follows.*" The Rev. Francis Hawley, pastor of a Baptist Church in Colebrook, Litchfield County, Connecticut, resided fourteen years in North and South Carolina. His standing and character may be judged from the fact that the Baptist State Convention of North Carolina, appointed him a few years since their general agent to visit the Baptist churches within their bounds, and to secure their co-operation in the objects of the Convention. In the course of a narrative, published under his own signature, he relates this incident:

" I will now give a few facts showing the workings of the system. Some years since a Presbyterian minister moved from North Carolina to Georgia. He had a negro man of an uncommon mind. For some cause, I know not what, this master whipped him most unmercifully. He next nearly *drowned* him; he then put him *in the fence.* This is done by lifting up the corner of a 'worm' fence, and then putting the feet through. The rails serve as *stocks.* He kept him there some time, how long I was not informed, but the poor slave *died* in a few days; and if I was rightly informed, nothing was done about it, either in Church or State. After some time he moved back to North Carolina, and is now a member of ——— Presbytery. I have heard him preach, and have been in the pulpit with him. May God forgive me ! "

The same witness relates the following :

" One of my neighbors sold a speculator a negro boy about fourteen years old. It was more than his poor mother could bear. Her reason fled, and she became a perfect maniac, and had to be kept in close confinement. She would occasionally get out and run off to the neighbors. On one of these occasions she came to my house. She was, indeed, a pitiable object. With tears rolling down her cheeks, and her frame shaking with agony, she would cry out, ' *Dont you hear him, they are whipping him now, and he is calling for me.*' This neighbor of mine, who tore the boy away from his poor mother, and thus broke her heart, was a *member of the Presbyterian Church.*"

The Synod of South Carolina and Georgia, embracing all the clergy of those States, give this testimony:

" Those only who have the management of servants know what the *hardening effect* of it is upon *their own feelings toward them.* There is no necessity to dwell on this point, as all *owners* and *managers* fully understand it. He who commences to manage them with tenderness and with a willingness to favor them in every way, must be watchful, otherwise he will settle down in *indifference, if not severity.* "

We add but one other item, from a *volume* of the same sort in our possession, all of the most unquestionable character. The Rev. Charles S. Renshaw, of Quincy, Illinois, formerly a resident of Kentucky, testifies as follows, in speaking of the Presbyterian minister and church where he resided :

"The minister and all the church-members held slaves. Some were treated kindly—others harshly. *There was not a shade of difference* between their slaves and those of their *infidel* neighbors, either in their physical, intellectual or moral state; in some cases they would *suffer* in the comparison.

"In the kitchen of the minister of the church a slave was living in open adultery with a slave woman who was a member of the church, with an 'assured hope' of heaven, while the man's wife was on the minister's farm in Fayette County. The minister had to bring a cook down from his farm to the place in which he was preaching. The choice was between the wife of the man and this church-member. He *left the wife* and brought the church-member to the adulterer's bed."

We present these as mere specimens of the *actual* condition of the slave. These facts exhibits his treatment by *Presbyterians* in the South—the ministers, and elders, and members of that church which Dr. Humphrey boasts is in sympathy with the people's passionate love of liberty! We present one other fact illustrative of the spirit of the General Assembly itself. A member of the Assembly of 1849, which sat in Pittsburg, relates the following :

"There is a fact that occurred in connection with the Assembly of 1849, which sat in the city of Pittsburg, that is worthy of notice. In the providence of God, a poor African female slave presented herself at the door of the Assembly, with a paper certified by a number of respectable ministers, begging some pecuniary aid to help her to purchase herself, her husband and her children, who were all owned by a master in Virginia. I, being a member of the Assembly, endeavored to do what I was able for her by my own contributions, and by circulating her paper. Among other means the thought occurred to me that it might do good to have her papers read before the Assembly ; and, accordingly, I suggested it to a number of the members and the moderator, but they all disapproved of the suggestion, and her papers were *not* read."

Here, a poor suppliant, begging the means to secure herself and family from this worse than Algerine bondage, is *denied even a hearing.* Jesus Christ always received kindly and listened tenderly to the petition of the very poorest. Yet this General Assembly, boasting through Dr. Humphrey of its devotion to freedom and justice, turns coldly away from the humble petition of a broken-hearted mother.

But to exhibit the full effrontery of this vain boasting, we present another extract from the sermon of Dr. Humphrey. Among the objects of home missions, he mentions these very outraged victims of wrong. Strange that a sense of shame did not crimson his brow and choke his utterance. In the course of his remarks on the subject, this passage occurs:

" They are the poor of the land, and to the poor the gospel is preached. ' For I am a debtor ' said the apostle, ' both to the Greeks and to the barbarians, both to the wise and unwise.' Further, they are accessible to us. We cross no sea or mountain to reach them ; we acquire no barbarous jargon ; we visit no inhospitable shore to bear to them the unspeakable riches of Christ. They are here ; they are all around us ; they speak our language : they cultivate our fields ; they sit with us in the house of God ; they wait in our houses ; they come even into our bedchambers. *Thousands of them are under service to the communicants or worshipers in our congregations,* and our ministers may have access as easy to the servant as to their masters."

Here is the admission from this boaster of Presbyterian devotion to freedom, that "thousands of immortal human beings are under service to the *communicants* or worshipers in their congregations." The nature of this service is exhibited in the extracts already given, and in thousands of similar facts in our possession. The whole power of the Assembly is wielded to sustain the system that licenses and perpetuates these oppressions and outrages on the defenseless poor. The oppressors are taken by thousands to the communion table, and their Christian (!) character indorsed. Northern ministers, and many of them abolitionists, sit down with them to partake of the symbols of the Saviour's passion, and thus lend their influence and character to uphold the wrong. And then doughface and slaveholder together, go to the hall of the General Assembly to listen with self-complacent pride to the praises of Presbyterian devotion to liberty.

SOUND DOCTRINE.

The *New Haven Register* has a report of the speeches at the Union meeting held in New Haven. Among the addresses was one by the Rev. Dr. Taylor, Professor of Didactic Theology in Yale College, which can not fail to be productive of good. We make extracts from it.

"I am happy to be here. I am glad to see the indifference to party ties, when the great interests of the nation are in issue. Long enough has this subject been trifled with. Long enough have the enemies of law and order had this subject all on their side, and reasoned it all the wrong way. I am, therefore, most ready to express my entire dissent, and unqualified disapprobation of all those attempts to degrade that article in our Constitution, upon which so much has been said, and to trample on the law, which all Northern men are bound to stand by and support in good faith to the very last. (Cheers.)

"I say in good faith; and I ask if the compact between the Northern and Southern States—independent sovereignties—was not a lawful compact? Had not the North interests at stake to justify them? I will not go into the question whether slavery is a sin. Be it so if you please. Had they not reason, and good reason, for entering into this compact? I will make a supposition: Suppose Russia and her hordes, combined with Germany, Austria, Prussia, France, and England, were threatening to conquer and devastate our country, and there is slavery in Spain; suppose for our own protection and safety, we deem it necessary to enter into an alliance with Spain. Now there are slaves in Spain and Cuba, and if this combination is made for our protection, Spain says some of her slaves will get among our people, and our people will not deliver them up.

"War is coming, desolation is coming; it is a sin, if you please, for Spain to have slaves; may we not lawfully, and for our own safety, enter into such a compact, and agree to deliver up these slaves. We have not made the slave; she is independent, and it is made by her own local laws, in the enjoyment of those local rights which she, as an independent sovereign has a right to exercise, so far as we are concerned. Whether she is right so far as her responsibility to the Judge of the earth is concerned, is another question. But, so far as we are concerned, she has a right to make these laws. What! may I not buy a piece of meat from a butcher, because he is profane? May I not make contracts with men whose characters, in some respects, are marred by evil? May I not consult my own safety by numerous acts of a defensive and confederate character, because the men who are engaged with me are not as good as I wish they were? Is this the principle in neighborhoods? Will it do in the family? Will it do better among nations? What right have we to make laws for the Southern States? I am the friend of slaves; I am sorry for slaves; I wish them well with all my heart and soul; and as I wish them well, I say, cease these agitations. Who are the friends of the slaves at the North? The agitators of this subject do more to injure the slave and perpetuate their chains at the South, than their true friends can do to terminate the evil for half a century. (Cheers.)

"As to the higher law principle: You expect me to admit of course, that we are all the subjects of Him who reigns amid the grandeur and glory of eternity, and that when his will is known, we, as mortal beings, are bound to submit. There is no question on that point; here is the point: Is that article in our Constitution contrary to the will of God—contrary to the law of nature, of nations, and the will of God? Is it so? Is there a shadow of reason for saying it is? I have not been able to discover it. Have I not shown you it is lawful to deliver up, in compliance with their laws, fugitive slaves, for the high, the great, the momentous interests of these States? And if it is lawful to do it, is it not in accordance with the Constitution to make a law providing for that result? Is there any law of God against this? Is there any law of God against doing lawful things, which every man must do in the course of his life? I do not so understand it.

"Stand, my fellow citizens, by law! stand by the Constitution of our country; that Constitution, which, like the atmosphere around us, blesses every breath we draw; we walk, we sleep, we exist every moment under its influence. What would become of us if the Constitution were trampled in the dust? No, sir—as has been said, so say I, with all my heart and soul, if any of my fellow-citizens do not value the Constitution enough to defend it, they are not worthy of the blessings it gives them. (Cheers.) I say again, let us stand by the Constitution and the law, and as somebody has said, as near as I can remember, 'I would not merely protect it with the shield of honest Ajax, I would protect it also with a wall of brass; and when this would not serve the purpose of protection, then would I circle it with the living hearts of my countrymen, and in its defense rally, till the last drop of blood were expended in defending the Constitution.' "

We take the above from the *Presbyterian Advocate*, which expresses the conviction that it "can not fail to be productive of good." It is just such "sound doctrine" as we look for in the *Advocate*. Its mingled obtuseness and wickedness fit it most admirably for the columns of that journal. It is another melancholy exhibition of the infidelity so rife among the D. Ds. of the popular churches of this country. When such sentiments are put forth by professors of theology, and imbibed by their pupils, alas! for the churches that are to sit under their ministry.

The leading idea of the above extract is, that, on the supposition of slavery being a sin, the North had a right to enter into a compact with the South, to deliver up the escaping slave, and is now both religiously and politically bound to fulfill the bargain "in good faith." Now if it be a sin to hold men in slavery, it must be right for the slave to escape if he can; and, therefore, it must be a sin to return him to his bondage. Admitting that the slaveholder sins in holding his fellow-man as a chattel, Dr. Taylor contends, that another man does not sin by entering into a contract to help him to do so, if there are what he considers sufficient inducements for so doing. It may be sin in the principal, but not in the accessory, if said accessory has "interests at stake to justify" him in aiding and abetting. What is this but "doing evil that good may come?" It is sin to hold the slave, but to secure certain "interests at stake," it is not sin to help the slaveholder to do the wrong. If this regard to "interests" may bleach one vice into a virtue, it may another. If I enter into a contract with another to help him commit murder, and have good reasons for so doing, it is my duty, according to this theory, to carry out my engagement in "good faith." Men have only to conjure up what they may think good reasons for forming a compact to commit any crime, and Dr. Taylor's principle justifies them in standing to the bargain.

But exclaims the sagacious Dr. "What! may I not buy a piece of meat from a butcher, because he is profane? May I not make contracts with men whose characters in some respects are marred by evil?" The object of this illustration is to justify a contract with the South to return the fugitive. It, therefore, betrays unpardonable stupidity, or a willful intention to deceive. No one denies the right to buy meat from the profane, or to make contracts with the wicked. But we do deny the right to make a contract to *aid them in their wickedness*. It is not making a contract with slaveholders that the abolitionists condemn, but making a contract to aid them in holding their slaves, which Dr. Taylor admits (or does not deny), is sinful. To make his illustration avail anything for his purpose, he ought to show that it would be right to enter into a contract to encourage his profane butcher in his profanity. He ought to show that it is sinless to make contracts with "men whose characters are marred by evil," the stipulations of which bind him to "aid and comfort" them in their evil ways.

The reasons which the Dr. alleges for the North entering into a wicked compact to deliver up slaves is purely a fancy sketch. (We say wicked compact, for, in the sense in which it is commonly understood, the article of the Constitution in question is wicked. We deny, however, that it is rightly construed.) But admitting the conditions do exist—that war and desolation are coming on this country, and that the only way that appears to human view to prevent this is to enter into a compact to do an admitted wrong, we utterly deny the right to do so. To assert the right is only an exhibition of rank infidelity. It is a most insulting distrust of God. What does it amount to? Plainly this: that God can not preserve a nation from destruction and the ravages of war, except they enter into compact with another nation to do an acknowledged wrong. This doctrine, coming from an infidel politician, might not surprise us, but coming from a professed believer in a superintending and omnipotent Providence, its infidelity is astounding. God is so straitened (that is the idea) for means to accomplish his ends, that he can, in a given case, preserve a nation from war and desolation only by its entering into a bargain with another nation to aid in doing an admitted crime. What course would a simple Christian faith dictate in such circumstances? A prudent use of all lawful means of defense, and then a committal of the whole case to that "God who presides over the destinies of nations." All such crooked expedients as the one lauded by Dr. Taylor are exhibitions of the grossest form of practical unbelief. May God save the country from the prevalence of such teachings.

AN ACCOMMODATING D. D.

There is, in Holidaysburg, in this State, a certain doctor of Divinity named McKinney, who has recently enlightened the world with a sermon entitled, "The Union Preserved, or the

Law-abiding Christian." The way this doctor in Israel blows hot and cold must rejoice the hearts of that very large class of modern Rabbis who are found on all sides of moral questions at once. Speaking of the Fugitive Bill, he discourses as follows :

"There is *another view* of this subject which may be presented for a moment. A law may be neither unconstitutional nor immoral, and still it may be ODIOUS. It may enjoin something repulsive to the feelings, and which a man would not perform, though at the risk of great personal suffering to result from his refusal. Such a law, *if esteemed needless*, he would naturally and strongly desire to have erased from the statute book. The thought of its existence is painful, and from its execution his soul revolts.

"And such, with some minds, is the Fugitive Slave Law. They regard it as hard—very hard toward a fellow-being—as discordant to the great law of love, and severely oppressive to the unfortunate. The poor negro is a slave *from no fault of his own*. He has a human soul, with human aspirations. He is bound down. The chain is galling. He pants for liberty. He has heard of a land of freedom—an asylum—a lap of plenty, where the poor of all lands find a home—a refuge for the oppressed—a rest for the weary—a land where the fundamental principles are freedom, equality, protection, 'life, liberty, and the pursuit of happiness.' Hope lights up his soul. He bursts his bonds, and flies thither. The fugitive is in our midst, weary, famished, seeking safety, and still pursued. Shall we stop his progress? Shall we deny his fainting soul a morsel of food? Shall we seize him, and bind him with thongs, and with irons, and force him back to remediless servitude, to agony, and despair, and death? And shall *these* hands—at man's bidding—touch the fugitive? Shall they do the foul deed? No: never—*never*—NEVER! No: my brother, though your face is strange, and your body dark; yet that face bears the lineaments of man, and that body encases an immortal spirit, and that bondage was for no crime of yours. Here is food, and there is the way.

"But his master is speedily at the door, also. Well, here is bread for the master; and there is the same way by which the servant passed. The flying slave plead the claims of humanity. The pursuing master has the protection of legal enactments. Each departs from me refreshed, and with his limbs unfettered. And for each there is the same path without an obstacle."

Food for the slave, and food for the master alike! An open way for both. Both leave his hospitable threshold equally refreshed. Liberty and slavery share alike in his sympathies. The fugitive seeking the priceless boon of freedom, and the slave-catcher striving to rob him of it, and to thrust him back to the horrors of slavery, are alike welcome under the hospitable roof of Dr. McKinney. To both he points the way, and stands by to see the race, like the woman watching the fight between the bear and her husband, not caring a fig which beats. "Good Lord, good Devil." What's the use to take sides in a controversy between slavery and freedom? A world of responsibility and trouble is avoided by treating both parties in the contest alike.

This "aid and comfort" to the man-catcher, in the circumstances supposed by this *impartial* D. D., will be entirely gratuitous. The fugitive law (so called) does not demand it. It is not stipulated in the bond. That "commands good citizens" to help catch the runaway, when summoned by the marshal, but not feed the kidnapper, or show him the way.

When professed teachers of religion are thus indifferent as between right and wrong—when they accord equal favor to justice and injustice—to the authority of God and the Devil, what can be expected of those under their instruction? When such teachers are rife in the land, it is not strange that the depravation of public morals should be rapid and alarming.

"The Spirit of Abolitionism."

The *St. Louis Presbyterian* commenting on the resolution of the Home Missionary Society, "that in the disbursement of the funds committed to their trust, the Committee will not grant aid to churches containg slaveholding members, unless evidence be furnished that the relation is such as in the judgment of the Committee, is justifiable, for the time being, in the peculiar circumstances in which it exists," remarks:

"We see in this resolution the true spirit of abolitionism. The Bible is no rule of faith and practice for its advocates; and the good of slaves is no part of its aim. All admit that the apostles of Christ preached without hesitation to just such churches as the Committee refuse to send the gospel to ; and all admit, that the very best way of ameliorating the condition of slaves, and of securing their freedom, is to preach the gospel both to masters and slaves. If abolitionism could prevail generally, among ministers, the gospel would be wholly removed from the slaveholding States; and the condition of the slaves would become unspeakably worse than it has ever been. Practically there are no enemies to the slaves whom they have so much reason to dread, as the men who would take from them the light and hopes of the gospel, and leave them in the hands of men wholly destitute of its beneficent influence."

It would be hard to express more untruths in as many words. There are five sentences in the above extract, and there are five distinct falsehoods. The second sentence contains two: "The Bible is no rule for its advocates, and the good of slaves is no part of its aim." The Bible *is* the rule of the class of abolitionists referred to, and the good of slaves *is* a main part of their aim. The declaration that "*all* admit that the apostles preached without hesitation to just such churches as the committee refuse to aid," is a stupendous falsehood. "All admit" no such thing. There is not an impartial Christian in the land, who has thoroughly investigated the subject, that admits that the apostles ever preached to churches that received habitual and unrepentant slaveholders. There is not one jot or tittle of evidence to show that they did, but a mass of overwhelming evidence to prove they did not. The declaration, that if abolitionism could prevail the gospel would be taken from the slave States, is utterly false, and Dr. Rice knows it. He has lived in Kentucky and knows that the abolitionists have been preaching the gospel there, amid persecution and reproach, for years. He knows moreover, that they have tried earnestly to introduce the gospel into North Carolina and other slaveholding States, and that they have endured all manner of persecution in the effort.

All that the Christian antislavery men of this country have opposed in this matter, is the preaching to slaves and masters of that false and spurious gospel which teaches that the Bible sanctions slavery. They regard such preaching as a libel on Christianity, and an unmitigated curse to master and slave. But they have done what they could to send the *pure* gospel of Jesus to the South. The work to which Christ declares he was specially anointed was "to preach the gospel to the poor, to heal the broken-hearted, to preach deliverance to the captives, and to set at liberty them that are bruised." This true aud loving gospel the abolitionists would preach all over the South, were it not that infidels, like Dr. Rice, in the church, and ruffians in the world, combine to drive their missionaries away.

INJUSTICE TO THE DEAD.

A work has been recently published by the Rev. Joseph Smith, D. D., giving a history of the rise and growth of the Presbyterian churches of Western Pennsylvania. This work has been made the text of a long article in the *St. Louis Presbyterian* on the same subject. After sketching the lives and labors of the prominent ministers of that period, the writer in the St. Louis paper remarks that " several character-istics of the *times* and the men who founded the Presbyterian Church in Western Pennsylvania, deserve bright notice." The first of these " characteristics " was the abundance of the labors of the ministers of that period. The second charac-teristic, which we are told " deserves *bright* notice," we give in the words of the writer, and of· Dr. Smith, whom he quotes :

" 2. But what will doubtless startle a class of good people, is the fact that most of the early ministers in Western Penn-sylvania were slaveholders! We let their historian tell the story. (Page 274.)

" ' The plain, frugal habits of the times did not impose upon the ministers then the necessity of any thing further than the cheapest furniture and the plainest style of living. Most of them assisted in much of the work that was done on their farms. With but one or two exceptions they owned colored servants, both male and female, who were carefully instructed and kindly treated. Most of these servants were members of the church. This statement may surprise some readers, and, if they are abolitionists, will be rather an unwelcome piece of information, but it was truly so. At least six of the early ministers, and almost all their elders, were slaveholders. We never heard that their consciences were disturbed on the subject. They provided well for their servants, and those born after 1780, were, in due time, entitled to the benefit of the act passed that year by the Legislature of Pennsylvania, ' for the gradual abolition of slavery.' "

Now, why do not Mr. Smith and his annotator tell the

whole story? Why do they not tell us that these same ministers, whose memories they venerate, were also whisky makers and whisky drinkers? Such was really the fact. Almost every farm in Western Pennsylvania had at that time a distillery, and the use of whisky was universal. Preacher and layman, saint and sinner, alike used it habitually. Drunkenness was common, and even the ministers sometimes drank to the verge of intoxication. Western Pennsylvania was the seat of the famous "Whisky Insurrection." This Insurrection was only quelled by the United States Government marching an army of fifteen thousand men to the scene of the rebellion, and not by the minister's reasoning, in imitation of Paul, of "*temperance*, righteousness and a judgment to come." These pioneer ministers had no penchant for such "reasoning" so far as "temperance" was concerned, for authentic legends tell us that some of them dearly loved the "good creature."

This the historian might have recorded with as much propriety as the fact that these men were slaveholders. And if their example proves any thing for slavery, it proves as much, or more, for whisky guzzling.

But it did not suit Dr. Smith's purpose to tell the whole truth. Whisky drinking and vulgarity are now regarded as rather low and disreputable vices. But slavery is the corner stone of our "Republican Institutions," and of our large ecclesiastical organizations. It has been pronounced by the Assembly of the O. S. Presbyterian Church, to be the bond of their union—the very cement that holds the stones of their Zion together; for they declare in so many words that to put it out of their church "would be to dissolve their organization." Moreover, unless common fame does Dr. Smith outrageous injustice, his own fingers have handled the price of the bones and souls and unpaid toil of some of his fellow-men. Hence the example of the fathers of the Presbyterian Church in Western Pennsylvania is quoted in favor of the practice of slaveholding. This "peculiar institution" is covered with the shining mantle of the real or supposed piety of these venerable men, and thus commended to our admiration, in order that their sons in this day may justify themselves for their complicity in this horrible system.

This conduct of Dr. Smith is a foul injustice to the dead. They lived in a period of profound ignorance, or of utter thoughtlessness in regard to the evils of slavery and drunkenness, and at a time when the refinements and amenities of our present social life were utterly ignored. "The times of this ignorance," we would charitably hope, "God winked at." Their education and the spirit of the times in which they lived, may palliate, if they will not entirely excuse in these men what would be utterly intolerable in their descendants. But to tear off this mantle, which that charity which covers a *multitude of sins*, would throw over these dark spots in their lives, and hold up their deformities to the gaze of posterity, is a work which does no credit to the head or heart of Dr. Smith. The time is not far distant when the fact that they were slaveholders will be as carefully concealed as the fact that they made and drank whisky. But to hold up their example as a barrier to that tremendous tide of opposition to slavery now setting in, is dishonorable alike to the living and the dead.

SLAVERY IN THE OLD SCHOOL GENERAL ASSEMBLY.

The vexed question was brought before this body by the Congregational delegate from Maine. The moderator of the Assembly responded, and the reporters placed him in a false position. The following is his explanation :

"The moderator (Rev. Francis McFarland, D. D., of the Presbytery of Lexington, Va.,) said : I beg to be indulged in a few remarks upon a subject in which I am peculiarly interested. Last evening I was greatly surprised to find in the *Commercial Advertiser* of this city a report of my remarks made yesterday in response to the delegate from Maine, in which I am made to say : ' As to slavery, Sir, I never heard remarks upon the evils of the system which I could not subscribe to.' [Laughter.] The Assembly will bear witness that I never uttered such a sentence. Had I uttered such a sentence the Assembly would have taken me out of this chair. Had I been considered capable of uttering such a sentence the Assembly would never have placed me in this chair. If it were believed that any minister had uttered this sentiment it would destroy his influence in the South."

" Dr. Prime.—And in the North, too, Sir."

Dr. McFarland also published a card in the *Commercial Advertiser* correcting the blunder of the reporters. Alluding to the above sentiment which they had put in his mouth, he says :

"The moderator never uttered such a sentiment—it would constitute him an abolitionist of the first class, from the principles of whom he utterly dissents. IIc expressed no opinion of his own, but said 'that he was extensively acquainted in the Southern States, and that he never met with man or woman who did not admit that slavery was an evil, till the Abolition controversy drove them in self-defense to take different ground.'"

Can pro-slavery truckling go beyond this? Had the moderator been capable of assenting to remarks on the evils of slavery he would have been taken out of the moderator's chair. Had he been considered capable of uttering a conviction that slavery is an evil, he would never have been placed in that chair. To admit that slavery is an evil is a bar to all promotion in the Old School General Assembly. This statement is made from the moderator's chair, and so far as appears, not a tongue is lifted in dissent to the disgraceful statement. But then it is consistent with the position of that Assembly since 1845. They then declared slavery to be their corner-stone and bond of union, and, of course, no one should be permitted to breathe one syllable of opposition to the peculiar institution. To doubt its Divine origin and holy character is to strike at the foundation of the General Assembly; and if a man, capable of such treason to slavery, should, by mistake, get into the moderator's chair, he must expect so soon as the mistake is discovered, to be dragged out in double quick time! The Old School General Assembly is becoming more and more besotted in its devotion to slavery, year by year. It is literally "drunk with the wine of the wrath of the fornication" of this great American harlot. How much longer will *Christian* people adhere to such a reprobate body?

The statement which Dr. McFarland *did* make, though very old and stale, is very peculiar and intensely foolish. What he did say was, that he never met a man or woman in the South, "who did not admit that slavery was an evil, till the abolition controversy drove them, in self-defense, to take different ground." That is, they admitted that slavery was an evil until the abolitionists of the North arose and agreed with them in that admission, and urged them to put the admitted evil away! Then, in self-defense, they changed ground, ate their own words, stoutly denied that slavery was an evil at all, and began to swear by it as a household god! And this statement is solemnly put forth before a grave assembly of doctors of divinity and others, apparently without a suspicion that it represents the men and women of the South as both knaves and fools. Dr. McFarland, of course, would have us believe that they were both honest and intelligent in formerly admitting that slavery is an evil. Did the rise of the abolition controversy, then, change the character of slavery? Is not the present denial by Southern men and women that slavery is an evil, both foolish and dishonest? Or did the magic wand of the abolitionists touch the unclean devil of slavery, and transform it into an angel of light? If the abolitionists have performed this miraculous service for the slaveholders, in all gratitude they should cease to curse them. Just look at the position in which the statement of Dr. McFarland puts the Southern people. There are men and women who freely admit to the world and to themselves that slavery is a great evil. A society of men and women is formed in the North who say to them, Yes, brethren and sisters of the South, slavery *is* undoubtedly a great evil, and now we propose to do what we can, in a friendly manner, to help you put it away. Let us set about the great work of abolishing this admitted evil at once. But presto! change! The words of these Northern fanatics, or rather their repetition of Southern words, has instantly changed the whole aspect of the case. The Southern people at once rise up and say, "You Northern fanatics are meddling with what you do not understand. Slavery is not an evil. It is a divine institution. ' It is the corner-stone of our republican institutions.' Our churches are based on the conceded principle, that it is no bar to Christian communion. Away with your intermeddling! In 'self-defense' we take back our former admission, and affirm that to be good which before we freely and honestly admitted to be evil." It is surely time that *men* should cease uttering such transparent folly.

The Dr. Prime who holds, as reported above, that a man will lose his influence in the North by declaring slavery an evil, is the editor of the *New York Observer*, the "Satanic press" of the religious world.

MISDIRECTION OF ANTISLAVERY EFFORT.

It is a curious and undeniable fact, that the success of the Slave Power, in this country, in its aggressions upon freedom, has kept pace with the growth of the antislavery sentiment.

The acquisition of Texas, the Mexican War, the enactment of the Fugitive Slave Act, and the repeal of the Missouri Compromise, have all transpired since the commencement of the antislavery movement. The abolitionists have for years been more numerous than the slaveholders. In 1848 they polled 300,000 *votes*, while the whole number of slave-owners in the country, including men, women and children, does not exceed 250,000. Yet the two worst acts of slaveholding tyranny— the passage of the fugitive bill, and the Nebraska swindle— have been perpetrated since that time. What adds to our surprise in contemplating this phenomenon, is the fact, that the abolitionists had all the advantages of having truth and conscience on their side, while the slaveholders have been warring against both.

It will be both instructive and profitable, if we can ascertain the true cause of this phenomenon. Without further preliminary, we state our belief that one principal cause has been, the misdirection of antislavery effort. The movement, of late years at least, has been too exclusively political. It has aimed at the defeat and destruction of the slave power through party tactics and political machinery. The stronghold of the system of slavery has not been much disturbed, but the strength of the hosts of freedom has been wasted in skirmishing attacks upon its outposts. And hence, with the advantages of superior numbers, and a righteous cause upon their side, they have been generally defeated. A few points in regard to this matter, are perfectly clear to our mind:

1. Slavery lives and flourishes in this country because the public sentiment of the nation either approves of it, or is indifferent. The great majority of men are governed by the opinions and sentiments of others, and *all* are to some extent influenced thereby. There are a few who make the law of God the supreme rule of their conduct, but the vast majority shape their course by the popular will. Hence the surest way to compass the overthrow of any existing custom or institution is to make it unpopular. "Better out of the world than out of the fashion," is the motto of millions. It is true that with a strong sense of duty and of the favor of God in their hearts, men may and do brave the terrors of an opposing public sentiment. But it is even then the hardest enemy with which flesh and blood ever grapples. No doubt the stake and the fire are less terrible to the martyr, than the concentrated scorn and contempt of his fellow-men. Mere animal courage can brave the former, but nothing save the

sustaining grace of God can nerve the heart to overcome the latter.

It follows that when men have not this deep consciousness of Divine favor to sustain them, they will abandon any practice against which a determined and hostile public opinion can be concentrated. Now no men know better than the slaveholders, that their system is inherently wicked; an abomination to God, and a loathing to all good men. Hence, having no inward consciousness of rectitude to sustain them, they will give up their oppression just so soon as it can be made thoroughly and universally unpopular.

2. In the second place, the great agencies which create and direct public sentiment in this country, are the Church, the School, and last, but not least. the Press. This proposition scarcely admits of a doubt. The political party may have some influence in molding the opinions of the people, but the politicians are much more frequently the followers than the leaders of public sentiment. Let the Church put the ban of her reprobation upon slavery by refusing to receive those in the practice of it to membership. Let the schools inculcate the love of freedom, and the hatred of oppression in the minds of the young; and let the press speak out in tones of stern denunciation of the great crime, and there is no political party on earth that could sustain it one hour. Slavery is made respectable by taking it into the church, by teaching its divinity in the school (especially the theological seminary), and by marshaling prostituted presses to its support. The slaveholders understand this well. Hence their unceasing vigilance in seeking the control of the great church organizations of the country, in expurgating every word of antislavery sentiment from the school-books, and in pensioning the most influential presses in the land to speak in praise of their institution.

3. It follows from this, that so long as slavery is fellowshiped in the Church, and so long as our schools and presses are the nurseries of proslavery sentiments, slavery will retain its respectability, and its power to rule in the State. It is perfectly idle to talk of denationalizing slavery, until it is unchurched. It is the hight of folly to talk of preventing its ingress into the territories, while it has a free passage into the sanctuary of God. It is worse than folly to try to cast it out of the political party, so long as a seat is freely accorded to it at the communion table.

This is the highest sanction that can be given to any human

practice or institution. The holiest place on earth is the table of the Lord. It is there the disciple makes the nearest approach to the communion of the upper temple; and that which does not disqualify for a seat at the Lord's table on earth, does not disqualify for a place in heaven.

But the practice of all the large and wealthy church organizations is to receive slaveholders freely to communion. There is not a case on record, that we know of, in which the mere fact of owning human beings has been made a ground of exclusion from church-fellowship in the Methodist, Baptist, Episcopalian, or either large branch of the Presbyterian Church. All the talent, moral worth, influence and piety of these large ecclesiastical bodies are thrown around the institution to make it respectable. To expect therefore, to break the dominion of slavery, and ultimately to abolish it by political action, so long as it is sustained by these other influences, is as idle as to expect to kill the tree by lopping off a few of its branches.

4. There is another consideration which should show the folly of expecting to abolish or even restrain slavery by mere political means. The slaveholders enjoy an undisputed superiority over Northern men in political cunning and management. Politics is a *profession* in the South. Being free from the necessity of labor, the slaveholders make it their constant study. They are familiar with all schemes of political intrigue; they understand all the crooked mazes of party tactics; and are perfectly at home in managing the wires by which the machinery is directed and controlled. In addition to this they are completely united on this question, and work in perfect harmony. To expect, therefore, to beat them at their own game, is vain. The antislavery men of this country constitute the great majority of the honorable and truly upright men. Were the intrigue and corruption by which the political affairs of this country are mostly managed, weapons which they could lawfully use, they must yet be beaten at this game by those who have made it their constant and earnest study.

It is true that we advocate political action on the subject of slavery. But it is political action based upon, and growing out of high moral and religious conviction. A political action which instead of shuffling, equivocating and compromising, will assert and maintain the absolute right, as the only true policy of government. But such a political action will spring naturally from the moral and religious regeneration of the people. Hence it is unwise and injurious for the opponents of slavery to devote their strongest efforts to mere political measures, to the neglect of that which is higher and more essential.

There is yet one other fact which in connection with those already stated, goes far to explain the comparative failure of political abolitionism :   That is, that many of those who are most active in the political movement, are holding religious fellowship with slavery.   The inconsistency (to use no harsher term) of this is so great, that it must weaken and paralyze any cause in which they are prominent.

The great want of the antislavery cause is a moral earthquake among the pro-slavery churches of the country.   Let the Church be shaken and purified, let the moral and religious sentiments of the people be thoroughly reformed, and the politics will take care of themselves.   The oft-quoted saying of Albert Barnes will then be verified : " That there is no power out of the Church which could sustain slavery one hour, if it were not sustained in it."

If these things are so, there can be no difficulty in determining to what point the efforts of the enemies of slavery should be mainly directed.

" No Apology for Schism."

The editor of the *Presbyterian of the West*, alluding to our article on his controversy with Dr. Rice, says of our humble self and others :

" He and others of his church, have no other apology for schism but the action of 1845, and they are not to be easily brought back."

Our cotemporary is as wide of the mark in this statement as he is in his efforts to harmonize the action of 1818 and of 1845.   He never was more mistaken in his life.   The action of 1845 is the smallest part of our " apology for schisms." (Let the reader take notice that in the vocabulary of modern doctors of divinity, the word schism stands for practical obedience to the command, " Have no fellowship with the unfruitful works of darkness.")   If the action of 1845 were repealed this day, and that of 1818 reënacted in its stead, we would have substantially the same reasons for separation from the Old School Presbyterian Church that we now have.

The *conduct* of a church as of a person, is immensely more

important than its *professions*. It is on account of what the
slaveholding churches of this country *do*, far more than on
account of what they *say*, that separation from them is duty.
Practically it is all one whether slavery is approved or censured in words by the Old School Presbyterian Church. The
simple fact is that all kinds of slaveholders are received freely
into that church. The avaricious and the benevolent, the
cruel and the merciful, alike enjoy the fullest toleration. This
is the explicit testimony of Southern Presbyterians themselves.
We gave in our last article on this subject the testimony of
Rev. James Smylie, an Old School Presbyterian minister in
good and regular standing, that three-fourths of all the Presbyterians, Baptists, Methodists and Episcopalians of the
Southern States, buy, sell, own and work slaves for gain, and
hunt them when they run away, for the same end. The whole
Synod of Kentucky testify, that brutal stripes are inflicted by
church-members on their slaves, and that " cases have occurred
in their own denomination in which professors of the religion
of mercy have sold the mother from her children, and sent
her into merciless and returnless exile, and yet no discipline
followed." We have a volume of testimony to the same effect.
Now, while such is the practice of the Church, it matters very
little what is its profession. A thoroughly antislavery testimony from a church guilty of such crime in practice, would
only expose her to the charge of inconsistency and hypocrisy.

This is the kind of slaveholding which the Assembly of
1845 declared to be no bar to Christian communion. No
amount of ingenuity or Jesuitism can make their resolutions
mean anything else. No torture of the English language can
extract from them any other signification. They say that
" *slavery as it exists in the Southern portion of the country*, is no
bar to Christian communion." Not slavery divested of all its
offensive and criminal features, but slavery as it is, with all its
actual robbery, cruelty and uncleanness.

To say, as does the *Presbyterian of the West*, that the object
and effect of the action of 1845 was merely to condemn the
abolition doctrine that slaveholding without regard to circumstances should be a cause of discipline, is sheer folly, for no
abolitionist that we ever heard of holds such a doctrine. We
hold that it is sometimes a man's solemn duty to become a
slaveholder, if becoming the legal owner of slaves makes him
one. For example, a few years ago James G. Birney became
the owner of a number of slaves by inheritance. He accepted
the ownership, and immediately commenced the work of set-

ting them free. But days and probably weeks elapsed before the legal forms necessary could be executed, and the work accomplished. During those weeks Mr. Birney was technically a slaveholder. He owned slaves by the laws of Kentucky, and could have sold all his possessions if he had chosen to do so. Now, we never heard of an abolitionist who condemned Mr. Birney's conduct in this matter. They all hold that he not only acted innocently, but discharged an imperative duty. Yet there was guilt somewhere even in reference to his slaves. The makers and upholders of the laws which made them his property were guilty, although he was innocent in accepting the ownership.

To affirm that the Assembly of 1845 merely meant to say that such slaveholding as that of Mr. Birney, should not be a subject of discipline, is simply absurd. Nobody ever contended that it should be. The Assembly were doing a work of foolish supererogation if that was their sole object. But no man in his senses who reads the document of 1845, can believe any such thing. It was the selfish and wicked slaveholding, in which Rev. James Smiley declares three-fourths of the Presbyterians of the South are engaged, which they *meant* to say, and which they *did* say, was no bar to Christian communion, the editor of the *Presbyterian of the West*, to the contrary, notwithstanding. Our cotemporary, we meekly suggest, is writing too much on this subject. He is in danger of repeating the trick which has made the name of Dogberry immortal, if he continues to write until he understands the subject better.

"CANDID ANSWERS."

The *Free Presbyterian* copies our article entitled "Choosing Slavery," and appends an answer. We said :

"The queries of our cotemporary of the *Presbyterian of the West* are certainly pertinent and pointed. But there are a few other questions which may be asked, which, perhaps, might prove as embarrassing to him as his must be to his Virginia brother. For instance: 1. Did not his General Assembly resolve in 1845, that it 'was organized on the conceded principle that the existence of domestic slavery, under the circumstances in which it is found in the Southern portion of the country, is no bar to Christian communion?' 2. Are not the so-called laws by which these men are sold

into slavery, and the public sentiment that enacts and exe-
cutes such statutes, some of 'the circumstances in which
slavery is found in the Southern portion of the country?'
3. Suppose a minister of the Old School Presbyterian Church
should preach a sermon justifying the infamous laws of Virginia on this subject, and should then purchase the two men
alluded to above, when the State puts them up at auction,
would his conduct in the case compromise his standing as a
minister in the least degree? and is there the slightest probability that his Presbytery, Synod or General Assembly would
censure him? 4. Would not the State of Virginia and the
Presbyterian minister in this case be guilty of the very crime
which God commanded to be punished with death, when he
said, 'He that stealeth a man and selleth him, or if he be
found in his hands, he shall surely be put to death?' 5. If
the editor of the *Presbyterian of the West* were a delegate to
the General Assembly of his church, which meets in Lexington, Ky., this month, would he not meet in council and
eat the Lord's Supper with ministers and elders who have
bought and hold in their hands men who have been stolen
and sold by somebody? 6. Is it consistent with the old
adage about folks that live in glass houses for a man in his
position to throw stones at his brother editor of Virginia?
We should be very glad to have *candid* answers from the
editor of the *Presbyterian of the West* to these questions."

That paper replies :

These questions are by no means "embarrassing," and our
answers shall be " candid " in every sense.

1. The resolution of the Assembly of 1845, quoted above,
is understood to not refer to the law of slavery, but to such
slaveholding as existed in the Church in the South. The
Assembly do not approve slavery or slave laws in that resolution, much less any of the cruelties of slavery. We have
already said that Dr. Lord of Buffalo, is the author of the
resolution referred to, and we have, moreover, intimated that
we would have been better suited if that resolution had said
"slaveholding as it prevails in our church in the South."
We do not believe that slaveholding, as it existed in our
church in the South, should have hindered the organization
of the Assembly, nor that it should lead to a division of the
church. We depend upon the church in the South more
than any other agency to bring slavery to an end.

2. The circumstances in which slaveholding exists in our
church are not such as that the church is the apologist or

bulwark of slavery; but, on the contrary, the pledged opposer and destroyer of the system within its own bounds, and, "if possible, throughout the civilized world." Before and since the organization, the church has denounced slavery as "a grievous wrong," "a gross violation of the most sacred rights of human nature, utterly inconsistent with the word of God, and totally irreconcilable with the spirit and principles of the gospel of Christ," and this has never as yet been repealed.

3. Any minister in our church who will justify slavery, or any "infamous laws" on that subject, we believe will be censured. The man who puts slavery in the same category with marriage, as a heaven-ordained institution, to be perpetuated, will be censured. There is not the "slightest probability" that he can escape censure. Men who would buy freemen wishing to be sold into slavery, we presume would not be censured by the majority of our church rulers. A man's deep abhorrence of slavery might dispose him, in some circumstances, to buy a slave as the best way of saving him from hopeless bondage. Such things have often occurred, and will, no doubt, happen again.

4. The State of Virginia might be guilty of man-stealing in the case alluded to, but the minister might be guilty in heart of no greater sin in buying such a slave than adopting the only expedient in his power for emancipation.

5. Yes! We might, and, indeed, we presume we shall "eat the Lord's Supper with ministers and elders who have bought and hold in their hands men who have been stolen by somebody." The *prima facie* evidence is that slaveholders in our church abhor the system, and we are bound to treat them as if this were the case. If our name had been Simon Peter, and if we had been at the first Lord's Supper, we would have eaten with Judas Iscariot. We should have taken for granted that he was a good man until we found it otherwise. We greatly fear that there are in our church some whose views of slavery are such as to deserve excommunication, but we know of no rule by which we can treat such "as heathen men and publicans," until we have obeyed the inspired injunction, "tell it to the church." We feel bound to treat all in the church as holding and practicing with our church on slavery as our faith and practice are set forth in the public deliverances of our chief judicatory. Schismatics can charge men with heresy and immorality without judicial proceedings, but we have not so learned our duty. The church should not be regarded as corrupt, or as having departed from the faith

until judicial process has failed to bring offenders to justice. Our Free Church friends are like Samson, shorn of his strength, unable to accomplish any thing since their exit. They have not only produced a schism, but they have surrendered their arms, and their largest trouble seems to be that we can not see cause also to become " aliens from the commonwealth of Israel."

6. If our five "candid answers" above are just, our reply to the last question is, that we are not of the "folks who live in glass houses."—*Presbyterian of the West.*

There are few things which a man can not prove if he has the privilege of choosing his own premises and making his own facts. We have no doubt that our brother is "candid" in the above answers, and believes all he states. We have just as little doubt that the most important statements made above are without any solid foundation in fact.

What the resolution of 1845, so often alluded to, meant, must be learned from its language. It says, in the plainest possible terms, that slavery as it exists in the southern portion of this country, is no bar to Christian communion. It is slavery *as it is* in the country, not slavery divested of all alleged abuses ; nor even " slavery as it prevails in our church in the South." Were this the language of the resolution as the editor of the *Presbyterian of the West* wishes, it would not help his case at all. For if there is any reliance to be placed on the testimony of Presbyterian Synods, Presbyteries and ministers in the South, slavery as practiced by church-members is just as wicked in all respects as the slaveholding practiced by the men of the world. See the testimony of the Synod of Kentucky, of the Harmony Presbytery, of the Rev. Jas. Smylie, etc., etc.

Our cotemporary "depends upon the church in the South more than any other agency to bring slavery to an end!" A church, three-fourths of whose members and ministers, according to Mr. Smylie, own, buy, sell and work slaves for gain, and hunt them when they run away, is certainly rather a poor dependence for bringing " slavery to an end." We might just as reasonably depend on the distillers, grogsellers and drunkards to bring intemperance to an end.

Our friend's reply to our second query is mere assertion without a shadow of proof. It is true there is a testimony on the minutes of the Assembly to the effect that slavery is a " grievous wrong," " a gross violation of the most precious and sacred rights of human nature," etc. But that testimony to Old School Presbyterians is musty and worm-eaten. Nearly forty years have passed since it was adopted, and not the first step has been taken toward carrying out its recommendations by their church, notwithstanding slavery has grown with their growth and strengthened with their strength. This old testimony would be a dead letter to Old School Presbyterians, even if it had not been virtually repealed in 1845.

Our friend's reply to our third question shows a faith in him that might move mountains, if, unfortunately, it were not utterly without foundation. Will he point us to a single instance within the past twenty years, in which a single minister of his church, among the multitudes who *have* "justified slavery and its most infamous laws," has been censured in the slightest degree? Will he, with the examples of such men as Drs. Junkin, Hodge, Plummer, etc., etc., before him, deny that any Old School ministers *do* justify slavery? Will he deny that the fugitive slave act of 1850 is a most "infamous law," or that it was justified and defended by Drs. Lord, Boardman and other Old School Presbyterian clergymen? And will he tell us when a hint was ever given in any Old School paper, Presbytery, Synod or General Assembly of censuring these men?

But our friend's reply to our fifth question is, of all the rest, the most preposterous. "The *prima facie* evidence is that slaveholders in our church abhor the system!!" My dear brother, where was your conscience when you penned that assertion? The *prima facie* evidence in *all* cases is, that what a man, or at least a professing *Christian*, habitually practices he loves and approves. When a man habitually drinks rum, the *prima facie* evidence is that he likes it. When a nominally Christian minister habitually chews tobacco, goes to the theater, drinks wine, etc., the *prima facie* evidence is that he loves and approves these practices. By what process of logic the man who habitually practices slaveholding is made an exception to this universal rule, it would puzzle a modern doctor of divinity to tell.

But further: If our friend's "name had been Simon Peter, and he had been at the first Lord's Supper, he would have eaten with Judas Iscariot. He would have taken it for granted that he was a good man until he found it otherwise." Exactly so. But would you have eaten the Lord's Supper with Judas Iscariot after you *did* find it otherwise? If your name had been Simon Peter, and Judas Iscariot, after betraying his master, instead of hanging himself, had come to the second Lord's Supper and claimed a place, would you have eaten with him then? If you answer "yes" to this question, and can prove that it would have been right, then you will have proved something in favor of eating the Lord's Supper with slaveholders, but not otherwise. The evidence of their guilt is open, palpable. The stolen men and women are "found in their hands," and if they lived under the Mosaic law, they would every one be put to death. There are three specifications of the crime of man-stealing in that law, each one of which was punished with death. 1. Stealing a man. 2. Selling him. 3. Holding him—having him in the hand. Of the last of these specifications of this capital crime, every habitual and voluntary slaveholder in the land is guilty. The excuse put in for these men, that they sometimes buy men to save them from perpetual bondage, would be valid if they emancipated them after they bought them. But to buy a man to save him from perpetual bondage, and then hold him in that very bondage, is as unique a performance as compelling a man to volunteer. It is the same thing in principle as for a minister to buy the liquors of a grogseller for the purpose of preventing them from being drunk, and then openly drinking them himself.

Finally: Our friend intends to stay in fellowship with slaveholders until a judicial process has been tried and failed. He will get his process issued and tried about the same time that the Southern Church "brings slavery to an end." Forty years is a long time to wait for a process of discipline. As to Free Presbyterians, they did all they possibly could for long years to bring the discipline of the church to bear on slaveholders, and left only when the last hope of success was utterly gone. Failing, after every effort, to get the menstealers put out of the church, they did the only righteous and consistent thing that remained—left the church themselves.

SIDNEY PRESBYTERY AND REV. WILLIAM PERKINS.

The *Presbyterian of the West* quotes the action of the Sidney Presbytery on the application of Brother Perkins for dismissal, and comments on our notice thereof as follows:

"The *Free Presbyterian* treats these proceedings of Sidney

Presbytery sportively, if not ill-naturedly. The editor says: 'A single member of the Ripley Presbytery has probably forgot more theology than the whole Presbytery of Sidney ever knew.' Indeed! If he has forgotten the theology which the members of the Sidney Presbytery know, and retains what these never knew, and if his theology is the same with the other members of Ripley, we don't wonder that the Sidney brethren are 'not in possession of any definite knowledge of their doctrinal belief.' There is one item (not of theology, but of Church history) which it would be well for Mr. Perkins and the editor to forget; for, after it is forgotten, they will hold as much truth as they now hold. They say:

"'In 1845 they (the Old School Assembly) declared if slavery were put out of the church it would be dissolved; hence it is an essential element in all churches. The Free Church is without this element; therefore, it is no church, and they can not send any minister to it.'

"Our Free Church friends are not willing to believe that we are doing anything for the African; and they seem to regard their mission as mainly accomplished by a bitter opposition to us. They will not allow that we are in favor of teaching slaves to read the Bible, or of emancipation, or of making Kansas a free State. A large part of the preaching of the gospel with them consists in warning us to flee from the church of our fathers. We sometimes wonder if they think we ever had any religion, or if their view is that we have fallen from grace. We are clear that they are guilty of schism, and that they have cut themselves off from what influence they might have enjoyed and wielded for the good of the slave. Has it never occurred to them that there has never been, in any case, judicial proceedings against any man for cruelty to slaves, or for holding that slavery is a Divine institution and a blessing? The foundation of the Free Church is the abstract question: 'Is slavery a sin *per se?*' That church affirms and has more charges to make against those that deny than against slave-drivers. Like the infidel abolitionists of New England (the party of whom Garrison and Phillips are the leaders), who have been led by their abstractions to turn their batteries away from slavery, against the Church and the State, against the Bible and the ministry, our Free Churchmen are turning their arms against the church they have left and the old ministers who have taught them and their children the way of the Lord. Their violent dealings will come down upon their own pates.

"A sensible and pleasant young man said the other day: 'My father and mother taught me to believe that a certain old minister was as perfect and pure as any living man could be. My reverence and respect for him was almost man-worship. Now they are in the Free Church, and they speak bitterly and reproachfully of him as if they sought his downfall. In conversation with one of their ministers, all seemed to glory in the prospect that he would soon die, and, if not before, his church would then be scattered.' The inquiry was made of the young man: 'Well, what do you think of the old man now?' He replied: 'I shall always know that he is a wise and good man, but I begin to doubt whether he or they who talk about him have any religion; or, rather, whether there is any such thing as religion.' Whenever, for any moral reform, we get so far along that we can sacrifice the peace and purity of the Church, and affiliate with all who agree with us in our '*one idea*,' there is but little hope for us or our children. Presbyterianism, its doctrines, its order, and its worship, is our highest admiration and our chief hope for our children; and we shall stand in our lot and testify, and watch, and pray, and work, until she is purified from intemperance, and oppression, and every sin; or until we are by unmerited grace permitted to join the purified Church on high.

"In regard to the translation of ministers in such cases, it may be said, letters of dismission should not be asked or granted. A certificate of good standing ought not to be refused, and it is all that is needed. Dismissions to join other bodies are only proper where the body granting them approves of the translation."

We are not aware of anything specially "sportive or ill-natured" in our notice of the proceedings of the Presbytery of Sidney in this case. Their confession of ignorance of the doctrinal views of our church, we thought was rather discreditable to their general intelligence, and we said so. But let this pass.

The editor of the *Presbyterian of the West*, thinks we ought to forget that his General Assembly in 1845 resolved in substance that if slavery was put out of their communion, their church would be dissolved. Doubtless the editor and many others would like to have this dark transaction forgotten. It does no credit to his church or to the cause of Christ. We, too, would gladly forget it if fidelity to God and his oppressed poor admitted. Let the editor put forth all his strength for the repeal of these flagitious resolutions, and when he *succeeds* we will try with all our might to forget that they were ever passed by a professedly Christian body.

The editor says, the mission of our churches is mainly to manifest bitter opposition to Old School Presbyterians. We think we have a higher and holier mission, and that is to present the gospel of Jesus to the world as uncompromisingly hostile to slavery, intemperance, and every form of sin. It is not thus presented to the world by a church which declares that its very existence depends in fellowshiping slavery.

He complains that we will not admit that they are in favor of teaching the slaves to read the Bible, or of emancipation, or of making Kansas a free State. We will gladly admit all this when we have *evidence* to prove that such is the fact. It is only a few months since one of the editors of the *Southern Presbyterian*, a minister in regular standing in the Old School Presbyterian Church, came out fiercely in opposition to teaching slaves to read the Bible. If he has ever been censured by his Presbytery, we have never heard of it. We find nothing in any of the publications of the Old School Presbyterian Church which we read, to convince us that any considerable body of its members desire the abolition of slavery. But we do find some of their leading doctors of divinity—their Rices, Lords, Boardmans, Plummers, etc.,—justifying both slaveholding and slave-catching from the Bible; we find the last named of these doctors declaring that abolitionists ought to be burned at the stake, and after this atrocious declaration has been before the world for years, we find its author elected by the General Assembly to a professorship in one of its theological seminaries. It may be that the editor of the *Presbyterian of the West*, and other members of the church, would like to have Kansas made a free State, though we can not see why; for if slavery is good enough to be kept in their church they ought to think it good enough to go into Kansas.

The editor "is clear that we are guilty of schism." *We are* clear that the real schismatics are the members of the Assembly of 1845, and those who indorse their action. The sin of schism consists not in leaving a corrupt church, for God expressly commands his people to come out from such, but in *corrupting* the church and thus *compelling* God's people to withdraw; and this is just what the slaveholders and the Assembly of 1845 have done. So "clear" are we on this point that if the editor of the *Presbyterian of the West* will open his columns to its discussion, we will publish *two* columns of what he may write on the subject, for every *one* that he publishes for us. We make this offer in good faith. Will it be accepted?

Our brother editor next asks a very singular question. He inquires, " Has it never occurred to them (Free-Churchmen) that there has never been in *any* case judicial proceeding against any man for cruelty to slaves, or for holding that slavery is a Divine institution and a blessing ? " Yea, verily, it has often occurred to us, and it is just this fact that shows his church to be utterly corrupt and guilty on this subject. The most atrocious cruelties may be practiced by Old School Presbyterian slaveholders on their slaves, without calling for any judicial proceedings. The whole Synod of· Kentucky testify explicitly to this point, as follows :

" Cases have occurred in our own denomination in which professors of the religion of mercy have sold the mother from her children, and sent her into merciless and returnless exile, and, *yet discipline has rarely followed."*

The Rev. James Smylie, an Old School Presbyterian minister of Mississippi, says :

" If to buy, sell and hold slaves for gain, *to advertise, pursue and apprehend them when they run away,* be a heinous sin and scandal, then three-fourths of all the Presbyterians, Methodists, Baptists and Episcopalians in the South are of the Devil."

The running away of a slave is *prima facie* evidence of cruel treatment, and so consequently is the pursuing and apprehending of the runaway ; and yet, according to the testimony of one of their own ministers, and he an apologist for slavery, three-fourths of all the Presbyterians of the South are engaged in this cruelty and wickedness. And yet they are never disciplined for it. Can *anything* show more clearly the heartless guilt and corruption of the Old School Presbyterian Church on this subject than these facts?

" The foundation of the Free Church is the abstract question, ' Is slavery a sin *per se ?* ' " The foundation of the Free Church is " the apostles and prophets, Jesus Christ being the chief corner-stone." That is the truths taught by prophets and apostles, and especially by Jesus Christ. Among these truths are some very explicit commands, one of which runs on this wise : " Have no fellowship with the unfruitful works of darkness, but rather reprove them." If slavery is not an unfruitful work of darkness, then no such work was ever done under the sun. And yet our brother's church declares that if it puts slavery out of its fellowship, it will thereby dissolve itself. Another of the foundation truths of our church, and of every true church, is " not to keep company, if any man that is called a brother be a fornicator, or covetous, or a drunkard, or an extortioner ; with such an one no not to eat." If the slave-holder be not a covetous man and an extortioner, then no such man can be found on the earth. Yet, with them, Old School Presbyterians eat every time they set down to the Lord's Table.

We pass over the story told by "a sensible and pleasant young man," which, *if true* in all its parts, which we very much doubt, is not pertinent to the points in issue. A "young man," no matter how "sensible and pleasant" he may be, who " doubts whether there is any such thing as religion," and who is capable of holding up his own parents to public contempt, is not likely to be the most truthful witness in the world.

The insinuation that Free Presbyterians affiliate in church fellowship with all who agree with them in the one idea of opposition to slavery, is simply false. We defy the editor of the *Presbyterian of the West* to show a single instance in which our church has given up one doctrine of Divine revelation, or a single principle of genuine Presbyterianism, in theory or practice. But if we had affiliated with opponents of slavery, our friend is not the man to throw stones at us. We would like to know which is the worst, to affiliate with opponents of slavery who may not be able to speak plainly on all our theological shibboleths, or with men who, according to the fathers of his own church, are guilty of the highest kind of theft, and are ranked along with murderers of fathers and murderers of mothers. The editor of the *Presbyterian of the West* affiliates with the latter to the extent of communing in his church with *ninety thousand* of them. Free Presbyterians affiliate with neither class.

Finally, our friend is going to "stand in his lot and testify, and watch, and pray, and work, until his church is purified from intemperance and oppression, and *every sin*," etc. So, then, intemperance and oppression, and *every sin* are found in his church, are they? Had a Free Presbyterian said so, he would have charged him with "slander," "bitter opposition," and a multitude of other offenses. But now our brother editor owns up to it all. Let us not, therefore, be charged with falsehood when we assert the same thing hereafter.

But we are glad our brother has come to this determination. We hope he will go to work vigorously and perseveringly; and as soon as he despairs of success, as he soon will if he labors in *earnest*, he will be ready to come to us, into a Presbyterian Church that is *already* purified from intemperance, oppression, and every gross and open immorality.

HARD NAMES.

We have no partiality to *hard* names, but we think there is an evident propriety in calling things by their *right* names. Hard words are generally the expression of angry feelings; right names must be used in the faithful reproof of sin. If a man commits a murder, we see no good reason why he should not be called a murderer. There is no unkindness in the use of the right term. If society has agreed to call his crime by some other name, that is no cause why those who see it in its true character should not call it by its proper name. In such a case it will generally be found impossible to convince the man of his guilt by the use of any softer term. Yet it is the highest kindness to try to convince him of his sin. We think the Christian rule is to treat him kindly as a man, while treating him justly as a criminal. If a man commits the crime of theft, we likewise see no good reason why he shall not be called a thief. Christian charity and courtesy are not violated by the application of this term.

Now, there are certain practices and institutions in this country which society has said are legal, and which many people have agreed to treat with respect, which we can not possibly recognize as any thing else than murderous and dishonest. Among these are the practices of selling liquor, and of waging war, and the institution of slavery. We are not alone in our estimate of these wrongs. But, authority aside, let us look calmly at them in the light of Scripture and reason.

What is murder? It is not only taking life suddenly, and with malice prepense, *but also pursuing a course the natural and necessary tendency of which is to shorten life.* A no less orthodox authority than the Shorter Catechism informs us that "the sixth commandment forbiddeth the taking away of our own life, or the life of our neighbor unjustly, *or whatever tendeth thereunto."* Now, take a simple case. Suppose two men of equal health, and strength, and age. The one uses intoxicating liquors habitually; the other abstains entirely from their use. There is not a grog-seller in the land who does not know that, other things being equal, the latter will live longer than the former. Yet he deliberately furnishes the liquor which he knows *has a tendency* to shorten life. It is, therefore, simply false to call his practice anything else than murderous. Yet in designating it thus we would do no injury, and no unkindness to the rum-seller. We desire only that he might be brought to repentance, and to forsake his guilt. He should be charged with murder, only to convince him of sin, and to warn others against being ensnared, by his influence, into intemperance.

Again: It is but reiterating a truth, which great names have indorsed, to say that every man has a right to own himself. It follows that he who deprives him of that right, takes what belongs to another, and is, therefore, guilty of theft. Why, then, should he not be called a thief? To say that this term is too harsh, is simply ridiculous. It is the only appropriate term. In applying this term to slaveholders, however, we would not charge them all with possessing the *feelings* and *motives* of man-stealers. With hidden motives and feelings we have nothing to do. To God they are known, and by him will be rewarded or punished. But the crime of man-stealing is there; a man is deprived of his inalienable right to liberty; and he who deprives him is guilty of the theft. If his motives and feelings are good, he can plead that before the bar of his Maker. Our business is to try to convince him of the guilt of his practice, and to do so we must call it by the right name.

We have the highest examples of the use of very strong, not to say hard, names toward a very respectable class of people. When the Pharisees and Sadducees came to John the Baptist to be baptized, he addressed them thus: "O, *generation of vipers*, who hath warned you to flee from the wrath to come?" If any one wishes an example of the Saviour's use of right names, he can find it by reading the twenty-third chapter of Matthew entire. The Apostle John uses this language: "Whosoever hateth his brother is a *murderer*, and ye know that no murderer hath eternal life abiding in him." "If a man say I love God, and hateth his brother, he is a *liar*."

To say that Jesus Christ and these inspired men used such language, in view of the secret wickedness of heart of those to whom they applied it, is not true. The language was based on their outward conduct, not on their hidden motives and feelings. It was because the Scribes and Pharisees "devoured widows' houses, and bound heavy burdens on men's shoulders," that they were denounced as a "generation of vipers, fit only for the damnation of hell." It is not very easy to see why those who now, not only devour widows' houses, and rob them of their substance, but who also take the *widows themselves* and reduce them to property, should be called by any milder terms than those employed by the "meek and lowly Jesus," and the most gentle of the apostles.

If these terms were applied to those guilty of these wrongs, why are they not still more applicable to *churches* which, with greater light, receive those practicing them, without opposition or rebuke, and thus encourage them in the wrong?

A Standing Testimony.

In the recent action (or rather *non*-action) of the Synod of Pittsburg on the Fugitive Slave Bill, we find the following:

"Whereas, This Synod has already and repeatedly borne its testimony in strong language in opposition to chattel slavery as a great political and social evil, involving great and deplorable moral evils in its history, and which testimony would not be strengthened by repetition," etc.

We refer to this not for the purpose of showing the utter insufficiency of a testimony against slavery, merely as a *political* and *social*, and not as a *moral* evil. This is the position of the Synod. It refuses to declare slavery a *sin*, and holds constant religious communion with those living in the open, constant practice of the wrong. But it is to the principle stated in the last part of the above extract we call attention: "Our testimony *would not be strengthened by repetition*." The principle taught here is, that if a church once bears its testimony against an evil, that is enough. There is no obligation to repeat it. "It would not be strengthened by repetition." If this be a sound principle, it will apply in other cases. We see no good reason why it will not apply in *all* cases. Now, if the Synod of Pittsburg honestly hold this doctrine, why do they not bear a comprehensive testimony against *all* evils and sins, and then disband themselves, and give up all their agencies and instrumentalities for disseminating truth and opposing error? Let them appoint a committee to prepare "a testimony" against every form of political and social evil—slavery, war, intemperance, profanity, sabbath-breaking, licentiousness, etc. Let them include in this a testimony against all the heresies in doctrine, past and present, which have ever troubled the Church and deceived the world. Let them testify at the same time against the depravity of the human heart and all the evils that flow from it; and in favor of all truth and all duty; and then, at the close, resolve, that "whereas this Synod has already and repeatedly borne its testimony in strong language in opposition to *all* wrong, and in behalf of *all* truth, and all duty, *which testimony would not be strengthened by repetition;* therefore, resolved, that our work is done, and that we hereby dissolve our organization, inasmuch as there is nothing more for us to do."

Look at the advantage of this step. *All* the institutions of religion—a ministry, religious papers, books, tracts, etc., are for the purpose of bearing testimony on the various subjects we have named. By the step above named, which consistency with their own avowed principle calls the Synod to take, all the vast expense, and labor, and trouble of these agencies would be saved. An army of missionaries would be ready to go forth into other lands and bear the same testimony there. Their congregations, relieved from their support at home, could donate the amount of their salaries to sustain them abroad. A letter to the people showing the advantages of this step would be all that would be necessary. Such a letter would be a standing injunction to benevolence and liberality, "*which would not be strengthened by repetition,*" and, therefore, would do just as well in leading the people to contribute liberally and constantly as all the multiplied appeals with which they are now wearied through agents and newspapers, and the preachers in general. Such an arrangement, if generally entered into, would soon supply the whole heathen world with missionaries; and in heathen lands a single "testimony" against their idolatries, and other evils and sins, would be all that would be needed, seeing such "*testimonies are not strengthened by repetition.*" Such a testimony could in this way, in the course of a year or two, be brought to bear on the minds of all the inhabitants of the globe, and under its influence the millennium be expected to commence about the time of the next presidential election. These *legitimate* consequences of the Synod's principle furnish one test by which to try its accuracy.

Let us look at it now in the light of Scripture. In the 28th of Isaiah, 10th verse, we read : " For precept *must be* upon precept, precept upon precept; line upon line, line upon line; here a little, *and* there a little." This is repeated in the 13th verse: "But the word of the Lord was unto them, precept upon precept, precept upon precept; line upon line, line upon line; here a little, *and* there a little."

The prophet Isaiah seems not at all to have understood or embraced the ethics of the Synod of Pittsburg. He might have avoided a world of trouble and a violent death if he had. After having "lifted up his voice like a trumpet, and shown the people their transgressions, and the house of Jacob their sins (the very same sins against which the Synod of Pittsburg refuse to repeat their testimony), he might have retired to private life, cultivated his vineyard, sat in safety under his fig-tree, and left his testimony, which could "not be strengthened by repetition," to do its work. Why might it not have done as well? His repeated testimonies seem to have been to a great extent disregarded; for toward the close of his prophesy he utters the complaint, "Who hath believed our report, and to whom is the arm of the Lord revealed?"

In the 21st chapter of Matthew there is a Divine proceeding related in a parable, which might have been managed much better if the principle of the Pittsburg Synod be correct. A certain householder planted a vineyard, fixed it all in good order, and let it out to husbandmen. At the appointed time he sent his servants to receive of the fruits. The husbandmen made summary work with the first that came. They "beat one, and killed another, and stoned another." A second company was sent, which fared no better than the first. Lastly, he sent his son, "his only begotten and well beloved." "The husbandmen caught him, and cast him out of the vineyard, and slew him."

All interpreters of Scripture agree that this parable represents the treatment which the Jewish nation gave to the prophets, and the Lord Jesus Christ. These were sent repeatedly to the Jews to testify against their sins, and call them to repentance. The violent death of one company did not deter Jehovah, the Lord of the vineyard, from sending others; or from lastly sending his "only begotten and well-beloved Son."

Now our brethren of the Pittsburg Synod would have managed this matter differently. Having sent forth one messenger, or issued one paper testimony, they would have resolved that this message or testimony could not be strengthened by repetition; and by conducting the enterprise on these *prudent* principles, would have saved many a valuable life.

Let us look at this matter a little further. The latest testimony of the Synod of Pittsburg, on the subject of slavery, was (we think) in the year 1845—five years ago. How long this testimony is yet to last the Synod do not tell us. From the fact that they refuse to repeat it, it is evident that they think it will answer the purpose for a while to come, at least. Now, suppose the Synod had, five years ago, uttered their testimony against the evils of intemperance. We will suppose this to have been a faithful, earnest testimony; not a half-way, pitiful sort of thing, like that which they *did* adopt on the subject of slavery. In the meantime intemperance goes on increasing its victims, extending the sphere of its operations, intrenching itself more firmly in the legislation of the country. In the year 1850 it finds its victims escaping more rapidly than usual. The Washingtonians are abroad. It sends forth its emissaries to "recapture the fugitives"—the poor drunkards, who are breaking their chains and fleeing from the toils of the destroyer. These emissaries find their work extremely difficult of accomplishment, through the interference of the Washingtonians. The grog-sellers get a law passed imposing a fine of $1,000, and six months imprisonment on any one who will aid, "*directly or indirectly,*" the drunkard to reform. It also "commands all good citizens" to aid the grog-seller's agents in forcing back the poor drunkard to the place in which the temptations to drink will be spread out with perfectly irresistible power—where he is sure to fall again, if he enters. Now, such a law would be in no whit more devilish than the Fugitive Bill of the late Congress. There is this important difference between the cases. The bondage of the drunkard is voluntary; that of the slave is forced.

The Synod of Pittsburg is, then, respectfully asked to express its opinion on this law, and tell its members whether to obey or disobey. That body, after due consideration, resolves, that as the law is not well understood, and as they have "already repeatedly borne their testimony against intemperance, which testimony will not *be strengthened by repetition;*" therefore, no action is called for at their hands. Such a decision would be no worse (if it would be as bad), than the decision on the Fugitive Slave Law. The duty of the Church is to witness against wrong, and in behalf of truth, just so long as wrong exists, and truth is trampled down. To bear one testimony against an evil, and then seal the lips in silence while that evil goes on increasing in power and extent, and then make their past testimony an excuse for present silence, is simply by that silence to consent to the wrong.

NUMBERS AGAINST PRINCIPLE.

In an article in the *New York Evangelist* these sentiments occur:

"There is sometimes, it is true, an earthquake power in a simple solemn separation from a corrupt body. Luther's heaven-adjuring protest dealt a blow at Rome from which she never will recover. The Free Church of Scotland was a sublime movement, not only justifiable, but of greater moral power than the thunderings of a hundred Chalmerses in the established pulpits could have exerted. But the impressiveness of such separations lies in their being right and unavoidable. They become pitiful and weak when they awaken no echo in the public sense of right. The scores of ruptures that have filled Scotland with petty sects, though made with great earnestness and under solemn forms, have exerted no moral power, because they had no grand justifying reason before God and men. When secession becomes the sole remaining resort, and the moral power which finds no way of exercise, gathers itself into a last act of solemn adjuration, then reason and truth find an echo in the conscience of mankind."

We were aware that many men were in the habit of judging of the right or wrong of principles by the numbers that embraced them. That a majority in any case adopt a doctrine is, with very many, an all-sufficient proof of its truth. But that this rule of judgment should be formally set forth by a religious paper claiming sympathy with the reformatory spirit of the age, we did not expect. The truth has, in all times, been rejected by the majority. The friends of God have in every age been few and feeble. Therefore. if anything is to be argued from this, the fact that the believers in any particular doctrine are but few, is rather an argument for its truth. This, however, is a false mode of reasoning in all cases. Whether few or many embrace a principle is no criterion of truth. That is to be tried and decided by another standard; and the honest man when convinced that any proposed dogma is true, will not inquire whether few or many receive it.

In the case of Dr. Chalmers and the Free Church of Scotland, suppose that instead of five hundred ministers seceding but three besides Chalmers had left (as was the case with Erskine and his adherents more than a hundred years before), would that have made their secession wrong? The causes of separation are supposed to be the same as they were—all the reasons that impelled Chalmers and his adherents to secede were in existence—but the Established Church was so corrupt that only four men could be found with conscience enough to break the tie : would that fact have changed the question of duty? This is the doctrine, or a necessary inference from the doctrine of the *Evangelist.* But so far from this being correct, the very opposite would be true. If the hundreds that left with Chalmers had approved the.evils for which they left, it would have added fearfully to the corruption of the established church, and would have vastly diminished the hope of a reformation. It would, therefore, have added incalculable weight to the reasons for a secession. But according to the doctrine of the *Evangelist,* it would have rendered their withdrawal "weak and pitiful." What a difference with some people numbers *do* make! That the world would have scoffed at the " Comeouters," is certain ; but that the holy eye of God would have looked approvingly upon them, is equally certain.

This case of the Scottish Free Church secession is the most conclusive of all proof of the hopelessness of reforming a corrupt church by remaining in it. If all the influence of Chalmers and the powerful body that sustained him, with all the powers of wealth, talents and piety which they wielded, could not reform the church, then when can such reformation be hoped for? Is the prospect in the American churches better? The evil is ten-fold greater, for in comparison with the guilt in these churches for sustaining the crime of slavery, the evil existing in the Established Church of Scotland dwindle into insignificance. The numbers that seek for reformation in the American churches are far less, while the numbers arrayed against them are almost incalculably greater. If then the Established Church of Scotland, after more than a hundred years effort, could not be reformed by the mighty influences of Chalmers, and his five hundred associates, the hope of reformation from worse evils, and against immensely greater odds in the American churches, is the very madness of folly

20.

POSITION OF THE NEW SCHOOL PRESBYTERIANS.

As the time for the meeting of Dr. Ross's secession convention approaches, it becomes more and more evident that a portion of the slaveholding members and ministers of this church will remain with the North. The fire-eaters of the church will alone withdraw, and as they are divided in counsel, perhaps not all of them. All along the border slaveholding churches will adhere to the Northern General Assembly, at least for the present.

As we have shown in former articles there is nothing whatever in the action of the late General Assembly to prevent this. It is but justice to our New School brethren to say that they do not claim to have made any advance. Their action was really and avowedly only a reiteration of the old testimonies. It was left to persons outside of that body to discover the wonderful progress which it is vainly alleged has been made. It is urged by the Northern portion of the New School Presbyterian Church, in their own justification, and in condemnation of the Southern factionists, that the latter have withdrawn simply because the former have adhered to the old landmarks.

Now the difficulty with both the Old and New School Assemblies has not been the want of a true testimony on the subject of slavery. For twenty years they kept a note in their confession of faith, ranking slaveholders with murderers of fathers and murderers of mothers, with whoremongers and adulterers, and pronouncing them guilty of the highest kind of theft. Since 1818 slavery has stood branded on the minutes of the Assemblies as "utterly inconsistent with the law of God, and totally irreconcilable with the spirit of the gospel of Christ." Murder and piracy are not more than this, and therefore according to the testimony of the Presbyterian Church of both branches, these crimes are no worse than slavery. And yet, with all this testimony against it, slavery has grown with the growth and strengthened with the strength of both the Old and the New School. With these burning words blazing in their faces, they have received the men guilty of this stupendous crime to their fellowship, they have indorsed their Christian character, and raised them to the highest posts of honor in their gift.

Again, as formerly shown, it is the South that has made progress downward, and not the North that has made progress upward. It is the growth of the South in wickedness and not of the North in virtue, that has brought about the present posture of affairs in the New School Assembly. Had not moral madness seized Dr. Ross and his apostate adherents, they might have remained quietly in the fold of the so-called "Constitutional Assembly." They may, indeed, now nestle down in that fold if they will just cease uttering their horrible blasphemies against the Holy Ghost by claiming that his pure word sanctions the foul pollutions of slavery. They may hold slaves to their heart's content in the New School Presbyterian Church, if they will only not try to justify the sin from the Scriptures.

The bearing of these remarks on the question of a union of Free Presbyterians with the New School is obvious. There is precisely the same reason for *remaining* separate that there was for *becoming* separate at the first. So far as the question of slavery is concerned, the position of that church is just what it has always been. Until they pass an act explicitly cutting off all slaveholders from their communion, the Free Presbyterian who returns to them will simply stultify himself. He will acknowledge by his acts that he had no just cause of secession at first, and that his course was schismatical and sinful.

But suppose the slaveholders to be cut clear off, what then? Grog makers and sellers, Free Masons, Odd Fellows, etc., remain without even a *testimony* against them. Now we regard grog makers and sellers, and Free-Masonry, as just as bad as slavery. These practices being all wholly and entirely sinful admit of no comparison, and by God's grace we will never belong to a church that does not at least testify against them.

It is said that as the toleration of these sins was not the ground of our secession at first, it ought not to prevent a reunion now. This is anything but a logical conclusion. If these sins were not the ground of secession at first, it does not follow that they are not *just* grounds of secession. Again, admitting that the fact that drunkard-making and Freemasonry were no bar to Christian communion, would not have justified secession ten years ago, it does not follow that that fact is not good ground for maintaining separation now. Much light has been diffused on these subjects in that time, and there is, therefore, less extenuation of the sin of fellowshiping these evils now than then.

The simple and only question on this whole matter is this: Is the position of the Free Presbyterian Church on these subjects right? If right, as it is, why should we abandon it?

If we are right in excluding liquor makers and dealers, and the members of secret societies from fellowship, then the New and Old School Presbyterians are wrong in receiving them. Now, if union is wanted, surely it ought to be on the right platform and not on the wrong one. If the position of our church on these questions is right, then the sin of schism, and the acknowledged evils of division, are not chargeable on her, but on those who refuse to unite with her on her Scriptural platform. If we stand on God's truth on these points, then are we false to our vows if we step off of that truth onto any rotten platform of error.

Again: It is said that members of secret societies are now in the Free Presbyterian church. If this be so, they are there in violation of our public testimony, and through the faithlessness of the sessions of the churches to which they belong. They are, moreover, guilty of the sin of open hypocrisy, professing adhesion to a church which pronounces their conduct worthy of discipline, while by that conduct they trample down the testimony to which they profess to adhere. That the Synods and General Assembly of the New School Presbyterian church would sanction a session which would expel from communion a member of a secret society, is to our mind very doubtful. The Old School Synod of Cincinnati recently *compelled* a Presbytery and Session to receive an Odd Fellow to communion, and we know of no reason whatever to suppose that a New School Synod would act differently. To say that a session and a minister are just as free to discipline members for these sins, in that church, as they are in a church which, through its highest court, has pronounced these practices a bar to communion, is certainly to talk very much at random.

We doubt not that the mind of Christ, to the Free Presbyterian Church, is expressed in his message to the church of Thyatira: "That which thou hast already, hold fast till I come."

APOSTASY.

That the religion which passes under the name of Christianity in the slaveholding States has become utterly corrupt and spurious; and that the mass of the nominal Christians of that section have totally apostatized, is becoming evident beyond all reasonable doubt. This corruption and apostasy are the work of slavery. The "little leaven has leavened the whole lump." With a few exceptions, the professing Christians of the slave States give the most overwhelming evidence that they have no part or lot in the religion and spirit of Jesus. The vast majority of the so-called churches of that section of the country have just as little claim to the character of true churches of Christ as the church of Rome. This is not the judgment of censoriousness, but a calm and sad conviction forced upon us by the most undubitable evidence. Let us look a little at this evidence.

In the first place, most of the nominal Christians in the South have become active propagandists of slavery. They are laboring with the rest of the Southern people to extend and perpetuate what Dr. Breckinridge once called "the most atrocious of all human institutions." They are not merely passive spectators of the efforts of others in this work, but actively co-operate therein. They no longer silently tolerate slavery as an evil which they deplore, but know not how to get rid of; but they cherish it as a blessing, and seek at the cost of civil war to extend slavery indefinitely over free territory. Among the most active promoters and participants in the infernal outrages of the slaveholders in Kansas, are the missionaries of the Southern Methodist Church. Professed ministers of the gospel have taken a leading part in planning and executing the murderous forays of the Missourians on the defenseless citizens of that unhappy territory. And the religious press and the pulpits of the South silently indorse or openly justify this matchless villainy. The religion of this section has no rebuke for arson, robbery, rape and murder, when perpetrated on the Free State settlers of Kansas; but, on the contrary, cheers on the vile miscreants by whom these crimes are perpetrated.

The religionists of the South are also among the most unscrupulous and lying slanderers of those who are seeking by peaceful and proper means to put an end to those crimes. The basest misrepresentations and the foulest lies, in regard to the measures and candidates of the political party that is seeking to stay the progress of the overflowing scourge of slavery, that we have seen during the present campaign, we have seen in Southern religious newspapers. There is no epithet of abuse against the antislavery people of the country too low and vile for them to repeat, and no political falsehood against the Republican candidates, too absurd and palpable for them to utter. Their whole influence is thus thrown with the propagandists of slavery and against those who seek its present restriction and final extinction.

The outrage upon Mr. Sumner—an outrage of which it is hard to say whether the meanness or the wickedness is greatest—is also sanctioned by the mass of Southern professors of religion. But one of all the religious papers in the South, so far as we know, has uttered a word in condemnation of that infamous act; and the editor of that paper (the *Lutheran Observer*, of Baltimore) has been denounced for so doing by professing Christians, and threatened with assassination. The vast majority of all the nominal Christians of that apostate region silently or openly approve the deed. A minister of the gospel has just been driven from Charleston, South Carolina, for refusing to sanction it.

Another item of evidence upon this subject will be found in the article from the *St. Louis Christian Advocate*, on our first page. In that article the settlement of pious, industrious and peaceable people (as the Welsh are generally known to be) is openly denounced, and mob violence virtually invoked on their heads, simply because they are unfriendly to the diabolical system of Southern slavery. The editor scents danger to the beloved peculiar institution as the raven scents carrion, and croaks as dismally as that filthy bird, over the prospects of the death of slavery.

It is evident from these, and a thousand similar facts which might be adduced, that the attitude of the Southern churches and professors of religion toward the "sum of villainies," has totally changed within a few years. Formerly, with few exceptions, they admitted it was an evil, professed to deplore its existence, but could not see how to get rid of it, and were, therefore, reluctantly compelled to tolerate it for the time being. Now they carefully cherish it as a blessing, claim for it the full sanction of the word of God, labor to extend it over our free territory, and sanction all the brutalities which it perpetrates in Kansas, Washington, Mobile, and elsewhere.

The question then arises, is a religion which justifies and cherishes American slavery, and which will extend it over all this continent and perpetuate its existence through all time, the religion of Jesus Christ? Then does the religion of Jesus Christ sanction, cherish, tend to extend and perpetuate robbery, man-theft, concubinage, adultery, arson, rape and murder. To say so is to blaspheme the Son of God. Are those true and living followers of the Divine Redeemer, who say to

Brooks, Atchison, Stringfellow, and their followers, Well done good and faithful servant? If so, then Christians and assassins are in nothing essentially different. Just as well might we regard Beelzebub an angel of light, as to recognize as true followers and ministers of Christ, those who aid, abet, and approve and perpetuate the system of slavery and the crimes it is now enacting in Kansas, Washington and all the South. The popular religion of the South is a devilish counterfeit of Christianity, and the mass of its professors utterly apostate. We speak only of the majority. That there may be seven thousand or more in the South who have not bowed the knee to Baal, we should be very sorry to doubt.

If such be the true character of slaveholding churches, and a slavery extending religion, it is not hard to determine what attitude true Christians should maintain toward them. *They should be utterly disfellowshiped.* They can never be reformed. Backsliders may be reclaimed, but apostates never. When the mass of a human body is utterly corrupted with disease, it is inevitably dead, notwithstanding there may be a few sound spots at the extremities. When meat is thoroughly rotten, salt can not restore it. God has still a people in Babylon, but she is, notwithstanding, "the hold of every foul spirit, and the cage of every unclean and hateful bird," and God's people are imperatively commanded to come out of her. The few faithful ones that may be left in the Southern churches can no more redeem them from apostasy and destruction, than can the few in the church of Rome.

Another consideration ought to be solemnly pondered by those Northern Christians who are in fellowship with this great Southern apostasy. The *leaven of unrighteousness is still working*, and it *may*, ere long, reach and corrupt them. That it has corrupted many of the free States already, there is sad evidence to believe. Border ruffianism with its arson, horse-theft, rape and murder, has its friends and supporters among northern as well as Southern professors of religion. "A little leaven leaveneth the whole lump." The downward course of the slaveholding churches of this land, like that of the country, is swift and steady. "Evil men and seducers shall wax worse and worse, deceiving and being deceived." "Evil communications corrupt good manners." There is no safety for true Christians in these ecclesiastical bodies, but in obeying the command of God. "Come out from among them, and be ye separate, and touch not the unclean thing, and I will receive you saith the Lord."

MISCELLANEOUS ARTICLES.

ANOTHER BENEVOLENT SOCIETY NEEDED.

A recent number of the *New York Tribune* suggests another benevolent society, in addition to the many that now hold their anniversaries in New York in the month of May. Its object shall be to promote the welfare of the remains of the Indian tribes in our country, and to try to save them from extermination. The suggestion is worthy of consideration by the benevolent. Following the example of the *Tribune*, we suggest that still another society is needed for a purpose more feasible, if not more important, than the one proposed above. *That is for colonizing the poor laborers of the Eastern cities, and settling them on the unoccupied lands of the West.* Let us look at some of the considerations bearing on this scheme.

It is a fact of great importance that the equilibrium between the demand and supply of labor in this country is greatly disturbed. The supply exceeds the demand in the Eastern cities, while in the West, the demand is greatly in advance of the supply. To restore the equilibrium is essentially necessary to a healthful condition of labor and capital. Then the high price and ready sale which all articles of food command, and the great scarcity of food in some parts of the country, show that too little labor is devoted to the culture of the soil, and too much to other pursuits. Few kinds of labor now pay better than agriculture, and this will undoubtedly continue to be the case for many years to come.

Again, it is notoriously and sadly true that the surplus of laborers in the large cities tends not only to cheapen labor, but to cheapen life, and also to multiply crime and pauperism. The capitalist of New York who hires labor at one notch above starvation point, as really works up his employees into material for his Fifth Avenue palace, as the Southern planter converts his negroes into rice and cotton. The difference is in the mode of operation, not in the results. From the same source, it is well known, springs by far the largest amount of the crime and pauperism so rife in our large cities. For one man who takes to thieving and other crimes through sheer depravity (if this ever occurs) doubtless ninety-nine are driven to it by want. By the utmost tension of toil continued through seven days of the week, many a poor laborer is barely able to keep together the souls and bodies of himself and his family. If employment fails, or sickness overtakes him, beggary or theft is all that is left for him and his children. Then the utter joylessness of the life he is thus compelled to lead, tempts many a poor victim to the rum shop to drown his sorrows in the intoxicating bowl, while the gnawings of hunger drive his daughters to the loathsome life of the prostitute.

The tendency of this state of things is to perpetuate itself, and to aggravate all its worst evils. It is a well known law of population that the poor multiply faster than the rich. The son is born to the condition of the father, or to a condition growing gradually worse, as population increases. And in addition to this natural increase, the tide of foreign emigration, sweeping like the Gulf Stream across the Atlantic, is adding its thousands monthly to the already overstocked market of city labor.

Thus the evil has gone on increasing until it has already reached a magnitude before which society stands appalled. If not arrested it will increase till the very foundations of society are upheaved, and the whole fabric thrown into chaotic and terrible ruin. It will be a fearful day to the grasping capitalists as well as to the Southern oppressor when the explosion comes, as come it must, and will, if the present order of things continues.

Now the remedy we propose for all this is the organization of a society for the purpose already specified—that of colonizing these surplus laborers on the unoccupied lands of the West. That this work must be done—if done at all—by a society, or some agency other than that of the laborers themselves, is very certain. It is utterly impossible for men who are compelled to toil all the time for barely enough to purchase the plainest food and clothing, ever to accumulate enough means for their own removal. By the cheapest mode that can be adopted, it still costs something to travel. It will cost more to purchase land, even at the low price of $1 25 per acre, and more still to fence it, to build a cabin, to buy farming tools, seed for the first crop, and food for the family while that crop is growing. And, although, the whole amount needed for all these purposes by each family is comparatively small, it is still utterly beyond the reach of those who are compelled to toil, day by day, for a bare subsistence. One hundred dollars is a fabulous sum to him who has nothing, and who is never able to have five dollars of his earnings at one time.

Our plan, then, is this : Let a society be formed and chartered with power to raise a certain amount of capital. Let this society purchase lands in large or small quantities, wherever it can buy them cheap. Let it donate ten, twenty, fifty, seventy-five, one hundred, or one hundred and sixty acres, to each poor laborer who will agree to live on it and cultivate it. Let the society furnish him the means of moving his family, building his house, buying his tools, seed, etc. Let the land be donated on condition that the man live on it and cultivate it a certain number of years; that he abstain from all use of intoxicating liquors, and other gross vices. The land, tools, etc., to be forfeited by him and revert to the society if any of these conditions are violated. Let the society reserve in its own possession every second, third, fourth and fifth section, as the case may be. And let the most intelligent, virtuous and thrifty of the very poor laborers be selected as the first settlers.

We may now contemplate far a moment the working of the scheme. Every laborer taken from the city leaves his place there for some one else. Slowly at first, more rapidly afterward, as the surplus labor is drawn off, and the number of paupers and criminals, made such by want, is diminished. They can find work and earn bread. The prices of labor in the city, as the supply decreases, will go up till they reach the true standard. Gradually but surely the dens of pauperism and infamy will be cleared of their inmates. The children of the poor as they grow up, find work that will enable them to buy not only the necessaries, but some of the luxuries of life, thus having been removed, to a great extent from the temptation to steal, drink rum and commit whoredom. If the old paupers and criminals prove irreclaimable, they would soon die off. Thus, as the scheme is worked out, the cities will be gradually rid of all the crime and pauperism that result from want of work and food, which is probably nine-tenths of the whole.

Turn we now to the other scene of the operations. On the broad prairies and under the blue sky of the mighty West, are placed thousands of the poor, crushed toilers of the city with the means of their own sure and rapid elevation in their own hands, and with the strongest motives of a worldly character that can be brought to bear on human beings, to impel them to a life of industry, thrift and virtue. Their labor in tilling the soil pays well from the first. A high price and ready sale for all they can produce are at their command. By degrees they gather round them the comforts of life. Then follow in sure succession the school-house, the book, the newspaper, the meeting-house, and other means of intellectual and moral improvement. It is absolutely certain that the great majority of the poor emigrants, under these circumstances, would rise rapidly, morally, socially and intellectually.

By the improvement of their lands, those portions reserved by the society would rapidly enhance in value. Settlements of farmers soon call for the mechanics, the merchants, physicians, etc. Some of the reserved lands would serve as sites for the villages that would grow up. Through their increase in value they would sell for enough to replenish the treasury of the society, and thus enable it to repeat the process of colonization year by year. But if this should not be the case, and it should all be a work of benevolence, we know of none more likely to be blessed of God, or to yield richer fruit.

An objection or two may be noticed here. It will be said, perhaps, that the poor laborer of the city will not go West. That can be ascertained in advance of the organization of the society, by a little inquiry on the part of those disposed to act in the matter. The offer can be made them, and if they *do* refuse, their future sufferings and crimes will be doubly chargeable on themselves and society will be in a great measure freed from whatever blame now attaches to it for these crimes and sufferings. But the objection is without any foundation. There is not the least doubt that the vast majority of the best poor of the cities would hail the offering with unspeakable joy.

It may be objected again that many who would go, would prove lazy and worthless, and starve after they were taken West. That this would be the case with a few, and only a few, may be expected. But what is lost? Their lands would revert to the society, to be given to others more worthy. Then it is starvation or something worse, if they stay where they now are. Surely they may as well starve, if starve they will, in the open country, with God's pure air and sunlight around them, as starve and suffocate both, in the subterranean dens and styes where they now burrow and wallow in filth, and stench, and darkness.

We have not space in this article to anticipate and reply to other objections.

Of the feasibility of this scheme we have no doubt. The work of colonizing poor children in the West is now prosecuted by a society in New York, with marked success. This work is kindred to the one we propose, although our plan is far more radical and thorough. Instead of merely removing children we propose to remove whole families. Instead of taking them to the homes of others in the West, our plan is to give them the means of making homes for themselves. Instead of trying to remove a few of the results growing out of the evil condition of the poor in the cities, the scheme we propose, will go down to the *cause* of those evils and remove that. That this work *can* be done we are sure. We wish we could say with equal confidence that it *will* be done.

The motives that should prompt to this work lie on the surface, open to the view of all. We may be pardoned, however, for briefly alluding to one of the mighty forces as addressed to the Christian. The pauperism and crime growing out of the surplus of poor laborers in the cities is one of the most difficult and appalling problems presented for solution to modern civilized society. The means hitherto employed by the churches to reach and elevate these classes, have been wholly inadequate, and have signally failed. Many of the poor of the cities are as stark heathen as ever danced around a human sacrifice in the heart of India or Africa. The fact that they are almost wholly uncared for by the churches which expend millions for the salvation of foreign heathen, has been the standing reproach of the church, and the perpetual scoff of the infidel. Now the scheme we propose will be adopted and carried out by *Christian* benevolence, if at all. It will, therefore, redound to the glory of our holy religion and of its Divine Author, and to the honor of the Church of God. It will take off the reproach that has lain as a mountain on the bosom of the church. It will add beyond calculation to her moral power. It will thus tend mightily to hasten the time when "the earth shall be full of the knowledge of the Lord and nothing shall hurt or destroy in all his holy mountain."

Publication of the American Reform Tract and Book Society.

We acknowledge the receipt of several new publications from the corresponding secretary of this Society. One of them is a Sabbath-school book of 134 pages, entitled :

"*A Home at the South, or Two Years at Uncle Warren's.*"

This is another in the series of antislavery Sabbath-school books which this society is issuing. It is a pleasant and attractive story. The book, like other issues of the society, is deeply religious in its tone. Sympathy for the slave, and efforts for his emancipation, are represented as the offspring of true religion—as the fruit of love in the heart for the Saviour. This is the true teaching. The abolitionism of some people constitutes their religion. They profess a strong and often uncharitable zeal for the freedom of the slave, while the whole current of their lives bears testimony that they are governed by the same spirit and principles that actuate the slaveholder. True zeal for the cause of the slave's emancipation—the zeal that will stand trials and persecutions—can be found only in the truly regenerated heart. At the same time every heart that *is* truly regenerated *will* have this zeal. It is impossible for a true Christian not to feel for the poor, and not "to try to remember those in bonds as bound with them." The pretended piety, in this land especially, which is utterly indifferent to the condition of three millions of slaves, is, of necessity, spurious, whatever zeal for the conversion of men and the glory of God it may affect. We are glad to see these truths set forth in this work. The book also illustrates the declaration of the Saviour, "Out of the mouths of babes and sucklings hast thou perfected praise."

We have also received three tracts from the society entitled respectively, "Have we any need of the Bible." "Is God Everybody and Everybody God." "Did the World Make Itself." These tracts are an able and spirited discussion of the themes indicated in their titles. They are intended and well adapted to meet some of the most popular and prevalent forms of infidelity and atheism of the present day. The exposition of the folly and impiety of Pantheism is particularly good. The writer shows conclusively of this system, to use his own language, that "it has rotted and putrified among the worshipers of cats and monkeys, and holy bulls, and bits of sticks and stones, on the banks of the Ganges, for more than two thousand years, yet is now hooked up out of its dunghill, and hawked about among Christian people as a prime new discovery of modern philosophy for getting rid of Almighty God."

The Reform Tract and Book Society is doing good service to the cause of truth in the issue of these tracts. The current infidelity of our time is specious and dangerous, at the same time that it is exceedingly superficial, and in many of its phases unspeakably absurd. It is dangerous, not because of any real force in its arguments, but because the human mind, especially in the young, is thoughtless, and averse to careful investigations after truth, and because the human heart in its carnal state is averse to truth. To expose clearly the sophistry, absurdity and falsehood of the theories which men adopt to get rid of the Bible is a most useful and important work. This work is well done by the writer of these tracts on the points which they discuss.

The Reform Tract and Book Society is going steadily forward in its great work. It deserves the prayers and contributions of all friends of truth and right.

What is a Religious Newspaper.

Some of our exchanges are discussing this question with considerable warmth. A few of them that claim to be religious journals themselves, occasionally exhibit a spirit which is not a very beautiful exemplification of that religion, the essential element of which is charity or love. This discussion is mainly in the form of an attack on the New York *Independent*, which is read out of the list of religious journals because it devotes a portion of its space to questions of politics and humanity. It is assumed that politics and religion are two things entirely, and totally separate and distinct; and that a religious newspaper is out of its sphere, and loses its character when it meddles in any way with political subjects.

This question is one of great importance, but one which is, we think, not hard to settle. The proper business of a religious newspaper is to teach religion. Its appropriate work is to expound the theory and enforce the duties of true piety. Now, if we know what religion is, we can be at no loss to know what a religious newspaper is. Fortunately we have a most explicit and beautiful definition of religion in the word of God :

"Pure religion, and undefiled before God and the Father, is this, to visit the fatherless and widows in their affliction, to keep himself unspotted from the world." James 1: 27.

Certainly a newspaper which breathes the spirit of this passage, and inculcates the duties therein enjoined, is religious in the only true sense.

But we have another inspired definition of true religion even more summary and comprehensive than this:

"Therefore all things whatsoever ye would that men should do to you, do ye even so to them, for this is the law and the prophets." Matt. 7: 12.

This is the sum of all duty between human beings. The other great duty of true religion is to love the Lord with all the heart. That is surely a truly religious journal which inculcates the duty of supreme love to God and of equal love to men. But the evidence of love to God is love to men. "If ye love me," says Jesus Christ, "ye will keep my commandments; and this is my commandment that ye love one another."

With these fundamental and indisputable principles before us we are prepared to consider the question whether it is within the province of a religious journal to meddle with what are called secular and political questions. By visiting the fatherless and widows we are to understand the general duties of benevolence and love to all human beings, with especial reference to the weak, and poor, and afflicted. It is surely and strictly a religious work to comfort the distressed, to relieve the suffering, to deliver the oppressed, to establish and execute justice and judgment among men. Hence it is the appropriate work of a religious newspaper to point out and enforce these duties. But the performance of these offices of justice and love very often requires political action. Widows and fatherless children are as often wronged under the forms of the law as in any other way. Shall the Christian, therefore, not visit them in their affliction, and try to relieve them lest he shall be compelled to come in contact with political institutions? The protection of the weak and the delivery of the wronged and oppressed, is the work for which civil governments are instituted. But they are often prostituted to the very opposite purpose. Shall the religious newspaper, then, not expose the wrong and demand the right because the questions are mixed up with politics? Was William Wilberforce any less a devoted Christian because he sat in Parliament and used every honorable means to accomplish the suppression of the African slave-trade, and the abolition of slavery by political action? Was Dr. Beecher any more out of his sphere, as a minister when he urged the suppression of liquor-selling by law, than when he urged moral suasion against the traffic?

The truth is to the *true* Christian there is no act of his life that is exclusively secular or exclusively political. *Whatsoever* he does, he does for the glory of God. He buys and sells and votes for this end, just as much as he prays and preaches for it. His Bible teaches him not only that it is his duty so to do, but also instructs him *how* he may do it. But it is the business of the minister of the gospel and of the religious newspaper to explain the Bible, and therefore just as much in their proper province to show men *how* they may *vote* for God's glory as how to pray acceptably.

The idea that politics and religion should be kept entirely separate is practical atheism. God's law is the supreme rule of man's conduct *everywhere*. It is to be obeyed in *all* our actions; in those which are secular and political, as well as in those more distinctively religious. God has made no division of authority with human governments or political parties. He has not set over one part of the domain of human conduct to their exclusive control, and kept another part for himself. Civil government and political parties have but one proper function, and that is to execute the will of God. When they fail to do this they ought to be abolished. When they oppose their edicts to the law of God, the Christian must disobey and oppose them on peril of his soul's salvation. Hence it is indisputably the duty of the Christian minister and the religious journal to show men when the enactments of civil governments, and the measures of political parties are in conflict with God's law, and to warn them against obeying those enactments and supporting these measures. They should unceasingly urge the duty of obeying God rather than man, and they are false and faithless to their trust when they fail to do so.

We do not hold that political questions should occupy all, or even the greater part of the attention of religious teachers and journals. The *great* object of Christian labor in all departments is the conversion and sanctification of men. To make mankind wise and good, and thus glorify God, is the one great end of all religious instrumentalities and efforts. But the first step toward making men good is to convince them of sin. This can be done only by showing that their conduct is in violation of God's law; by placing their lives alongside of its requirements and thus exhibiting the conflict between them. Now if a man's besetting and grossest sins are *political* villainies, they should be held up in all their blackness, and the severest judgment of God should be denounced against them. No man is a symmetrical Christian whose *whole* heart and life are not governed by the Divine law. The true Christian as already remarked, will make his business and his politics a part of his religion. But how shall he do this unless he understands the requirements of God's law on those subjects? And whose business is it to expound to him the claims of that law, if it is not the business of the minister of the gospel and the religious editor? The really religious journal will strive " to declare the *whole* counsel of God ; " and those professedly religious journals which teach that it is no matter what a man does politically, if he only attends church and prays with fervency, are teaching the worst and most dangerous form of irreligion.

Cheap Newspapers.

Low priced articles are usually the dearest that people can buy. A prudent dealer pays far more regard to the quality than to the price of his purchases. An article of the best quality is generally the cheapest, though it may cost twice as much as one of an inferior quality. While the price is only double the service will usually be fourfold. This will be found true as a general rule of articles of dress, agricultural and mechanical implements, and, in short, of everything of a material character.

Still more true and important is this rule when applied to that which pertains to our mental and moral interests. Here eminently quality is the one thing all-important. The price, with a wise man, will be altogether a secondary consideration. The books that he reads, the teachers that he employs for himself or his children, will be the best within his reach. When the formation of the character and even the eternal destiny of the soul may depend on the influences and agencies brought to bear upon us, surely it is the part of wisdom to see that they be pure and right, rather than cheap. And if this be true of books and teachers, it is equally and even more true and important of the newspaper, which in our day is one of the most powerful of all agencies for the formation of character, and molding of heart and life.

But many people strangely lose sight of this obvious truth when books, and especially newspapers, are in question. With them a book is a book and a newspaper is a newspaper; and the *size* of each is the great consideration. The more printed matter these persons can buy for a given sum, the better off they think themselves. The more news they get in their paper the more they think they have gained. Quantity and cheapness are everything, quality is next to nothing.

But no idea can be more false and pernicious than this. If ever close and accurate discrimination is required it is in regard to what we read. Especially is this true in this age when the press is groaning with the issues of " cheap literature." (Dog cheap it generally is in price, though often costing in the end the loss of the priceless jewels of virtue and purity.) He who would guard his own mind and the minds of his children from moral poison, must beware of the *cheap* periodicals, and other issues of the press at the present day.

Now the cheap mammoth weeklies of the large cities are no exception to this remark. The best of them all, the *New York Tribune*, may be had by clubs, for a dollar a year. It is the strongest paper in the world, and, in some respects among the best. And yet, even the *Tribune* publishes huge masses of matter which no pure minded parent would think of putting in the hands of his children. For instance, New York city was convulsed with excitement during the past winter, over the murder of Dr. Burdell (a murder, in regard to which we have published nothing, because we deemed the details unfit for our columns). Much of the testimony taken before the coroner's jury was of the filthiest character. The coroner himself is a Dogberry of the Dogberries, and his examination of witnesses abounds in excrutiating attempts at wit, and in the most obscene and blackguard illusions. And yet of this mass of essential nastiness, of which murder, fornication, adultery, etc., form the seasoning, the *New York Tribune* published, by its own statement, no less than one hundred and fifty columns! And *naively* remarked, in view of that fact, that "it could have been filled with nothing so satisfactory to its readers!" Nor is this a solitary case, but rather a sample of what occurs daily. Very much of the police reports, and of the reports of the trials in the criminal courts of the cities, is of the most abominable character. The details of crime are spread out with a disgusting minuteness which can gratify nothing but an itching and prurient curiosity, and which can foster nothing but a most depraved and vicious taste. Surely the man who buys large masses of such trash, though it costs him only a dollar a year, is paying dearly for his whistle.

But morality out of the question, there is a deal of humbug in this matter of cheap newspapers. The quantity of matter in the mammoth dollar weeklies of the cities which is of any use to persons of almost all occupations in country or village, compared with the whole contents of the paper, is as "two grains of wheat to two bushels of chaff." To get the items he needs, the farmer, or mechanic, or country merchant, must often wade through solid columns of stuff that is of no moment whatever to him. Now the man who will sift out the wheat from the chaff, selecting what is valuable and rejecting what is worthless, and presenting the information that is really useful in condensed form, is surely doing a good service for his readers. This is an important part of the work of country journals of limited circulation. And it is cheaper for the farmer and mechanic to pay three dollars for one of these papers, which presents him just the matters in which he needs to be posted, than to buy a mammoth weekly for one dollar, and glean from the mass of irrelevant matter the items he needs for himself.

But the moral aspect of the case is vastly the most important. The newspaper has become a power of the age. It is doing a mighty work in molding public sentiment, and in shaping the destinies of men and nations. A weekly journal of elevated literary, moral and religious tone, presenting truth with all the variety and freshness necessary in such a medium, and adapted to form a chaste and cultivated taste in its readers, is an instrumentality of unspeakable importance in a family. The worth of such an educational agency is above rubies.

LECTURE OF RALPH WALDO EMERSON.

This gentleman lectured before a large congregation of citizens and students, in the College Chapel, on Thursday evening last. Mr. Emerson is tall and slender in person; viewed by lamp-light he is not handsome. In lecturing he has an upturning eye that is particularly unpleasant. He is awkward in his postures and gestures; hesitates, blunders, and occasionally stutters in his speech. His command of language is not copious. He frequently begins a sentence, stops after uttering four or five words, goes back and takes a fresh start. Occasionally he gets something more than half through a sentence apparently without knowing how it is to close—then, pausing briefly, and perhaps thinking it easier to go forward than backward, he grinds out with seeming difficulty the concluding member of the sentence. In such cases the conclusion is usually inelegant and confused. Mr. Emerson *excels* in obscurity. He is master of the art of mystification. He is an adept in the trick of "darkening counsel by words without knowledge." His lectures have been compared to constellations of stars flashing through mist or fog. The mist and fog, we can testify, were very thick on Thursday evening. The starlight was not so palpable.

These, however, were the least faults of the lecture. Its end and aim, if we could gather them from its loose, involved and shadowy sentences, were to exalt the intellect " above all that is called God, or that is worshiped." This was to be expected, as a development of the Pantheism (in other words, the Atheism) of which the lecturer is one of the modern prophets. Holding, as he does, that "God is every thing, and every thing is God;" teaching, as he does, that "he, himself, is part or particle of God," and that "God attains self-consciousness only in the human soul," it is, of course, to be expected that he should exalt the human soul as an object of religious worship. Hence, he represents it as endowed with creative power. "If the sun and moon were annihilated," exclaims the lecturer, "the intellect could begin to re-create them!" This arrant nonsense, we suppose, passes with some people for profound wisdom. *How* the intellect could begin the creation of a sun, the lecturer did not condescend to inform us. Where it would get the materials, by what means it could arrange these materials in order, how it would impress upon them the laws by which matter is now governed, are questions on which the prophet of Pantheism was equally silent. To talk of the human intellect, which is utterly incapable of prolonging its own existence for a moment, and which feels in its deepest consciousness its total dependence on a being above itself, as endowed with creative power, is the most downright foolery that we ever heard from human lips. Yet of this transcendental folly the lecture was full.

But there was one thing worse even than this, taught by the lecturer. That was the *infallibility* of the human intellect. He represented it as the sole guide of the individual in all the conduct of life. "Give free scope to thought;" "*trust your intellect*," were exhortations emphatically impressed upon his audience. There was no hint given that this lauded intellect ever had or ever could wander into mazes of error and falsehood. Being part of God, according to the lecturer's creed, how could it? He totally ignored the fact that the working of the human intellect in science, religion, politics, and every thing else, is mainly a history of teeming follies, absurdities, errors and lies, of which it has been the prolific parent. He gave no hint of a difference between true and false thinking. In fact one would infer from the lecture that such a thing as false thinking was utterly impossible. In this, again, he was consistent with himself. The intellect being "part and particle of God," being that, in fact, in which "God attains self-consciousness," and God being infallible, of course the human intellect is so likewise.

Man's *moral* nature, and the existence of laws governing both his intellectual and his moral faculties, were completely ignored by the lecturer. The intellect with him is the all in all. It is to be unrestrained; it is to be a law unto itself; its vaguest dreams are to be reverenced as the voice of God. Whether it works for the glory of God and the salvation of men, as in the pious essays of Hannah More, or prostitutes its powers to the overthrow of faith and the undermining of the foundation of all virtue, as in the infidel blasphemies of Voltaire, it is alike divine. "Write a verse of poetry," says Mr. Emerson, "and society will adore you." But it is no matter at all, according to him, whether that poetry glows with the fire of hell, as in the stanzas of Byron, or shines with the light of heaven, as in the radiant lines of Milton.

From this apotheosis of the human intellect the transition is easy and natural to the worship of monkeys and crocodiles, for they too, according to Pantheism, are "part and particle of God." Accordingly we find, in fact, that this brute worship is the grand achievement in which the system of the Hindoo philosophers has culminated; and from these Hindoo philosophers Emerson and the other modern Pantheists have borrowed their creed. The identical doctrines which are given out oracularly by Mr. Emerson, as something profoundly original, were taught in India two thousand years ago. They have found their full development in the adoration of apes and alligators among the present inhabitants of that country. In this grossest of all idolatries, and in the fathomless degradation to which it has plunged its votaries, we have a demonstration of what Pantheism can do for mankind.

Perhaps some reader is ready by this time to ask, had the lecture no good points? It had an occasional witticism which made the people laugh, and a few good hits at some of the prevailing follies of the times.

We have thus expressed our opinion somewhat freely of the lecture and the creed of Mr. Ralph Waldo Emerson. His admirers, if he has any among our readers, will of course set down all we have said to the credit of our own stupidity, and we are perfectly willing they should. We hope to be always too stupid to see the profundity of wisdom in moonshine rhapsodies.

LECTURE BY BAYARD TAYLOR.

Bayard Taylor, of New York, lectured before the Yellow Springs' Lyceum in the College Chapel, on Saturday evening last. The spacious hall was well filled with an attentive and intelligent audience, showing that our citizens are disposed to patronize a course of lectures by men of ability. Mr. Taylor is quite youthful in appearance—tall, straight and handsome. His delivery is unimpassioned and somewhat uniform in tone and gesture, but pleasant and attractive withal.

His subject was India. He began by saying that however far particular races of men might wander from their birthplace, they still traced back their pedigree to the cradle of the race in Asia. The natives there had a tradition that Adam's paradise was in the centre of that division of the earth. Mr. Taylor thought that the vale of Cashmere might have been its seat, if beauty of scenery was evidence.

The geography and topography of the country were briefly sketched. The beauties of its valleys and the sublime grandeur of the Himmalaya mountains—its Northern boundary—were beautifully described.

The lecturer represented the people as weak and cowardly, but deeply religious. They have always been conquered when attacked, and have often been governed by foreign powers. This he attributed mainly to their vegetable diet.

They have a superstitious regard for animals, and a special veneration for the cow. Hence they look upon beef-eating as an abomination. We should think, however, that the climate had as much to do with the character of the nations as their diet. We find most of the energy and enterprise of the human race in the temperate zones. In the high Northern latitudes where they use almost exclusive meat diet, men are dwarfed and feeble, as in the tropics, where their diet is purely vegetable.

The religion of the Hindoos consists first in the worship of Brahma, the supreme and omnipotent God, creator of heaven and earth. Associated with him are Vishnu, the preserver, and Siva, the destroyer, making the Hindoo Trinity. Then there are other inferior Gods, who, with their progeny, amount to thirty-three millions. The faith of the Hindoo is intense. This trait, the lecturer thought, was an assurance of their sincere devotion to Christianity so soon as they can be brought to embrace it. But the great barrier in the way of their religious, as well as social and political improvement, is *caste*. In addition to the four principle castes, there are innumerable subdivisions. Every branch of labor has its caste, and every caste shuns contact with those below it, as they would the plague.

The influence of British rule in India was next treated of. In regard to this, he stated that one class of witnesses, the employees and dependents of the East India Company, represented it as all that is good and paternal. Another class, the philanthropists and reformers, described it as wholly barbarous and wicked. The truth, he thought, lay between these extremes. The rule of the East India Company *was* despotic, and its course had been marked with blood. But some good had already resulted from its government, and more might be expected. By the extinction of the native sovereignties, intestine wars were totally suppressed. The Suttee and the immolation of victims beneath the wheels of Juggernaut were no longer known. As the natives come more and more under the influence of the English, and as civilization and Christianity have freer scope, great progress may be expected. Much evil and suffering may attend the correction of existing abuses. But all things are under the control of a wise Providence, which slowly works out its designs through cycles of ages. In fulfilling the purposes of Providence, men often commit great crimes. The "Vox populi" is frequently "Vox Diaboli." But the voice of *ages* is the voice of God.

This sketch is only a glance at a few of the points in the lecture, and does it no manner of justice as a report. It occupied an hour and a quarter in its delivery, and was listened to with undiminished atttention to the close.

COLONIZATION.

We have spoken our opinion freely of this scheme. In doing so we are actuated by no feeling of hostility to the existing colony of Liberia. On the contrary, we most sincerely desire (though we can not expect) that it may prove as great a blessing to the colored people of this country, and the natives of Africa, as its most sanguine advocates predict. We most heartily rejoice in all *reliable* accounts of the prosperity of the infant colony. If it has been the means of checking the slave-trade along the coast, we can feel as honest a gratification as any other in the fact. If the colony is disseminating, to any extent, the blessings of civilization and religion among the natives, it must rejoice the hearts of all the humane; though, to do this, there must be a better spirit between the colonists and the natives than there was in 1840, when Missionary Brown and his coadjutors—to use his own language—" peppered the hams of the Africans with buck-shot," and sent home a letter recounting the deed with triumph.

Again, we would not throw a straw in the way of any colored man, who feeling deeply the grinding power of caste and prejudice in this country, should seek in Liberia that social and political equality which is denied him here. To assist persons who, with these feelings and an intelligent understanding of the facts in the case, should desire to emigrate, would be praiseworthy and benevolent.

But these considerations do not affect the character of the Colonization Society, as an organized association claiming to advance a wise and philanthropic scheme for the benefit of the free negro, the slave, the native African and the white race. The past and present influence of the Colonization Society, we honestly believe, was and is evil. It has its origin and existence in the spirit of caste, and the self-interest of slave-holders, and is one of the bulwarks of these evils.

The reasons set forth by the friends of the society in its favor are utterly contradictory, and must be so from the nature of the case. Of this some recent examples have arrested our attention.

In his speech at the late anniversary of the Colonization Society, the President, Henry Clay, uses the following language:

"I have said, and recently on another occasion, that I sincerely believe that, of all the projects of the existing age, the scheme of colonization of the African race on the shores of Africa is the greatest.

"In saying this, I did not look into its present condition; I do not look at what it may be ten, fifteen or twenty years hence; but I endeavor to throw myself in advance, and look into what it will be fifty or a hundred years hence; what it will be when the continent of America shall have discharged itself mainly of the greater portion of the African race, and shall have returned them back to the continent of Africa, and shall have rewarded Africa for the injuries which her sons have suffered, *by sending back a race of men endowed with all the attributes of civilization, Christianity, the arts, and all the benefits, in fact, which belong to our own race.*"

This language was used when the object was to show that Africa is to be redeemed by the colonization of the free people of color from this country. Then this portion of the population is, with one sentence of the orator's speech, "endowed with *all* the attributes of civilization, *Christianity*, and the arts." Four paragraphs from this the speaker was trying to show the benefits of colonization to this country, and then quite another note is struck. The free negroes are stripped of the "attributes of civilization and Christianity," and described as follows:

"With regard to the free people of color, do you not all know (I wish to say nothing but what is warranted by daily experience) that it is not their fault that they are a degraded set. It is not their fault that they are more addicted to crime and dissolute manners than any other portion of the population of the United States. It is the inevitable result of the law of their condition. The whites themselves, if placed in the condition of the free people of color would, like them, be exposed to the perpetration of crime in the same way they are. Look at the annals of criminal jurisprudence in our country—and in this very city—and it will be seen, that of the proportion of those who commit crimes, the free people of color is infinitely greater than that of any other class which compose our population."

It is a significant commentary on the character of the whole scheme of colonization, that a person of the speaker's intelligence should thus flatly contradict himself in half a column of his speech.   It shows a large drawing on the imagination for facts, for truth is ever harmonious.   It is only falsehood that thus contradicts itself.   By what process " a degraded set " (to use the elegant language of Mr. Clay) is to " learn Christian ethics in the salt sea's foam," is a mystery which the colonizers have never yet explained.   This contradiction has been exposed a hundred times, and yet it is paraded with all the confidence of a new and indisputable truth.

There are other points of contradiction quite as glaring as this.   In regard to the influence of colonization on slavery, the most opposite teachings are prevalent.   For instance, Mr. Clay says:

" This society has, with consistency, protested from its origin to the present time, that it has not, does not, and never will, interfere with the subject of slavery as it exists in the several States.   It is no part of its object or office to do that."

R. J. Breckinridge, D. D., in a late speech before the Kentucky Colonization Society, declares that " *no well informed person believes that the number of slaves will be reduced by the action of the Colonization Society.*"   This is what the abolitionists have always asserted.   Yet we find in this day, *religious* papers (so called) the editors of which would, no doubt, like to be thought " well informed persons," gravely setting forth the colonization scheme as the remedy for slavery.   For instance, the *Cumberland Presbyterian*, a paper of the Cumberland Presbyterian Church, published at Brownsville, Pa., uses this language:

" It may be asked, as we are opposed to slavery, and also to denouncing it in the Church, what measures we adopt as proper to secure ultimate emancipation?   To this we answer, we are decidedly in favor of the colonization scheme, as set forth and carried out by the American Colonization Society.

" The measure adopted " by men who boast that they " have availed themselves of *all* the light that has been cast on the subject," to " secure ultimate emancipation," is the colonization scheme; this, too, in the face of the declaration of the most distinguished advocates of the cause, that the society " has not, does not, and *never will*, interfere with the subject of slavery," and that " no well informed person believes that the number of slaves will be reduced by the action of the society."

The foregoing are mere specimens of the opposite teachings on this subject, which have been current for many years. Yet this scheme of contradictions and absurdities is extolled as "the greatest enterprise of the age." A persevering effort is made to induce Congress to tax the people for carrying it on ; and Christian people are exhorted to support it as God's own chosen means for removing slavery, converting Africa, and saving the free people of color from degradation and ruin.

Co-Existence of Liberty and Slavery Impossible.

The following is from the *Richmond Enquirer*:

"Social forms so widely differing as those of domestic slavery, and (attempted) universal liberty CAN NOT LONG CO-EXIST IN THE GREAT REPUBLIC OF CHRISTENDOM. They can not be equally adapted to the wants and interests of society. The one form or the other must be very wrong, very ill suited to promote the quiet, the peace, the happiness, the morality, the religion and general well-being of the community. Disunion will not allay excitement and investigation, much less beget lasting peace. The war between the two systems rages elsewhere ; and will continue to rage TILL THE ONE CONQUERS AND THE OTHER IS EXTERMINATED."

This is the exact truth, clearly and definitely stated. It is truth which abolitionists have been preaching for years. When they first announced it they seemed to the nation as those that mocked. Now, however, this truth is becoming manifest to all. The slaveholders see and assert it— and at last the besotted North begins to realize it. The Christ of liberty can have no concord with the Belial of slavery. The conflict between them is joined, and one or the other must perish. The war on the side of slavery is one of extermination. It will give no quarter to freedom. It will, if successful, leave it no foothold on this continent. It will hunt the fair form of freedom from every inch of territory between the Atlantic and Pacific oceans. Already the death's head of this piracy gleams balefully over Central America. It is compassing sea and land to plant its black banner on the plains of Kansas. Already its deadly folds wave over New Mexico, and the home of the modern Sodomites in Utah.

From there, if its other schemes succeed, slavery will push its conquests to the Pacific. That point gained and all Mexico and Central America will be speedily absorbed. Then the rapacious hordes of despotism will turn north, and soon the feeble remnants of freedom left us in the free States will be trodden to death under their bloody feet.

Such are the purposes of slavery, and such the spirit in which they are prosecuted. Would that the same uncompromising spirit actuated all its professed opposers. Would that the avowed friends of freedom were as resolutely bent on hunting the demon of slavery from its last resting-place. Would that they too were resolved on a war of extermination. But such, alas! is not the case. The vast majority of the professed friends of freedom in this country are at the utmost pains to disclaim all purpose of interfering with slavery where it now exists. They vehemently deny that they have any intention of driving slavery from the strongholds—political, social and ecclesiastical—in which it has already entrenched itself. They will share the empire of this continent with the slave power. They ask only a part of the fair heritage, which should all be the birthright of freedom. They will leave to slavery the undisputed power it now exercises over the Church and the State, if it will just forego the privilege of extending its domain into free territory.

We rejoice that slavery rejects this compromise, and now claims universal sway. It will, by so doing, *drive* the free States into the same policy on the other side. It will convince them that they must exterminate this piracy, or be exterminated by it. It will force time-serving politicians into a decided position. It will explode the paltry schemes of timid ecclesiastics, who think by "capping the volcano" to prevent an eruption, while the fire is left burning within. It will turn to folly all worldly-wise projects for "settling the question." It will show that slavery will never be quiet until dead and buried, and will set all hands, not willing to be subjugated, to the work of digging its grave. When the North is at last unanimously forced to that position, the work will be cut short in righteousness. May God speed the day.

SLAVERY AND THE SLAVE-TRADE.

It is one of the inconsistencies of human nature that men are often shocked with one form of a particular sin, while they will practice another form of the very same sin without the least compunction. The clerical wine-bibber, who goes to bed every night half-fuddled on his aristocratic beverage, is piously exercised over the intemperance of the poor wretches who get drunk out-right on vulgar whisky. The genteel swindler who embezzles thousands of his employer's money, would feel insulted if placed on a level with the poor thief who steals a penny loaf from a baker's window. The woman of French morality, in "high life," grows eloquently indignant over the low debauchery of the Five Points.

Very similar to the conduct of these worthies is the opposition manifested in certain quarters to the reopening of the foreign slave trade. This opposition, in many instances, comes from those who are living in the closest political and religious fellowship with slavery; and who openly defend that system, or silently acquiesce in its existence. Their opposition to the slave-trade is precisely on a par with the wine-bibber's opposition to intemperance. Governor Adams, of South Carolina, has expressed a logical and inevitable truth, when he says that "If the slave-trade is piracy then slavery is plunder." On the other hand, if slavery is right, so, also, is the slave-trade. The one is the parent of the other. The slaves were originally stolen from Africa. The Virginia and Carolina planter bought only the slave-trader's title to his chattels. That was only a pirate's title. The slaves being stolen, and the buyers knowing that fact, became partakers of the theft by purchasing the stolen property. Evidently he could transmit to his posterity no better title to his human chattels, or to their offspring, than he possessed himself. Hence, we repeat, if the slave-trade *is* piracy, the slaveholder, down through a hundred generations, is a man-stealer—"a thief of the highest rank."

But there are those in this country who insist that the slave-trade shall still continue to be branded as piracy, and yet that the slaveholder may be a very exemplary and pious Christian—fit for the pulpit, and for the very highest stations of honor in the church. They still cling to him in religious fellowship. They still hold fast to church organizations which declare that slavery is the corner-stone on which they are built, and the cement that binds their spiritual stones together.

Our brother of the *Presbyterian of the West* is anxious to know if the Southern pulpit and religious press will come out in opposition to the re-opening of the foreign slave-trade.

Without any pretension to prophetic lore, we can inform him that they will do nothing of the kind. We venture the prediction that outside of Maryland and Virginia, in which States public sentiment, for the most mercenary reasons, is opposed to the foreign slave-trade, not a whisper of opposition to its re-opening will be heard from Southern pulpits or religious presses. Why should they oppose it? Do not the nominal Christians of the South openly practice and defend, or silently indorse a worse traffic in human flesh than that from the coast of Africa? On this point hear the testimony of a Virginia statesman. During the debate in the year 1832, in the Virginia House of Delegates, on the abolition of slavery, Thomas Jefferson Randolph, the grandson of President Jefferson, spoke as follows:

"The gentleman has spoken of the increase of the female slaves being a part of the profit: it is admitted; but no great evil can be averted, no good attained without some inconvenience. It may be questioned how far it is desirable to foster and encourage this branch of profit. It is a practice, and an increasing practice, in parts of Virginia, to rear slaves for market. How can an honorable mind, a patriot, and a lover of his country, bear to see this Ancient Dominion, rendered illustrious by the noble devotion and patriotism of her sons in the cause of liberty, converted into one grand menagerie, where men are to be reared for market like oxen for the shambles? Is it better, is it not worse than the slave-trade— that trade which enlisted the labor of the good and the wise of every creed and every clime to abolish it? The trader receives the slave, a stranger in language, aspect and manner, from the merchant who has brought him from the interior. The ties of father, mother, husband and child, have all been rent in twain; before he receives him his soul has become callous.

"But here, Sir, individuals whom the master has known from infancy, whom he has seen sporting in the innocent gambols of childhood; who have been accustomed to look to him for protection, he tears from the mother's arms, and sells into a strange country among strange people, subject to cruel task-masters. In my opinion, Sir, it is much worse."

The Southern Church and ministry have no word of rebuke for this home traffic in slaves; why then should they be expected to brave public sentiment in opposition to a milder traffic from a foreign shore? The Southern Church and clergy daily see mothers torn from their children, and children torn from their mothers; they see husbands and wives separated by brutal force, never to meet more on this earth ; they see virgins sold for whoredom, and they breathe no whisper of rebuke of these crimes. Many of the members of Southern churches are themselves engaged in the infernal traffic, and do not thereby compromise their standing as church-members in the least. To expect these men, therefore, to enter upon a Quixotic crusade against the foreign slave-trade, is as vain as to expect the priests of Baal or Juggernaut to oppose idolatry.

It is surely no violation of charity to say that this Southern slave-breeding and slave-trading religion bears but a very faint resemblance to the religion of Christ.

PERVERSION OF SCRIPTURE.

The exigencies of a bad cause compel the advocates of communion with slaveholders to resort to the most gross perversions of the Holy Scriptures. As an example of this, the *Central Christian Herald* opposes secession from slaveholding churches, because " it is taking the leaven out of the meal-tub and keeping it by itself, where," he smartly observes, " all experience shows it is apt to become very sour." The figure of Christ which is referred to here is entirely perverted from the sense in which it is used by the Saviour. His language is as follows :

" Another parable spake he unto them : The kingdom of heaven is like unto leaven, which a woman took, and hid in three measures of meal, till the whole was leavened."—*Matt.* 13 : 33.

The kingdom of heaven means Christ's spiritual kingdom, the Church. This is placed in the *world*, as leaven is placed in the meal, until the whole be leavened. Its sense is very clear and very beautiful. As the little leaven works on silently, but powerfully, until the whole mass of meal in which it is placed is pervaded by its influence, so the spiritual kingdom of Christ, placed in the great mass of corruption, the world, will work on, slowly, it may be, but mightily and surely, till the whole corrupt mass is brought under its purifying influence.

Now see the gross perversion of this figure by the *Herald.* According to its doctrine, the evil-doers are to be kept in the Church, that they may thus be brought in contact with the leaven; thus completely breaking down all distinction between the Church and the world. Christ's kingdom, while in the world, is not of the world. The idea is presented, in every proper place in the Bible, that the Church is to be kept separate from the world, and thus being kept pure in itself, is to exert its saving power. But the *Herald*, admitting, as it does, that slaveholders need the converting and sanctifying grace of the gospel, insists on keeping them mixed up with God's people in the Church, in order to bring them in contact with the leaven. On the same principle, the whole world ought to be brought into the Church; otherwise, the leaven will be outside of the meal-tub. Suppose the New School Presbyterian Church should admit gamblers, and drunkards, and debauchees to her communion, as she now admits slaveholders; and suppose the opposers of these sins, after fourteen years of hard but ineffectual labor in trying to have the sinners expelled, should conclude that the only way to free themselves from the guilt of communing with gamblers and adulterers was to leave the New School Church. When they propose this last resort to their brethren, up starts the editor of the *Herald*, and says, "No, brethren; if you leave the Church, the leaven will be taken out of the meal-tub, where all experience shows it is apt to become very sour." This argument would be just as powerful in this case as in reference to slaveholders, who, according to the standing testimony of the Presbyterian Church, New and Old School, are far greater sinners than gamblers and debauchees.

If this interpretation of the Saviour's parable be correct, it forbids all discipline as completely as it does secession. When a church court is about to expel an incorrigible offender, for whose reformation all efforts have failed, a member of the court, with the *Central Herald* in his hand, stands up before them, and says, "If we put this man out of the pale of our church, the leaven can no longer affect him. Let us retain him in our communion, and thus it will work upon him till the whole mass of his incorrigible obstinacy and corruption is leavened."

The use that is made of the figure of leaven, by the enemies of the Free Church movement, involves a theory of church fellowship and church action in direct opposition to that which is revealed in the Bible, and which has been generally received in the churches. The idea is, that to separate ourselves from the communion of wrong-doers, in the only way that is possible in a church which steadily refuses to discipline them, viz.: by separation from the church, is taking the leaven out of the meal-tub. The doctrine of the Bible, and it is the old-fashioned theory of the Church, is that the Church should keep herself entirely pure and free from open and gross offenders; and that her power for good in the world is just in proportion to the degree of her purity. The leaven is powerful in proportion to its freedom from admixture with that which destroys its power. "If the salt have lost its savor, wherewith shall it be salted." "If the light that is in you be darkness, how great is that darkness." If the leaven be mixed up with that which destroys its efficacy, it is useless when applied to the mass of human corruption. But to receive or retain the open and unrepentant sinner in the Church, is destructive of all the ends for which a Church has been established in the world. It is in this way alone that the salt loses its savor, and the light becomes darkness. Yet the argument of the *Herald* requires this. It must surely be a bad cause which compels men to resort to such monstrous perversion of Holy Writ.

ANTI-SLAVERY MEN IN PRO-SLAVERY ORGANIZATIONS.

In a previous number of our paper, we expressed the opinion that anti-slavery men in pro-slavery churches are the most efficient supporters of slavery. As this will probably strike many minds at first sight as an unfounded proposition, it may be worthy of additional consideration. We believe it susceptible of the clearest demonstration. By a pro-slavery church, we mean a church which permits its members to hold slaves without censure; a church which does not use its aggregate influence against the system, but for its support; for " he that is not against it is for it."

Now, if the aggregate influence of a church be in favor of oppression, it is self-evident, that the greater that influence, the greater the support that will be given. The aggregate influence of a body is made up of the individual influence of its members. There is in such case a *common treasury* of moral power, into which each member contributes all he has. The leaders of the church, or those having control of this treasury, take the influences concentrated there, and use them to uphold slavery. Whatever of moral power, then, antislavery men have, they put into this common treasury; whence, despite their efforts to the contrary, it is taken and used in support of the system. The power of numbers is almost, if not altogether, the only power now exerted in this country by the large and popular churches over the world ; hence, it inevitably follows, that the increase of numbers is the increase of power. For instance, if a church consist of one thousand members, and one thousand more join it, its influence is doubled; if five hundred leave it, it is reduced one-half ; therefore it follows, that every man that *belongs* to a pro-slavery church, increases its numbers, and therefore the power by which it upholds oppression. In this way, professed abolitionists in pro-slavery churches give their influence in favor of slaveholding. They support the church that supports slavery. By sustaining the *prop*, do they not sustain the fabric that rests upon it ? This influence for slavery, abolitionists, in the churches of which we write, exert in common with other members. But there are peculiar circumstances in the case, which increase their influence, in consequence of their antislavery principles and professions· To some of these we adverted before.

1. They shield the church from the reproach of being pro-slavery, and thus increase her power to uphold the system. A church's power for good or evil depends to a considerable extent on the degree of confidence reposed in her by the world. Now, the moral sense of men generally revolts at the enormity of slavery, though for selfish reasons many practice and defend it: hence, it is a reproach for a church to be considered pro·slavery, and really weakens her influence ; hence, by the way, also, the sensitiveness on this point witnessed in many quarters, and the labored efforts to prove that this charge of the abolitionists against different churches is false.   Just at this point, and for this purpose, the fact that professed abolitionists belong to these churches is of singular service. This *fact* alone is considered a triumphant refutation of the charge. The new School Presbyterian will point to men like Barnes and Beecher ; the Old School man to men like Carothers and Thomas, and ask with an air of triumph, *if our church is pro-slavery, why is it that these thorough-paced abolitionists belong to it?* Thus these antislavery men become Issachars to bear off the burden of reproach that would otherwise press upon their churches, and in return, generally get the usual reward of the patient animal to which the Patriarch likened his son — "more kicks than kisses."

II. In the second place, the influence of antislavery men in the position of which we write, tends to quiet consciences that would otherwise be aroused by antislavery truth. It is a weakness perhaps of human nature, in determining questions of duty, to look more at the conduct of others than at abstract truth. Hence, when the conscience of the slaveholder becomes through any means aroused to the wrongs of his practice, or the conscience of the non-slaveholder to the sin of a connection with pro-slavery organizations, they at once look to the practice of the abolitionists. Seeing them holding church-communion with slavery, both conclude that their rebukes of it are hypocritical; that slavery, after all, is not so bad; and hence, both continue on at their ease in sin. Thus these men stand between the consciences of slaveholders and their defenders and the truth, and shield them from its barbed arrows.

III. But the worst influence of the men of whom we speak is in weakening the efforts of those who are consistently laboring to free the Church from the sin of slavery. We put this question to every man and woman who may read this article, and ask them to answer it dispassionately: Suppose all the large influential churches of this country—Methodists, Presbyterians, Episcopalians, Baptists, etc.—should take the ground occupied by the Free Presbyterian Church—make slaveholding or its defense a term of communion—*would not this be the death-blow to slavery?* This question is its own answer. It is too plain for proof. There is no power on earth that could hold up slavery a year against the united, earnest condemnation of the whole Church. So says Albert Barnes, and so says every man's *common sense*. It follows inevitably, from this fact, that slavery lives and strengthens through the support of the Church. It draws its life-blood from her bosom, and kills the spirituality of the Church thereby. How, then, can the churches of this land be brought to use their power for the destruction of slavery? *Not in the mass.* The whole history of the world furnishes *not one* instance of the majority of a church once radically wrong becoming right *en masse*. How, then, can this be accomplished? Simply and only by each individual, whenever he embraces antislavery truth, leaving and uniting with those churches which do exclude slavery from their communion. Their leaving is a testimony which raises up others to fill their place, and in turn withdraw; while their staying in paralyzes their own consciences and the consciences of others. Their example is quoted against those who secede and form anti-slavery churches, and thus they weaken their hands. If the Free Presbyterian, Wesleyan, and other churches making slaveholding a term of communion, had all the professed abolitionists that hold the same faith on other points, and yet stay in slaveholding churches, their power would be "mighty to the pulling down of the strongholds" of slavery. However much contempt may be affected for these churches, they are now more feared and hated than despised, by the friends of slavery. Their growth is justly looked upon as the sure pro-gress of a sentiment that is destined inevitably to overturn this great evil. By all, therefore, by which their increase is retarded, is the day of its downfall protracted; and by nothing is this so much hindered as by the example and influence of those who profess anti-slavery principles and retain pro-slavery connections.

We have no wish to use harsh language or hard names; but we ask such of our antislavery friends as are yet in the situation of which we write to look candidly at the case we now present. Suppose that by some strange fortuity the sin of horse-stealing should become legal and organic in this country. Suppose in that case the church to which you belonged should pronounce this sin "no bar to Christian communion," what would be your course? Perhaps remon-strance would first be tried. But we fancy your remonstrance would be stern and brief, and if it failed to secure a repeal of the decree of the church, you would then withdraw at once, to escape participation in the guilt of horse-stealing. But suppose you still hope for reform, and stay "a little longer," and while you are laboring for this, a portion of your brethren secede and form a church, on precisely the *same principles* as the one they left, save that it made horse-steal-ing a "bar to Christian communion." Now what would you do? Are you not ready to say that the man who would stay after that would be in fact one of the worst horse-thieves in the land?—"*Mutato nomine de te fabula narratur.*" Change the name and the tale is told of yourself. Substitute in the foregoing sentences the word "slaveholding" for "horse-stealing," and you have an exact description of your present position. And it has a familiar sound to antislavery ears, to say that slaveholding, which is man-stealing, is as much worse than horse-stealing as a man is of more value than a horse. The principle asserted in this last sentence is incontestibly true. It has never been questioned, and never will be successfully. Where, then, does it place the American Church? Just as much deeper in guilt than a church which should receive known horse-thieves to her communion, as the horse ranks lower in the scale of being than man.

We use the term horse-stealing in this connection by way of illustration, not by way of reproach. We would use no term unnecessarily harsh. But the points presented in the illustration are *simple truths;* and the "truth should be spoken, though the heavens should fall." We repeat the indisputable truth, therefore, that a church which allows her members to hold slaves, is worse than a church which should permit her members to steal horses. We press this truth upon the consciences of all who retain membership in such churches. It is time this subject were looked full in the face; and honeyed phrases are not the sounds to arouse from sleep so death-like as that of the American Church. Especially is it time that professed friends of the slave, in churches that enslave him, should understand their position, which we look upon as peculiarly dangerous. The inconsistency of men holding connections with churches, the principles of which are at war with their own, is so obvious, that violence must be done to their moral sense by retaining those connections. The Temperance man in a grog-selling and drinking church, the believer in the Trinity in a church of Unitarians, and the abolitionists in a slaveholding church, are so obviously out of place, that they retain their relations at the risk of a seared and hardened conscience. God's express command to all is— " Come out of her, my people, *that ye be not partakers of her sins,* and that ye receive not of her plagues."

SENTIMENTS AGAINST SLAVERY.

A most interesting and suggestive article on the sentiment of Great Britain, on the subject of slavery, will be found in another part of our paper. It is from the London *Morning Advertiser,* said to be the second paper in circulation and influence in England. This article gives a painful but truthful account of the position and influence of the clergy of this country on the subject of slavery; and warns the people of England against the corrupting influence likely to be exerted on the public mind of Great Britain, by an influx of the pro-slavery clergy of America at the World's Fair. This article is interesting in several respects, but we allude to it mainly as suggesting the most feasible and certain way of abolishing the blood-stained system of American Slavery—*that is, by combining the public sentiment of the civilized world and especially of the Free States of this confederacy, against it.* The moment that witnesses correct views and feelings on this subject, approximating to a universal adoption in the civilized world, and also an appropriate expression of those views and feelings, will witness the freedom of every slave on American soil. This will be the case if not a single conscience in the slaveholding States is convinced of the sin of slavery. A regard to reputation, if not to justice, will compel the slaveholder to relax his grasp. Let us look at some of the reasons for this belief.

A regard to the opinions of others is a much stronger motive, with the mass of men, than regard to right and justice. What will the world say? is a much more common question than what says the Word of God? Men are often deterred from the performance of known duty by the fear of incurring the ill opinion of their fellow-men. It has been, in all ages, but a very small portion of the race that have been actuated in the main course of their lives and conduct by the naked consideration of right and duty. Against the combined influence of a general public sentiment nothing can sustain a person for any length of time, but a deep consciousness of right, and a strong abiding sense of duty. This idea is not abolition fanaticism, but most orthodox sentiment, preached from the pulpits of all denominations, in the ten thousand warnings to sinners and Christians, against the influence of evil associates, and against the fear of the world.

Now, when any thing like a general public sentiment is concentrated against an evil practice or institution, there being no strong sense of duty in its supporters, but just the reverse, it must be abandoned. There being no innate vitality, the system must perish under outward pressure. This truth might be illustrated and confirmed by reference to past and present reforms. The cause of temperance has been advanced to its present stage, not by convincing the consciences of all or most of the distillers and grogsellers who have abandoned their business, but by bringing the force of a public sentiment, hostile to their practices, to bear upon them. The abolition of the slave-trade, and of slavery in the West India Islands, the repeal of the corn laws, and the reformation of the penal code, by the Parliament of England, are all examples of the operation of the same influence. They were all *unwilling* concessions to a prevalent, controlling public sentiment.

The prevalence of an antislavery sentiment would, in like manner, strike the fetters from every slave in the United States. It could not live a single year surrounded by a healthful abolition atmosphere in the free States. Public sentiment would seal its doom. Make it unpopular, and its days are numbered. This consideration derives additional force from the peculiar character of the Southern people. They are proverbially jealous of their honor. An imputation of dishonorable conduct to a Southern man, is an insult to be wiped out only with blood. This is peculiarly the case with slaveholders, for, are they not a "chivalrous" race? Now, let every one of these once realize that his fellow-men, in all civilized communities, look upon him as a thief— as having appropriated to his own use, as property, human beings whose right to own themselves is inalienable—let them

> "Writhing, feel where'er they turn,
> A *world's* reproach around them burn;"

and he who believes slavery can survive, must be blind indeed. This matter is well understood by the slaveholders. The ablest and most far-seeing of Southern statesmen, John C. Calhoun, once declared, that what the South had to fear from the abolitionists was not an attempt to liberate the slaves by force, but appeals to their consciences, and to the sentiment of the world against them. " *Their warfare*," said he, "*is not upon our persons, but upon our characters.*"

This is a perfectly legitimate influence, to bring to bear against slavery. It does no injustice to the slaveholders. To affirm that it does, would be more absurd than to say that the public sentiment which brands the common thief with infamy is unjust. We say *more* absurd, because we believe with the General Assembly, that "slaveholding is the highest kind of theft." Proportionally strong should be its condemnation and the infamy attached to its perpetrators. It is God's will that crime should be unpopular. He regards it with infinite abhorrence, and men have no right to regard it in any other way. The abhorrence of the crime *must* attach to the criminal, so long as he willfully continues in its commission. This is a law of God's own enacting, and it is inexorable. In but one way can the sinner escape the disgrace of the sin; that is, by repentance and reformation. While he continues on in a willful course of wrong doing, God intended that he should feel, both for his restraint and punishment, the reproach of the virtuous burning into his soul. It is this influence we would concentrate on the slaveholder and his sin. It is not violence we advocate. We would not have a hair of his head injured. But would rouse against him the calm, yet deep abhorrence of every soul that loves liberty. Let the slaveholder, when he turns his eye to a free State, behold the light of freedom, as a wall of fire, throwing its rays far into the depths of the dungeons of slavery. Let him, as he sets his foot on the soil of a free State, read in every countenance the deep loathing for himself and his crime, which ought to be felt. Let the cry of "shame on the man-thief" ring out till the very heavens reverberate with the sound, and roll it back in echoes of thunder; and that sound will be the trump of jubilee to the slave.

Do some timid doughfaces say they will dissolve the Union if this state of sentiment is created? Will that make slavery more respectable, or diminish the abhorrence with which all freemen regard it? Will that hush the voice of indignant remonstrance from the civilized world? Will a dissolution of the Union pile up inaccessible mountains, or stretch impassable deserts between the slave States and the free? It would but aggravate the thing complained of by the South, in every particular. This the slaveholders know full well, and hence, notwithstanding all the bluster with which they are wont to affright the serviles of the North, would rather liberate the last slave they own, than suffer one link of the chain that binds the States together to be severed.

It is needless to remark that the very reverse of this spirit of abhorrence for slavery prevails in the nominally free States. It is the opponents of slavery generally that are the objects of reproach. This is no more strange than true. In the land boasted as the freest on earth, those guilty of practicing "the vilest system of oppression that ever saw the sun," are the most caressed and popular class in the nation, while those who oppose the bloody system, are the most reviled and hated. Antislavery survives this ordeal because it is of God. The reform is based on truth that can not die, and "the eternal years of God are hers." But let the tide once be reversed, and slavery—containing as it does within itself the seeds of death—will die under the consuming breath of a nation's scorn. It lives now because cherished by a prevailing sentiment in its favor in the so-called free States.

It is in view of this indisputable fact that the guilt of the American Church is seen in all its magnitude. *The Church creates and controls public sentiment in this country.* With one hundred thousand ministers, preaching weekly to more than ten millions of people, her power over public opinion must be almost omnipotent. Her combined attacks, with the weapons of truth, on slavery or any other system of crime, would be perfectly irresistible. Hence it is that the American Church has been correctly denominated "the bulwark of American slavery." "She holds the key of the prison-house of the slave," and not only refuses to unlock it, but is busy forging additional bars and bolts to hold him more securely in his chains. The plea, so often urged in defense of the Church, that she has no power to abolish slavery, is false. If true, it would be to her disgrace, that, with such vast resources of numbers, wealth, learning and talents, she was thus powerless. But it is not true. In regard to political power, with half a million voters in her communion, she holds the balance between the parties in the country, and if true to her duty in the exercise of this power, she could make it tell mightily on the cause of freedom. But when this is combined with her moral power over the public heart and conscience, it is no exaggeration to say that no system of crime in this land could stand one year against it.

In view of this power in the hands of the Church, the anti-slavery men turned to her for help in the early stage of the cause. A few glorious spirits responded, and the Church to her honor has furnished some of the most devoted laborers, and some of the martyrs in the cause. But the vast majority of her ministers and members "knew not the day of their merciful visitation." They rejected the call of God to this glorious work, and joined hands with the oppressor; and in accordance with an invariable rule of Divine precedure, have been left to "blindness of mind and hardness of heart" on this subject. As the consequence, we find the Church and the clergy now, in the van of the defenders of slavery, and the fugitive slave bill, with all its unspeakable atrocities. Their reformation is therefore hopeless.

There is, hence, but one course left to the friends of God and his oppressed poor—that is to destroy the present large ecclesiastical organizations of the country, and substitute others in their place which will do the work for which God instituted his Church. Having become welded indissolubly to the foul system of slavery, they must sink with it, under that tide of universal execration, which is rising to overwhelm the bloody abomination. As a significant indication of the rise and direction of the current, the article from the *London Advertiser* possesses special interest.

Religious Instruction of Slaves.

As the text of a short discourse on this subject, we copy the following paragraphs from one of our exchanges:

"Colored Presbyterian Church.—The congregation of the Second Presbyterian Church, Rev. Dr. Smyth's in Charleston, South Carolina, have erected a house of worship for the use of the colored portion of their congregation—their galleries having become to small to accommodate the congregation that desired to assemble with them.

"The house of worship is in a simple Gothic style, and in the shape of a capital T—the transepts or wings being appropriated for the use of white persons.

"The entire cost of this church, including the lot and a small building in the rear used for Sunday-school purposes, will be about $7,700; of this there are about $1,600 due over and above funds that are now in hand.

"Those who may become church-members will be received into the Second Presbyterian Church, by its session, after careful examination, and remain always under the ecclesiastical watch and control of that body. The congregation therefore will be part and parcel of the Second Presbyterian Church.

"The session is to appoint the minister and provide for his salary. They have secured the services of Rev. J. B. Adger, a returned missionary of the American Board. The Sabbath-school connected with the church numbers 150 pupils, taught by twenty-five to thirty of the white members of the church. The Rev. Dr. Thornwell, preached the dedication sermon, on the 26th of May, to an immense congregation. The *Southern Presbyterian* says: 'It was one of the most masterly discourses we have ever heard from him. *It was a powerful vindication of the rights of Southern slaveholders and the duties of Southern Christians.*'"

This fact is interesting and instructive. Dr. Thornwell, as is well known, is one of the most talented, popular and influential ministers of the Old School Presbyterian Church. Three years ago he occupied the Moderator's chair in the

General Assembly. It is reasonable, therefore, to suppose that his preaching to slaves is a fair specimen of the kind of religious instruction they generally receive. The points selected by a man of Dr. Thornwell's standing, at the dedication of a church for the use of slaves, no doubt occupy a most prominent place in whatever of religious teaching is ordinarily given them. What, then was the Doctor's theme? "*A vindication of the rights of Southern slaveholders and the duties of Southern Christians*"—that is, of course, the rights of Southern slaveholders to *hold* their slaves. This is the *only* right slaveholders, as such, claim or exercise. If, therefore, other rights were meant, they would be called the rights of Southern men, or citizens, or Christians, not "the rights of Southern slaveholders."

In regard to the general object of the religious instruction of slaves, two facts can be indisputably established:

I. That any religious instruction for slaves, which claims for the master the right to hold them in slavery, and enjoins on them the duty to submit to his authority as lawful and right, is a positive injury to the slave;

II. That this *is* the kind of teaching the slaves *do* receive from Southern professing Christians.

The first of these propositions requires little proof. There is a principle implanted by God in every human soul, which tells the man he has a right to be free. This principle is stronger than any other conviction which it is possible to engraft on the soul. It rises above the authority of human law; and if a pretended revelation from God should assert that the man was born to be enslaved, he would feel that the writing of Deity on his heart, contradicted its assertion and stamped it as a lie. Hence, when the Bible is tortured into a justification of the Divine right of slavery, in the hearing of the slave, he comes inevitably to one of two conclusions: either, that the Bible is false, or that his teacher is falsifying its teachings. Either conclusion must be fatal to any good impression on his mind.

But it is not by argument that we purpose to establish this position; we have the most abundant and conclusive *testimony* on the point. To show that nothing can obliterate from the mind of the slave the innate consciousness of his birth-right to freedom, we present the following truthful and beautiful extract from the speech of James McDowell (since Governor of Virginia, and now a Member of Congress), in the Legislature of that State, in 1832.

"Sir, you may place the slave where you please—you may dry up, to your utmost, the fountain of his feelings, the springs of his thoughts—you may close npon his mind every avenue to knowledge, and cloud it over with artificial night—you may yoke him to your labor as the ox which liveth only to work, and worketh only to live—you may put him under any process which, without destroying his value as a slave, will debase and crush him as a rational being—you may do this, and the idea that he was born to be free will survive it all. It is allied to his hope of immortality—it is the ethereal part of his nature which oppression can not reach—it is a torch lit up in his soul by the hand of the Deity, and never meant to be extinguished by the hand of man."

In view of the truth so eloquently expressed in this extract, it is obvious that a religion which tells the slave that he was born for bondage, and that, therefore, this glorious *instinct* of his nature is not of God, must come to him with the evidence of its falsity on its very face; and, therefore, though through fear or flattery he may affect to receive it, in heart he utterly rejects it.

But on this point we have testimony still more directly in point. It is that of Rev. C. C. Jones, D. D., who has been devoted for years to the (so-called) religious instruction of the slaves. In his rules for the direction of others engaged in the same work, occurs this language:

"Do nothing without the master's consent. Teach them what Paul directed slaves to do and be; but beware of pressing these duties too strongly and frequently, lest you beget the fatal suspicion that you are but executing a selfish scheme of the white man to make them better slaves, rather than to make them Christ's freemen. *If they suspect this you labor in vain.*"

If to *suspect* this motive is to render the teacher's efforts vain, surely when they openly teach that the Bible sanctions the claim of the master to the body and soul of the slave, the effect must be something worse than vain.

Leaving this point, in proof of which we have abundance more testimony, we pass to consider our second point: That in the religious instruction which the slaves *generally* receive, the Divine right of the master to hold them in bondage, and their consequent duty to submit to his authority as right, is one of the most important elements, and that, therefore, this instruction is a positive curse, instead of a blessing. Let not our position be misunderstood. We do not object to the slaves being taught that it is their duty to submit peaceably, *for conscience sake*, to the wicked claim of their masters, until they can by lawful means get free; but to the inculcation of the *right* of the masters to enslave them, and that hence God has placed them and wishes them to remain in this situation. To the proof of this, furnished by the extract at the head of this article, we have already alluded. A sermon by the leading Presbyterian preacher at the South (for this Dr. Thornwell emphatically is), at the dedication of a church for their especial use, contains " a powerful vindication of the rights of Southern slaveholders." But we have other testimony, the character and quality of which establishes this point beyond a question, if human testimony can establish anything.

In the first place, the instruction contemplated is usually only oral. In an article on the religious instruction of slaves in the *Princeton Review*, extracts from a number of letters are given, which the *Review* says are from " clergymen of high standing in several different denominations; from lawyers, physicians, judges, members of Congress, intelligent planters and others residing in Virginia and Texas, and other States lying between them." From these letters, thus vouched for, we give the following extracts. One says:

" Under present circumstances, it is evident that they who engage in the delicate business of instructing our slaves, must confine themselves to the method of oral communication. But this limitation should not produce the slightest discouragement. Written documents bore but a small part in the early propagation of Christianity. Until the present age, indeed, the mass of the people have received by far the greater part of their religious knowledge and impressions from the mouth of the living teacher. Even now, perhaps, the majority in our own country have their religious principles and character formed mainly by oral instruction."

Another says:

" On the modes of communicating a saving knowledge of Divine truth to the colored population, best suited to their genius, habits and condition, we must remember that oral instruction is the kind of instruction alone that is universally allowed in slaveholding States. Hence, the question with us will be, in what mode can oral instruction be best communicated?"

The Synod of Virginia, a few years ago, passed the following resolution:

Resolved, That the Synod would recommend, wherever it may be practicable, the establishment of Sabbath-schools for the ORAL instruction of the colored people."

In view of the fact thus established, we see that Roman Catholicism is not confined to the Church of Rome. One of the worst features of the policy of that Church—the giving of mere oral instruction—has been deliberately adopted and openly recommended by the Protestant churches of this country in reference to the slave population. We now present a few facts illustrating the nature of this oral instruction. We have already said that one of the points most insisted on is the right of the master to hold his slave in bondage, and their consequent duty to submit to him as placed over them by God. In proof of this, we first present some extracts from a book of sermons, intended especially for the use of masters and mistresses, in the instruction of their slaves, by Rt. Rev. Wm. Meade, Assistant Bishop of Virginia. The *Princeton Review* indorses his discourse on this subject, calling it "a manly and Christian publication." Says the Bishop:

"Almighty God hath been pleased to make you slaves here, and to give you nothing but labor and poverty in this world, which you are obliged to submit to, as *it is His will that it should be so.*"

Again :

"Having thus shown you the chief duties you owe to your great Master in Heaven, I now come to lay before you the duties you owe to your masters and mistresses here upon earth. And for this you have one general rule that you ought always to carry in your minds, and that is, *to do all service for them as if you did it for God himself.*"

And again :

"Now, from this general rule, namely, that you are *to do all service for your masters and mistresses as if you did it for God Himself*, there arise several other rules of duty toward your masters and mistresses, which I shall endeavor to lay out in order before you.

"And, in the first place, *you are to be obedient and subject to your masters in all things.* * * * And Christian ministers are commanded to '*exhort servants to be obedient unto their masters*, and to please them well in all things, not answering again, or gainsaying.' You see how strictly God requires of you, that whatever your *masters and mistresses* order you to do, you must set about it immediately, and faithfully perform it, without any disputing or grumbling, and take care to please them well in all things. And for your encouragement, he tells you that he will reward you for it in heaven : because while you are honestly and faithfully doing your master's business here you are serving your Lord and Master in heaven. You see, also, that you are not to take any exceptions to the behaviour of your masters and mistresses, and that you are to be subject and obedient, not only to such as are *good*, and *gentle*, and *mild* toward you, but also to such as may be *froward, peevish* and *hard*. For you are not at liberty to choose your own masters, but into whatever hands God hath been pleased to put you, you must do your duty, and God will reward you for it."

In these passages, slavery, for the perpetrators of which, Adam Clark declared " perdition had scarcely an adequate penalty," is directly charged upon that God, the habitation of whose throne is justice and judgment." We present but another extract on this point:

"Rev. Joshua Boucher, formerly a minister of the Methodist Episcopal Church, states that the slaves of the South are told that God made them black with the design that they should be slaves ; and that, when traveling and preaching in the South, another preacher, belong to the same church, related the following conversation, which took place between himself and a slave boy :

" *Minister*. ' Have you any religion ? '

" *Boy*. ' No, sir.'

" *Minister*. ' Don't you want religion ? '

" *Boy*. ' No, sir.'

" *Minister*. ' Don't you love God ? '

" *Boy*. ' What! me love God, who made me with a black skin, and white man to whip me ! '

" A man, who had been held as a slave near General John H. Cocke's plantation, in Virginia, where a meeting-house was erected to afford slaves an opportunity of listening to special preaching, asked me if it was in the Bible that he should be a slave, and said they had always told him it was there, and said they (the colored people) should be slaves."

To complete the picture, nothing but a suitable *motive* is wanting to account for the zeal manifested for the religious instruction of slaves. This is clearly furnished by the following extracts, which are taken from letters written by a number of gentlemen in South Carolina and Georgia, in answer to a circular asking information on the subject of "the influence of religious instruction upon the discipline of plantations, and the spirit of subordination of the negroes."

James Edward Henry writes from Spartansburg district, May, 1845, as follows:

"A near neighbor of mine, a prominent member of the church to which he belonged, had contented himself with giving his people the usual religious privileges. About six months ago he commenced giving them special religious instruction. He used Jones' Catechism principally. * * * He states that he has now comparatively no trouble in their management."

Thomas Cook writes from Marlborough district, May, 1845:

"Plantations under religious instruction are more easily governed than those that are not."

John Dyson writes from Sumpter district, May, 1845:

"Upon the discipline and subordination of plantations, religious instruction will be found generally and decidedly beneficial."

William Curtis writes from Richland district, May, 1845:

"I have found the owners of plantations around not only willing but desirous that we should preach to their negroes; and they find, as they expected, a better spirit and subordination among them."

James Gillam writes from Abbeville district, May, 1845:

"*The deeper the piety of the slave, the more valuable is he in every sense of the word.*"

Nicholas Ware writes from Brownsville, Marlborough district, May, 1845:

"All our negroes have, to a great extent, grown up under religious instruction. * * * We scarcely hear of depredations upon stock, etc. They are more obedient and more to be depended on. We have few or no runaways, and corporeal punishment is seldom resorted to."

N. R. Middleton writes from St. Andrew's Parish, May, 1845:

"A regard to self-interest should lead every planter to give his people religious instruction."

John Rivers writes from Colleton district, May, 1845:

"Religious instruction promotes the discipline and subordination on plantations."

Our limits do not allow us to present further testimony, nor is it necessary. If there is one thing true beyond all dispute, it is that the slaves are habitually taught by preachers and others, that God has given their masters a right to enslave them, and hence, that they are bound to submit to all the hardships of their lot, as to his will. The inevitable conclusion, if they believe these teachings, is, that God is a partial tyrant, and therefore a being to be feared and hated, not to be loved. If, on the other hand, they do not believe their religious instructors, then they must set them down as hypocrites, and with ignorant minds, it will be a natural conclusion that their religion has made them such. In either case, therefore, the influence of such instruction must be fatal to any correct ideas of Christianity, and to all right religious impressions on their minds. We mourn that such should be the case. The consolations of the gospel of Jesus Christ are eminently fitted to sweeten the bitter cup of slavery. But the perverted and falsified gospel they receive only tends to make the bitterness more intense. To tell them they suffer unjustly, and exhort them to bear it meekly for the love of God, would be right. But to tell them God wills and approves their oppression, is to present him to their minds as a great Almighty slaveholder, and therefore a tyrant, hating and hateful in his character.

We take no pleasure in exposures of this kind. But one of the most common defenses now set up for the slaveholding churches of this land is, that their members and ministers are actively engaged in the religious instruction of their slaves, and thus doing all they can to ameliorate their condition and prepare them for freedom. That in rare instances this may be the case we do not deny; but any one who will look dispassionately at the facts we have presented, must conclude that the religious instruction of the slaves is only, in the vast majority of cases, a selfish scheme to make the slaves more docile and honest, and thus increase their value. This is *literally* making "a gain of godliness." Of all the crimes with which slavery stands convicted, one of the worst is its impious perversions of the Bible and its blasphemous misrepresentations of the character of God. This compound of lust and blood is represented as harmonizing with the teachings of the Bible, and therefore with the character of God, for the Bible is but a copy of his character. And to make the hold of the oppressor more secure, the sanctions of that Bible are urged in its support, and the religious susceptibilities of the slave are so trained as to rivet his fetters more firmly on his limbs.

Yet this kind of instruction is all that is compatible with

the condition of slavery.   Hence, the inevitable conclusion is, that the first step to the enlightening and Christianizing the slave is, his entire and unconditional emancipation.

BIBLE REVISION.

Our readers are probably aware that a portion of the Baptist Church in this country have a society of recent origin, called the Bible Union, the professed object of which is to get up a revised and improved translation of the Holy Scriptures.   We have never thought very highly of the wisdom of this movement.   In the first place we do not think the scholarship necessary to this work is to be found in this country, and least of all is to be found in the Baptist Church.   It requires a peculiar education to fit a man for the task of translating the Scriptures.   He ought, in the first place, to be familiar with the languages in which they were written— Greek, Hebrew, and Chaldee—as with his mother tongue. He ought to understand the cognate languages, Arabic, Syriac, Aramaic, etc.   He ought further to be intimately acquainted with the geography, topography, geology, climate, and natural productions of the countries in which the Scriptures were written.   He ought to be minutely acquainted with the state of the arts and sciences of the people among whom the sacred writers lived, and with their social and domestic habits, their political institutions, their modes and habits of thought, their manner of transacting business, their currency, commerce, agriculture, etc., etc., as all these furnish illustrations to the sacred writers.   In addition to all this he should know all that may be known from profane history of the nations among whom, and the times in which, the inspired penman wrote.

Now men with this training, and these acquirements, are not to be found in this age and country.   A few such might be found in the German Universities, but the majority of them are rationalists and infidels.   Certainly we should not look for them among the Baptists of this country.

In view of this fact it does not savor much of a becoming modesty in the Bible Union, to attempt a translation that shall supersede the one now in use.   That translation was made when the studies into the languages and literature of the Scriptures, which attended and followed the Reformation, bad reached their hight. A liberal education in that age consisted mainly of an acquaintance with Latin, Hebrew, Greek, and the pure mathematics. The *great* minds of the age were occupied with theological and exegetical studies, which is not the case now. As their minds were confined to a narrower range of studies than now make up a liberal education, they would of course acquire a more thorough acquaintance with what they did study. What they lacked in the extension of their field of investigation, they made up in the depth of their researches into what was open to their view. This kind of education admirably fitted them for the work of translating the Bible, and it is a striking illustration of the special providence of God, and of his care over his own word, that a large number of the most learned men of that age were brought together for the great work of translating into English the Holy oracles. The translation itself, moreover, illustrates the same thing. There is an accuracy, a beauty, a freshness, and propriety in its language that is not found in any of the current literature of the age in which it was made. A few obsolete words might properly be replaced by others, and in a few minor points the received translation might be improved. But as a whole it may be doubted if it will ever be amended to advantage. It has become interwoven with the whole frame and net-work—with the very foundations of thought and emotion in the minds of all Christian people who speak the English tongue.

In view of these, and other similar facts, the idea of a few smatterers in sacred literature in this day attempting to get up a translation that should supersede the magnificent one now in use, has appeared to us as one of the greatest exhibitions of folly which the age has witnessed.

These *a priori* conclusions are singularly confirmed by recent developments in the history of the Bible Union. Its president, and most efficient agent, was the venerable Dr. Archibald Maclay, of New York. He has recently resigned his office in the society, and given as reasons some facts which the papers call "astounding developments." Such in fact they are, as the following extracts from his pen will show. We quote his language, with the comments of one of our exchanges. He says:

"On being elected President of the Union, in October, 1855, I found myself in a position of more direct and unqualified responsibility; and under these circumstances I felt the importance of becoming more particularly acquainted with the operations of the body.   I then, for the first time, ascertained who the revisers were; and found, to my astonishment, that instead of there having been about forty individuals actually engaged in translating the New Testament, as I had understood from the Secretary, and often stated, there had not been more than twenty-three or twenty-four. Instead of these all being competent scholars, as I had supposed, and as the plan of the Union required, and as is often reiterated in the official documents of the Union, some unquestionably lacked the essential qualifications of a translator."

The receipts of the society now amount to $50,000 per annum. This sum is expended upon this new translation, and the Rev. Dr. Maclay informs us how it is done. "Prof. Conant, of Rochester, has a contract with the society 'which secures to him, *in addition* to a salary of $1,200 from the Theological Seminary, $2,000 a year for the portion of time not required in his professional duties, *till he shall have completed the Old Testament*, with a copyright interest, and a percentage on future sales of his translation, when published with notes.'   Prof. Conant has already received nearly $6,000, or three years' salary, and has not completed one of the books of the Old Testament.   This contract is binding on the society till he has finished the whole, and he is only to give his leisure time to it!"

Dr. Maclay complains of the translation as very much at fault.   He gives specimens.   Here are some:

"He it is that immerses in a holy spirit." John i: 33.

"If any one be not born of water and spirit." John iii: 5.

"The Son can do nothing of himself, if he see not the Father doing anything." John v: 16.

"But this he said of the spirit which those believing on him were about to receive; for there was not yet a holy spirit." John vii: 39.

"And I give to them eternal life, and they shall not perish, forever." John x: 28.

"Jesus, therefore, when he saw her weeping, and the Jews, who came with her, weeping, he groaned in the spirit, and troubled himself." John xi: 33.

"Who were begotten—not of blood, nor of a will of flesh, nor of a will of man—but of God.   And the Word became flesh and dwelt among us (and we saw his glory, a glory as of one only begotten of a father), full of grace and truth." John i: 12–14.

These are by no means the most objectionable renderings.

In this and other books are some *which I would not disclose to the public eye.*

Dr. Maclay found that the rule of the Board, in regard to the received text, had been violated, and the revisers had, without authority, undertaken to decide, each for himself, in regard to the various copies or texts. He says:

"And on a closer examination in the department of revision, I found that, in addition to the shocking translations already referred to, the misguided hand of the reviser had been rashly laid upon the original text, as it seems to me, without any authority of the Board. It will be recollected that in the famous Amity street letter, Dr. Williams charged the Bible Union with improper secresy, in withholding from the churches a knowledge of the Greek text to be used as the standard of revision; and in a reply, written by Dr. Judd, and adopted by the Board, it was said:

"'This subject received our early and prayerful attention, and after obtaining the most satisfactory information respecting it, with the counsel of competent advisers, and our own mature deliberation, we determined to use the "received text," as critically edited by the best scholars of the age, and published by Bagster & Sons, London, octavo edition, 1851.'

"Previous to this, the Board had established certain 'General Rules for the Direction of the Translators and Revisers,' of which the third reads thus:

"'Translations or revisions of the New Testament shall be made from the received Greek text, critically edited, with known errors corrected.'

"Also certain 'Special Instruction to the Revisers of the English New Testament,' of which the first reads as follows:

"'The common English version must be the basis of revision; the Greek text, Bagster & Sons' octavo edition of 1851.'"

These are all the rules of the Union respecting the Greek text; neither of them has ever been abrogated or altered; and as they stand, they admit of no departure from the "received text," as critically edited (not by revisers of the Bible Union, but by distinguished scholars in times past) and *subsequently* published by Bagster & Sons in 1851. Yet it appeared, on examination, that some revisers had undertaken what seemed to me to be even more presumptuous than the selection of some other text, such as Griesbach's, Sholz's, Tichendorf's, and more unsafe than the preparation of a new, independent recension by competent hands from original sources; viz., a revision of the "received Greek text," by weighing all the different manuscripts, to ascertain the relative value of their various readings, as given by second-hand authorities, varying or modifying these readings by ancient versions and patristic writings, collating and comparing the opinions of different editors, then selecting or rejecting any particular reading, according as it was found to be, in the reviser's judgment, genuine or spurious; his English version being conformed to this eclectic edition of the Greek text. In one book, which came under my observation, after it had been stereotyped, a cursory examination showed that the reviser had deviated from the "received Greek text" in two places by adding something to it; in twelve places by rejecting something of it. And one of the portions rejected as *spurious* embraced twelve *consecutive verses!* In another place the following passage is cast out of the Bible:

"For an angel went down at a certain season into the pool, and troubled the water; whosoever then first after the troubling of the water stepped in, was made whole of whatsoever disease he had."

Where the common version reads:

"That whoever believeth in him should not perish but have eternal life,"

The received Greek text has been so critically edited that, in the revised English version, the same passage reads thus: "That every one that believes on him may have eternal life." And the rejection of "Jesus," "John," "Christ," and "Amen," are specimens of the smaller changes, which have resulted from this revision of the Greek text.

When Dr. M., being a conscientious man, got into trouble over the maladministration of the society, of which he was now the head and most responsible officer, an effort is made to divert him from any further examination of the working of the Union. He says:

"The Secretary urged me to leave New York and travel abroad as an agent. I informed him that, with the views which I then entertained, I could not conscientiously act in the capacity of an agent; that among other things, I had assured the people that we have competent scholars to translate the Scriptures, and that the funds of the Union were judiciously and economically expended, but I could do so no longer; that I had aimed to live an honest man, and I meant to die an honest man; and if I were to go out and publish my honest impressions regarding the operations of the Bible Union, I should only damage its reputation, which, under existing circumstances, I was not prepared to do. One would have supposed that such a statement would have precluded any further request from the Secretary for me to go abroad as an agent of the Union. His subsequent reiteration of this request, besides the imputation of a disbelief in my own statement which is conveyed, exhibited such a solicitude for the services, and such an indifference for the conscientious views of an agent, as equally surprised and pained me. I was the more resolved to examine thoroughly the whole policy and conduct of the institution; to inquire more fully into the character and qualifications of our revisers, the practical working of our plan for the production of a revised English version, the condition and effect of our periodical publications, and the appropriate economy of our expenditures."

After further examination and further finding, he gives up all hope of reform and resigns. He says:

"Being fully satisfied from personal examination, that the funds which I have done so much to collect, and which I know have been most sacredly devoted, by the rich and the poor, to one of the holiest purposes of Christian charity, are being squandered; that a vast amount is expended for operations remote from the one great object of the institution; that men are employed to translate the word of God who are not qualified for the work; that unwarrantable translations have been made, which, if published, must bring into discredit the most precious doctrines of my faith, sap the fundamental truths of Christianity as indubitably revealed in the Holy Scriptures, and shake the confidence of the people in the canon of the sacred writings; that such revisions are likely to be published for indiscriminate circulation without the previous precautionary examination, provided for, and *required* by the plan and rules of revision, as originally adopted by the Board; that the controlling power of the institution has become completely centralized in one man; and that the exercise of that power is not only such as to forbid the hope of reform, but also to blast the name and influence of every one who advocates reform: feeling perfectly assured of all this, I am compelled by a stern sense of duty, to abandon the enterprise, and to free myself, as far as possible, from all further responsibility in its operations. And I can not doubt that my friends, when rightly informed, will justify me in so doing."

These developments will doubtless put a *quietus* on the

whole movement. It is to be hoped that the funds and the labors of the Bible Union will now be devoted to more sensible and useful purposes.

THE FORM OF GODLINESS WITHOUT THE POWER.

The strictest observance of outward forms in a church is entirely compatible with its total apostasy. We know that the popular belief is, in this day, opposed to this truth. It is a prevalent idea that so long as a Church holds essential truth in her creed, and keeps up the public worship of God in a serious and orderly manner, that church can not be other than a Church of Christ. This idea is held by many honest people, and serves as a veil to hide the moral deformity that is often found in the character and conduct of the Church. Hence, when their church is charged with supporting systems of the highest crime, they regard the charge as false and slanderous. They think of the public congregation where Jehovah is, to all appearance, devoutly worshiped. Their minds revert to the fervent prayers and earnest exhortations of the preacher. His solemn warning to sinners, and beautiful exhibitions of the blessedness of the righteous, come back to mind. The serious, attentive faces of the congregation, as they listen to these proclamations of truth, are present to their view. The conclusion from these things is that there must be reality in all this. This must be true religion. God must surely own the church as one of his, where he is thus worshiped in the solemn convocation. Hence it can not be that their church is one of the bulwarks of any system of crime.

The Bible furnishes abundant evidence that all these outward appearances of piety are strictly compatible with the worst practical crimes, and may be found in churches that are utterly apostate. Passing by, for the present, other instances of this in the Bible, we select one from the prophet Micah. In the third chapter of his prophesy we find this language :

"Hear this, I pray you, ye heads of the house of Jacob, and princes of the house of Israel, that abhor judgment, and pervert all equity.

"They build up Zion with blood, and Jerusalem with iniquity.

"The heads thereof judge for reward, and the priests thereof teach for hire, and the prophets thereof divine for money : yet will they lean upon the Lord, and say, *is* not the Lord among us? none evil can come upon us."

That these verses describe an apostate church, under the influence of apostate religious teachers, is evident. Zion, or the Church, was built up with blood, and Jerusalem with iniquity. The religious teachings were utterly depraved. Yet great apparent devotion to the interests of Zion was manifested, and loud professions of piety were abundant. While the heads of Zion judged for reward, and the priests thereof taught for hire, and the prophets divined for money, they yet "*leaned upon the Lord, and said is not the Lord among us.*" While abhorring judgment (or justice) and perverting all equity, they felt so secure in the Divine protection that they said "*none evil can come upon us.*" These hypocrites could point to what they considered certain evidences of the Divine presence and favor: Is not the Lord among us? Are not these the tokens of his gracious regard? Do we not have a numerous attendance on our ministrations in the solemn services of the sanctuary? Are we not "building up Zion," lengthening her cords and strengthening her stakes? Drawing from these considerations a presumptuous confidence, they felt safe in God, at the very moment that his heaviest curse was impending over them.

A more exact description than this of the leading churches of this land could not be written by the prophet if he lived in our day, and was an eye-witness of current events. Let us look at some of the details in this prophetic picture. The first is, "they abhor judgment and pervert all equity." The pulpits of this land have rung and are now ringing with defenses of the system of slavery and the Fugitive Slave Bill. The religious press is teeming with similar justifications. Now slavery and the Fugitive Slave Bill are the most monstrous "perversions of *all* equity" that were ever framed into law. The provisions of the Fugitive Bill are drawn with an eye solely to the establishment of injustice. A bribe is paid for a decision against natural right, and evidence is taken as sufficient to consign a man to the endurance of life-long robbery, which would not establish a claim of property to a dog. Now, if the defense of this iniquity by the Church and clergy is not overwhelming evidence of an "abhorrence of justice," and a desire to "pervert all equity," there never can be any evidence of the existence of such disposition.

Another particular in the description is, "they build up Zion with blood and Jerusalem with iniquity." As a striking exemplification of this process take one or two authentic advertisements. The *Savannah Georgian* of the 3rd of March,

1845, contains the notice of a public sale. After describing the plantation the advertisement adds:

"Also, at the same time and place the following negro slaves, to-wit: 'Charles, Peggy, Antoinette, Davy, September, Maria, Jenny and Isaac, levied on as the property of Henry T. Hall, to satisfy a mortgage, issued out of the McIntosh Superior Court, *in favor of the Board of Directors of the Theological Seminary of the Synod of South Carolina and Georgia, against said Henry T. Hall.* Conditions cash.

"'C. O'NEAL, Deputy Sheriff, S. C.'"

The *Charleston Courier*, of February 12th, 1835, contains the following:

"FIELD NEGROES, *by Thomas Gadsden.*

"On Tuesday, the 17th instant, will be sold at the North of the Exchange, at ten o'clock, a prime gang of ten NEGROES, accustomed to the culture of cotton and provisions, belonging to the INDEPENDENT CHURCH in *Christ's Church Parish.*"

The next notice of a bequest of negroes for the benefit of the heathen is from a Savannah (Ga.) paper:

"*Bryan Superior Court.*

"Between John J. Maxwell and others, Executors of Ann Pray, complainants, and Mary Sleigh and others, Devisees and Legatees, under the will of Ann Pray, defendants. } IN EQUITY.

"A bill having been filed for the distribution of the estate of the Testatrix, Ann Pray, and it appearing that among other legacies in her will, is the following, viz.: *a legacy of one-fourth of certain negro slaves to the American Board of Commissioners for domestic missions for the purpose of sending the gospel to the heathen, and particularly to the Indians on this continent.* It is on motion of the solicitors of the complainants ordered that all persons claiming the said legacy, do appear and answer the bill of the complainants within four months from this day. And it is ordered that this order be published in a public gazette of the city of Savannah, and in one of the gazettes of Philadelphia once a month for four months.

"Extract from the minutes, December 2nd, 1832.

"JOHN SMITH, c. s. c. b. c."

These advertisements are mere specimens of multitudes of others of similar character, and serve both as indications and illustrations of a general practice. Human beings are bought

and sold, held and bequeathed, for the benefit of theological
seminaries, the support of preachers, and the sending of
missionaries to the heathen. The wages paid for the labor,
and the price paid for the bodies of slaves, is both literally
and figuratively, the price of blood. This price of blood the
leading denominations of the American church take and
apply to the support of all the various means employed for
building up the Church at home and extending it abroad. If
this is not "*building up Zion with blood*," then how and where
can the world furnish an example of such spiritual masonry?
Yet do the sanguinary builders of this structure of blood put
forth, as in the days of Micah, abundance of pious pretenses.
They say with their ancient prototypes, " *Is not the Lord
among us?* " Look at our revivals of religion, our extended
missionary operations, our numerous theological seminaries,
our presses, and pious ministers and devoted people. Then
elated with the survey of their extended boundaries, flowing
wealth and multitudinous adherents, they triumphantly ex-
claim with them of old, " *none evil can come upon us.*"

To the churches thus cemented together by the blood of
the tortured slave, comes the terrible denunciation which the
prophet thunders against the wicked Church of his day :

" Therefore shall Zion for your sake be ploughed as a field, and Jerusalem shall become heaps, and the mountain of the house as the high
places of the forest."

Similar to this is the language of Isaiah :

" To what purpose is the multitude of your sacrifices unto me? saith
the Lord : I am full of the burnt-offerings of rams, and the fat of fed
beasts, and I delight not in the blood of bullocks, or of lambs, or of
he goats.

" When ye come to appear before me, who hath required this at your
hand to tread my courts ?

" Bring no more vain oblations: incense is an abomination unto me;
the new moons and sabbaths, the calling of assemblies, I can not away
with, it is iniquity, even the solemn meeting.

" Your new moons and your appointed feasts my soul hateth; they
are a trouble unto me; I am weary to bear them.

" And when ye spread forth your hand I will hide mine eyes from
you; yea, when ye make many prayers I will not hear: your hands
are full of blood."

DECREASE OF THEOLOGICAL STUDENTS.

Recent statistics exhibit the fact that there are fewer candidates for the ministry in the Protestant churches of this

country than there were in 1840. In the Theological Seminaries of the Congregationalists and Presbyterians there are fewer by seventy than ten years ago. During this period the population of the country has increased six millions, and one million of square miles have been added to its territories.

These facts furnish food for reflection to the thoughtful. A truly evangelical Protestant ministry is one main hope for our country and the world. A *true* minister of Christ is the fast friend and staunch advocate of all those principles of freedom, justice and religion which form the only solid basis of good government, and which alone can promote the highest well-being of mankind in time and eternity. The *true* minister is, of necessity, the friend and advocate of freedom, for his great business is to preach and follow Christ and his doctrines, and the mission of Christ is to " proclaim liberty to the captive and the opening of the prison to them that are bound." He is necessarily, also, the enemy of intemperance, because he is ordained to warn men against those sins which exclude from the kingdom of heaven, and the Bible declares that " no drunkard hath eternal life abiding in him." He is by the same necessity the friend of peace and enemy of war, because his master is the Prince of Peace, and the elements of his kingdom are " righteousness, *peace* and joy in the Holy Ghost." He is also, of necessity, the friend of sound education, for the mission of the gospel of which he is a minister is to enlighten the world. God's true Church and ministers are the light of the world, and as his religion is disseminated through the earth, so will the cause of true learning progress. In short, the true minister of Christ is the friend of every principle and every measure which makes men wiser and better, and the opposer of every principle and system which has the opposite tendency. He is governed by a spirit alike the opposite of that of the despot or the slave. He has no desire to be lord over God's heritage ; but feeling his own unworthiness, and imbued with the spirit of genuine humility, he preaches Christ the Lord, and himself the servant of the flock for Jesus' sake. At the same time he has none of that spirit of craven fear and cringing sycophancy which would induce him to hold back one jot or tittle of the counsel of God, for fear of offending his people. He is too deeply penetrated with a sense of his high and solemn obligations to his own master, to stoop to court the favor of rich and haughty sinners in his congregation. Perfect weakness in himself, he is strong in the Lord and in the power of his might. An ambassador of God, he will be true to his mission, and declare to the utmost letter the whole of God's terms of reconciliation with men. With his treasures and hopes in heaven, he will be proof alike against the frowns of power and the seductions of flattery.

Such a minister will never perjure his soul by forging lying apologies for crimes like slavery and drunkenness. He will sooner perish at the stake in the fiercest fires of persecution, than throw the mantle of his religion around the criminals that traffic in intoxicating poisons or in the bodies and souls of men. Such a minister will never fawn on the great or despise the lowly. His voice will be raised in stern rebuke of the titled profligate, and in words of consolation to the suffering and the dumb.

A ministry of this character will *command* the respect of the world, however much it may be opposed and hated. It will draw to it the gifted and the pure, and embrace the best mind and deepest piety of the Church. It will possess elements of irresistible attraction to the strong-minded and the pure-hearted, and will, by the force and operation of this principle of moral attraction, inevitably perpetuate itself.

Is this the character of the American clergy as a class at the present time? Every intelligent man knows it is not. As a class they are the most dangerous foes to freedom and the strongest body-guard to oppression. They fawn on the vicious great and refuse to plead for the poor and the dumb. They are the conservators of many of the errors of the past, and the enemies of practical reform. They are the friends of education only so far as it consists in the induction of the youthful mind into the cast-iron thoughts and systems of former generations. They have expunged from their creed the idea of progress, and ignored *living* themes in the discussions of the pulpit. They shrink from grappling manfully with the great social and moral questions of the day, and content themselves with teaching the forms of a faith from which the life and spirit have departed.

What is the consequence of all this? The ministry of the present day, as a class, have lost the respect of the world. The wicked have not respect enough to oppose them, and the good are not attracted to their support and sympathy. These facts, if we are not greatly mistaken, account, in part at least, for the decrease in the number of the candidates for the ministry. The gifted and the good among the youth find the attractions to other pursuits stronger than the profession of the clergy. They find in other departments freer scope for the development of their mental energies, and a wider field for the exercise of Christian benevolence. Through the many reform societies, organized to do the work of the Church, the very existence of which is a burning reproach to the ministry, they devote themselves to the good of their race. To the investigation of weighty questions of science, morals and religion they devote their energies. They are thus throwing a flood of light over the laws and relations of mind and matter, revealing the wondrous wisdom and power of God in all his works, and thus showing forth his glory. They are thus preparing the materials and facilities for the construction of the glorious temple of the Redeemer's worship; and these works, so full of promise to the race, are often pursued under the ban of the clerical profession. Not strange is it, therefore, that the respectability and the numbers of the ministry are decreasing together. The discussion of the remedy for this state of things, we must reserve for another article.

Trouble in the Episcopal Church.

A man of decided note, in his way, is Bishop Doane, of New Jersey. He is a leader, and one of the most ultra members of the High Church, Divine right, Puseyite party in the Episcopal Church. He delights to be known by the sounding title "His Holiness Lord George, Bishop of New Jersey?" Various rumors and charges against the moral character of Mr. Doane have for some time been afloat. He is charged openly with such slight peccadilloes as "obtaining money under false pretenses," "defrauding his hired men," etc. "Wine bills, to the amount of $1,000," contracted by the Bishop and unpaid for, are also talked of. These rumors have become so notorious that the bishops of Maine, Virginia and Ohio have thought it their duty to interfere. On the representation of four laymen of New Jersey, these bishops have written a letter to Bishop Doane, in which they declare that "such and so many are the charges against him, that they do not feel at liberty" to let the matter pass without an investigation. They wish the Bishop to request an investigation, and declare that if he declines doing so, they will feel bound to have the matter inquired into. "His Holiness Lord George" responds wrathfully and indignantly to the letter of the three Bishops. He and his party are firm believers in the doctrine of an "official sanctity" pertaining to an ordained minister, entirely distinct from his personal character. Accordingly Bishop Doane, like his illustrious prototype, a bishop of the Church of England who, when reproved for swearing, answered that he "swore as a man, not as a bishop," holds that he cheated his workmen and obtained money fraudulently as a man, not as a bishop. He opens his protest in the following grandiloquent style :

"In the name of the Father, and of the Son, and of the Holy Ghost, Amen. The undersigned, George Washington Doane, D. D., L. L. D., by Divine permission Bishop of the Diocese of New Jersey, humbly ministering before God, in the twentieth year of his Episcopate, in the name of His crucified Son, and in the power of his sanctifying spirit; and not without tokens of the Heavenly blessing on his unfaithful and unworthy ministration; makes now, as in the immediate presence of the Holy Trinity, adorable and ever to be blessed, his solemn protest, as aggrieved by the Right Reverend Wm. Meade, D. D., Bishop of the Dioceseof Virginia ; the Right Reverend George Burgess, D. D., Bishop of the Diocese of Maine; and the Right Reverend Charles Pettit McIlvaine, D. D., Bishop of the Diocese of Ohio, by their *uncanonical*, *unchristian* and *inhuman* procedure in regard to him, as heretofore set forth in the document bearing their signatures."

To our poor comprehension there seems to be a decided spice of blasphemy in this language ; but not being versed in the mysteries of "Apostolic succession," "official sanctity," etc., we would not venture to speak with much confidence. Not content with this protest, Bishop Doane proceeds to call a special convention, not to sit in judgment on his own conduct, but on that of his brother bishops. As this convention will be mainly composed of the partizans and creatures of Bishop Doane, it is pretty certain that they will clear him and condemn his accusers; and as Bishop D. is a leader in the High Church party (*low* enough is this *high* churchism, one would think), it will be very hard to convict him. The affair may bring to a crisis the elements of antagonism that have long been at work in the Episcopal Church. Ultimate disunion of the two opposite principles and parties may be the issue. We note these things as items of news, and also as affording a rather poor commentary on the boasted "unity in diversity" of the Episcopal churches. The facts are also interesting in another view. Bishop Doane is one of the lower law, pro-slavery, fugitive slave law advocates. He venerates Daniel Webster, as is natural. That he who advocates the stealing of women and children should obtain money under false pretenses, and cheat his hired laborers, is not at all strange. Bishop Doane and his party are pointed illustrations of the description of the American clergy, as a class, in the previous article. His case is another indication of a degree of corruption in the popular religion of this country which can be purified by nothing but a moral revolution.

As a literary curiosity, we insert the close of the Bishop's reply to the charges of the accusing bishops:

"And these are the four persons, and such the charges, upon whose authority three bishops in the Church of God, without acquaintance with the men or inquiry as to their allegations, have relied, as the ground of criminal proceedings against their peer. Fearful, indeed, the reckoning they will have to meet. For the inroad which has thus been made upon the sacred sorrows of a desolated hearth; for the interruption of the daily duties of an office which adds to the care of a Diocese, the care of a parish, and the care of two institutions, in which two hundred of the sons and daughters of the church are nurtured; for the storm which now must burst upon the peace and quiet of the church — for this aggression on the Diocese of New Jersey — for this invasion of the rights of its convention; for this injustice, indignity, and cruelty toward its bishop; for the whole amount, and all the shapes, and every incident and consequence of this enormous wrong — the undersigned holds as responsible the Bishops of Maine, Virginia and Ohio; accuses them before Christendom, and summons them in all solemnity and sorrow, before the judgment seat of God."

CATHOLICISM AND CIVIL LIBERTY.

Dr. O'Connor, the Roman Catholic Bishop of Pittsburg, recently delivered a lecture on this subject. This address is published at length in the columns of the *Pittsburg Catholic*. It contains many queer things. The Bishop labors hard to prove that all of freedom embodied in the political institutions of this country, is owing to the Roman Catholic Church. The attempted proof of this is quite novel. He tries to show that the common law of England, which is the basis of our free institutions, is of Catholic origin, because it grew up in Catholic times! The same logic would prove the Reformation of Luther, and the astronomical discoveries of Gallileo to be due to that church, which was the relentless persecutor of both. The common law of England originated in the civil institutions of Alfred, before the papacy assumed the control of the temporal kingdoms of the earth.

But it is not our purpose to review this remarkable production, but simply to present a sample or two of its style and matter. The two following paragraphs afford a rare instance of the coolness with which Roman Catholic ecclesiastics can distort the facts of history:

"Every one will admit the importance of religion for the government of society, since all know if it were withdrawn, the mainspring of the vast machine would be broken. Constitutions would be but as chaff before the wind. Laws will be swept away wherever a sense of duty and the force of moral obligation are not embedded deeply in the bosom of society. This truth will explain the origin of those convulsions which we have lately witnessed. Men have succeeded in plucking from the hearts of the multitude a love of religion —in many cases even a religious belief was banished. But man is not a mere machine. Unless his actions are governed by the laws of God, his institutions will be like buildings erected on the sand, which will be swept away by the torrent. We have seen this effected, within the last few months in France by the hand of one man, and such will be the fate of all governments in the heart of whose people religion is not firmly implanted.

"The religious training necessary for this is imparted with peculiar efficacy by the Catholic Church. She does not merely announce her doctrines and her precepts. She embodies them, as I have already stated, in institutions which bring them home to all ages, all classes; makes them sink deeply into our very nature, and thus, at trying moments as well as in days of prosperity, they exercise a powerful influence on the mind and on the heart."

France contains a population of about 36,000,000. About 30,000,000, or five-sixths of the whole population are Roman Catholics. From the days of Pepin and Charlemagne down to the present time, France has been one of the firmest supports of the Roman Hierarchy. In no country have Protestants been more ruthlessly persecuted than in France. The revocation of the Edict of Nantes, and the slaughter of St.

Bartholomew, are familiar passages in the "Catholic chapter" of the history of France. Charlemagne was crowned Emperor of the West, by the Pope, as the reward of his services in sustaining the interests of the latter. The bayonets of Louis Napoleon are now the only prop to his tottering throne. In no country has the education of the people been more fully under the control of the Roman Catholics than in France. In that country, therefore, if anywhere, we may look for the legitimate effects of that system of religion and education. What are those results? According to Bishop O'Connor's own confession, infidelity controls France, and the people are the supple tools of the little tyrant who now rules them. What Catholicity can do for any country, where it is supported by the Government, and has had for ages the almost entire control of the education of the people, it has done for France. The very socialism, communism, and other isms, which are the professed abhorrence of the Catholic Church, have sprung from her bosom as from the arms of their nursing mother. The "Infallible Church" has there had the completest scope to develop what it can do for the political freedom, the social morality, and the religious training of mankind. Behold the result in the infidelity, the recking licentiousness of the people, and the infamous despotism of Louis Napoleon. It is hard to tell which predominates, the the folly or effrontery of Mr. O'Connor, in pointing to France as an example of the want of the Roman Catholic religion.

SECTARIAN SELFISHNESS.

We know of nothing on earth more meanly selfish than the attempt to use instrumentalities established by the labors of different denominations of Christians, to promote the sectarianisms of one. All co-operation of different sects proceeds on the assumption that there are certain great principles which they hold in common, and certain important objects which they are mutually desirous to accomplish. It is always understood that the object of combination is to advance these common principles and objects, and that all the funds contributed, and all the instrumentalities established, shall be honestly devoted to this purpose. It is likewise either tacitly understood or expressly stipulated, that sectarian peculiarities shall be held in abeyance, in so far as respects the action of the parties in their associated capacity. It matters not that one sect contributed more to the funds than another, or that it has a larger number of members concerned in the management of the affairs of the society. It only adds to the meanness of the thing to take advantage of the power of a majority to pervert the resources of the common society to sectarian purposes. If but a widow's mite has been contributed by any one party, it is given with the express understanding that it will be faithfully devoted to the common cause. To use it for another purpose, however praiseworthy in itself, is a violation of plighted faith. To use it for a purpose which the giver does not approve, is both robbery and sacrilege, as it is taking that which was consecrated wholly to the Lord for another purpose which the giver does not believe to be well-pleasing in his sight. From this it follows that the man who will avail himself of the opportunity afforded by a particular position, to thus pervert the agencies established for the propagation of a common faith, to the narrow purpose of building up his own sect, is capable of any other act of baseness or fraud. He is a man who would not hesitate to rob the temple of the Lord of its golden vessels, if he might coin them into money for the promotion of his own selfish schemes.

Yet we have met such men in our day, and unless some of the larger sects of the country slander each other, they are trying to perpetrate this very baseness. Some of the most rabidly sectarian newspapers that we know of, were established and have been sustained by the contributions of various denominations; some at least of which would have rather thrown their offering into the sea, than to have had them thus perverted. If we may believe the New School Presbyterians, and the Congregationalists, each party is trying to use the Home Missionary Society to propagate its ecclesiastical isms, rather than preach the truths which both hold in common. And indeed we know of no instrumentality for extending the Gospel, established by the mutual efforts of different denominations, in regard to the management of which suspicions of sectarian unfairness have not at some time been excited.

It may be said, and it has been said, that although the constitution of a society may be Catholic in its character, and may invite the co-operation of various sects, yet if one denomination gives most of the funds, they thereby acquire a right to use those funds to build up their own sect. This plea would be false, if every cent of the funds were given by one sect. They are asked and obtained for a specified purpose, and it is *practicing* a falsehood to ask money for one object and then use it for the promotion of another. It is assuming that the contributors *all* feel more desirous to extend the power of their sect, than to preach the *common* salvation—an assumption which, if true, stamps the character of the sect as essentially anti-Christian, but which, if false, involves those thus using their contributions in the crime of deception, and of obtaining money under false pretenses. If any portion of the funds, even the smallest, are furnished by other denominations, then the meanness and wickedness of perverting them to sectarian purposes are too manifest to need exposure.

All sects profess to value the great principles of Christianity which they hold in common, far higher than they do their peculiar sectarian principles. The gospel was "the power of God unto salvation," before the distinctions of Presbyterian, Methodist, Episcopalian or Congregationalist were known in the Church. The gospel will survive the obliteration of the sectarian lines which separate these various branches of the Christian host. Hence, the man who values his sectarianisms more highly than the great fundamental doctrines of the Christian system, is not himself a Christian. His connection with the church is formed for the purpose of promoting some ambitious or lucrative purpose of his own, and not for the purpose of professing Christ before men, blessing mankind, and honoring God. Hence, the influence of such men is the greatest obstacle in the way of harmonious co-operation between different branches of the Church. They are usually men ambitious of leadership ; and having put on a profession of Christianity merely as a cloak, they are generally unscrupulous in regard to the means they use for the accomplishment of their ends. And as their great object is their own personal honor or advantage, they will ruin the common cause, if they can not use its funds and friends for their own purposes. We have known the most promising schemes of co-operation between various branches of the Christian Church, defeated by the unscrupulous ambition of such men. True Christians are usually unsuspecting and very forbearing. Hence these sectarian schemers have the greatest security and advantage in prosecuting their plans.

The remedy for this evil is not meekly to submit to the wrong, and palliate and excuse the conduct of the wrong-doer. The man who is capable of such a sacrilegious prostitution of the labors and offerings of simple-hearted piety, is not a man to appreciate a generous, Christian magnanimity in those whose confidence he has abused. This will only encourage him in his evil course. Such men will feel nothing but the indignant scorn and reprobation of those whom they seek to use as their tools. Let them know that their schemes and their character are understood; let them be deprived of all control of the agencies which they seek to pervert, and they will be rendered powerless for evil. Then such a high and fervent spirit of piety in the Church as will make it an uncomfortable place for the selfish sectarian, will finally deliver them from the curse of his presence.

SPEAKING EVIL OF DIGNITIES.

The Apostles Peter and Jude mention it as one characteristic of a class of false teachers who had crept into the Church in their day, that they were " not afraid to speak evil of dignities." By a common consent, these " dignities " have been supposed to be civil magistrates or the magnates of the Church. Hence we have heard this text gravely quoted to prove that it was wrong to call Franklin Pierce by his right name, or to characterize as they deserve pro-slavery Drs. of Divinity. Nothing, we think, is more incorrect than such an application of the passage. This is one of those errors of translation and exposition which was foisted into the Bible by the prejudices of the translators and of the time in which they lived. The divine right of kings was standard orthodoxy in politics and religion in the days of King James, when our present version of the Bible was made. Hence, the translators were ever ready to construe passages which had any *seeming* of this doctrine in them, in accordance with this prevailing opinion; and commentators of that era, sharing in the same belief, followed their example, and were themselves followed in turn by others, without critical investigation. Of this kind of translation and exegesis the passage in question furnishes an example. In our opinion it has no reference to magistrates in the State or to dignitaries in the Church—except so far as these office-bearers are types of Christ, and represent his authority. It refers, we fully believe, primarily to the Lord Jesus Christ in the dignity and glory of his mediatorial reign. We present a few reasons for this belief:

1. In the first place, the word translated dignities does not mean magistrates, so far as we know, in any other passage of the Scriptures. The Greek word is *doxa*, (in the plural

doxas) signifying *glory*.   It is the word most frequently used to express the glory of God.   Thus, Christ is called the "brightness of the Father's glory "—*doxas*.   Again, it is said that he for the suffering of death was crowned with *glory* and honor—the same word in the Greek.   In the Gospel of Matthew it is expressly applied to the mediatorial reign of Christ.   The request of James and John, the sons of Zebedee, was that they might sit the one on his right hand and the other on his left in his *glory*—that is, in his kingdom, which as Mediator he should set up.   We might quote a multitude of passages where the word is used in the same sense. But we know of no instance, unless it is the one in question, in which it is applied to civil magistrates or ecclesiastical functionaries.

. 2. Again, the word translated to "speak evil," signifies more properly to blaspheme.   It is indeed the same word with the English, blaspheme, with only a Greek termination. Hence the literal translation of the passage is " blaspheming glorious ones ; " and as the plural is sometimes applied to God to denote his dignity, it might without any violence to the laws of language, be rendered " blaspheming the Glorious One."   But blasphemy can only be against God.   Men may slander and revile each other, but can not be properly said to blaspheme each other.

. 3. In the third place, the Apostle Jude, speaking of the doom of these false teachers, declares that " the Lord cometh with ten thousand of his saints to execute judgment upon all, and to convince all that are ungodly among them of all their ungodly deeds which they have ungodly committed, *and of all their hard speeches, which ungodly sinners have spoken against him.*"   The Apostle is in this passage giving an epitome of the crimes which he had detailed more at length in the previous part of his epistle.   Hence the conclusion is clear and convincing, that the *hard speeches* against Christ were the very same as the speaking evil of dignities, to which he had referred before.   They " blasphemed the Glorious One," that is, " uttered hard speeches against Christ."

We have other reasons in favor of this exposition of the passage, but have not now time to adduce them.   We have only space, in conclusion, for a remark or two in regard to the common understanding of the text.   We do not deny that civil magistrates and office-bearers in the Church, in so far as they execute the duties of their offices in accordance with the will of Christ, are to be held in high honor.   Civil and ecclesiastical governments are Christ's ordinance, and civil and ecclesiastical rulers are his ministers. So far as they conform to his law, they represent his authority, and to speak evil of them is·to blaspheme Christ. But that *any* form of civil government, no matter how it is administered, is Christ's ordinance, is a prevalent but pestilent heresy. To affirm that Franklin Pierce is Christ's minister, in any other sense than the Devil and all wicked men are his ministers, is to our mind a most monstrous and impious proposition. He possesses not a single qualification which God requires of the civil ruler. The Government under his administration contravenes and tramples down God's law in every important act. God's civil ruler is a terror to evil-doers, and a praise to them that do well. Franklin Pierce, so far as he has the power, is a terror to *well* doers, and a praise to them that do evil. To crush the poor, to burn defenseless villages and render hundreds of women and children homeless, to break down the barriers, that the overflowing scourge of slavery might pass over vast territories of free soil, are the important and characteristic acts of his administration. The idea that God Almighty regards the man and his government with any other feelings than those of intense loathing and profoundest contempt, is to our mind horribly blasphemous. And we know not by what authority we are required to express reverence for that which God abhors.

The same is true of corrupt ecclesiastic rulers. Jesus Christ certainly did not commit the sin of "speaking evil of dignities," when he denounced such as serpents and vipers. According to the prevalent notion of our times, this language was very wrong and irreverent. But he was holy and harmless, neither was guile found in his mouth. The Bible everywhere teaches that it is a duty to call things by their right names; and when a ruler in Church or State is base and mean and cruel, in his public acts, it is right to say so, and to hold him up to the scorn of all the good. When we come to entertain correct views of the character of God's rulers in Church and State, and to have proper ideas of the true functions of civil and ecclesiastical government, we will not blaspheme these Divine ordinances by supposing that they are found in our covenant-breaking President, in our slave·trading Government, or in any of the corrupt pro-slavery ecclesiastical organizations of the land.

The New Pro-slavery Church.

By the proceedings we published last week, our readers will have learned that the Southern seceders from the N. S. Presbyterian Church, have perfected their schism by giving it organic form. The salient point of this whole affair is that the new church has really and avowedly but one distinctive principle, and that is, the sanctity of American slavery. The seceders allege no other ground of difference with their brethren from whom they have separated. They profess to agree with them on all points of Christian doctrine, and church order. The sole offense laid to the charge of their former associates is, that they will not recognize slavery as approvingly ordained of God, and as in all circumstances a holy and desirable institution. We say in *all* circumstances, because the N. S. General Assembly have always admitted that in *some* circumstances slavery is innocent. In the Detroit resolutions they specify three circumstances which, in their judgment, justify the holding of men as property by the members of the church, and their last Assembly enacted nothing inconsistent with this. But because they hold that slavery, under other circumstances, is evil, Dr. Ross and his schismatical adherents, have withdrawn, and organized what they call a church, on the ground that slavery is always and only good, and shall enjoy the fullest and most undisturbed fellowship and sanction. Slavery is therefore their corner-stone, their sure foundation, their bond of union. The right of the master to buy, sell, work, scourge, and kill his fellow-men, to separate them from wives and children, parents, brothers, and sisters, is the sole right, for the maintenance of which the new organization has been formed.

It is difficult to find words to adequately characterize the moral enormity of this whole proceeding. Slavery, in the abstract, and in the concrete, and under all circumstances, is a crime that stands alone in unapproachable atrocity. It is literally the "sum of all villainies." There is not a crime on the catalogue of human guilt—sacrilege, blasphemy, idolatry, murder, incest, adultery, robbery, rape—which slavery does not license; and all of these crimes are perpetrated from time to time by masters upon their slaves. Some of them are perpetrated habitually, from the very nature of the case, others of them occasionally. All of them *may* be perpetrated with perfect impunity by masters on slaves, at any time and at all times. Yet here we have a convention of professed ministers and members of Jesus Christ, in his name, and ostensibly by his authority, separating from those with whom they have long associated, on the sole ground that this atrocious system shall not be discussed, and shall not be condemned. And after separation they proceed to form an organization, and call it a church, on the avowed principle that God sanctions this concentration and embodiment of all conceivable guilt and infamy.

And these men have the terrible effrontery and blasphemy to call themselves Christians, and Christian ministers! Christians indeed! What possible point of affinity can be traced between them and the meek and holy Jesus? Behold that Divine Saviour, as seated on the mountain side, with his mild eye all burdened with the weight of human sympathy, he proclaims, "Blessed are the merciful, for they shall obtain mercy." "Therefore all things whatsoever ye would that men should do to you do ye also to them, for this is the law and the prophets." Behold him again in the synagogue with the book of the law open before him, proclaiming, "The Spirit of the Lord is upon me, because he hath anointed me to preach the gospel to the poor, he hath sent me to heal the broken-hearted, to preach deliverance to the captives, and recovering of sight to the blind, to set at liberty them that are bruised." The very soul of love and pity for the poor and oppressed breathes in his words and acts. "All bore him witness," we are told, "and wondered at the *gracious* words that proceeded out of his mouth." Their souls were lost in delightful wonder at the more than human love, that, like a halo of heavenly light, pervaded his presence, and breathed around him. His distinguishing mark of his own divinity and Messiahship, was his love for the poor, and his zeal to preach to them the gospel. Wherever a human heart lies crushed under oppression, there yearns his bowels of mercy. Wherever a soul toils wearily under the weight of sin and sorrow, there sounds his voice of love, bidding the weary and heavy laden come to him and be at rest.

Turn we now to the other side of the picture. In the city of Richmond, where day by day the hammer of the auctioneer falls heavily on the crushed and broken hearts of the scattered and peeled poor ones of this land, assembles a convocation of the nominal disciples of this blessed and compassionate Saviour. Do they, like him, feel that their mission is to "preach deliverance to the captives, and the opening of the prison to the bound?" Nay verily. Their open and avowed, and only object is, to perpetuate the captivity, and bar more securely the prison doors of the oppressed. Under the shadow of the lofty temple where they meet, the Saviour, in the person of some of his poor, heart-broken disciples, lies chained and bruised in the loathsome slave-den. These professed embassadors of that very Saviour, meet for the sole purpose of organizing a nominal church, in which those who buy, and sell, and chain, and lacerate Jesus Christ, may be fellow-shiped as good Christian brethren. In that fetid slave-pen lies the wife and mother. She has been ruthlessly parted forever from her husband, and from her arms has been cruelly torn the babe, over whose little form her heart yearns with all the deathless love that the mother only knows. As she lies there in chains, memory brings back the image of the little one. She sees the sweet smile upon its innocent face. She feels its warm breath, and the pressure of the dimpled hand upon her bosom ; and then, as she recalls the dreadful truth that she will see it no more in this world, she sobs as if her very heart-strings would burst asunder. And there, almost within hearing of her wail, those professed ministers of the loving Jesus are ordaining that the fiend in the shape of man, who inflicted all this terrible weight of woe, does nothing whatever inconsistent with the character of the Christian! And these men preach, and pray, and talk pious cant, and then, like the adulterous woman, wipe their mouths and say, "We have done no wickedness."

Let these men fill up their cup of iniquity, and, by all means, let them be consistent, and open wide the doors of the sanctuary they are founding. Let them send one delegation to the leprous saints of the Salt Lake Valley, another to the seething brothels of the Five Points of New York, and a third to the Thugs of India, bidding the Mormon adulterer, the New York prostitute, and the Indian assassin come to their fold, and aid them in celebrating this marriage of death and hell. We can conceive of but one reason why they might not thus greatly increase their somewhat meager number, and that is, that the Mormon, the prostitute, and the Thug, might spurn the invitation, and resent as an insult the attempt to place them on a level with Dr. Ross and his adherents. We can hardly say that they would not have just cause so to do.

Movements in the Roman Catholic Church.

The appointment of John Hughes to the rank of Archbishop of New York, and the delivery of a lecture by that high functionary, soon after, On the Decline of Protestantism, are facts with which our readers are already acquainted. Nearly cotemporaneously with these events, the Pope of Rome (*Pio Nono*) issued a bull, appointing an English Archbishop, and dividing the country into twelve dioceses, and appointing bishops to several of them, accompanied with a promise of a full supply. This was done without respect to, or leave of the English Hierarchy, and the Queen, the Head of the Church, "by the grace of God, defender of the faith," etc. These several movements of "His Holiness" have severally excited quite a commotion, both in this country and in England—much greater in the latter country than in this, however. The excitement in this country exhibits itself in lectures, sermons, newspaper comments, etc. In England not only these weapons are used, but meetings are being held through the kingdom, resolutions and addresses are adopted, invoking the interference of the Queen and Parliament, to arrest the threatened subjugation of the country to the See of Rome.

We do not apprehend serious danger to the Protestant cause, from these or any other popish demonstrations. Whatever injury may result from them will be owing, not to the inherent strength of the papacy, but to the inconsistencies, and consequent weakness of some of the leading sects of Protestants. It is the leaven of popery working *in* the Protestant churches, not its outward assaults, that endangers the citadel of truth. The most prominent and violent opposers of the recent pretensions of the Papal See, are the Puseyites, of England, and the pro-slavery Protestants of the United States—the very sects that embody most of the errors of popery. The proclivity of the first of these toward the embrace of "Holy Mother" is a matter of notoriety throughout Christendom. Hence their opposition to the pretensions of the papal bull is not founded on religious convictions—not the offspring of an honest, conscientious persuasion of the errors and corruptions of the Catholic Church. They have embraced and propagated some of the most dangerous and wicked dogmas of the Vatican. That the Bishop of London, "Pope Henry of Exeter" (as the bishop of that diocese is

called), and other Puseyite bishops and ministers are influenced by deep religious sentiment of opposition to the doctrinal errors, or practical corruptions of the papacy, is probably
not suspected by themselves or any of their followers. Passions
of another sort are the cause of their vehement demonstrations
of hostility to the papal bull. That they, by the grace of
God, and laws of the realm of England, the Lords spiritual
of the Church, and Lords temporal, moreover, occupying seats
in Parliament and other worldly perquisites, should be coolly
thrust aside by a proclamation from the Vatican, to make way
for others sent over from the banks of the Tiber to fill their
places, rouses all the pride of place and power, for which the
clergy of established churches have ever been distinguished.
The motives for their fierce opposition are palpable—" known
and read of all men." That they are not the men to rebuke
the arrogance of Rome—that their testimony is powerless to
convict and convert the deluded votaries of the papacy—all
can see. It savors too much of " Satan " reproving sin.

Now, the same thing is true of the slaveholding, and
slavery-defending churches of this country. They have
deliberately adopted some of the very worst principles of the
great apostasy. Some of these are openly proclaimed, others
insensibly insinuate themselves into the policy of the churches,
and, to an extent not suspected by many, control and influence their doings. Let us specify some facts in proof of this
point.

1. In reference to a portion of the population of this country, the policy of withholding the Bible, and giving them
mere oral instruction has been publicly adopted, and openly
proclaimed. It is true that this is owing in part to the fact,
that the civil laws of some of the States prohibit the slaves
from reading the Bible. The fault of the Church in the
matter consists in permitting her members to uphold these
laws in their capacity of citizens, and in succumbing and giving in to those unholy enactments, which, in so many words,
nullify God's express command to " search the Scriptures."
By a silent acquiescence in such laws, individuals and
churches consent to the wrong. But in many cases, churches
have openly proclaimed this as their settled policy, in regard
to the religious instruction of slaves. The proof of this
assertion has been repeatedly published in our columns.
While launching anathemas against the Pope and his Cardin-
als, for withholding the written word from their followers,
they coolly announce that " oral instruction " is all, under

present circumstances, that they are called to impart to the slave population of the United States.

2. Again : the Protestant churches of this country have, in many cases, virtually adopted the popish doctrine of indulgences. Slavery has been condemned as a sin, in the *teachings* of nearly all the sects of this land, yet toleration to continue in the practice of it has been granted to the same extent. The plea for this is, that though slavery is abstractly wrong, yet *circumstances* justify the practice. This is, to all intents and purposes, an indulgence to commit sin. *Circumstances*, instead of the Pope, grant the license, and those circumstances are the creation of the fancy of the Church—they have no existence in fact. We state simple truth when we say that there is scarcely a social crime which does not find shelter in the Protestant churches of this country, to a greater or less extent. Slavery, war, intemperance, fraud, falsehood, immoral voting, connection with oath-bound, secret societies, and many other practices, at war with the very plainest precepts of Christianity, are generally no bar to Christian communion. Now, the refusal to exercise discipline for these evils, is the fullest indulgence to those engaged in their practice. Yet the creeds of all the churches in which these things are tolerated condemn them as sinful. Yet for sake of members, of wealth and influence, those practising them are freely admitted to the communion of the Church. *The price paid for the indulgence*, is the only difference between those of Popery and Protestantism—the principle is precisely the same in both cases.

3. That "the end justifies the means," is another doctrine (originating with the Jesuits) of the Church of Rome. We find traces of it in many a development of the pro-slavery Protestantism of this country. The facts already referred to furnish an illustration. The end proposed by many a church, is to build itself up in numbers, wealth and power. This is a holy object, provided the numbers are all good Christians, and the wealth and power are all used for benevolent purposes. But among the means used for this purpose, is the toleration of those wrongs and sins which we have named. That this is really the motive, is evident from the excuses put forth when the duty of casting out these evils is pressed upon the church. It will divide the church, diminish our numbers, deprive us of many contributions which now flow into our treasury, etc. These are the standing pleas for continued fellowship, in many cases, with the very worst of sinners. The

end proposed, the prosperity of the church—the means, the toleration of sin in its communion—the end sanctifies the means.

In many other things the working of the leaven of popery is seen in Protestant churches. The prevalent notion of schism—that it consists merely in leaving an external church organization—is purely popish. The constant appeals made to the Fathers and their traditions—to the principles and practices of a past generation—instead of the Bible, is of the same character. Whether or not, the ministers of many Protestant churches exhibit any of the characteristics of the popish priesthood, our readers can judge. That spiritual pride, impatience of contradiction, a disposition to guard most sedulously all the prerogatives of their class, a desire to hold and exercise all possible control of the consciences and wills of their hearers, and to suppress free inquiry on many subjects, are, to a considerable extent, found in the ministry of many of the Protestant churches, would not perhaps be a very hazardous assertion. That these things are marks of the popish priesthood, all Protestants believe.

It is needless to pursue these remarks further. If they are true, the conclusion is inevitable, that the popery of Protestantism is fraught with most danger to the cause of truth. This is our painful conviction. In this country, popery finds its appropriate ally in the institution of slavery. They are kindred systems. One enslaves the mind, the other both mind and body. Both deny the Bible to those under their control—both discourage free inquiry, and "love darkness rather than light." Popery robs its victims; slavery does the same. By its penances, masses for the dead, indulgences, etc., popery extorts money without rendering an equivalent; slavery robs men of all their earnings, their wives and children, and their own souls and bodies. The same evil passions, avarice, and the lust of power uphold each. The Pope, "as God, sitteth in the temple of God, showing himself that he is God;" slavery makes the master the God of the slave. The slave's right to worship God, to read the Bible, to discharge all the duties of religion, is denied. Thus both systems, as far as possible, dethrone Jehovah, and set up an idol in his place. Popery denies the sacredness of the marriage tie, by "forbidding to marry;" slavery *annihilates* the institution of marriage.

This analogy might be run out to the end of the chapter, but enough of it for the present. That a church, which proclaims slavery "no bar to Christian communion"—which takes it to the baptismal font and the communion table—is not the church to denounce popery, or to convince its votaries of error, and turn them to the ways of truth, is the inevitable conclusion.

———

EFFETE ORTHODOXY.

The *Christian Press* quotes Dr. Chalmers as saying, that "The orthodoxy of the Church, in this day, has become effete, a body of ceremonies and doctrinal formulas, from which the life and the power have departed." It needs not the high authority of Dr. Chalmers to assure every intelligent and considerate man that this, with few exceptions, is so. Forms and statements of doctrine which were pregnant with meaning, and instinct with life, in the minds of the reformers, of the men composing the Westminster Assembly, and the fathers of the orthodox church in this country, have become to the men of the present generation meaningless and lifeless words. While professing to hold these doctrines, the life of the churches is a daily denial of their truth. Numerous specifications of this fact might be given; we name but one or two.

In the Calvinistic system God is all in all, so far as "dominion over the creatures" is concerned. His absolute and undisputed supremacy in all things—the affairs of the Church and of the State, and in the individual life of every intelligent being—is one of the fundamental doctrines of this system. But by none more than the professors of this creed has the authority of acts of Congress, and other legislative enactments been exalted "above all that is called God, or that is worshiped." For men like Drs. Lord, Boardman, Spencer, etc., to mouth the formulas of the creed of John Calvin is a heartless mockery. Had they lived in his day they would have been among the most servile worshipers of the Beast, and the most devout and sanctimonious persecutors of Calvinists. This language does them no injustice. They bow, at this day, in obedience to the ruling powers of this land, which is more profligate and devilish than ever was the harlot of Rome in her worst estate. Surely the orthodoxy of these men is effete, a mere formulary, without life or power.

Another foundation article in the orthodox creed is, that the doctrine of gratuitous justification leads necessarily to

holiness of life—that he who has been justified will also
become sanctified, and that the only evidence of pardon is
entire separation from all known sins. That consequently
the man who habitually follows any sinful practice is unfit for
the communion of saints. This is the theory: what is the
modern practice? We wish to speak of this in all candor,
and to state nothing but facts. The practice of the orthodox
churches of this country is to admit pretty much every body
that applies. All that is generally required of a professor of
religion is to avoid breaking the laws of the land, and shun
unpopular sins. If he keeps out of the clutches of civil law
he is pretty safe from all ecclesiastical censure. He may buy,
sell, whip, and rob his fellow-beings. He may sell intoxicating liquors, vote for the vilest of the vile for civil office,
and commit divers other similar offenses, and retain his full
standing in any of the large branches of the orthodox or het-
erodox churches of this country. And when these churches
are censured for these things, the plea is put in (and men
like Albert Barnes are not ashamed to use it), that we must
not expect perfection in the Church on earth, and that if the
principle is once admitted, of separating from a church because
she tolerates one sin, it will bind us to separate on account of
the toleration of every sin. Surely that article of orthodoxy
which holds sanctification to be the only evidence of justification, is effete—"Thrice dead, plucked up by the roots."
Waiving other illustrations of the fact in the case, we pass
to another consideration. This effete orthodoxy is the triple
chain that binds men with the strength of a cable to their
pro-slavery churches. It is the *form* of sound words that they
regard as valuable in their ecclesiastical organizations. Deluded by their leaders into the belief that the prime articles of
their creed have been renounced by those who seek to free
the Church from her connection with abounding iniquity, the
masses in churches are held by their attachment to these formulas of faith. When the question of separation from the
communion of slaveholders and other criminals is presented,
they are told that they must choose between a renunciation of
their theological creed, and a continuance of their present
church connections. The orthodox tenets of faith laid down
in the confessions of past generations are extolled and magni-
fied by the men who practically give them the lie every day of
their lives. Whether orthodoxy in the minds of the people
e real and living, or formal and dead, does not materially
ffect its power to hold them in an organization. Men cling

to forms even more tenaciously after the life is gone than before. When the rites and ceremonies of religion are *all* that any people possess, they can the less afford to lose them.

In view of this fact the mission of the religious reformatory spirit now abroad is immensely increased in importance. It is not only to destroy those particular evils, in opposition to which it first manifested itself, but also to infuse life into the dead forms of faith in the nominally Christian world. So far from orthodox Christians being required to renounce their religious belief when they leave the large and corrupt ecclesiastical organizations of this country, the exact reverse is true. Only the men who hold to the doctrine of no religious fellowship with open iniquity, manifest a real faith in the orthodox tenet, that " every sin deserves God's wrath and curse, both in this world, and in the world to come." None but those who hold to a higher law than acts of Congress or Parliament, can really indorse the Calvinistic doctrine of God's supremacy. So with other points.

In the light of this subject we see the delusion under which honest people labor when they cling to the large and corrupt church organizations of this country, through devotion to the great doctrines of the orthodox faith. They embrace the body from which the vital spark is fled.

COVENANTING.

The subject of public covenanting, at the present time, has been brought to the notice of our readers by our correspondents, in this and last week's paper. It is perfectly evident, we think, that if those denominations, which profess to believe in the divine obligation of solemn, public covenanting, at particular times, permit the present occasion to pass without entering into a solemn bond to obey God in opposition to the wicked demands of the slave-power, they will find it hard to convince the world that their testimony, in behalf of covenanting, is anything else than a dead letter. But, leaving controverted points on this subject out of view, we confess we should love to see the friends of God and the slave, in all Protestant denominations, unite in a public bond at the present crisis. This bond should embrace a distinct assertion of the supremacy of God's law over all mere human enactments, and a pledge to obey the former and disobey the latter, in all cases where they conflict one with the other. As instances of such a conflict, it should specify those parts of the fugitive slave bill which command the citizens to join the *posse comitatus* to aid in recapturing the escaping bond-man, and those parts which forbid them to aid, directly or indirectly, in his escape. The bond should pledge its signers to use all *peaceful* means in opposing the execution of this enactment, and to secure its repeal. It should also pledge them to oppose by all right means, the election of any man to office who is not opposed to slavery, and all laws made to sustain it, and who is not known to possess Bible qualifications for the office of civil ruler. It might embrace a testimony in favor of peace and in opposition to preparations for war, also in favor of temperance, and in opposition to all laws intended to give a legal sanction to the selling of intoxicating liquors. Other things might be added in different localities, as might be thought best.

It would be a sublime spectacle to see the friends of God and liberty, all over this land, meeting together in convenient places, by preconcerted agreement, on the same day, and there solemnly entering into covenant with Almighty God, to choose his service, and obey him, in opposition to the behests of the Government of the United States, which violate his laws. If, forgetting slight denominational differences, members of all churches could thus unite in publicly swearing allegiance to him who alone is Lord of the conscience, it would be a transaction to go down in history with the leagues of the Scotch Covenanters, in the reign of the Stuarts. Such a movement would arrest, if any human agencies can, the downward progress of this nation. The signs of the times indicate that it is rapidly traveling in that pathway that led to the French Revolution. The law of God has been openly insulted and cast out of the American Senate. The man who asserted its supremacy was obliged to make a virtual retraction. The licentious and the drunken occupy the high places of power; duelists and murderers are the chosen law-makers of this people. It is but within a week that two of them tried to blow out each other's brains in mortal combat. "The vile are exalted," and consequently "the wicked walk on every side." Crime is increasing with a rapidity which is exciting the attention and the fears of many who are called to execute the laws. If these things are not arrested, the man is blind to the teachings of the past, and the signs of the present, who can not foresee the result.

Patriotism, then, to leave higher motives out of view, ought to unite the friends of righteousness at this crisis. The perpetuity of this Government, as a government of justice and liberty, must be dear to all friends of God and man. The hopes of the present generation and their posterity are deeply involved. Yet if the present downward tendency is not reversed, the ruin of this nation is inevitable. The great want of the friends of righteousness, it seems to us, is organization—union. As a means of promoting this, the measure of public covenanting of which we speak, is worthy of serious consideration.

MODERN INFIDELITY.

If the denial of the *plenary inspiration* of the Scriptures is infidelity, then there are no doubt infidels among the advocates of the most important modern reforms. They are found chiefly among that class of antislavery men who—for want of a better term—are called Garrisonians. (We use the term for convenience, not by way of reproach.) That *all* who hold Garrison's views of the United States Constitution, and of Christian non resistance, deny the plenary inspiration of the Bible, is not true. Whether or not a majority of them do, we do not know, nor is it important we should. Neither do we know what is Mr. Garrison's own opinion on this subject. That some of the most prominent of the class to which we refer, do deny the doctrine alluded to above, is certain. They generally make no secret of their views. For whatever is frank and open in the avowal of their sentiments, they deserve credit. That there are, besides these, many *Socialists*, and advocates of other real or pretended reforms, who repudiate the doctrine of plenary inspiration, is true. The influence of these varied classes is extensive and powerful. They embrace men of the finest intellect, and of admitted purity of moral life. Many of them are also men of great natural kindness and benevolence of heart; and many of them exhibit a philanthropy and expansive benevolence, which ought to put to the blush many, of orthodox creed, who rail most loudly at their theoretical infidelity. That the views of these various classes, on moral, social, and political questions, are gaining ground, and that along with these views their opinion of the Bible is spreading, in many directions, it is useless to deny.

It becomes, then, a matter of vital moment, to ascertain the cause and the remedy of this species of unbelief. As the Bible reveals the only hope for man, in this world and the next, and as the authority of the Bible rests on the doctrine of its plenary inspiration, to know how this doctrine may be most fully established, and how the progress of the opposite belief may be most effectually arrested, are questions which must lie near the heart of every friend of God and man. It is obvious to all, acquainted in any degree with the subject, that the former modes of argumentation are insufficient. It is of course true, that the way of proving the inspiration of the Bible is the same in all ages. The arguments proving the genuineness and authenticity of the books of the Bible, the proofs from miracles and prophesy, are essentially unchangeable. The only effect of time on these various proofs, is to increase their weight, as fuller investigation developes the accuracy and purity of the sacred text, and as prophesy becomes more and more completely fulfilled. The force of these evidences will only increase by the lapse of time.

But these, to the mass of men, are not the most accessible or the most conclusive proofs of the inspiration of the Bible. The internal evidences, derived from the purity, holiness, and consistency of the teachings of the Bible, and from their effects in transforming human character, and controlling human conduct, are at once the most obvious and the most convincing. It is when mankind behold the Bible working an entire renovation of the whole moral and intellectual being of their fellow-men, that "the excellency of the power" of the Holy Scriptures is seen "to be of God." We are then brought directly to what we conceive the principal cause of the infidelity of which we have spoken, and consequently to its remedy. It is the failure of the Church to exhibit the fruits of this radical transformation, and the exhibition of their very opposite, that has filled the land with unbelievers in the inspiration of the Bible. An entire change, therefore, in the whole spirit and practice of the churches, is the only effectual remedy. It will not do, in this age, for the Church, or her ministers, to denounce infidelity, and argue, as she once could, from the known bad character of infidels. She dare not challenge comparison between the conduct of her own ministers and members, and those whom she denounces as unbelievers. The advantage is here against the Church and with the infidel. This is a humiliating confession, but truth *compels* it to be made, and being true it is useless to disguise it. Hence the argument, from the glorious effects of receiving the Bible as inspired, is lost to the believers of that doctrine, and turned against them. What ought to have been their mightiest weapon of defense, is the most fatal implement in the hands of the unbelievers.

The interpretation of the Bible, by the prominent commentators of the country, has had a similar effect with the practice of the Church. Instead of showing (which is really the truth), that its teachings harmonize with, and really inculcate all true reform, the interpreters of the Bible have generally made it, on these subjects, the minister of sin. They have distorted its holy pages into a seeming justification of the most atrocious social and political crimes. Drunkenness, war, slavery, caste, passive obedience to government as of Divine right, have fled for refuge to the perverted precepts of the Scriptures. The Church has furnished, and now furnishes, commentators in abundance, who forge from the armory of eternal truth, weapons for the defense of all these grievous wrongs. Now, the innate sense of right, which God has implanted in every man's soul, revolts at these practices. Hence the abhorrence which every one, except those who for selfish purposes practice or defend them, feels for these evils, is easily turned against the Bible, from which a seeming justification for them is extorted. The enemy of slavery, war, etc., has to encounter at every turn, the perverted teachings of the Bible. He has to urge his appeals against the prevailing exposition of that book, and against that reverence for its authority which all religious persons feel—a reverence, not founded on an intelligent understanding of the teachings of the Bible, but on the prejudices of education and habit.

Thus meeting, at every point of attack, the alleged authority of the Bible—finding a garbled text ready as an answer to every argument, and every appeal which he urges in behalf of the wronged and suffering slave, the antislavery man, who has not been deeply imbued with the teachings and spirit of the Holy Scriptures, almost inevitably conceives a strong disgust against them. Now, the guilty authors of his infidelity are the preachers and church-members, who so obstinately thrust forward the Bible to cover and excuse the unspeakable atrocities of slavery.

The temperance man, with his soul alive to the evils of drunkenness, goes to the haunts of its victims. He finds there the besotted husband and father, once respectable and virtuous, now a hardened and imbruted savage; the crushed and heart-broken wife and mother, the hungry, ragged, squalid children. He listens to the oaths and blasphemies of the drunkard, the heartrending sighs of the suffering wife, and the sobbings of the worse than fatherless children. With his heart melted by the sight of all this misery, he goes into society to urge an appeal for the rescue of the victims. The first thing he meets is the grog-seller, who has been the guilty cause of all this woe, a respectable member of a professedly Christian church. Then a tippling deacon, or a hypocritical preacher, who has "stolen the livery of the Court of Heaven to serve the devil in," "quotes Scripture for the deed." In answer to all his appeals in behalf of the poor victims of drunkenness, garbled extracts of holy writ are thrust in his face. That he should curse the Scriptures, and their professional expounders, is a deplorable, but almost inevitable consequence. Then, to help matters along, the hypocrites who have driven him into unbelief, stand up and with solemn sneer cry, "Infidel!" "Infidel!"

The same course, substantially, is pursued toward the advocates of almost all other benevolent reforms. The friends of peace, with hearts brooding in agony over the horrors of war, have to encounter the same opposition from the expounders of, and professed believers, in the Scriptures. The advocates of political rights, and the opposer of despotic government, when urging the right and duty of establishing righteous civil government, are met by the language of Paul, "The powers that be are ordained of God, whosoever, therefore, resisteth the power, resisteth the ordinance of God," etc. These texts, says the Church, teach passive obedience to the existing government, though it may be the despotism of Nero or Nicholas. It is, therefore, infidelity to try to subvert these, and establish those which will protect instead of crushing the liberties of the people.

Thus it is, and has been with every reform. The Bible has been pressed into the service of every form of error, and every abomination in practice. And now, to cap the climax, its holy pages are tortured into a seeming justification of the present unspeakably atrocious slave-catching bill of Congress. The most important cause of the current unbelief in Scripture is, therefore, obvious. We have, for one, no hesitation in saying, that if we believed the prevailing interpretation of the Bible, in regard to the various evils of which we have spoken was correct, we should be an infidel. A book which justifies, by direct precept, or by fair inference, slavery or drunkenness,

or war, or the divine right of kings, is a book of abominations, and, therefore, not a revelation from a God of immacu-
late justice and holiness. The Church and the commentators
say, that the Bible does contain this justification of these
evils; the opposers of them accept the interpretation which
they give, and consequently reject the Bible. We reject both
the premises and conclusion.

The Bible not only does not sanction, but most pointedly
and terribly denounces all these evils. In that fact we find
evidence of its inspiration. The remedy for the form of
infidelity of which we have spoken is, then, perfectly evident.
That remedy is simply a true interpretation of the Bible—an
interpretation which will exhibit its teachings, in harmony
with all practical benevolence, and all true reform. If the
Bible is left in the hands of those who are now, by pro-
slavery and other false interpretations, bringing it into contempt, infidelity will continue to spread. To rescue the Scriptures from their professed friends, who are thus distorting
their pages, is the work of those reformers who believe in
their inspiration.

The Waiter-Killer Acquitted.

Herbert, the California ruffian who killed Keating, an
Irish waiter in a Washington hotel, in an affray excited by
his own insolence. has been acquitted. No one, we presume,
acquainted with Washington society and Washington courts,
expected anything else. " Moreover," says Solomon, " I saw
under the sun, the place of judgment, that wickedness was
there, and the place of righteousness that iniquity was there."
Were the Jewish sage living now, he would find that in this
particular, there is nothing new under the sun. It costs a
member of Congress $300 to beat a Senator nigh unto death,
and an Irish laborer, whose only offense was resenting a foul
insult to the mother who bore him, may be killed by " honorable" murderers for nothing. The wife of the murdered
man has died broken-hearted—killed by her great sorrow.
From the shock which she endured when the bloody and
lifeless body of her husband was brought to her presence,
she never recovered. She had loved that piece of lifeless
clay. Beneath the coarse garment of honest poverty a warm
heart had throbbed, on which she had often nestled her head

in the confiding trust of a happy love. Far away over the
blue ocean, in green old Ireland, they had plighted their
troth in the glad days of youth. In search of a home they
had crossed the broad sea together. By humble but honest
toil the husband was earning bread for his wife and little one.
Peace smiled upon their home, which though lowly, was all
the world to them. But in a moment the husband and father
is stricken down, because he could not meekly endure the
most foul and galling insult to himself and his mother. He
is carried breathless and bloody to the presence of his wife,
whose heart breaks with the shock; and now the bodies of
both molder to dust, side by side. Their child survives, a
fatherless and motherless orphan.

But the murderer walks free, ready in his pride of place
and power, to shoot down the next poor man who may have
the manliness to resent his insolence. He sits as a legislator
for a professedly Christian people. He, with his brother
assassin, Brooks, is a delegate to the Cincinnati Convention,
and both are prominent members of the party. The assassin,
with the blood of a double murder upon his hands, sits as a
law-maker in the national Congress, and the members of his
own party vote almost unanimously against an inquiry into
his crime. Thus his party indorses his guilt, and makes it
its own.

This case is another mournful evidence of the deep corruption which is pervading the courts of justice, and the public
sentiment of this land.

www.ingramcontent.com/pod-product-compliance
Lightning Source LLC
Chambersburg PA
CBHW031037120726
47905CB00007B/2222